G

A R I M A R M E L L

TIME OF JUDGMENT

Act one of the Time of Judgment

Vampire: The Masquerade
Fiction from White Wolf

The Clan Novel Saga

A comprehensive, chronological collection of the fourteen-volume best-selling Clan Novel Series. Includes all-new material.

Volume 1: The Fall of Atlanta — foreword by Stewart Wieck; new material by Philippe Boulle

Volume 2: The Eye of Gehenna — foreword by Eric Griffin; new material by Stefan Petrucha

Volume 3: Bloody September — foreword by Anna Branscome; new material by Lucien Soulban (forthcoming)

Volume 4: End Game — foreword by Gherbod Fleming; new material by Janet Trautvetter (forthcoming)

The Victorian Age Vampire Trilogy

A Morbid Initiation by Philippe Boulle
The Madness of Priests by Philippe Boulle
The Wounded King by Philippe Boulle

The Clan Tremere Trilogy

Widow's Walk by Eric Griffin
Widow's Weeds by Eric Griffin
Widow's Might by Eric Griffin

The Clan Lasombra Trilogy

Shards by Bruce Baugh
Shadows by Bruce Baugh
Sacrifices by Bruce Baugh

The Clan Brujah Trilogy

Slave Ring by Tim Dedopulos
The Overseer by Tim Dedopulos
The Puppet-Masters by Tim Dedopulos

The Dark Ages Clan Novel Series

Dark Ages: Nosferatu by Gherbod Fleming
Dark Ages: Assamite by Stefan Petrucha
Dark Ages: Cappadocian by Andrew Bates
Dark Ages: Setite by Kathleen Ryan
Dark Ages: Lasombra by David Niall Wilson
Dark Ages: Ravnos by Sarah Roark
Dark Ages: Malkavian by Ellen Porter Kiley
Dark Ages: Brujah by Myranda Kalis
Dark Ages: Toreador by Janet Trautvetter
Dark Ages: Gangrel by Tim Waggoner (forthcoming)
Dark Ages: Tremere by Sarah Roark (forthcoming)
Dark Ages: Ventrue by Matthew McFarland (forthcoming)
Dark Ages: Tzimisce by Myranda Kalis (forthcoming)

For all these titles and more,
visit www.white-wolf.com/fiction

GEHENNA
THE FINAL NIGHT

This is the Time of Judgment

Since the earliest nights, the undead have stalked the living, feeding off their blood to survive. According to the oldest stories, these vampires descend from Caine, the Biblical first murderer. Passing on their curse when they choose to remake another, the Cainites have become a parasitic culture existing in the shadows of history. In the modern nights, they lurk unseen among the mortal herd, forming their own sects and societies. For centuries, the greatest of these—the Camarilla—has enforced the Masquerade, a grand tradition enforcing secrecy and discretion on the undead. Even the Sabbat, the other great sect, built on the precepts of vampiric supremacy, enforces its own version of the Masquerade, lest the mortal herd rise and destroy the parasites among it.

But greater threats loom on the horizon for the undead. The same stories that tell of the Curse of Caine also speak of his return, and that of the Antediluvians, the ancient vampires he first spawned and who will rise to consume the young. *The Book of Nod*, most celebrated of all ancient vampiric texts, calls this terrible time Gehenna, and lays out signs that will presage its coming, signs that many say have come true.

These are the Final Nights and, at long last, judgment is at hand.

A Matter of Perspective...

Each act of the **Time of Judgment** trilogy adopts the point of view of the supernatural creature whose story it tells. Astute readers will note nods and small references to the larger supernatural world, but most vampires, werewolves, and even mages find their attention drawn to their own problems in these terrible last days. Thus, the three acts of this trilogy are more akin to three facets of a larger happening than sequential sections of a single tale. Each builds upon the others, but tells its own story.

prologue:
twilight

Quiet! Hear the raven's cry!
The stillness of the wind rising on the street
the towers hide
the darkness of the day.

When Lasombra's dreams come true
on the day when the moon runs as blood
and the sun rises black in the sky,
that is the day of the Damned,
when Caine's children will rise again.

And the world will turn cold
and unclean things will boil up from the ground
and great storms will roll, lightning will light
fires, animals will fester and their bodies,
twisted, will fall.

—*The Book of Nod*, "The Chronicle of Secrets"

Taurus Mountains
South-southwest of Kayseri (and Mt. Erciyes),
Turkey

And on top of everything else, it was hot.

It shouldn't have been. This late at night, the temperature in the mountains and the desert surrounding them should have dropped substantially. Tonight, though, the heat clung stubbornly to the mountainsides, refusing to let the setting sun drag it down, and the desert winds succeeded only in pushing that heat around in pockets of warmer air, rather than dispersing them entirely.

The heat made an already difficult task that much more uncomfortable, and Beckett took a moment out of his preparations to scowl at no one in particular.

Beckett wouldn't really stand out in a crowd. Brown hair just a bit longer than was currently in vogue, brown jeans, a white denim button-down that wasn't currently buttoned, hiking boots and a backpack nearly large enough to crush a man who tried to put it on at the wrong angle. About the only truly unusual feature were the sunglasses he wore even late at night, an attention-getter he'd never have worn if they hadn't served the very specific purpose of hiding his inhuman eyes from mortal observers. For similar reasons, he wore a pair of gloves to conceal the coarse hair and thick nails that marked his hands, a further legacy of his blood's bestial heritage.

Still, these oddities aside, he looked for the most part like a hiker, perhaps a European traveling the globe to "find himself." Actually, Beckett knew exactly where he was. He was, in fact, traveling the globe to find something—or, in the more recent past, some*one*—else.

The wind that was doing such a poor job of cooling the area was proving far more efficient at kicking up the dirt and sand that coated the shallow mountainside on which he stood. Beckett had abandoned the jeep he'd purchased as surplus from the Turkish military—which probably made it Russian surplus if one followed its pedigree back far enough—some miles ago. Even a four-wheel drive in top condition would have proven incapable of climbing some of the slopes Beckett had been forced to cross on his route, and the jeep was rather distant from top condition.

He knew there wasn't a chance in hell he could finish what he needed to do and still get back to civilization before sunrise, but he also knew the area. It wouldn't be difficult to find a cave deep enough to shelter from the lethal inconvenience that was the sun. Of course, in an emergency, Beckett didn't *need* shelter; just a patch of earth deep enough for him to sink into—that was one of the benefits of his particular undead pedigree, and a fair trade for the inhuman features. Still, he'd have had to leave all his gear out in the open, and while the odds of anyone passing by were slim, it was a risk he'd rather not take.

Right now, though, he had an entirely different cave in mind. He hadn't been back to it in some years, but the route was indelibly etched into his mind. He probably could have found it with his eyes closed.

The wind lessened as he approached it, but a look behind showed that it was blowing as strongly as ever just a few dozen yards away. The place itself seemed somehow to shrug off the worst of nature's fury.

"Well," Beckett said to the world at large, "that's convenient."

He paused a moment.

"I *really* don't trust 'convenient.'"

For several long moments, Beckett stood unmoving—far more than any mortal could have managed—and let the sight before him burn itself into his mind, overlapping vivid memories with current reality.

It hadn't changed. He stared at a cave entrance that gaped open in the mountainside like the mouth of some great beast; had Zeus buried the monstrous Typhon under this mount, rather than Mt. Etna, it might have explained a maw like this. A dozen people standing shoulder to shoulder could have walked inside without touching either wall. At one point in the distant past, they could have walked blindfolded, and been certain of the smooth and even floor beneath them, but even this place wasn't entirely immune to the passing years, and rocks and other debris now presented obstacles to easy footing.

From here, a mortal could not possibly make out the ancient writing across the rim of the cave. It was too small, too worn away by centuries of wind-flung sand. Beckett, however, could read it as clearly as if he stood right beside it on the night it had appeared.

According to legend, no hands, human or otherwise, had carved those words, words in a language that few alive (or undead) could read. Words that had appeared, chiseled into the stone, even as the ancient master of this place spoke them.

Let no childe of Caine ever leave through this passage. Let no son of Seth enter.

Beckett stood, as he had so many times before, at the entrance to Kaymakli, ancient city—and ancient tomb—of a long-dead clan.

But this time, he intended to do more than just stand. This time, for the sake of a vampire named Okulos, a friend—or a companion as near to being a friend as Kindred nature would allow—he would challenge the might of a departed Antediluvian.

Assuming he was nuts enough to actually go through with it.

One Year Earlier
Princess Caroline Library
Monaco

Beckett was not especially happy to be in Monaco. The entire country always felt like one sprawling tourist trap to him. There was nothing to explore, no deep cultural secrets to unearth. Oh, certainly the nation's history went back hundreds and even thousands of years, as far back as its settlement by the Phoenicians, but the Kindred played very little part in it, and that was always Beckett's first concern.

Besides, most of the people there spoke French.

But that was where Samir dwelled, and that was where Samir wanted to meet. So that's where they met.

Muhsin Samir—most assuredly not his real name—was Moroccan born, and could certainly never go home again. He was Tremere, a warlock as well as a vampire, and that made him more than a little unpopular among the Assamite clan who held quite a bit of influence in Morocco.

He was also an old associate of Beckett's who was willing to trade information, at least when he could do so without interfering with Tremere interests. Beckett had gone to him more than once on matters thaumaturgic and arcane, for while Beckett himself had a greater mastery of blood magic than most, it still paled beside the knowledge of a true student of the occult.

Samir arranged the meeting, not at some fancy hotel or casino like the Monte Carlo, as Beckett expected, but in the Princess Caroline Library, known far and wide for its specialization in children's literature.

"Because it will not seem unusual for us to be trading tomes," the Tremere, clad in American Levis and an old Garth Brooks T-shirt, said in response to Beckett's unasked question. He paused long enough to step aside as a flock of children brushed past them at just slowly enough the staff couldn't yell at them for running. The children clearly had at least one more stop they felt they had to make before the library closed. "And because it gives us only a short amount of time to make our exchange, and thus precludes any last-minute renegotiation."

Beckett scowled, but chose to let the implied insult pass without comment. Instead, he stuck a hand into the satchel he carried at his side—one that had not been easy to slip past the library's new security—and removed a book. The cover was thick leather, cracked in various spots but otherwise in relatively good condition.

"You didn't tell me," Beckett growled, jerking the book back out of reach as Samir reached for it, "that the previous owners were going to object quite so strongly to me making off with it."

"It's a tome on Hermetic magic, Beckett. What did you expect?"

"I expected to find the temple abandoned, seeing as how someone who shall remain nameless told me it would be. I did not expect to have to slice my way through a Hermetic wizard while the rest of his chantry tried to bring the roof down on me, crash my car, or otherwise explode my head with their various and sundry rhymes from hell!"

"You know very well that Hermetic incantations don't rhyme, Beckett."

"You want this damn book or don't you?"

"Language, Beckett! There are children present." Then, when his companion's nostrils actually flared, Samir decided it was time to stop teasing his guest. "All right, Beckett. You have my sincere apologies. I honestly believed the temple *was* abandoned. I didn't find out that the order was attempting to recover the texts until you were already out of contact. Now, may I please have the book?"

Another moment of hesitation, and then Beckett finally handed over the prize. "What did you want this for, anyway? I thought you Tremere already had the entire Hermetic collection."

"Ah, no. There are still secrets that we do not—well, it doesn't matter. We wanted, and you delivered. Thank you."

"Don't thank me. Just hold up your end of the bargain."

Samir glanced around to ensure that no curious children—or adults—were within earshot. "Beckett," he whispered, and all hint of teasing was gone from his voice, "it's taken me years to dig up this ritual. It's old, older than most of my clan. I mean no offense by this—you're quite skilled for one who hasn't devoted his existence to the mysteries—but I have serious doubts that you've the power or experience necessary to invoke this rite."

Beckett leaned forward, as though preparing to share some great secret with the Warlock. "Samir…"

"Yes?"

"I doubt it, too." He grinned, then, a grin with little humor in it. "Guess I'll find out for sure."

The Tremere could only shake his head. "As you will. Come with me outside. The materials are in my car."

The Present
The Taurus Mountains
South-southwest of Kayseri (and Mt. Erciyes),
Turkey

And now he was here, standing at the very brink of eternal imprisonment, staring down the mouth of a cave and past an invisible barrier that had imprisoned God-knew-how-many Kindred—including two of Beckett's companions. It had taken him almost a year after receiving the ritual from Samir to gather the necessary components. (It wasn't as though werewolf blood or a key carved by one of the fair folk were easy to come by—and those weren't even the rarest items on the list.) Clearly, Samir hadn't been exaggerating about either the age or the power of the ritual Beckett contemplated. The rite had certainly been created in an age when magic and the world were very different from what they were now.

Beckett glanced at his watch. He needed at least an hour to prepare the ritual, another three to carry it out. And even assuming it worked, he didn't have the slightest hint how long it would take him to explore what lay beyond; nights, probably.

He had just enough time before dawn to tear down the barrier, if he pushed.

So he'd push.

The backpack dropped to the ground with a muffled thud, sending a rolling cloud of dust and sand in all directions. From within, Beckett pulled two smaller bags, stored within the first to keep his mundane equipment separate from his other, more esoteric possessions.

In the first bag, the same shoulder-satchel in which he'd carried Samir's tome, was all the gear to be expected of an archeologist and explorer: a set of tiny precision tools, from brushes to chisels to paper and crayons for making rubbings; a vintage World War II Colt .45 with four fully-loaded extra clips (Beckett had far more effective ways of dealing with any Kindred who got in his way, and he'd never been particularly fond of firearms, but when it came to dealing with hostile mortals in large numbers, he'd still found nothing better than lead moving at very, very high speeds); a heavy flashlight and several flares (Beckett could see in the dark, but he often traveled with companions who couldn't, and he'd simply developed the habit of carrying them); a night-vision camera, so he could snap shots of any valuable or informative finds without exposing them to the harsh glare of a flashbulb; an advanced GPS reader, capable of telling the user his precise position (a device Beckett *really* wished that he, and more appropriately his companions, had brought with them the last time); a spade—not in the bag, but strapped to it—with the very end of the handle broken off, apparently through hard use (that the break gave the wooden grip a particularly pointed end was not, however, coincidence). In a rather grotesque tribute to preparedness, Beckett also included an insulated thermos filled with some fresh AB-negative, something few other archeologists would have any use for. All this he'd take with him past the mouth of the cave, assuming he decided, when push came to shove, that he had sufficient balls—and insufficient common sense—to take that fateful step.

The contents of the other bag would, of course, be left behind—those that weren't consumed by the ritual, at any rate.

Assuming he could make the ritual work.

Assuming the ritual didn't consume *him*.

Assuming—*ah, fuck it. Time to stop assuming, Beckett*, he thought grimly. *Ante up or go home.*

With as much precision as any surgeon, Beckett began—using the index finger bone of a hand that was cut off its owner as punishment for stealing, back in the days when such was common practice—to draw symbols in the dirt. Candles (not all made from wax) and even more peculiar ingredients would follow, and after that…

After that it was time to pit his magical abilities against a ward put in place by Cappadocius himself, one of the thirteen forebears of the entire Kindred race. And those abilities were suddenly starting to seem very, very limited.

The Taurus Mountains
South-southwest of Kayseri (and Mt. Erciyes),
Turkey

Beckett hadn't really needed oxygen (speech notwithstanding) for nigh onto three hundred years now, yet instincts long dormant but not fully purged had him gasping with the exertion. In the depths of his soul (or whatever passed for it these nights) he could already feel the sun beginning to drag its way, hand over fist, toward the horizon. The dawn was less than an hour away.

Around him lay scattered the remnants of his ritual. Puddles of wax, melted and allowed to dry once more, formed strange patterns in the sand. The winds that had sprung up out of nowhere about midway through his casting (and he still hoped those were signs of success, not random occurrences that might well have disrupted his concentration at a crucial moment) had completely obliterated the sigils he'd so carefully drawn in the dust. The lupine blood was gone, absorbed into the solid rock against which he'd ritually splattered it; the key forged by the fae was buried deep, the sand above it stained a deep red-brown as though turned to rust. Beckett himself was coated in a sheen of blood-sweat, his formerly white shirt plastered to his chest and already beginning to dry and crack. It smelled wrong, almost tainted, as though something unnatural (even more unnatural than Beckett himself) had invaded his system.

Yet for all the wind, for all the blood, for all the strange happenings and bizarre quirks, he saw no sign that the ritual had succeeded. Frankly, he'd expected no more. Parts of the ritual were scribed in languages that he hadn't even recognized, let alone understood. Samir was good enough to provide phonetic notes so Beckett could at least stumble through the motions, but it was no substitute for actually knowing what the hell he was doing.

Still, his earlier pessimism notwithstanding, Beckett couldn't help but feel an acute disappointment. Okulos had been a good companion, one of the few in several centuries Beckett might have called friend. He could well be destroyed, or at least in torpor, but Beckett had felt obligated to make at least one more concerted effort at keeping his promise, at finding a way for his friend to escape a trap laid centuries ago by a dead demigod.

"I'm sorry, my friend." It was the first time in a great while Beckett had apologized. It was the first time in even longer that he meant it. He bent down to collect what few occult components might be salvageable, determined at least to leave no evidence of his presence.

When his fingers brushed against the rust-colored spot

upon the sands, he felt as if a volcano had erupted from the earth—through him. A surge of power the likes of which Beckett had never felt literally lifted him off his feet and hurled him half a dozen yards back from the cave entrance. Beckett couldn't immediately try to determine what had happened; he was too busy fighting down the Beast within him, which seemed determined to drive him into either a blood frenzy or a headlong instinctive flight away from this spot and anything that reminded him of it. Beckett had once done a goodly amount of his traveling in the company of a woman named Lucita. An elder in the blood and a renegade from many of her fellows, she'd told him tales of the Sabbat, and of how they "coaxed" information out of those unwilling to give it. She'd been particularly impressed, in a disgusted sort of way, with the creativity of one inquisitor who had developed a system involving white-hot pins, sugar-water and an entire colony of fire ants. At the time, Beckett couldn't imagine what being simultaneously burned and consumed from within could possibly feel like.

Now he knew.

He also knew, however, that if he frenzied now, or succumbed to the red fear, he might not have the presence of mind to locate proper shelter from the sun. He wanted to escape the pain, as the Beast did, but not by immolating himself and becoming one with the desert.

Had he not been so focused on overcoming his own pain, and his own inner turmoil, he might have seen the stone walls of the cave before him *ripple*, as though they were nothing but a watercolor painted on the wind. He might have seen the runes etched into that stone glow with a bright red light that could not possibly come from any natural reaction or process—and then fade from sight, their age-old power finally shattered.

But he didn't. And so it was only when he'd gotten himself once more under control, when he stopped seeing the world around him through a haze of red, that he looked upon the cave face—and he *knew*. Somehow, against all hope, against all logic, he'd done it. The ward had fallen.

Beckett wished he could take the time to confirm, despite his certainty. Examinations with heightened and even preternatural senses, thaumaturgic rituals…

But he did none of these things. With the fatigue of dawn already creeping up on him, and the sun lurking so near the eastern horizon that the clouds were turning pink, Beckett scrambled to gather his equipment and dove into the welcoming shadows of Kaymakli just before slumber overtook him.

Elsewhere…

Above Kaymakli, the Red Star shone.

QThe ward came tumbling down, and as it fell, it triggered an invisible surge of power that flowed outward like a shockwave.

The Red Star shone, and beneath it barriers weakened. The Red Star shone, a hellish light at the end of a very long tunnel.

The collapse of Cappadocius' barrier echoed over the mountains and the deserts of Turkey, out into the Orient and the Middle East.

Somewhere, deep beneath the sands in a cave that only partially existed in any world human or Kindred minds could comprehend, the echoes disturbed the dreams of something that had slumbered since the world was young.

It had stirred before, this impossible thing, this relic of old that monsters feared. Stirred—but never before awoken.

It awoke now. It awoke to a world of nothingness, aware of nothing, seeing nothing, feeling nothing.

Nothing but a hunger so all consuming, so pervasive that nothing could possibly exist outside it—for anything that was, was only to be consumed.

Hunger… and a single, rational thought, couched in terms impossible to comprehend, from a time when language did not exist.

Loosely translated into mortal concepts, it was simply: *It is time.*

And above it all, the Red Star shone.

Kaymakli,
under the Taurus Mountains
Eastern Turkey

In the darkened entry hall of the great underground city of Kaymakli, sheltered from the burning gaze of the sun, Beckett dreamed...

He stood, not within the cave, but once again outside it. Some hundred yards away, its rotors having finally drifted to a complete halt, was the Bell Industries helicopter—the same model sold to militaries and police forces across the globe, though lacking many of those agencies' more interesting offensive modifications—that had brought them here.

In that strange partial awareness that so often comes to dreamers, Beckett wished he'd had such a means of transport, or the ability to pilot it, for *this* visit. He also had the presence of mind to wonder where the dream came from, since he was quite certain he hadn't dreamed since he was a mortal.

He was not alone, a fact for which he was profoundly grateful. This—this could well be the greatest archeological discovery, at least from a Kindred perspective, of the modern era. Beckett was glad to have valued companions with whom to share it; some things were simply too big even for him. There were no mortals to be seen for miles, so the two Nosferatu who traveled with Beckett had long since dropped the illusory masks of humanity so many of their clan wore to hide their monstrous features.

Korenna, childe of Okulos and thus, in some respect, godchilde to Beckett, couldn't repress a sigh of delight as she translated the words that ringed the cave's mouth. "This is really it, isn't it?" She had in her voice the tone of a child who has just received the one thing she actually wanted for her birthday or Christmas. "This is the entrance to Kaymakli."

"If it is not," Okulos told her with a sidelong wink at Beckett, "it's the most skilled forgery I have ever seen."

"Not to mention the biggest," Beckett added.

For hundreds of years the children of Caine had searched for this place, spoken of in some of the most horrific of their legends but also a source of great knowledge—and possibly great power. For if those legends were true, literally thousands of vampires had been imprisoned behind their progenitor's ward. Though many had assuredly met their final deaths, many others might yet lie in torpor, awaiting only eager students of the past to awaken them—or eager diablerists to drain the souls from their already bloodless husks.

Anyone who made even the most cursory examination of the history of Kaymakli, its sister city Derinkuyu, and the Cappadocian clan that was master of both, knew the approximate location of the hidden city. (Of course, that itself was problematic, since few Kindred in the world knew enough of either of those cities or the Cappadocians to even begin such research, but Beckett and his companions ran in very select circles.) Somehow, though, nobody had ever succeeded in locating the entrance.

"Or at least," Okulos had remarked to Beckett one evening, "nobody ever reported finding it. It's likely that several Kindred are running around with this knowledge, but no notion of how to use it. It's likelier still that some of the Kindred trapped behind the ward are more recent tenants than the Cappadocians themselves."

They had determined that they were not going to be so careless. Years of research finally yielded the clue that would lead them to Kaymakli—hidden away in an otherwise unremarkable manuscript by a vampiric madman who had wandered the Near and Middle East claiming to be the reincarnation of one of Muhammad's wives—making a detailed record of his travels—and then leaped headfirst into a bonfire, supposedly to burn away his masculine exterior and reveal the woman beneath. Though excitement had flared within them all, they decided that their first expedition would serve merely to confirm the cave's location, and to study the entrance and—if possible—the ward itself. Beckett had a fair idea, culled from other accounts, as to exactly how far into the cave one could step before passing through the mystic barrier. ("Not far," was the general conclusion.) They hoped to find a means of testing that without putting themselves in danger.

Now that they were here, of course, it was far more tempting to

*throw themselves into the task, to learn everything they could and
damn the risks, but they maintained a level of professional calm.*

*"Okulos," Beckett told him, "why don't you and Korenna ex-
amine the cave mouth itself? I'm going to take a few external
measurements."*

"Well... Yes, Beckett, as you wish."

What? No! Beckett's dream-self was suddenly confused.
That wasn't how it had happened! Okulos had *insisted* on being
the one to examine the cave mouth, Beckett had never
wanted...

*He had set to measuring the density, and guessing about the age
and mineral composition, of the surrounding rock face when he was
interrupted by a pair of screams. The first was female, sharp, a high-
pitched cry of unbearable agony that was silenced as abruptly as it had
begun. The second was male, deeper, a wail of loss, and it continued
far beyond the point where the other had ceased even to echo.*

*When Beckett raced back around to stare into the cave, focus-
ing the power of the blood through his eyes so he could see clearly into
the darkened abyss, only a single figure, one hand still raised in a futile
gesture, remained.*

*"Beckett..." Okulos choked, his voice almost a sob. "Korenna
is gone! You must have misjudged the location of the barrier, Beckett!
My childe is dead! I am trapped! And it's your fault!"*

Again, Beckett's dream-self cried out in silent protest. His
calculations were not in question! And he'd never claimed they
were precise enough for use as a God damn yardstick! The Nosferatu
had gotten careless in their excitement, misread their location in
the dim glow of their flashlights. Nobody, Okulos included, had
ever blamed Beckett for it! It hadn't been his fault at all!

*But in the dream, Beckett stepped back from the entrance,
removed a notebook of transcribed phrases and calculations—
calculations that showed subtle marks of recent erasure and
rewriting—and exulted.*

Kaymakli, under the Taurus Mountains
Eastern Turkey

Beckett wasn't a large enough fan of clichés to allow himself to awaken, screaming and sitting bolt upright, from a nightmare like that. Still, the emotion was so powerful that he very nearly shifted directly from daytime slumber to maddened frenzy, and only managed to regain control through a supreme act of will. When his vision once more cleared, he glanced at the rivulets of blood that trickled down his arms from his clenched fists. His Gangrel ancestry had its advantages, but it had its drawbacks as well—the main one of which was the unfortunate tendency to adopt animalistic features when they frenzied too often.

That's twice in two nights you've almost lost control, Beckett. Unless you want to find yourself looking like Marmaduke, you'd better get a grip.

A quick slug from his thermos calmed his nerves, though it was something of a struggle not to drain the container dry. He felt a tingle in his eyes as his body focused the power of the blood within him. Instantly, the solid darkness around him faded like a gentle mist, and Beckett could see. He knew that other Gangrel's eyes glowed when they made use of their preternatural night vision; his own remained that way constantly. Under most conditions he'd be worried that this would allow others to spot him approaching in the dark, but that was another reason he'd brought the seemingly superfluous sunglasses. With them on, the gleam in his eyes was muted to near invisibility, yet he could still clearly see his surroundings.

Rocks. Stone walls. A cavernous ceiling above. The floor of a passageway that, while probably naturally occurring, had clearly been smoothed by artificial means.

All in all, not the most dramatic first sight of perhaps the largest find of his existence.

A closer examination revealed that what he'd initially taken for loose rocks consisted at least partially of bones. Mostly pig, but some dog, sheep and even a single human skeleton.

Beckett smiled sadly. Okulos was a neat freak about most things, but he'd always been a sloppy eater. Beckett had returned to Kaymakli on a regular basis for months after Okulos was first trapped within, bringing food animals for his imprisoned friend. He'd only stopped when Okulos stopped appearing in the tunnel to claim them.

His friend might be truly dead. But just maybe he lay somewhere, starved into torpor but revivable, and Beckett would keep his promise.

First, however, before he could go forward, he had to see if he could go back.

His hand very nearly shook with the vampire's instinctive fear of flame—Beckett had arrived too late to see Korenna immolated by the great seal, but he'd smelled the traces of her demise on the air. Still, one way or another, he had to know.

Beckett took one step back up the tunnel, a second, a third...

And nothing happened. Despite himself, Beckett allowed a single laugh of relief to well up from his throat. Somehow, God alone knew how, he'd really done it. The ward was down.

As for the inside, he didn't expect much. Reports and rumors about places like this were always exaggerated. He anticipated a small village, not a sprawling city, and expected that the dozens of inhabitants had been inflated, as legends often did, into thousands. Nevertheless, he was about to set eyes on a site few had seen, and fewer still had survived to tell. And just maybe, he was about to find his friend. His spirits brightened considerably, Beckett progressed down the passage.

Whatever cheer his apparent success with the ward might have brought him faded swiftly.

It began as a chill in the air. Caves were often naturally colder than their surroundings, and Beckett had delved into more than his share. A certain degree of cold was to be expected. This was different. Beckett had stood in the midst of blizzards that would have killed a mortal in minutes, but now he *felt* the cold. It didn't attack his flesh; rather, the blood within him seemed to chill, making him sluggish. Unable to focus, he let several minutes of progress pass without examining his surrounding—not a wise proposition, either in terms of learning or personal safety. Beckett shook his head violently, and wished emphatically for something to keep him focused, to distract him from the unnatural cold.

He should have known better.

It sounded like an echo of the blowing wind, carried down the passageway behind him by some trick of acoustics. It was incredibly faint, barely audible even to his inhumanly acute hearing. He wasn't certain how long he'd been listening to it. Beckett tensed, and his fingertips began to itch as his body instinctively transformed his inhuman nails into the talons that were his most potent weapon.

There were voices in the wind.

And it was clear, soon enough, that it wasn't wind at all, for they no longer came merely from behind, but from all other directions as well. Words, so muffled and distorted that he could not even recognize the language, grew louder and fainter as though the speakers were moving past him in the hall. Some were masculine, some feminine, and all had the same timbre to them. The speakers, whoever and whatever they were, were clearly puzzled about something.

About him, perhaps?

"Hello? If you've something to ask me, ask me directly."

When no response came—as he'd expected—he allowed his claws to slide back into his flesh and continued walking, more slowly, more warily.

At least he was no longer focused on the cold.

The cavern widened still further, and Beckett saw growing signs of ancient inhabitation—here a small niche, almost like a room of some sort, carved into the wall; there, an engraving from the Bible, specifically the ninety-first psalm: *He that dwelleth in the secret place of the most High shall abide under the shadow of the Almighty*.

Then the passage opened into a cavern larger than any Beckett could have imagined, and Beckett stared incredulously at the underground wonder—and horror—that was Kaymakli.

The legends, the rumors, the "exaggerations"—they were all true. There, stretching out before him like a model or a map, was an entire medieval city. Buildings constructed both of the native rock and of wood hauled in from the surface occupied vast portions of the cavern floor; they were even arranged into uneven but noticeable blocks, allowing a system of streets and roads to spread throughout the city. Most were in awful shape, evidence that the city had lain derelict for so many years. Even from here, Beckett could see the rotten wood, the crumbling thatch. Even those structures carved from the rock had gaping holes where doors and shutters once rested, and showed the wear and tear of the region's occasional quakes.

In the distant corners of the city, nearly too far for Beckett's unnatural sight, lay broken stonework that might once have been an aqueduct. Beckett could only assume that the ancient inhabitants had brought water from above, storing it for use when they could not conveniently travel to the surface.

The voices grew louder as Beckett progressed into the first of the narrow streets, standing in footprints and even wagon tracks that were clearly preserved from ancient nights. The sounds seemed now to be coming from various doors and windows, yet no movement accompanied the voices. Once and once only, Beckett suddenly twisted about and lunged through one of those gaping doors, determined to find the source. He found nothing but a broken table and a cloud of dust stirred up by his swift arrival.

They weren't merely louder, though. They were starting to sound angry. Well, Beckett had dealt with irritated ghosts before, and he wasn't about to let them turn him away now. Carefully watching his feet so he could pick his way through the heavy shadows of the buildings, he slowly made his way—

Shadows?

Beckett stopped dead, motionless save for a deliberate blinking of his eyes. The cavern was completely dark, without the glimmering of a single star or candle flame to illuminate it. He was able to see only because one of his familial traits as a Gangrel allowed his eyes to pierce even absolute night. No shadows could possibly exist, for there was neither light to cast them nor to see them by.

Yet even when he looked again, they remained. Dark and blurred reflections, stretched out across the street before him as though the sun itself shone from the cavern's depths. Houses, stables, a well, even the wreckage of large cart—all of these cast their images before him.

Everything had a shadow, everything except Beckett.

And that realization was followed by another: The voices he heard were coming not from the buildings, but from the buildings' shadows.

Ever so slowly, Beckett reached into the satchel he carried and removed the powerful flashlight. His own vision might be more efficient, but it was seeing things that clearly couldn't be, and he wanted to see if they still existed in "real" lighting.

Beckett clicked the light on, and the world went mad.

The meager beam of his flashlight somehow bounced off the surrounding shadows, as though it struck some reflective barrier, until it shone back in his eyes and threatened to blind him even through his sunglasses. The ground beneath his feet shifted from the dark brown he had seen with his night vision to a dull red. It was no longer solid but a thick mud that clung to his boots, and it was clearly not water but countless gallons of blood that saturated the floor. The charnel stench of a slaughterhouse assailed him, forcing its way through his nose though he drew no breath, threatening yet again to unleash the Beast within him.

Beckett staggered, tried to turn away from the blinding light. The voices rose around him, growing louder, deafening, their screams now a mixture of rage and panic, crying out for mercy, for forgiveness. Figures only vaguely human in shape detached themselves from the shadows of the buildings and hurtled down the narrow road, past Beckett, and *through* him, and each tore a sliver from his soul. Memories assaulted him. Only a bare few were his, and those were twisted beyond recognition, much as his dream had been.

He was a young woman, barely three years a Cainite. It wasn't his fault! He hadn't had time, hadn't had the opportunity to make something of himself! God, please, no, don't leave him down here, not in the dark, not in the…

Fury like he'd never known flooded him, granting strength to limbs that looked like those of an old man. Worthless, was he? Unworthy of the blood? He'd show that arrogant old bastard, show the lot of them! With the amount of power down here, he could take, and take, and—and what was that sudden pain in his chest, and why couldn't he move? No, damn it! His soul wouldn't go to feed some young scoundrel, he'd…

He was Beckett again, crouched beside the blond Malkavian, the oracle of horrors to come, and listening to yet another of his rumi-

nations on the Book of Nod. Only this time, when Anatole turned away, making some dramatic gesture or other, Beckett lunged at his throat, jaws agape…

He was nobody, he could remember no name, no identity, nothing but a crushing fear of enclosed places as the bodies pressed against him and the mighty rumble of the cave entrance sliding closed sent shivers through his gut…

"Mary? Mary, where are you? Mary, I can't hear, everyone's too loud. Why is the cave closing in? Mary, did we do something wrong?"

With the voice of a thousand doomed souls, Beckett screamed. It went on, far beyond the point where a mortal would have been forced to draw breath, went on even when the air in his lungs was fully depleted and no sound at all emerged from his throat.

Becket collapsed, his knees striking the sodden road, and it was the splatter of cold mud on his face that saved him. The tang of the vitae in the muck roused the Beast within, and when Beckett instinctively fought it down, struggled for calm, he regained not only control over the Beast, but over the images and memories as well. Around him the parade of ghosts, or memories, or whatever they were continued, but for at least a moment he was himself again. He glanced around, seeking a place of shelter, and saw only the tiny alleyway between two houses—and what, at first, he took for stacks of cordwood, laid out since Kaymakli was abandoned…

Except cordwood didn't have limbs, didn't have eyes. Dear God, they were Kindred! Ancient Kindred starved so thoroughly by years of torpor that they held not a single drop of moisture within—were literally nothing but bones and hardened, mummified flesh. He wondered, briefly, who had taken the time to stack them like this, and then decided he probably didn't want to know.

Beckett fumbled in the mud beside him, found the flashlight he had dropped, and thumbed the switch back so violently the plastic cracked.

Instantly, all was silent. Examined only with his preternatural night vision, Kaymakli was once more a place of strange movements and impossible shadows, but nothing more. The road on which he knelt was again merely ancient dirt, absent any trace or scent of spilled blood. Whatever it was that lingered here, it reacted most strongly to the light—so Beckett would give it none.

He took a few moments to calm himself, to regain his strength, to convince himself that nothing was lurking over his shoulder, prepared to rip his mind apart. He was no longer standing where he had been, but was much deeper into the city itself. He wondered if one (or more) of the ghosts had possessed him temporarily, but no—they'd all been fleeing this area, not moving toward it. Nor, he figured, had he frenzied and made his way here on his own, since his instincts would probably have carried him *away* from the city if he had. At least, he certainly *hoped* that was the case. Beckett had no interest in looking or acting like an animal, as so many elder Gangrel did after the Beast took control one time too many. Like some others of his clan, he had learned techniques of concentration and meditation that would allow him to purge his undead body of those animalistic traits, but they required weeks or months of effort that could better be spent in other pursuits. Nor were the techniques flawless, as Beckett's own monstrous eyes and hands attested.

He could only assume, then, that he'd come forward pushing against the spirits like a drowning man fighting the tide, that his struggle against them mentally had entailed a physical one as well.

In any event, he stood on a street corner that offered no particular features he might use to orient himself. From the cave entrance looking down on it all, every street looked very much like every other. Beckett had an unerring sense of direction, and if he'd been conscious for the walk here, he could have at least retraced his steps, but as it was…

Well, the phantoms of this place could damn well work *for* him. When he saw them moments before, they'd all been surging in the same direction, as though fleeing something, and whatever that something was, it was sure to be more distinctive than where he was now. Beckett chose the direction that most closely approximated the path of the torrent of spirits as he remembered it, and backtracked it.

He soon passed between two of the largest buildings he'd yet encountered down here—they appeared, on casual inspection, to be churches or temples of some sort—and stood before one of the cavern's great walls. A second cave, smaller than the entryway but still large enough to drive a car through, loomed open before him. Chunks of rock littered the surrounding area, rock that was strangely smooth on two sides. After a few minutes of placing pieces together like a remarkably heavy jigsaw, Beckett decided that this was once a massive circle of stone, probably used to seal this cave. Whatever had been on the other side had eventually broken through, but been unable to leave the city itself thanks to Cappadocius' ward.

This, then, would be the tomb. The metaphorical dining room of the so-called Feast of Folly. Within this cave, thousands of Cappadocians were entombed by their own progenitor, condemned to cannibalism and inevitable starvation for the sin of not living up to his ideals.

No wonder the ghosts were pissed.

From deep within the smaller cave, a light flickered. It wasn't steady enough to be electric. A fire? Beckett tensed, not so much at the thought of flame—he had to be pretty close to an open blaze before his instincts overrode his control—but at the notion that someone had been moving about in there recently enough that any fire they lit was still burning.

Whatever the source, the ghosts didn't seem to be reacting to that light as they had to his. Maybe they were accustomed to it. Maybe something about the "artificial" light of a bulb, as opposed to flame, set them off.

Or maybe whatever was moving around in there scared them.

A few steps in, Beckett's night vision faded, as his otherwise heightened senses required only the dim light of the distant fire to work with. In the brief moment he had to look around, he saw broken stone furniture, bloodstains so old and thoroughly soaked into the stone that they were permanent additions to the décor, more neat stacks of desiccated bodies like wood, a few other bodies scattered about as though discarded by an angry child…

Then something hard and heavy slammed into Beckett's side like an enraged bull.

Beckett tumbled, his jaw clenched in pain as he felt the bones in his arm separate with the initial impact, his other hip crack as he hit the floor. Only his supernatural resilience saved him from far worse.

Martial instincts honed in the best of schools—street fights and real combat, rather than any dojo or arena—sent him rolling under the impact. Even as dirt crunched under his shoulders he placed a foot against his attacker and shoved. He didn't have the angle or the momentum to send the foe flying, but he was able to knock him away and give himself room to stand. Blood flowed through his limbs, strengthening his flesh, tensing muscles to force broken bones back together with an audible crack. His nails hardened and slid several inches from his fingertips with the sound of tearing flesh. Teeth bared in a snarl, hands raised, the Beast lurking just behind his eyes, Beckett spun to face his attacker.

And his jaw gaped.

"Oh, shit. Okulos…"

The Nosferatu was barely recognizable. His granite-gray skin was paler than Beckett had ever seen it, and clung to his bones like wet cotton. His various scars and blemishes were more pronounced, in some cases open and oozing. Several of his twisted and uneven teeth were missing; the others protruded directly from bone, for the skin of his gums had completely rotted away. His heavy coat and pants were tattered, his shirt completely gone save for the cuff still buttoned around his left wrist. The leather bandolier that hung from his left shoulder was of the sort that had once been called a brace, used by pirates of long ago to carry multiple pistols at once. When Okulos had first vanished into the depths of Kaymakli, that bandolier had been full of flare guns, Okulos's favored weapon for use against other Kindred. Now only two remained, but these were still more than sufficient to cause Beckett some serious injury. Fortunately—if such a state could ever be called fortunate—Okulos appeared too far gone to the Beast to think of using them.

"Okulos, it's me. Do you remember me? I don't want to hurt you. I *sure* as hell don't want you to hurt me. I—"

Beckett hadn't really expected his words to penetrate his friend's starvation-induced frenzy, but he still barely hurled himself to the side as Okulos shrieked and leaped at him. Beckett backpedaled furiously, looking for a way to protect his own skin without destroying the one person he'd come to save. He knew he was faster than his friend, and capable of absorbing a great deal more punishment, but Okulos was undeniably the stronger of the two. Beckett blocked blow after blow, and each time his arms ached as though struck by a jackhammer. The newly healed bone in his left elbow began to separate once more, and when the maddened Okulos followed up a punch with a sudden thrust of his knee, Beckett felt numerous ribs give way and puncture organs that, thankfully, he no longer used.

Spitting blood he couldn't afford to waste and remaining upright through sheer stubbornness, Beckett knew he couldn't afford to hold back any longer. But damn it, he was *not* going to destroy the one for whom he'd gone to all this trouble! If nothing else, it was inefficient.

Using a technique he'd learned from Lucita, Beckett tensed one shoulder as though planning to throw a punch and then, as his foe twisted away from the attack, delivered a devastating spinning heel kick from the other direction. It wasn't the most precise technique; any halfway skilled opponent could avoid or block it. The point, however, was to drive the foe back a step or two, either through impact or their own dodge. And indeed, Okulos staggered aside even though his mighty arms absorbed most of the blow.

It gave Beckett just enough room to dive. Allowing his momentum to carry him, and grimacing in pain as the rocks and the dirt scraped a layer of skin from his chest, he slid between Okulos' legs.

Hope you'll forgive me for this later, Beckett thought grimly as he lashed backwards, severing both his friend's hamstrings with his claws.

With a shriek of pain and endless rage, Okulos toppled forward. It was not a permanent injury for a vampire but, delivered as it was with Beckett's unnatural talons, it would require many nights, and much blood, before Okulos could walk once more.

It was a mark of his insane hunger than he tried, even with two useless legs, to drag himself after Beckett, crawling hand over hand, face twisted and jaws agape. For his own part, Beckett allowed his nails to sink back into the flesh of his fingers, picked up the satchel that had fallen when Okulos struck him, and removed the heavy spade with the broken handle.

"Damn you anyway, Okulos. You'd better apologize for making me go through this."

Okulos shrieked once more as the wooden shaft plunged through his back, snapping ribs as it went, and penetrated his heart. Then he went limp, paralyzed by the intrusion of the natural world through his center of power.

Beckett knelt gingerly, his body aching, beside his paralyzed friend, and placed a surprisingly gentle hand upon his gray and scabby head. "Just like you to make me carry you out of here, you lazy bastard."

"Ah. You must be Beckett."

He spun, unable to hide his shock at the sound of a voice where no voice should be. One hand thrust into his satchel, closing around the grip of the Colt. The other began to itch as his talons once more began to sprout from his fingertips.

The newcomer didn't look especially imposing, as far as Kindred go. (And Beckett had no doubt that he *was* Kindred; even if his mere presence behind the ward that "no son of Seth" could enter wasn't sufficient, Beckett's sensitive ears could detect no trace of breathing or heartbeat.) The stranger was short, less than two inches over five feet. His hair was darker than Beckett's, and longer. He wore a thick beard that was barely a thumb's-width shy of qualifying as shaggy. He wore a simple knee-length tunic, apparently made from materials salvaged from Kaymakli itself.

No, he didn't look like much, but Beckett wasn't fooled. The vampire practically radiated a sense of controlled power. Besides, his features alone suggested that he might well have been Embraced some time ago. They were subtly different than those of a modern man, in ways that no mortal and few Kindred could have noticed. Beckett kept his gaze focused at the level of the other's chin and neck, unwilling to meet his stare for fear that his will might be overwhelmed by the elder's gaze.

"Who the hell are you? And how do you know me?"

"My name," the shorter vampire said, "is Kapaneus. And I know you because your friend spoke of you often. Back," he added, his voice turned sad, "when he was still capable of speech."

Kapaneus. It was a Greek name, but the accent with which he spoke didn't sound Greek. In fact, Beckett couldn't place the accent at all; it sounded like a mix, probably picked up through substantial travel. Of course, the fact that he was speaking English at all was stranger than any accent.

"Okulos taught me your language," Kapaneus continued, as though reading Beckett's thoughts. "He told me of many marvels of the modern age that I can scarce understand, let alone believe. He and I became close companions in the years we had, Master Beckett, and his friends are mine. I mean you no harm. In fact, I have been hoping you would appear."

Beckett removed his hand from his weapon, but he remained alert. "How did you get down here, Kapaneus? How long have you been trapped?"

"I passed through Cappadocius' ward in the year 1401. I was seeking a place where I knew the concerns of the world would not disturb me, for I had much to contemplate."

"What?!" Beckett's jaw dropped. "You *willingly* trapped yourself here?!" And then, suddenly, he thought he understood. "Oh, great, just what I need. Another one. You're Malkavian, aren't you?"

Kapaneus laughed, then, a loud, boisterous sound for one so small. "No, I am not of Malkav's brood—though I have, at times, wished that I were. It must make this world so much easier, being mad, seeing things only as you wish."

Beckett thought briefly of Anatole, the Malkavian prophet of Gehenna with whom he'd often traveled, learned from, whom he'd even considered, at times, an adopted sire. Anatole had spent his many years spouting prophecies no one wanted to hear, and had given his existence to find answers even his visions could not offer.

"Don't be so sure," he whispered softly. Then, louder, "How have you survived down here so long?"

"I call animals to me when I need them," the elder responded. "One grows tired of rat, lizard and the like, but they serve. I slumbered in torpor a great deal. And I have mastered certain meditative techniques that allow me to go longer than normal without feeding, if I am careful to conserve my energies. I tried to teach them to your friend, but it took me many mortal lifetimes to master even the simplest of them. I fear Master Okulos was lost before he could ever have learned."

Beckett once more knelt beside his paralyzed companion.

"He has been naught but a beast for some while now," Kapaneus told him, "and my powers only barely hid me from him in his madness. He may yet be savable—but I'd not be terribly hopeful of it."

"He's savable." Beckett stood, holding Okulos in his arms. "I've managed to come this far. I'll find a way to finish the job."

"So you have." Kapaneus seemed to ponder, and then smiled. "As you have been so kind as to tear down the ward, perhaps—with your permission—I'll accompany you for a ways. I would see what the world has become, and I would know that Master Okulos has, indeed, fully recovered."

It would be difficult, certainly. Kapaneus admitted he knew nothing about the modern world. Hell, did the elder even know of the Masquerade? Vampires who wished to survive stayed very well hidden indeed in these modern nights.

But the opportunity to speak to one so ancient, to ask questions of one who had actually seen so many years... Most modern elders had their own agenda, political reasons for refusing to answer, or answering with half-truths. The chance to speak with Kapaneus at length was worth almost *any* inconvenience. Hell, if it meant a shot at answers to questions he'd been asking for almost three centuries, Beckett might even risk the Masquerade itself.

Besides, even if he wanted to, Beckett was certain that trying to prevent Kapaneus from accompanying him would be more trouble than it was worth. To say nothing of the sort of damage an ignorant elder might do in the world *without* some sort of guide.

Beckett simply nodded assent, and began the long walk back to the open air.

part one:
nightfall

And if the day comes when they are so blind
or possessed by jealous rage
that they would root out the one true growth
from among their garden of weeds
then it will be their own souls they destroy.

—*The Erciyes Fragments, "Lamentations"*

Dew Drop Inn, off Interstate 10
Just outside Los Angeles, California

The room was as generic as motels come. Off-brown carpet, tan walls, a pair of twin beds, dresser, television with a menu of movies at least two months out of date. It smelled like cheap carpet cleaner.

The room's current occupants were somewhat less generic. To start with, none of them was living.

The first, a tall, gangly fellow by the name of Ebert, wore glasses and a pinstripe gray suit open at the neck. He was rising from a kneeling position, in which he'd crouched for over an hour before one of the room's badly upholstered chairs.

The second, looming over Ebert's shoulder, was tall, with unruly brown hair and a beard that had just begun to gray. Clad in heavy pants, boots, and a flannel shirt, he looked like an undead lumberjack.

Both of them stared down at the room's third occupant, a youngish blonde woman who sat motionless in the chair, her jaw slack, her expression vacant.

"That should do it, Samuel," Ebert said, his voice horse with fatigue.

"I need you to be absolutely certain," Samuel replied. "This is a very special young woman."

"Special?"

Samuel smiled broadly. "'Your savior is lost among the thousands,'" he quoted, "'And all your searching cannot find the secret mark upon her flesh, or know her name. Behold, the Lady's crescent guards the heavens. And down below, inscribed in flesh, marks the only path that leads from doom.'"

"Right." Ebert was unimpressed. "*Book of Nod*. You believe that crap? Think this girl's some kind of messiah?"

"Messiah? Not exactly. But she's going places, Ebert, and she's going to deal with a lot of powerful people. I can't have anyone stumbling across any signs of your presence."

Ebert scowled. "You came to me because I'm the best, and you know it. Nobody's going to find signs of what I've done. It's not blatant. She's not going to fall all over you, or act like you're bonded or anything. She's just going to be very inclined to listen to what you have to tell her."

"Good. Very, very good. And it'll be how long until she comes out of the trance?"

"At least an hour. You should have plenty of time to get your second coming where she needs to be. And, as I believe that concludes our business, I'll be on my way."

Samuel held up a hand. "Actually, if I could trouble you for just a moment more…"

The flannel-clad Samuel left the motel moments later, a young blonde draped over his shoulder. Everyone who saw them on the street, getting into a beat-up old car, assumed she was drunk. One young man even offered to help position her comfortably in the back seat.

Nobody ever found any traces of Ebert, but the cleaning crew did wonder about the prevalence of ash on the room's floor the next morning.

The Houston Ship Channel
Houston, Texas

Texas. Why did it have to be Texas?

Federico di Padua, loyal Camarilla archon and agent of the Nosferatu justicar Cock Robin, hated the American South and Southwest with a passion that could, in his case, be described quite literally as "bloody." It had all the downsides of his birthplace in Italy—hot, humid summers, and too many wide-open and featureless spaces—with none of the cultural high points. It was like a black-and-white copy of a Rembrandt.

To make matters worse, di Padua was only a few months awakened from torpor. He'd had the misfortune of facing Cardinal Polonia himself during the Camarilla's conquest of New York in 1999, and the Sabbat ancient had come painfully near to destroying him. Even now, years later, di Padua still felt an occasional twinge in his chest, still felt a bit stiff where his neck had finally healed shut, and wondered if he'd ever be back to his full strength.

Di Padua once more sent a string of curses in five different languages, all aimed at his fellow archon Zack Shale. Houston was *his* stomping ground, part of his regular theater of operations, and the current rumors of a Sabbat scouting pack having crossed over from Mexico should have been his concern, not Federico's. Federico should still be recovering, serving as part of Robin's entourage, or otherwise undertaking duties that didn't require him to strain himself until he was back at one-hundred percent.

Unfortunately, Shale had vanished. The justicars were fairly certain he hadn't been slain. It looked as though he'd taken the time to pack up and depart on some schedule. He'd even made the effort of sending a coded message through a series of phone relays, a message that meant, "Cannot complete assignment, send help." But after that, it was as if he'd vanished off the face of the Earth—no mean feat, when hiding from seekers with the abilities and connections of the justicars and their archons.

That meant somebody had to take over where Shale left off, and di Padua had the misfortune of being available.

So now he was crouched in the control booth of a massive crane sitting on the Houston Ship Channel. The power of the blood within him, augmented by the heavy shadows within the booth, rendered him completely invisible to mortal (and most Kindred) sight. Shale's notes, thoughtfully left for di Padua in a bus station locker, and di Padua's own investigations, led him to believe that the Sabbat border-crossers were planning to pick up a load of something or other from one of the freighters docked here overnight. He had no idea *what* they were receiving, and that—combined with the fact that he wanted to see precisely who he was dealing with—had spurred him out here tonight.

Unfortunately, though he'd spotted some initial activity down by the ships, nothing of any consequence was happening. He saw two figures—he thought they were Kindred, but couldn't be sure at this distance—standing around and talking, but nothing more.

When they suddenly vanished, not as though they'd melded into the darkness as he himself often did but as though they'd simply blinked out of existence, di Padua knew he had a problem.

When the first hole appeared in the crane's windshield, surrounded by an intricate spider web pattern and accompanied by a loud crack, he knew the problem had just grown a lot bigger.

And when he saw over half a dozen figures leaping or clambering down from atop nearby roofs and cargo containers, he knew he was pretty much fucked.

Di Padua hadn't come equipped for a running firefight. Stealthy reconnaissance followed by a quick spate of close-in violence, that was his style. The archon hurled himself from the crane, sprinted across an open road with bullets kicking up dust around his feet, and dove behind a shipping crate. He peeked over the shelter, ducked swiftly as one of the approaching Sabbat threw...

A rock? Why the hell would they throw a rock at me?

The rock hit the ground behind the crate, and two thoughts passed through di Padua's mind all at once:

One, the Sabbat pack obviously had a Ravnos among them, or someone who had mastered that clan's facility with illusions. It was the simplest way to explain the disappearance of the figures who had held his attention—a planned distraction, apparently—for so long.

Two, the rock hadn't thumped when it hit the ground near him. It had clinked. Like metal.

Di Padua, in a near panic, sent blood pumping throughout his body. Though he wasn't especially proficient in doing so, he possessed the ability to accelerate himself to inhuman speeds. It should be enough to get out of range before—

Nothing happened. No sudden acceleration, no burst of speed. The blood flowed through his body, and did absolutely nothing.

As Federico di Padua was sent hurtling by the explosion, his body torn by shrapnel, his flesh burned, he didn't wonder if he would have the strength to heal the injuries. He didn't wonder how he'd escape the pack that was assuredly even now closing on his broken and bleeding form.

No, only one thought penetrated his agony-drenched mind as he lay waiting for a seemingly inevitable end. His abilities—his invisibility and his speed both—had utterly failed him. And he didn't know *why*.

Allied Engine Works Factory (Foreclosed)
New Bedford, Massachusetts

"You may have fooled the others sent to find you! You may have run long, and run far from the site of your transgressions! But there is no shadow God cannot see through! There is no place to hide from His anger!"

The whip lashed out, stripping another ribbon of flesh from the back of one of the condemned, and the eyes of the vampire known only as Righteous Endeavor blazed in pleasure at the sight. He had removed the long-tailed jacket of his old-fashioned black suit, and stood behind the prisoners clad in trousers and a white shirt with the sleeves rolled up. The broad-brimmed felt hat, which he insisted on wearing as a symbol of his "sacred" past, hung idly from a jutting spine on one of the inhuman creatures who accompanied him. These *szlachta*—powerful and highly trained war-ghouls, shaped and twisted by the flesh-sculpting powers of the Tzimisce clan—served as both his protectors and his instruments in tasks such as this.

Both witch and witch-hunter from the darkest days of Salem, Righteous Endeavor had abandoned neither his faith nor his love of "confessing" heretics and sinners when he was Embraced. As a priest and informal inquisitor for the Sabbat, he had simply shifted his focus somewhat.

The four neonates kneeling before him were merely the latest "sinners" with whom he had to deal. Assigned the task of scouting the Camarilla strengths in the smaller cities and towns around New York, they had instead encountered a sheriff and her bruisers already prepared for their arrival. They had bargained with the Camarilla, trading Sabbat secrets for their own survival—a grievous transgression in the eyes of their superiors—and had only recently been run to ground. The room in which they were to suffer their fate was practically featureless: four cinderblock walls and a cement floor to which their chains were bolted. The air was heavy with the tang of blood, both shed from wounds and sweated from Kindred pores—quite literally the scent of pain.

"We are the instruments of the Almighty!" Righteous Endeavor continued, bringing the whip down again and again. "We are His hands!" *Crack!* "We are His wrath!" *Crack!* "'Vengeance is mine,' sayeth the Lord, and we *are* that vengeance! The Sword of Caine is the Sword of God, and God cannot abide a tool that breaks!"

Crack!

The neonates cried out in pain, yet they made no move to avoid the strips of leather braided with shards of broken glass. It wasn't that they were physically incapable. The chains that held them were weak, little more than ceremonial. It wasn't that they feared the *szlachta*, for a swift death at those beasts' talons was preferable by far to the endless torture the ranting preacher inflicted with the whip. No, it was the aura of the priest himself, an almost palpable sense of power and malevolence and fearfulness that shimmered from him like a heat mirage and forced them to their knees, kept their eyes turned to the floor and their limbs motionless. They could no more have forced themselves to raise a hand against Righteous Endeavor than they could have taken up arms against the rising dawn.

"You are flawed!" *Crack!* "You are weak!" *Crack!* "You are damned, as are we all, but you accept *not* your damnation! You flee from it! You flee from pain and death in God's service, and so you flee from Him!" *Crack!* "You have turned from Him! You have *scorned* Him! And you have *angered* him!" *Crack!* "Reap ye what ye have sewn, for I *am* the strong right arm of the Lord, I *am* the vengeance of the Lord and of the Sword of Caine, and I say unto thee, thou art twice damned!

"Members of the Silver Hammer Pack," the Tzimisce priest continued formally, coiling the whip without bothering to wipe the blood or bits of skin from it, "I find you guilty of heresy, against the word of God and the laws of the Sabbat. In mine eyes, and in the eyes of the Lord, you are already dead. In His name, I shall make it so.

"Finish them."

As the *szlachta* glided forward, Righteous Endeavor snatched his hat back and turned away, content to listen to the sounds of sinners being rent limb from limb.

He heard sounds, all right—but they weren't what he expected at all.

The preacher spun, eyes wide, to see his precious war-ghouls thrashing about as though poisoned. The larger of the two convulsed once, twice, and then died. The other suffered far worse, as though the powers that had shaped it into something both more and less than human were running amok. Limbs lengthened and shortened, twisted and distorted. Wounds gaped open, extruding stubs of flesh like tongues from gaping mouths.

Righteous Endeavor was struck almost beyond the capacity for speech. How could this be happening? "What—what…"

"*This*, you sanctimonious bastard!"

The preacher toppled to the floor, agony shooting through his skull. He looked up to see one of the prisoners, the chains that had tethered him to the wall now hanging broken from his wrists. Several of the links were covered in blood.

This wasn't possible! His power, the sheer weight of his supernatural presence, should have kept them cowering like children even with the death of their guards. Well, they were about to learn the dangers of interfering with the Lord's work.

Righteous Endeavor tensed, allowing the fury of God's most martial angels to flow through him. It *should* have transformed him into a fearsome creature, a demon of the Pit, with spines and green skin and hands capable of ripping through concrete as easily as through weak flesh.

Instead, the mighty Tzimisce witch-hunter fell to his knees as his body began purging itself of the blood within. He vomited it up in enormous gouts, until his mouth no longer provided wide enough passage and he felt it flow through his nose and even his tear ducts as well.

"My Lord," he choked, his voice nearly unintelligible through the blood. "Why have you…"—another choke—"forsaken me?"

"Probably," he heard the neonate standing over him say, voice filled with anger and hate, "because he's as tired of your bullshit as we are."

By the time the Silver Hammer pack grew bored of their sport and chose to end it all by drinking what remained of Righteous Endeavor's soul, the preacher could only thank God it was over.

Airport Hilton, Los Angeles International Airport
Los Angeles, California

The Kindred known only as Tara, former anarch leader and now Camarilla-supported prince, was not having a good year. All things being equal, she'd rather be back home in San Diego, her true domain, in spite of all its various problems and nightly catastrophes.

Instead, she was now entering her third month as "regent" of Los Angeles. The Cathayans, those strange Asian vampires who had claimed much of the West Coast for their own, had suddenly withdrawn, their manpower in LA shrinking to a fraction of its former size. The elders of the Camarilla didn't know if they'd been destroyed, returned home, or what—and they didn't care. Already, several anarch factions were moving to reclaim LA, which had once been the center of the so-called Anarch Free States. The Camarilla didn't want that either. The justicars weren't about to let another hostile faction form around LA, or leave it available for the Cathayans should they return.

Thus, when Prince LaCroix was slain around the same time the Cathayans began to vanish, they'd needed someone to step in. Someone experienced, someone who knew the area, someone who knew the anarchs.

As prince of her own city, they couldn't *order* Tara to do it. But she knew damn well they could make her existence a nightly hell if she didn't. So San Diego was held by her childer now—and she'd already promised all manner of eternal torments on them if they didn't handily turn power back over to her when she returned—and she was scrambling about madly trying to juggle the numerous Angelino factions.

"Raymond, I need you to deliver a message." She spoke into the receiver of an old telephone. Though little trace of it showed in her voice, save for the occasional wavering of a lone word here and there, the expression plastered across her face indicated just how thoroughly disgusted she was with what she had to do.

"Kindly inform Four Winds Conspire"—Gods, how she *hated* saying Cathayan names aloud; it always made her feel more than a little goofy—"that after careful deliberation, the sovereign domain of Los Angeles accepts the latest proposal delivered by his masters. We will pay the New Promise Mandarinate of Los Angeles a tribute of no less than five million dollars. In exchange, the NPM promises to refrain from interfering in our ongoing struggle with the anarch element, both the so-called MacNeils and Cross's thin-bloods. Tell him that I expect confirmation that his superiors understand and accept my agreement within the month."

Tara hung up before her ghoul could respond. The plastic casing shattered beneath her grip as rage threatened to draw her Beast out of her. The MacNeils—who had taken their name from Jeremy MacNeil, an anarch leader killed when the Cathayans had taken San Francisco back in 2000—were the primary anarch faction in LA, and still touted the tired anarch party line about abolishing princes and sects and running their own existences. As though they'd have the first clue how to do it! They were many, and they were well armed, but they weren't subtle. Faced with them alone, Tara knew she'd have come out on top eventually.

But now she had this other group of anarchs in the mix. These thin-bloods, vampires so far removed from Caine they were barely more than mortal at all, were a recent phenomenon in Kindred terms, and they'd been nothing more than a curiosity—until recently.

"Prince Tara?" Though clearly reluctant to face her leader under the circumstances, the only other vampire in the chamber—Tara's seneschal, a former anarch like the prince herself, who had accompanied her master from

San Diego—stepped forward. "Are you certain this is wise? One of the main reasons we're here is to keep the Cathayans from regaining—"

"*Don't you think I know that?!*" Tara shot to her feet, fists clenched. The bulges of protruding fangs horribly distended the normally round, soft contours of her face and jaw. The other vampire—actually the great grand-childe of Tara herself, as Kindred measure such things—retreated several steps and flattened against the far wall. "Damn it, Dionne, and damn you, I *know*!" The prince stalked forward, until the younger Kindred probably felt as though the force of Tara's anger, made manifest by her unnatural nature, would press her through the wall.

"I know what I've done! I know that if the Cathayans return in force, they're going to have a nice little power-base from which to start rebuilding. I know that I'm going to be kowtowing to those shit-sucking ugly bastards from now until Gehenna if I don't get *damn* lucky!

"You tell me what the fuck choice I have? The MacNeils set fire to Rodriguez's haven two nights ago. Jenna Cross and her damn flunkies have killed two more of my citizens and taken another nine neighborhoods in the past *three months*! I can barely fight a war on *two* fronts with the resources I have, Dionne. I can't possibly fight one on *three*! And the high-and-bloody-mighty Camarilla, after so politely requesting that I calm LA down for them until a permanent prince can establish himself, can't be bothered to send reinforcements! 'Too many unexplained activities in other parts of the world.' I have to deal with my enemies one at a time. I know I can handle the MacNeils—I know how they think, how they operate—so right now Cross's 'army of the oppressed' is the more immediate concern."

"There was a time," Dionne said softly, "when *you* were the oppressed."

Tara's teeth actually clicked and grated as she clenched her jaw. One hand rose, almost of its own accord, to Dionne's neck, and it was only with the greatest effort that the prince stopped herself from crushing her seneschal's larynx. It wouldn't do permanent damage to a vampire, but it would certainly shut her up for a while.

"Yes, there was," the prince growled. "And then I grew up.

"Call the surviving primogen," she ordered, turning away and striding toward the door. "I want the full council convened by early next week, no matter what they have to drop to make it. We're going to deal with Cross, and we're going to do it now."

Dionne stood motionless, staring at the door for several long moments after Tara had slammed it so hard the frame rattled. Then, with a very human sigh, she removed a cell phone—prepaid, disposable and untraceable—from the inner pocket of her suit jacket. Without even looking, she punched a sequence of numbers, one that had become quite familiar to her within the past months.

"It's me," she announced into the mouthpiece. "The expected meeting's been called for next week. Yes, I'll take care of it. Are you certain you're ready for… All right, it's your call. You do understand that if this goes sour, I'm going to be the one howling loudest for your head, right? Good, so long as we're clear.

"Good luck to you too, Jenna. I'll see you in a week."

Aljafería Palace
Zaragoza, Spain

"I'm sorry, Cardinal Mysancta is unavailable to speak with you at the moment."

"Yes." Lucita, ancient Lasombra, bane of so many Kindred throughout the centuries of her existence, and relatively newly appointed Archbishop of Aragon, practically hissed at the speakerphone that sat on the heavy mahogany desk. "So you've told me. Multiple times, even. I wish to know *why* he cannot speak with—"

"I'm sorry, Cardinal Mysancta is unavailable to speak with—"

A tendril of pure darkness, rolling shadow that moved independently of the ambient lighting, lashed out of the gloom behind Lucita. Only at the last moment did she regain sufficient control, of herself and the filament of nonexistence she'd conjured, to simply close the connection rather than reduce the speakerphone (and probably the desk) to so much rubble.

It took far more effort than it should have. The manifestation of such a tentacle—one of the so-called "arms of the Abyss"—was a simple matter to one as skilled in the arts of manipulating shadow as she. Yet Lucita felt vaguely worn, as though she'd just completed a mild workout.

It wasn't the first time she'd experienced such a variance in her power in the recent past. Not many years gone, she had encountered, and only barely defeated, an enemy capable of far greater feats of Abyssal summoning than she—one also capable of interfering with others' abilities to do the same. This wasn't the same, though. Then, she'd felt an active interference with her efforts. This time, and on several other occasions in recent weeks, she'd felt simply as though she were trying to lift a weight just slightly heavier than expected. Nobody was interfering with her. It was as if the shadows themselves resisted her efforts.

That alone was enough to concern, but not unduly worry, Lucita. The Abyss was a strange place, a strange *entity*, not fully understood even by those who had mastered the powers they drew from it. If the currents and ideas and concepts that were the closest thing the Abyss had to physical features were shifting—especially in light of what had happened a few years ago—it wouldn't be so surprising.

But recent irregularities were not limited to a single Lasombra's waning potency with the shadows. Lucita used her position as archbishop to keep tabs on events happening throughout the territories claimed—or desired—by the Sabbat. Reports had begun to trickle in, slowly but gradually increasing in pace, of Cainites experiencing weaknesses and outright failures of their abilities. Had they been more sporadic, Lucita might have dismissed them as flukes, vampires trying to do too much after too long without feeding, or else delusional fools who had begun to believe their own exaggerations.

They weren't quite that sporadic, however. In fact, her analysis showed a distinct and alarming trend. Elder vampires were displaying more frequent, and more severe, variations than were the younger. It was enough, combined with her own difficulties, to inspire her to inform the Sabbat cardinals of her discoveries.

Her failure to reach several of them was leading her to a more uncomfortable conclusion still—specifically, that several of the Sabbat's leaders were missing. Not all of them, not even a majority; but in the last few nights, Lucita had gotten the runaround from enough toadies who clearly had no clue where their bosses might be, and were desperate to hide that fact, to recognize that something was wrong.

And tonight, things had deteriorated even further. Reports were coming in hard and fast, by fax, phone and courier, of violence within the ranks. That in itself wasn't unusual; the Sabbat's doctrine of strength and power ensured that many internal conflicts ended in blood and destruction. The sheer number, however, was surprising. Entire packs had apparently wiped each other out, and several bishoprics and archbishoprics seemed to have declared war on one another, launching sieges of the sort normally reserved for Camarilla-held cities.

Hmm... Unusual violence. Disappearing elders. Lucita had a sudden thought, and decided to follow up on it. Deliberately using the shadow tendril where she could have done so by hand—she was going to maintain her full level of control even if it meant relearning her skills from the beginning—she depressed the intercom button on the speaker.

"Get me Aajav Kahn."

For a moment, she received no reply but silence. Then, "Excellency, could you—umm, repeat that please?"

"You heard me quite well. Seraph Aajav Kahn of the Black Hand."

"Excellency, I'm not entirely certain I know how to—"

"Then learn. And swiftly." Lucita clicked off the intercom.

The secretive, militant sub-sect of the Sabbat called the Black Hand was not easy to reach—even as compared to those cardinals who employed dozens of layers of secret transfers, encrypted data packets, and multiple code phrases, merely to answer a phone—but she knew that *someone* in the hierarchy knew how to reach its leaders. And if *someone* could do it, *she* could do it.

Several hours passed, in which Lucita alternated between reading further reports and practicing her control over shadows—sometimes both, as she attempted to use tiny tendrils of darkness to manipulate the pages. It was well after midnight when the intercom sounded.

"Have you got him?" Lucita asked, not allowing the other the opportunity to speak.

"I'm—I'm afraid not, Excellency. Very few of our contacts were willing to divulge contact information for the seraph. And those few connections I was able to attempt all led to dead ends. Either none of my leads were accurate, or Aajav Kahn is not currently accessible. To anyone. I'm sorry, Excellency."

Lucita practically hissed. "You know better than to apologize to *me*. Do better next time."

Still, Lucita couldn't really blame her assistant. It wasn't as though she herself had had the greatest luck in reaching people recently.

Something was clearly going on, something with potentially far-reaching repercussions. She'd walked the Earth for too long, seen too many moves in the Jyhad up close and personal, to even consider that this convergence of events—a strange spreading weakness of the blood in elders, a spike in violence throughout the sect, and the disappearance of several of the Sabbat's leaders—could possibly be coincidence. Someone was going to have to look into this, and though she spent a great deal of time attempting to come up with alternatives, the truth was that Lucita knew only one person she trusted enough to conduct such an investigation.

What the hell. She'd wanted some more practice anyway...

Another click of the intercom. "Please make arrangements for my extended absence, and have the plane readied. I'm going to be doing some traveling."

The Granite Steps Hotel
Savannah, Georgia

"You realize, of course," Anatole said calmly as he raised the cup of coffee to his lips, "that this can't really be happening."

"Oh, I know," Beckett replied, sipping at his own cup. He glanced around, staring at empty tables. He and his prophetic friend were the only people seated at the outdoor café. It looked Parisian, but for some reason Beckett couldn't see the rest of the block to confirm their location. "I'm not sure how I know, though. Why can't this be happening?"

"Because it's practically impossible to find a decent café open at this hour," Anatole told him. The cup in his hand had become a goblet, of the sort one often saw used for communion in the richest churches of the Middle Ages. "And if you could, it would hardly be empty."

"Ah." Beckett took another sip. It still tasted like coffee, but the liquid in his own mug—no, goblet—was thick and red. "You know, you sound different."

"Death does that. I've never met anyone who spoke the same after he died."

"That makes sense, I guess."

"You know you're in trouble, right?"

"Yeah, there's no cream."

"I'm serious. Look."

Beckett turned around, and realized it wasn't that he couldn't see the rest of the block; the rest of the block didn't exist at all. Even as he watched, the nothingness crept just a few inches closer, accompanied by the sound of chewing.

"What the hell is that?"

"I would tell you. But I'm dead."

Beckett awoke.

"That," he muttered to the empty hotel bathroom, "was odd."

For a few moments, he simply lay in the bathtub—the added safety of an extra wall between him and any windows, to say nothing of the extra lock on the bathroom door, made the discomfort of waking up cramped by porcelain worthwhile—and pondered. This was far from the first dream he'd had recently. It wasn't even the first one that had involved his old friend and mentor Anatole. Beckett was confused. Though he'd never admit it to another soul, he was also starting to worry. For his entire existence as one of the undead, Beckett's days had passed in dreamless slumber— or, if he *had* dreamed, they hadn't been memorable enough for him to recall after the sun went down. For the last several months, however—ever since the night he'd spent in the entrance to Kaỳmakli—Beckett had dreamed at least twice a week, sometimes as often as once a day. He had assumed, at first, the dreams were due to the memories dredged up and altered by the ghosts beneath the earth, but he'd expected them to fade. The fact that they hadn't was troubling. Beckett had seen too many prophets and prophecies vindicated in his time not to believe in omens, and he didn't like the ones he seemed to be experiencing now.

The sudden chirp of a satellite phone—specifically a personalized ring Beckett had assigned to only one individual—yanked him from what was threatening to become an all-night reverie.

Beckett grinned ever so slightly as he thumbed the phone on. "How are you feeling, Old Man?"

"I am older than you," Okulos informed him with exaggerated pompousness, "by less than a decade."

"Right. So how are you feeling, Old Man?"

The voice on the other end laughed. "Better, thank you. The physical injuries are long since healed. Including," he added, a wry tone creeping into his voice, "some fairly nasty gashes behind my knees."

"Consider that the alternative would have been your gut or your throat."

"Ah. Well, yes, the physical wounds are healed. I'm still—tired. Drained. I do not know how long I spent indisposed…"

Beckett grinned at that choice of phrasing. Okulos never liked to think of himself losing control, so he rarely used the word frenzy except when referring to others.

"…but it must have been long enough to really take a lot of out of me," Okulos concluded.

Beckett could only agree, though he wasn't about to say anything. Okulos had been in the grips of the Beast for months, according to Kapaneus. Beckett was truly impressed that his friend had the strength of will to reassert his humanity at all.

"I think," Okulos continued, "that I'd be all right, if I could just get some solid rest, if these damn dreams weren't keeping me up for half the day."

Dreams? Again, Beckett thought of saying something, but closed his mouth with an almost audible snap. He wasn't prepared to confide his own dreams to anyone, at least not until he'd puzzled out what, if anything, they meant.

"But enough of an old man's complaints," Okulos said with a chuckle. "How was Cairo?"

"Disappointing. And dangerous. Something's going on there. The cold war between the Assamites and Setites of the region seems to have heated up, and neither side is especially interested in dealing with outsiders."

"I see. But—disappointing? I've not been to Cairo as often as you, but I've never found it thus."

"Well, Kapaneus seemed to like it," Beckett acknowledged.

"He's still traveling with you?" Definite surprise in *that* question.

"Yes. He's in the next room as we speak." Beckett frowned. "Honestly, though, I'm not quite sure *why* Kapaneus is still with me. He's got a truly irritating way of not actually answering any of my questions about the past, and he's perfunctory with those he *does* answer. But every time I turn around, *he's* asking *me* questions about the modern world, and I'm answering them without thinking. I don't know why the hell I'm still putting up with it."

Actually, that wasn't entirely true. Beckett was fairly sure he *did* know why, and it wasn't just his lingering hopes of pumping Kapaneus for information. He hadn't done any great soul-searching recently, except in the matter of the dreams, but he suspected the true answer was simple loneliness. He had very few traveling companions left anymore, and it was nice to share the night with *someone*— even if that someone asked more questions than a three-year-old.

(And part of him wondered, given Kapaneus's presumed age, if he could make him leave even if he wanted to.)

"Anyway, the discovery itself was useless," Beckett explained, shifting the topic back to Egypt, and to a dig he'd investigated out in the desert. "Only one of the artifacts had the 'mysterious writing' on it, and it's just a common passage from the Book of Nod, one I've already got in three other forms. It's a valuable find—you wouldn't believe how much Ash was willing to pay for it, to add it to her collection— but useless so far as my own research is concerned."

"Ah, the delectable Victoria Ash. I was wondering why you were wasting your time in the American South. I trust you'll be leaving tonight, then?"

"Tomorrow." Beckett scowled at what was to come. "Before I left her offices, Ash received a phone call, asking for me. I'm supposed to meet with the Dutch Toady tonight. Something about the Camarilla needing my 'expertise.'"

It took Okulos a few minutes to stop laughing. "Does Pieterzoon know you think of him that way?"

"Jan Pieterzoon is a yes-man, a tool, and a blind Camarilla fanatic of the worst order. If he doesn't know how I feel, I'll be happy to tell him."

"Then why are you meeting with him?"

Beckett felt a very human urge to sigh. "Because he's also an agent of the Camarilla's Inner Circle and a childe of Hardestadt, one of the sect's founders—and it's easier for me to take a few hours to humor them than to take a few years waiting for their ire at being ignored to blow over."

"Sensible."

"Sensible, that's me. In fact, I'm so sensible, I'm running late. I'll talk to you later, Okulos. Glad you're feeling better."

The Thompson Plantation
Outside Savannah, Georgia

Beckett climbed out of the rented Land Rover and examined his destination with an expert eye. The mansion stood at the end of a long tree-lined drive and was perched in the midst of an enormous property. It clearly predated the Civil War. If he'd had to guess, Beckett would say that the building had probably been cleaned up and restored by the Historic Savannah Foundation during their sprucing spree of the 1950s. The main building itself was large enough to house a family of about fifty, and Beckett imagined the former slaves' quarters had been converted into some fancy guest houses.

A single guard, who appeared to be nothing more than an elderly, white-bearded black man, sat in a folding chair beside the gate, playing a hand of solitaire on a TV tray. Beckett, knowing full well that he was almost assuredly more than he seemed, kept his hands visible as he approached.

"Beckett, to see Ms. Ash. I'm expected."

The old (looking) man—no, vampire, Beckett realized from this close up—stared at him intently. Beckett had both seen and performed enough examinations with senses unavailable to mortals to know how thoroughly he was being sized up now.

"Right you are, Mr. Beckett," the guard said at last. He pressed a quick sequence of numbers into a keypad hidden on the wall behind him, and the gate swung open. "If you'll park by the main house, someone will see to your car. You just go right on in."

Beckett proceeded up the drive, noting that several groundskeepers—Beckett wondered briefly if they were ghouls or merely hired hands—wandered about the property even at this late hour, ensuring the various flower gardens thrived. At the manor itself, a wide, shallow flight of stone steps led to the main door, which was far taller than it needed to be. A bell jingled in the background somewhere as he pulled it open.

The interior of the house was far more opulent even than the exterior. A thick carpet created a path from the front door, beneath a sequence of massive crystal chandeliers, to a split staircase that curved up and around to meet itself at a second-floor balcony. Paintings and other artistic trinkets adorned the walls while statuettes occupied displays in isolated nooks, placed with the precision only a true aficionado of art could achieve. Somehow, though, the house also gave an impression of temporary inhabitation, as if the occupant, despite the apparent insistence on beauty and comfort, didn't anticipate being here long. Even if Beckett hadn't already known who dwelt here, he could have guessed by the foyer alone.

"You've a beautiful home, Ms. Ash," Beckett told his hostess as she descended the leftmost staircase. "I'm honored to be here."

He was also damn curious as to why he was there, since the business they'd conducted in the preceding nights had all taken place at her office. Why did Pieterzoon warrant a meeting room in her personal haven? Either he was throwing his weight around—something that Beckett, much as he disliked Pieterzoon, had to admit was unlikely—or Ash was simply ingratiating herself by according him every courtesy.

"Oh, Victoria, please. And thank you." Her deep red hair was pinned up in layers tonight, a modern echo of the style a true Southern belle might have worn to welcome visitors into this selfsame manor almost two centuries ago. Her gown, a dark red, left her shoulders bare, and she wore a black shawl over that. "I'm glad that you're here, Beckett," she told him, leading him back up the stairs. "Perhaps you'll help me find the right place to display the pieces I've just acquired from you."

"I'm sure I wouldn't have your skill at placing them, Victoria," he replied, enjoying the game despite himself.

Victoria and he had crossed paths a few times over the years, most notably in London over a century ago. That business had not ended especially pleasantly for either of them. "Or your eye for aesthetics.

"Still," he continued, as he set foot on the upper landing and proceeded, at his hostess's urging, toward an oaken door that probably led into an office, "if I can get away from Pieterzoon with a minimum of wasted time, perhaps we can examine—"

"You're not meeting with Jan Pieterzoon." Beckett heard just the slightest quaver in Ash's voice as she spoke. He froze, one hand already outstretched to open the door, and slowly turned his head to stare at her, unblinking. Come to think of it, was she a bit paler than normal, even for her?

Suspicion began to stir in the back of Beckett's mind, the Beast riding along with it. Had he been betrayed? Was this a trap of some sort?

"Victoria," he began, his voice low, "what's going on?"

"What's going on," a new voice answered as the office door was opened from within, "is that my childe became occupied with other matters. I trust I'll do in his place, Mr. Beckett?"

Beckett could feel his own face go pale—an instinctive reaction in Kindred physiology, as it concentrated all the blood in the body in preparation for fight or flight—and forced color back into his cheeks. He'd heard that voice, with its strange Germanic-but-not-quite-German accent, before. He knew, even before he turned back to the doorway, what he would see. Still, he paused for a moment, partially to let his flesh regain what little color it normally possessed, partly so as not to appear as startled as he truly was.

The man in the doorway was a few inches shorter than Beckett himself, though he had been considered quite tall during the age in which he was born and Embraced. Black hair, blue eyes, a chin nearly square enough for use as a straightedge… An insanely expensive, tailor-made black European suit, with a royal purple shirt beneath it… And an aura of power and authority so powerful that Beckett nearly had to squint against it.

"Hello again, Mr. Beckett."

Beckett *really* hoped the other didn't notice him swallow once before speaking. "Hello, Hardestadt."

The Thompson Plantation
Outside Savannah, Georgia

They stood alone, now, in the office. The Founder had cursorily dismissed their hostess from their presence with a brusque, "These matters do not concern you, Miss Ash." And while the Toreador might well have been angered or insulted at being so casually brushed off in her own home, she wasn't about to argue with the one doing the brushing. The office was comfortably furnished with several cushioned chairs, a large desk and several bookcases—all of which appeared to be as old as the house itself—but neither Beckett nor Hardestadt seemed inclined to sit.

Beckett stood as rock-still as he could manage, praying the Founder couldn't detect his inner turmoil. His dislike for officials of either sect—sanctimonious egotists, the lot of them, with no concern for anything but their own interests—clashed with a healthy dose of nervousness (Beckett wasn't quite honest enough with himself to call it fear) that any wise Kindred felt when dealing with a figure as powerful as this one. He knew, too, that part of his trepidation was an artificial result of the Ventrue's unnatural emotional aura, but that knowledge didn't make the feeling any easier to overcome. Beckett held the Beast down in the depths of his mind and soul with a grasp of iron.

"All right, Hardestadt, what's this about? I'm honored you've come all this way to see me, but…"

"Honored?" Hardestadt raised a disbelieving eyebrow. "Really."

"Well, maybe not so much honored as annoyed."

What the hell are you doing, Beckett? he felt part of himself ask the other, and he didn't actually have an answer. It was a fine line between masking fear and excessive bravado, and he was still thrown enough that he wasn't sure he could tell the difference.

Fortunately, other than a brief tic of one of Hardestadt's eyes, the Founder seemed inclined to let the insult pass without acknowledgment.

"Tell me, Beckett," he continued instead, finally taking a seat in one of the chairs, crossing one ankle over the other knee in a posture that absolutely radiated a sense of comfort and ease that both Kindred knew was a façade. "Have you noticed anything at all unusual in the past months?"

Beckett frowned, and rested his hands on the back of the other chair, though he remained standing. It wouldn't hurt to admit where he'd been recently—Ash already knew, after all. "I've been in Cairo most of the past months. Cairo's always a bit unusual. But yes, there have been signs of something not quite normal. The different factions of Cairo seem to have finally declared open war. And I think I heard a rumor or two about some blood sickness in a few elders, but I never had the chance to look into it."

Nor was Beckett certain he *wanted* to. He still had frightening memories of the *last* time some blood-borne disease capable of affecting vampires spread through the community, and the panic and violence that had ensued.

"Indeed." Hardestadt nodded. "In truth, it's somewhat more severe than that. This 'blood sickness,' as you say, hasn't afflicted only a few elders. It seems to have spread *substantially*. Nor is it apparently limited to those above a certain age, though it seems to strike older Kindred harder. Rumors are spreading, Beckett, and spreading swiftly. If you'd spent any length of time in Camarilla domains—or, I imagine, even those of the Sabbat,"—Hardestadt practically spit the word—"then I'm certain you'd have heard them for yourself.

"Nor is this the only issue at hand. Violence, both between and within the sects, is rising at a substantial rate. In two months, we've had no fewer than eleven reported border skirmishes with Sabbat domains, at least three open battles between rival Camarilla princes, and intelligence suggests that a number of Sabbat elders have either gone into hiding, or been removed from the field. The most recent instances have occurred here, in the Americas, but it is happening to a greater or lesser extent worldwide.

"Finally, Beckett, a number of our mystics are claiming that the Red Star has begun to glow more brightly when examined with anything beyond mortal senses."

Beckett suddenly thought he saw where the conversation was going, but he couldn't bring himself to believe it. "You, Hardestadt? Of all people, is one of the great Camarilla Founders, one who's spent the last five-and-a-half centuries claiming it's all just a myth, suddenly afraid of Gehenna?"

"Don't be absurd. Of *course* this isn't Gehenna. Unfortunately, as I was saying, rumors spread quickly. And many of those who hear them aren't as level-headed as I."

"All right, so why bring this to me? I'm not precisely a public relations expert."

Hardestadt grimaced. "I need people—famed and respected experts in the field—to start assuring the masses that this is not some pseudo-mythical apocalypse, but merely a spreading blood fever, perhaps combined with another cycle of hallucination and Gehenna hysteria. The Tremere may be unable to provide a satisfactory explanation."

"If they can't," Beckett said, "I'm not sure what—"

"So I'm approaching other acknowledged occultists and Noddists," Hardestadt continued, uninterested in Beckett's comments. "Unfortunately, that's not as easy a proposition as it once was, as most of the truly well-known such experts have a habit of disappearing. The Malkavian Anatole is dead. I've people searching for your companion Aristotle de Laurent, but we've had no luck locating him as yet."

"*Former* companion," Beckett growled low in his throat. He still hadn't forgiven Aristotle for attempting to steal one of the relics Okulos had passed to Beckett while trapped in Kaymakli, before he'd stopped communicating through the ward.

"Calebros has agreed to help, but his reputation in the field is still a new one. His word carries less weight than I require. And so, Beckett, occult scholar, archeologist and determined Noddist, we come to you."

Beckett felt the wood of the chair creaking beneath his grip as his fists tightened. *Here it comes…*

"Just so we're clear… You want me to do *what*, exactly?"

"Merely spread the word that what is happening now is *not* the forerunner to Gehenna. Calm people down. Travel with me for a time, perhaps. Speak in front of others, where I tell you to speak. Do this, and you may well prevent widespread panic, not to mention foolishness that could expose us to mortal attention. Those in the grip of panic have an unfortunate habit of disregarding our traditions of Masquerade."

"But I'm not a member of your Old Dead Man's Club, Hardestadt. Even if you were willing to trust me to do this, why would I want to?"

"All Kindred are part—"

"Oh, save it for the neonates, Hardestadt. If I hear any of that 'All Kindred are one with the Camarilla whether they know it or not' bullshit one more time, I swear to God I'm going to beat someone into torpor."

Oh, shit. I did not just say that…

Hardestadt's eyes blazed as he rose to his feet. Though the taller of the pair, Beckett suddenly felt as though he were looking up. Waves of awe-inspiring majesty and righteous fury poured from the Founder, and he appeared to grow, not physically larger but somehow more solid, more *real*, as though everything else was merely a painted backdrop. The air in the room gathered itself up and began pressing down on Beckett's shoulders, an impossible weight that made movement in any direction but straight down unthinkable. If Beckett thought he'd been shaken by the Founder's uncanny presence earlier, he was positively crushed beneath it now. His body trembled as he fought the urge to roll over and bare his throat.

Don't show fear. Don't show fear. Don't let him know how thoroughly he's got you…

"You," Hardestadt practically roared, and even his words seemed to land with the impact of a stream of bullets, forcing Beckett back toward the corner, step by step, "show a dangerous lack of respect for your elders, sir!"

A very substantial part of Beckett wanted to do what Hardestadt clearly expected. He wanted to swallow his pride, to allow his fear to show, and to simply apologize, maybe even grovel. It was undoubtedly the smart move.

But instead, Beckett listened to his well-honed instincts to *never* accede dominance, particularly to a member of the hierarchy of one of the great sects. Those same instincts told him that his fear was artificial, and for all he knew it was Hardestadt's own voice that was calling submission the "smart move." So, instead of an apology, Beckett spoke something uncomfortably akin to his own death warrant.

"You're not my elder by so many years as you lead people to believe, Hardestadt."

The room went utterly, deathly silent. The weight of Hardestadt's personality bearing down on Beckett grew suddenly ice cold. Whether it was this that caused a shiver to race through Beckett's undead body, or whether it was simply the awful, gut-churning realization of what he had just done, he couldn't say.

It was something Beckett, who had access to many historical perspectives and even firsthand accounts that most others did not, had figured out quite some time ago. Officially, Hardestadt had survived an assassination attempt by a revolutionary called Tyler during the Anarch Revolt, the Renaissance-era Kindred war that had indirectly spawned both the Camarilla and the Sabbat. Beckett, however, had pieced together the truth, a truth known only to a select few among the Camarilla's highest ranks: Hardestadt the Elder had indeed died at Tyler's hands and fangs. It was his childe, Hardestadt the Younger, who survived to this night, having taken his sire's place.

It was a secret that Hardestadt had assuredly killed to keep, on more than one occasion. And Beckett, unless he did something *very* quickly, had just neatly penciled his name onto that list.

He could very nearly have given thanks on his knees when Ash chose that moment to open the door.

"My apologies for disturbing you both," she said calmly, politely—almost as though she really meant it, "but whatever you're doing up here, I can feel it across the house. This is my home, and I'd appreciate it if my guests kept things civil."

Hardestadt gave her an irritated glance, but Beckett felt the weight of the Founder's presence ease just a little.

"Look, Hardestadt," he said quickly, praying that his voice didn't sound nearly as desperate as he felt, "I can't just be a propaganda mouthpiece for you. Without an in-depth examination of the circumstances, I wouldn't be able to sound believable, at least not to anyone who has the slightest clue what I'm talking about.

"Let me offer this, though. I'll look into what's going on, study it. Hell, I'd probably have decided to do so anyway, once I'd heard for myself some of these rumors you're talking about. And as soon as I learn anything about what's going on, I'll report it back to you, and we—that is, you—can decide where to go from there."

For several long seconds, the longest—and possibly the last—of Beckett's existence, the Founder continued to stare at him. The emotional pressure pounding into his mind, heart and soul increased once more. Then, with another glance at Victoria Ash, Hardestadt took a single step back. He seemed to shrink as he did so, and the air in the room palpably softened.

"Very well, Beckett. I've my own people investigating this, of course, but I imagine we could well use the insight of an expert. Look into it. Tell me what's happening, whether it's a blood sickness, a curse, or something more.

"But Beckett... *Everything* you learn comes to me. Immediately. If I learn you've left out a single detail, or that you've delivered any of this information to someone else, I give you my solemn oath you'll spend the rest of your existence begging for Gehenna to truly arrive."

Beckett wasn't much impressed with threats, but he knew that Hardestadt was quite capable of doing exactly as he promised. He nodded. "How do I contact you?"

"I'll be traveling a great deal. You'll have your—cellular device with you?" Hardestadt apparently wasn't entirely comfortable with modern technology, not an uncommon characteristic of an elder.

"Uh, yes. Is there a number I can call—"

"No. When you have something to report, leave word here, with Ms. Ash. She will let me know, and I will contact you." He turned. "I trust that is acceptable to you as well?"

Their hostess nodded. "You have but to ask."

And just like that, Beckett found himself working for the Camarilla. He wondered if it wouldn't have been better to let Hardestadt kill him.

The Thompson Plantation
Outside Savannah, Georgia

"What did he want?"

Beckett didn't really know what to say to that. He'd already gotten himself in enough trouble without breaking confidence with Hardestadt the Founder right off the bat. "You were there for most of it, Victoria. Anyway, I thought you knew everything that happened under your roof."

She gave him a sour smile. "How very back-handed of you, Beckett. What did you say about the Tremere?"

Beckett was honestly confused. Might as well be up front. "Not much. They're helping him on this business, or weren't able to actually."

"Don't you find that strange? That Hardestadt couldn't find a single Tremere to assist him in… whatever business brings him here?"

"I didn't say that, Victoria." She wanted to tell him something. He could feel it. "I just got the impression they were giving him an official stonewall is all. Standard operating procedure for that bunch, really."

Victoria didn't say anything for several long moments, and Beckett refused to break the silence. She was weighing pros and cons, trying to decide where her advantage was. Well, let her.

Finally, she spoke. "Beckett, I can't find the Tremere. *Any* of them. I don't think he can either."

Beckett swallowed. The Kindred were hardly numerous and the Tremere were but a fraction of that, but there were chantries in major cities across the world for God's sake. There were hundreds, maybe thousands, of them all told. "What do you mean? They've all gone to ground or something?"

"No. Beckett, the Tremere haven't 'gone to ground.' There were three blood sorcerers in Savannah and when I noted their absence I started making some inquiries. So far as any of my friends can tell, they're all completely gone. I can find no trace of them, here or in any city where I still have connections."

Beckett leaned forward. "They're gone? *All* of them?!"

"So it would seem. Beckett, what's going on?"

"Victoria, when I find out, you'll definitely be one of the first to know."

The Granite Steps Hotel
Savannah, Georgia

"You appear to be in something of a hurry."

Beckett, his hands buried in the large canvas satchel he was packing, practically leaped from his skin. "God *damn* it, Kapaneus! Stop *doing* that!"

The elder vampire—dressed now in an Egyptian cotton tunic and pants, as he'd expressed some discomfort with most modern clothing—stood with one hand on the doorframe of Beckett's room. "Are we going somewhere?"

"I am. And it's not that I'm in such a hurry to be anywhere, so much as I am to not be here. I've managed to talk my way into a hell of a mess, Kapaneus. And as big a mess as I'm in here, it's starting to sound like there's a bigger one out there." Briefly, he repeated the information both Hardestadt and Victoria had given him. Kapaneus actually looked concerned.

"It sounds very much like some of the prophecies, Beckett. 'There will come a time, when the curse of the One above will not be tolerated further, when the Lineage of Caine will end, when the Blood of Caine will be weak…'"

"I know the prophecies, Kapaneus. *The Book of Nod* is a hobby of mine, and I've been around the block enough times to have heard plenty of cries of Gehenna that turned to nothing. But I know *something* strange is happening, and when it comes to this sort of strange, I can't think of a better starting point than the Tremere."

"But both Hardestadt and Ash implied the Usurpers had all disappeared."

The Usurpers. Sometimes Beckett forgot just how old Kapaneus must truly be. Hell, with him as a companion, maybe he didn't have to worry quite so much about Hardestadt.

"So they did. I have no idea *what* the hell's going on, and it worries me. A lot. When the Tremere run for cover, something unpleasant this way comes. Either way, I've got Okulos trying to reach his contacts, and in the meantime, I know somewhere I'm almost certain we can still dig up a warlock."

"Ah. So it is 'we' now. Good. Egypt was fascinating, but I would still very much like to see more of this age. Where are we going?"

"A little country called Monaco."

Inside the cargo ship Salimah, dockside
Istanbul, Turkey

His name was Jibril, after the archangel Gabriel in the Arabic tongue. If he'd had any other name, he'd forgotten it in his centuries of unlife—and Jibril's nearly black skin showed that he had many such centuries behind him.

Jibril considered himself an Assamite's Assamite. The clan was, in truth, far deeper and more varied than its reputation suggested. Most outsiders saw it as little more than a band of blood-hungry assassins and cannibals. To judge by Jibril, they were right. He loved only the hunt, only the kill. When the ancient Ur-Shulgi arose and demanded all Assamites abandon their mortal faiths to worship only Haqim, their founder, many of the clan had chosen to go their own way, striking out alone or joining the Camarilla or Sabbat. Jibril remained loyal, and had taken it upon himself to hunt down those who had turned traitor. This was not out of any love for Ur-Shulgi or even Haqim, but for the sake of the kill. Assamite tradition forbade unauthorized violence within the clan itself, but Jibril now had an excuse to hunt down the greatest prey of all.

Thus had he smuggled himself here, to Istanbul, for Turkey was home to many of his weaker brethren, those who had thrown in their lot with the Camarilla. He would strike them down one by one, and revel in their—

It was impossible here, in a tiny room in the hold of a ship, yet somehow a sudden hot breeze swept through the room. It reminded Jibril of a desert wind, carrying with it the taste of sand.

It was followed almost immediately by an overwhelming scent of blood. The chamber smelled like an abattoir, so intense was the aroma. Jibril found his fangs lengthening of their own accord. The hunger awoke in him so intensely he began to sweat. Still the wind picked up, and still the scent grew stronger.

And then there was more. Though he saw nothing, felt nothing but the breeze, Jibril was aware of a presence with him in the room, something hidden.

Something awful.

"Who—"

When he began to speak, Jibril was perfectly fine, albeit somewhat nervous. By the end of the first word he was falling to the floor, his body utterly drained of blood, his soul sucked out to feed some ancient thing. And then he was naught but dust, whipped around the room for a minute or so before the wind faded away, taking the scent of blood with it.

More minutes passed, and then the door creaked open. The woman who stood in it was also dark-skinned, and just as in Jibril's case, that darkening was not the tint of melanin but the mark of advanced age as only the Assamites suffered it. Her features were fine, sharp, yet attractive. She wore loose clothes, pants and shirt that would not in any way interfere with her movements. Her hair was tied back with a cloth, and she carried no fewer than six blades secreted at various points on her person.

Her name was Fatima al-Faqadi, and she hunted something she prayed to Allah she would not find. For months she had sensed a growing presence in her mind, the weight or the echo of something that moved across the world. Sometimes she would feel it draw near, only to lose it again. Each time she would make haste to the spot where she felt it most strongly, only to find scenes such as this—evidence that someone who had once survived beyond death had finally fallen.

To whatever it was. Though she had her fears and her theories, Fatima was unprepared to settle on any conclusions without further evidence.

It was, however, time that she stopped trailing three steps behind whatever it was, but tried instead to move ahead of it. If vampires were dying suddenly, violently, then perhaps it would behoove her to speak with those who specialized in killing them.

Fatima departed the *Salimah*, undetected as she'd entered it, and began to arrange for swift travel to Juarez, Mexico.

The Thompson Plantation
Outside Savannah, Georgia

"I should have killed him."

Hardestadt sat in the same chair, behind the same desk, in the office upstairs in Ash's manor. He was alone; Ash was a polite enough hostess to offer her guests privacy when they desired it. More to the point, most sane Kindred would be too frightened of the consequences to risk spying on the Founder. He spoke to his absent and long-dead sire, the original Hardestadt. He did so often, when contemplating tactics where none could overhear. It was a habit he'd picked up not a year after Tyler's attack.

"But it would have raised too many questions, I think, at least with Victoria—and she has the ears of too many others. I'm trying to *avert* this damn Gehenna hysteria. For me to be directly involved in the death of so famous a Noddist as Beckett… The last thing I need is for it to appear as though I'm hiding something. Better to let him travel, to be far away from anywhere associated with me and mine."

It was too bad. Beckett's insight into current events could prove fascinating. He might even be able to help Hardestadt determine what was *really* happening. Hardestadt's current instinct was to blame the Tremere, to assume they'd either turned on the Camarilla or allowed their magics to get out of control—but it was all just theory until he had solid evidence. Beckett would have been useful in gathering said evidence.

On the other hand, Beckett was an occultist and an avowed believer in signs and portents. It was entirely possible that he'd be caught up in the spreading panic, that he might begin to believe this Gehenna nonsense. And as much trouble as Hardestadt, the Inner Circle and the justicars were going through to keep such rumors from spreading, the last thing he needed was a respected scholar adding fuel to the fire.

Plus, of course, Beckett knew too much about him as it was.

It was going to be difficult finding someone both loyal and strong enough to eliminate the Gangrel. Most of the Camarilla's archons were currently assigned to rumor control, even—in a few cases—to silencing those who spoke too loudly. But this was a priority.

Hardestadt eyed the telephone in the office, decided he couldn't trust Ash's manners *that* completely, and, with an expression of extreme distaste, removed an older model cellular phone from his coat pocket. He neither knew, nor cared, that the number he dialed passed through over a dozen relays and was scrambled and rescrambled almost as many times, using encryption technology that even the CIA hadn't yet adopted. He only knew that his advisors assured him it was secure, and that was sufficient.

"This is Hardestadt. I require one of your archons, on a matter of utmost urgency for the Inner Circle, and indeed the Camarilla entire. Yes, I know you're busy. Find someone anyway.

"What?" The Founder couldn't quite prevent an enormous grin from spreading across his statuesque features. "Yes. Yes, he'll do *perfectly*. Have him contact me directly, and I'll issue further instructions."

Hardestadt closed the repugnant little device with a loud click. Beckett was as good as dead.

The Thompson Plantation
Outside Savannah, Georgia

For the tenth night in a row, Victoria sat at her dressing table, using its mirror and a small hand one to examine the flesh behind her jaw line, on the left side of her neck. For the last four years, she had scrupulously avoided ever looking there, and favored hairstyles that kept that small space covered. During the fall of Atlanta to the Sabbat, she had been captured and given over to a monstrous creature named Elford, who had branded her. Elford—*may he rot in hell!*—had been an enthusiastic torturer and gifted in the horrific art he called fleshcrafting. Like many members of his clan—the Tzimisce—he could reshape bone and skin like clay. His ministrations were impossible for Victoria to recall without sparking a wave of rage, fear and disgust in her heart. That Elford hadn't survived their encounter was of little comfort to her—the raised ridge of flesh he's left on her neck had. Like a snake eating its own tail, the circle of unnatural skin was a constant reminder that she could never fully escape those terrible nights after her city fell to the so-called Sword of Caine. The mark had been as undying as she was.

Until now.

For the last ten nights, she'd watched this *thing*—more than a mark, more a parasitic growth—blister, crack and finally bleed. Now there was a raw, seeping mark on her skin that refused to heal despite all her best efforts. Only by using small compresses and changing them several times a night, had she managed to keep this her secret.

She'd deigned to seek out the Tremere for help, but that had led only to another worrisome discovery.

"Good luck, Beckett," she said, and put down the hand mirror.

Airport Hilton, Los Angeles International Airport
Los Angeles, California

Prince Tara was scowling as she entered the conference room on the fifth floor of the Airport Hilton. Distracted as she was by the tactical concerns of her growing campaign against

Jenna Cross and her misfits, to say nothing of the destruction caused by the MacNeils and the dramatic diplomatic hoops she had to jump through with the remaining Cathayans, it took her several seconds to recognize that all was not right with the room.

It was, in most respects, a typical example of its type, a conference room with a large window (equipped with heavy curtains, just in case Tara or one of the primogen were forced to use the chamber for daylight sanctuary), a long wooden table (polished oak), and a number of chairs (precisely none with wooden legs). The carpeting was thick, the walls and ceiling soundproofed. A large wooden entertainment center on one end held a TV and VCR, and a small door on the left wall near the window led to a smaller room for private conversations.

All this was as it should be. The problem was that all the chairs, save the one in which Dionne sat, were empty.

"Where is everyone?" Tara asked, her voice calm.

"I'm afraid the primogen will not be attending this evening, Prince Tara," Dionne said.

"And why is that?"

"Any number of reasons, I suppose. I imagine the primary one is that I told them the meeting was tomorrow."

"I see." Tara began slowly but steadily making her way around the table toward her errant seneschal. "You're playing a dangerous game, Dionne, and it's not one you have a hope in hell of winning."

"Tara," Dionne said, rising to her own feet and beginning to pace around the table (and not coincidentally out of the prince's immediate reach). "Don't do this. You were among the greatest anarch leaders once. You knew what Kindred society should be. You should be working *with* the thin-bloods, not—"

"Oh, God, here it comes," the prince snarled through bared fangs. "Damn it, Dionne, I thought you were different. When I first declared myself prince, every other Camarilla official in the region told me the same thing. 'Don't keep the Caitiff as your advisor,' they said. 'She's never going to be as loyal to you as she was to the nonsensical dream you've grown out of,' they said. I told them they were wrong. I *swore* to them they were wrong! *Damn you!*" Tara's fist landed on the heavy table with the sound of a gunshot. The wood around her hand cracked.

Tara was capable, as were most Kindred, of increasing her physical strength several times over, of pumping blood through the limbs to heighten their power and speed. The only problem was, she hadn't yet done so—and at her normal strength, she should never have been able to damage the table like that.

She was, however, too busy battling down frenzy—and wondering if she should bother—to notice. She saw Dionne's look of sudden fear, and attributed it to her obvious rage. Had she noticed the damage to the table, she'd have been at least as puzzled as her seneschal seemed to be.

"Tara," Dionne continued desperately, "you can do this. Throw the city open to the thin-bloods and the other pariahs. Make this a safe haven for them. With all the chaos and weirdness happening in the world right now, the Camarilla couldn't possibly spend the effort necessary to object in any meaningful way. Hell, they might grow to like it, at least it wouldn't be Cathayan territory—"

The prince let loose a single scream of primal rage, grabbed the nearest chair from the floor and hurled it across the table. Her movement was so fast, the throw so powerful, Dionne couldn't quite leap aside in time. The foot of one of the legs caught her across the forehead and sent her sprawling.

"Is this why you arranged for us to be alone together?" Tara growled, stalking around the table, hands curled into fists that, considering her seemingly enhanced strength this evening, could shatter cinderblocks. "So you could try to 'talk sense' into me? Or were you just feeling suicidal?"

"Neither." The door to the side-chamber opened, and Tara turned to face the muzzles of half-a-dozen firearms. "She arranged for you to die. She just hoped—like a dumbass—that it wouldn't be necessary."

The woman who had spoken stood at the forefront of the group. She was, on casual inspection, easily dismissed as some *American Idol* wannabe—except for the competent, no-nonsense manner in which she gripped the dull back Tec-9. Her long hair, falling around her face, was an obviously bleached blonde. She wore a tight purple midriff shirt and jeans that appeared as if they would fall off her hips at any moment.

A more thorough observer—one who looked deep into

the fire in her eyes, or stopped to notice the strange crescent-moon shaped mark on her shoulder that might be either tattoo or birthmark—would know better even without the weapon.

Prince Tara's heightened senses often alerted her to danger before any mortal could possibly have been aware of it. Tonight, either her intuition had failed her or—more likely, she acknowledged to herself—she'd been too enraged at Dionne's betrayal to pay attention. For a gaggle of children to catch her by surprise like this was intolerable!

It was also fixable. Jenna Cross might be a lot of things, but she, and most of those who followed her, was still inexperienced. They still thought as mortals, still had no true comprehension of what a vampire could do.

Even as the first bullets roared from their barrels, Tara was hurling herself backwards at several times the speed even the most highly trained mortal could move. Rather than striking her about the head and chest—which would hardly have put her down in any permanent way, but might well have incapacitated her long enough for the others to finish the job—most of the barrage passed by harmlessly, to strike the far wall. No way the soundproofing was going to muffle *that*. They had only a matter of minutes, now, before someone came to investigate.

Several of the bullets still connected. They tore through her right arm and shoulder, spraying blood and long-dead flesh out across the floor. She felt one lodge in her shoulder bone, and clenched her teeth to avoid crying out in pain. Her body instinctively began pumping blood into the wound, trying to heal; with an instant's concentration, Tara stopped it. She could work around the pain for now, and she might well need the blood before this was over.

The prince hit the floor and rolled, coming to rest under the table as the last of the bullets spent themselves against the wall. She had only seconds, if that, before another metal-jacketed swarm would be coming her way. She heard the thin-bloods moving through the doorway, even heard one drop to the floor for a better shot at her. Tara's veins burned as the blood ran through her at inhuman speed. She twisted around and kicked up with both legs.

She only meant to overturn the heavy table, granting herself far more effective cover from the gunfire. Instead, the table cracked down the middle where her feet struck, though it held together as a single piece. The heavy wooden monstrosity did indeed flip over. It also hurtled across the room, knocking Cross and one of the other thin-bloods back through the doorway. The childe who had dropped to fire under the table had barely an instant to scream before hundreds of pounds of oak landed edge-down on his spine.

A vampire could, given time and blood, recover even from a wound such as that. Tara didn't let him. She rolled to her feet, stomped once hard on the crippled thin-blood's head—barely even noticing the spray of bone and brain-matter that soaked her ankles—and picked up his weapon, a Mac-10 converted to full auto. She fired once, blindly, over the table and into the doorway. Her objective wasn't actually to hit anyone (though she certainly wouldn't mind), but to keep the thin-bloods back for another moment.

There. Dionne was trying futilely to press into a corner, to remain unseen. With a gust of wind, Tara was on her, lifting the seneschal to her feet with one hand tight around her throat. "Didn't expect me to survive this long, did you, you bitch?"

"Tara, please, I—"

One quick burst of bullets to the gut to shut her up and render her temporarily immobile. Then, discarding the weapon and holding the Caitiff in both hands, Tara charged forward even as Cross leaped over the table and once more opened fire.

Dionne's body shuddered once as it hit the plate glass window. The sound of cracking bones was very nearly as loud as the gunfire and breaking glass. Shards of the latter fell to the street fifty feet below. Tara and Dionne followed.

Airport Hilton, Los Angeles International Airport
Los Angeles, California

"Fuck!" Jenna Cross raced to the window, fired a few swift bursts downward, but she knew it was useless. Even injured by the fall and clearly limping, Prince Tara was down the block and around a corner with unearthly speed. Several passersby stared in shock at the body that lay broken on the pavement. Dionne might not be well and truly dead, but she was definitely not waking up for months, if not years.

"What do we do, Jenna?" one of the others asked from behind her. "This is a complete pooch-screw."

"Not completely, Laurence." Jenna Cross turned away from the window. "The bitch escaped, that's true. But she's not going to accomplish anything out there, alone and injured. We have a few nights before she can come back at us. Dionne gave me the addresses of most of the elders' havens around here. Let's make sure Tara hasn't got anyone to turn to once she's healed up. Someone call Samuel, tell him what's going on, and arrange a meeting."

The thin-bloods swiftly wiped down the weapons, just in case they'd left any fingerprints—unlikely, given that vampires have no skin oils, but possible—and discarded them. Then it was simply a matter of running out of the building in a near panic, along with the kine who'd heard the gunfire.

Too bad about Dionne, Cross thought as she jogged alongside some overweight accountant with a bad complexion. *She could have been useful. But then, Caitiff or no, she wasn't a so-called "thin-blood," so it wasn't like she was* really *one of us.*

Cross glanced sidelong at an alley beside the building, yanked the accountant in after her, and fed deeply both in celebration and in preparation for the night's work to come. First, deal with the primogen and other elders to whom Tara might turn. After that, she was going to have to start positioning her people throughout the city, and try—again—to come to some arrangement with the MacNeils. She wasn't certain what sorts of reinforcements Tara might come up with when she discovered her local powerbase destroyed, but Cross was determined to be ready for it.

Trafalgar Square
London, England

"But it's the end! The end is here!"

"Right you are, sir. The end, I'm certain." The bobby shook his head in amusement, even as he gently but insistently prodded the scruffy fellow before him with his baton. "Going to have to be the end somewhere else, though. You're causing a stir out here, and we've enough of you doomsayers about as it is. Why you lot didn't just give it up with the turn of the millennium, I don't—"

The instant the lights of Trafalgar were behind them, the ranting fellow—clad only in faded jeans, old Converses, and an overcoat—spun about, smacked the officer's baton aside with a blow that shattered the man's arm, and latched onto his throat. For several long moments as they huddled in the shadows between street lamps, the only sound to be heard was a horrible, messy slurping.

"Evenin', Rufus."

His chin stained by a trickle of blood that had, so far, escaped his notice, the disheveled vampire turned at the sound of his name. In the alley behind him, illuminated only by the faint glow of her cigarette, was a woman built to give the average longshoreman a run for his money. Her black hair was tied up in a tight bun behind her head, and she wore jeans and a man's flannel shirt. Rufus didn't see it on her, but he'd no doubt she was also carrying the baton she'd inhered from her father, one of the first of London's metropolitan police so many years ago. The weapon, which she'd carved to a fine point, had developed its own savage reputation throughout London's Kindred underground.

"What do you want, Liza?"

"Going to have to take you in, Rufus. Queen Anne and the sheriff ain't happy with what you've been about lately."

"What, this?" Rufus dropped the bobby. "He'll live, see? Still breathing and all. He'll just figured I knocked him out trying to escape."

"Not about the bobby, Rufus."

Rufus blinked. He hadn't *done* anything else! He'd done nothing in the past nights he wasn't *always* doing! Rufus considered himself something of a prophet, and he'd taken it upon himself to warn his fellow Kindred of the approaching Gehenna—always couched in terms so as not to give any secrets away to the kine passing by, of course. They didn't tend to listen, but he warned them anyway. And in these last nights, when some vampires were acting all peculiar and the Red Star shone bright, he'd only increased his—

Oh, God. They were after him because he *knew*. He must be right! And if that was the case, he couldn't let them silence him now!

To his credit, Rufus gave the sheriff's bruiser a good run. He made it almost three blocks, and halfway up a fire escape, before the impact of the baton against the small of his back caused him to fall from the ladder with a cry of pain. He didn't scream long. Even as he rolled over, the sharpened end of the wooden weapon plunged through his ribcage and into his heart.

It might have made Rufus feel better to know that he was far from the first Kindred to vanish off the streets of a Camarilla city in recent nights, and that he would be even further from the last.

Might have—but probably not.

A warehouse in Midtown
Houston, Texas

"Ah, Archon di Padua. So good to see you up and mobile."

The speaker, Karen Suadela, looked like a severe businesswoman, probably in her forties. Her dark hair was tied back, and she wore a well-pressed pants suit of deepest blue. For decades, Suadela had been a guiding force in Houston's primogen. She might even have had the clout to challenge Prince Lucas Halton for the princedom, but she'd always been content to remain a lesser target.

That all changed several weeks ago, when Prince Halton disappeared along with the rest of the Tremere in the city. Suadela, deciding that the opportunity was simply too good to pass up—and also concerned that any *other* prince might not be as easy to work around as Halton had been—wasted no time at all in stepping forward to claim the authority, and none of the other primogen had sufficient means to stop her.

It was just as well Halton had vanished when he did. Suadela didn't think he'd have had the strength of will to do what needed to be done anyway.

Di Padua, for his part, returned her greeting with little more than a stiff nod. He shuffled into the room, the mincing and unsteady gait of a wounded man trying to limp on both legs. Wounds, completely dry of blood, still gaped open on his arms, and his face and shoulders still bore both the burns and lacerations of the grenade. A week since the incident, and he still hadn't managed to heal any but the slightest of his injuries. His blood simply didn't seem as potent as it had been—which, if true, would also explain the failure of his abilities when faced with the Sabbat pack in the first place. If he hadn't alerted Prince Suadela and Sheriff Reno to his operations ahead of time, and if they hadn't sent their own people to back him up, the Sabbat would have finished him. As it was, Reno and his people had barely scooped him up before one of the bastards put a machete between his head and his shoulders.

Less knowledgeable vampires might consider it good fortune that Suadela was going out of her way to help him out, arranging for a safe haven while he recovered. Now, out of the blue, she'd sent one of her ghouls in a limousine, along with an "invitation" to join her in this rundown warehouse. He'd been led up a flight of stairs, and now stood on a balcony—more of a wide catwalk, really—overlooking the warehouse floor.

"Up, Prince Suadela. Not quite what I would call mobile yet. What, if I may ask, am I… doing…"

Di Padua stared out over a scene ripped from Dante's nightmares. A handful of heavily armed Kindred stood at attention or walked steady patrols through the warehouse, which was empty of anything resembling wares. Instead, several short rows of Kindred lay spread neatly across the floor. Each lay motionless, paralyzed by the lengths of wood—ranging from broom handles to thick branches to arrows to actual stakes apparently carved for no other purpose—protruding from their chests.

"Prince Suadela, what *is* this?"

"Criminals, Archon di Padua, every one. They have been found guilty of violating the traditions, and acts of sedition against my rightful rule—and the Camarilla's."

"Specifics?" Technically, di Padua had no right to demand details. This was, after all, a local matter of the prince's law. But he was curious.

"In most cases, spreading lies of the coming of Gehenna and the rise of the Antediluvians. Given the strange blood sickness going around now—to which you seem to have fallen victim, Archon di Padua—I cannot afford to allow doomsayers to cause widespread panic. Most of the neonates are just gullible enough to believe it."

"I see. And they are here, as opposed to exiled, blood bound or darkening the sunrise… why?"

"Walk with me, Federico." Di Padua noticed the sudden shift to his Christian name, but chose not to comment. He followed, silently grateful that Suadela kept her pace slow as she descended the steps toward the main floor.

"You are not the only victim of the curse, or sickness, or whatever it is that has afflicted us, in my city. Several individuals close to me have also suffered."

That probably meant that she herself had suffered, di Padua figured, but refrained once more from comment.

"And we have discovered a remedy, Federico."

Di Padua's feet touched the floor—and he was instantly assaulted by the scent of Kindred blood, as it leaked through the wounds left by the incapacitating stakes. It struck him as no hunger ever had. The Beast within him didn't merely stir, it launched itself to the forefront of his soul without a moment's warning. The personality that was Federico di Padua blacked out, one hand still on the railing of the stairs. When his vision cleared even slightly—when he could once more see the world, even if it was through a haze of blood and rage and unending need—he was kneeling beside the first of the staked criminals. His fangs were fully extended, almost painfully so. He quivered with the desire to plunge them deep into the exposed flesh of the helpless vampire.

But this wasn't the way! Diablerie, vampiric

cannibalism, was the worst of all sins. It was everything that an archon like di Padua was supposed to stand against. The destruction of not merely another's body but his *soul*—Federico didn't think he could survive with that on his conscience.

Eyes wide, lips and jaw actually trembling, he twisted his head back to stare at Karen Suadela, standing beside him. "It's the only way, Federico. Regain the power that is yours! Feel the blood flow through you, as it should! If you do not heal, you cannot help us face what is to come. The Camarilla needs you, Federico."

His soul twisting within him, Federico di Padua looked down at the helpless Kindred on the floor beside him. And slowly, ever so slowly, he bent forward.

It had to be done, and if it *had* to be done, he'd find some way to deal with it and move on. It was only going to be just this once…

Somewhere over the Atlantic Ocean

On casual examination, the plane looked average enough. A General Dynamics Gulfstream model 400, it was one of the jets of choice for wealthy individuals and private businesses that needed to make transatlantic flights without relying on commercial airlines. Normally capable of seating eight comfortably, this particular G-400 boasted a few internal modifications that cut down its passenger space but made the ride far more comfortable for its owner. The rear half of the passenger compartment was completely sealed off from the front by a thick bulletproof wall and a heavy door that bolted from the inside. This internal compartment lacked windows, but was otherwise equipped with just about anything a discriminating traveler could ask for, up to and including a satellite phone and Internet connection. Several chairs, a sofa, and a work desk with a custom-built personal computer gave the small room the feel of an office. The small refrigerator and television gave it a more personal touch, though the bags of blood in that refrigerator might be somewhat more startling. A padded metal coffin of the sort used to transport bodies overseas rested along the rear wall, along with a sleeping bag for Beckett's guest.

Beckett rather disliked the melodrama of sleeping in a coffin. Give him a comfortable Sealy Posturepedic, or else a nice patch of dirt, any day. If the plane were to go down during daylight hours, however, he wanted some means of avoiding the sun (on the minuscule chance he survived the crash), and a sealed metal box was simply the best way to do that. He wasn't about to spend multiple millions on an aircraft without taking every possible precaution.

Of course, he hadn't really wanted to spend the money in the first place. Though hardly poor, Beckett didn't have the sort of resources that many Kindred of his age did—he was far too concerned with his own personal crusade to worry about playing stocks or manipulating corporations. Even with his various Swiss accounts, the money that had gone into this jet hit him hard. He was still making sales of his less-than-helpful archeological finds (such as the one he'd concluded with Victoria Ash) to replenish his flaccid accounts. Still, given the amount of continent-hopping he did, he'd needed to do *something*. His own two feet (or four feet, or two wings, depending on his form at the time) were sufficient for traveling state-to-state, but not so effective at crossing large bodies of water. Flying commercial wasn't an option for someone like him—all he needed was a single delay to keep his plane in the air past dawn to generate a whole mess of problems—and boats, while safer, were not particularly swift. Just a few years back, he'd finally decided it would be more efficient to acquire his own means of transportation.

The intercom buzzed once, like a startled bumblebee. Beckett reached up and depressed a button. "What is it, Cesare?"

"You asked me to notify you, Signore, when the authorities located the attendants. They have done so."

Beckett nodded, only then remembering that the

ghoul couldn't see him from the cockpit. He and Kapaneus had left a trio of baggage handlers stuffed into a janitor's closet back at Savannah/Hilton Head International. He'd even stolen their wallets, just to make things look a bit more natural. The men, when they recovered, would tell a tale of being jumped from behind and knocked unconscious.

If they recovered, Beckett corrected himself internally with a quick flash of guilt. He'd lost his head somewhat when drinking from the third man, and he might have taken too much. It was always risky to feed in so public a place as an airport—if the bodies were discovered before they took off, they might be denied permission to leave—but riskier still to embark on a long-distance flight while hungry, with none aboard to feed from save the pilot. True, he had his emergency stash in the refrigerator, but why take the chance?

No doubt the airport would shut down for hours, as authorities strove to ensure that the attack wasn't indicative of some sort of terrorist infiltration of the facility. Beckett had Cesare listening in to airport radio chatter—and God bless the friend of Okulos who had sold them the long-range eavesdropping equipment they now used—just in case anyone tied the attack to the private flight that departed the airport some two hours ago. It wasn't likely, but Beckett wasn't one to ignore the possibility.

"Very good, Cesare. Let me know if anything comes of it."

"Of course, Signore."

Beckett frowned as he clicked off the connection. He'd never wanted a ghoul. The very idea—a human made an emotional slave through the consumption of vampiric blood—always made him feel vaguely unclean. He was a predator, and he'd accepted that centuries ago. Killing humans, though something he avoided as much as possible, was part of his nature. He'd never developed the taste for controlling them, however, that so many other Kindred did.

Still, when he'd purchased the plane, he'd also been

well aware that he'd need someone to fly it. Cesare was an out-of-work pilot Beckett ran across in Venice while attempting (unsuccessfully) to buy a certain heretical text from the collection of one Pietro Giovanni. Cesare was quite skilled, but he was also a slave to the bottle. Beckett figured that if the man was going to enslave himself to something, he might as well be made useful while he was at it. The alcoholism was gone now, replaced by another, far less natural addiction. Beckett disliked the necessity, he disliked the obligations it placed on him, and frankly he wasn't all that fond of Cesare on a personal level—but ultimately, it was still the best of a number of bad choices.

"You were telling me," Kapaneus prompted him when it became clear that Beckett was lost in thought, "about this Hardestadt, and why you have chosen to work for him."

Beckett blinked, then grinned a grin with absolutely no humor to it. "'Chosen' is, I think, not the most accurate term, Kapaneus. I had no choice at all."

"Because this Hardestadt is a powerful member of this Camarilla of which you've spoken?"

"Powerful? Hardestadt was one of the Camarilla's founders," Beckett explained. "He's also almost assuredly a member of the Inner Circle. Or if he's not, he pulls the strings of many who are. Frankly, I'd as soon rip out both my fangs with a Leatherman as work for him, but—well, I managed to put my foot in my mouth something fierce when speaking to him. It's in my best interests to keep him happy with me right now, and if that means playing errand boy for a little while, so be it."

If Kapaneus had any difficulty with the modern metaphors, he hid it well. "Why not simply hide? His reach cannot possibly be infinite."

"No, not infinite. But close. For me to hide from him, I'd have to go somewhere *really* obscure, and stay there. And if I did that, I couldn't conduct my own investigation."

"Ah." Kapaneus leaned back, his expression suggesting that this was the point toward which he'd been maneuvering. "So you do not do this merely on his behalf, but also on your own. It is part of the same quest you were on in Egypt, yes?"

Quest. Interesting choice of words. Beckett had to smile again. *In the end, pretty accurate, though.* "Yes, I suppose that's right."

"So why do you do it? It is not as another's agent, obviously. Why do you travel so, search so? What do you hope to gain?"

Does he actually want me to answer that question? They'd been traveling companions for months now, but that did not make them friends. They were Kindred, and trust was practically as foreign a concept to them as sunbathing.

Still, Beckett rarely had the opportunity to discuss his motivations with anyone. If nothing else, it would allow him to keep it all straight in his own mind.

"A large part of it," he began, idly fiddling with the sunglasses he held in his left hand, utterly unaware of the very human gesture, "is the process of problem-solving itself. Piecing together puzzles. I find the intellectual and emotional stimulation almost as gratifying as a good feed. It keeps me sharp, keeps me from becoming jaded." His expression quirked. "Makes me feel useful, like I'm actually accomplishing something with immortality."

Kapaneus smiled shallowly. "Always a noteworthy accomplishment, that. But that is not your only reason, is it?"

Beckett took a moment to marvel at the vampire sitting before him. Though restrained by mortal standards, Kapaneus was downright exuberant for an elder Kindred. Most elders eventually came to appear inhuman, not due to physical changes, but to their actions, their movements. They ceased making all those little incidental gestures that humans made, ceased fidgeting, blinking. Some even stopped making expressions at all, unless they consciously reminded themselves to do so.

Beckett himself had a few more mortal mannerisms than most vampires his age. He cultivated them deliberately, mostly to counteract the inhuman features and habits he'd developed over the years. But Kapaneus was very nearly as expressive as Beckett, and he was substantially older.

"You're right," Beckett finally answered, giving himself a mental shake. "No, that's not the only reason I do what I do. I'm looking for the truth of our past, and of our origins, as a means of understanding us. More than us, myself."

"How do you mean? How will knowing Caine, or the Third Generation, aid in this?"

"I believe," Beckett said, leaning forward as he warmed to his subject, "that 'Caine,' as the Kindred know him, didn't exist. The tales of Caine, and Abel, and Gehenna—they're all apocryphal. Myth and metaphor."

Kapaneus' eyes widened. "In my time, such a thing could never even have been considered. Our history, as related in the Book of Nod and by our ashen priests, was as certain as tomorrow's dawn."

"Right. And that's the problem. Most Kindred who concern themselves with it at all look at it as history. Nobody stops to figure out what it *means*."

"And you wish to know what it means."

Beckett nodded. "I may not believe that we descend from a homicidal farmer, but we came from *somewhere*— and given the rather unusual nature of our abilities, it sure as hell had nothing to do with evolution or natural selection. Something created us. Maybe it was God. Maybe it was something else. I don't know. I *do* know that there must have been some *purpose* behind it. That we were created for a reason, and it was more than just to be a scourge set to the back of the sinning humans by a wrathful deity.

"I have to understand where we came from, Kapaneus, because only that way can I understand *why* we are. I honestly believe this lack of understanding is at least partially responsible for our inability to cooperate with one another for any length of time, for the constant schemes and machinations and wars of people like Hardestadt. Immortality without purpose has to be the greatest curse imaginable, and it's one from which I intend to free myself—and the rest of the Kindred, if they'll listen.

"Without understanding, Kapaneus, everything else is so much ash and empty sound."

Any response Kapaneus might have made was rudely interrupted by the sudden sense of lethargy that swept over them both. They barely had time to crawl into their respective beds—Beckett in the coffin, Kapaneus in the sleeping bag—before the rising sun sent them into slumber.

Sforzesco Castle
Milan, Italy

Once a mighty fortress ready to repel almost any attack, Sforzesco Castle was besieged in the modern era by a mob of a different stripe: tourists. Containing multiple museums and libraries, including the famed Museo d'Arte Antica, the stone floors echoed from dawn to dusk with the footsteps of staff and thousands of people who traveled from near and far to see these relics of bygone eras.

At night, of course, Sforzesco Castle was completely closed to the public. Those who stood within its high-ceilinged galleries now were not "the public." Any other night, several of Milan's Kindred population might well be roaming these halls, feigning delight at the art and sculptures in order to impress their brethren with their taste and culture. Sforzesco Castle was declared Elysium, one of several in Milan, a spot where Kindred could gather without fear of violence or hostility—at least of an overt nature. It wasn't where Prince Giangaleazzo held court, but it was the city's next most popular gathering spot for social-climbing vampires.

Tonight, it was largely empty. Giangaleazzo had called a court gathering elsewhere to begin at midnight, and the city's upper-crust Kindred were taking the early hours of the night to prepare themselves. That left Giangaleazzo time to travel to Sforzesco for a meeting of his own. He stood now in one of the smaller galleries, occupied largely with busts and other small sculptures of Italy's past, scattered throughout the room on pedestals that seemed almost randomly placed. Their presence interfered with his near-manic pacing, but he managed nonetheless, his footsteps ringing a regular beat against the floor.

The epitome of Italian gentry, Giangaleazzo kept his dark hair tied back. He wore a navy blue suit made of the finest silk. A ring set with an onyx stone that flashed even in the room's faint lighting was his only other adornment.

The chamber's other occupant, who looked longingly at the kneecaps of the pacing vampire and entertained various brief fantasies of breaking them, couldn't have appeared any more out of place. He was clad in jeans, running shoes, and a leather jacket—though, as a nod to the formality of the occasion, he'd replaced his usual biker jacket with a leather sports coat. For the same reason, he was without his customary baseball cap, and his head felt naked without it. He carried a canvas gym bag over his shoulder. Some things he never traveled without.

Finally, already impatient waiting for the prince to speak, he couldn't deal with the steady pacing any longer. "Cool beat," he said, putting himself in Giangaleazzo's path, "but I can't dance to it."

"Tell me, Archon Bell," Giangaleazzo snapped, drawing up short to avoid walking into the larger vampire, "what do your superiors propose to *do* about this?"

It required every trace of willpower for Theo Bell, archon to justicar Jaroslav Pascek and—it seemed in recent nights—all around errand boy to the Camarilla, to avoid saying "music lessons." Instead, *manners* and *diplomacy* echoing in his head, he offered a wan smile.

"My superiors are looking into it. We've dealt with curses and blood illnesses before, and this time shouldn't prove any—"

"Spare me the platitudes, Archon! I am not some ignorant neonate to be placated by empty promises of miracle cures, or to be fooled by transparent falsehoods of plague and pestilence! This is no mere pathogen and the Inner Circle damn well knows it!"

Christ, here we go… "And just what do you think *is* happening, Prince Giangaleazzo?" Bell asked through gritted teeth.

"Are you truly so blind, Archon Bell? The signs all show themselves. Elders in the blood are dwindling night by night, and if rumor is to be believed, only the blood of other Kindred serves to mitigate their weakness. The Red Star shines brightly—more so, I am told, to those with the gift of superior sight, but it is obvious even to me. Can you truly not see that Gehenna is upon us?"

"Gehenna is a myth, Prince. We're looking at a pretty damn big upheaval, I'll grant you that, but—"

"Bell, I abandoned the Sabbat because I could not stomach what it had become, and what it was forcing me to become. I had assumed, however, that your superiors were prepared to deal with the Ancients when they arose, that their protestations of myth and legend were meant only to pacify the younger generations. If it is not, if the Inner Circle is going to bury their heads in the sand even with such blatant evidence held before them, perhaps I should rethink my earlier decision. At least the Sword of Caine has eyes."

Bell blinked once, slowly, a deliberate indication that he was pondering what he'd just heard. Then, equally slowly, he took several steps forward until he was standing almost literally nose-to-nose with Giangaleazzo.

"Prince," he said, his voice low and quiet. "I didn't want to be here tonight. I've spent several month dead center in a shit-storm of fairly epic proportions. I've been sent to Europe without any clear idea of what my job is gonna be, told to wait for further Goddamn instructions, and *then* they tell me, while I'm at it, that I need to swing by Milan and deal with your complaints. 'Try to assuage his concerns,' they told me. Well, after what I just heard, I got *no* interest in 'assuaging.'

"I'm tired. I'm used to the sun being up right now. I have no fucking clue why I'm *on* this side of the ocean, except that every damn archon over here was too busy with something else to do whatever the fuck it is that I'm doing. And now, suddenly, I've got a Camarilla prince telling me straight up he's thinking of rolling over.

"So let me tell you how it is, Prince. It was a major coup for the Camarilla when you came over and brought your city with you. It would be a major blow if the justicars discovered that it was actually a Sabbat ploy, and that you had to be put down as a spy. A lot of people would lose face, big time. *But*—and here's where it gets fun—that would be less of a blow than if you actually *succeeded* in going back to the Sabbat.

"Am I crystal-fucking-clear?"

"You—you can't talk to me that way!" Giangaleazzo was actually spluttering, something rare indeed for a vampire of his age and usually perfect composure. This was the elder who had calmly turned his entire city over to an enemy sect, and had his own people slaughter all Sabbat loyalists in Milan at the time. For him to be this shaken, Bell realized, he must honestly believe the end of the world was nigh.

That, or he's also been affected by this blood-whatever that's going around. Either way, he still needs to get my point.

"I can, and I just did. Since I'm going to do you a favor and pretend I didn't hear this conversation—unless you do something stupid later on to make me remember it—I think you owe me some slack on the finer points of diplomacy."

Bell took two strides back from the flabbergasted prince. "Now," he continued, "I assure you the Camarilla is looking into this matter thoroughly and seriously, and they appreciate the concern shown by the *loyal* and *trustworthy* Prince of Milan. We'll keep you informed, and if you come up with anything that might aid the ongoing investigation, please feel free to step forward with it at any time."

Giangaleazzo snarled once, then spun on his heel and stalked through the nearest doorway, leaving Bell to wonder if that had really been the best way to handle the situation.

Fuck it. It was the best way I could handle the situation. They want finesse, they can damn well get someone else here. I've got other things to…

Only the slightest narrowing of his eyes, utterly invisible to anyone not staring directly at his face, belied Bell's sudden tension. He moved casually among the busts and sculptures, stopped to examine one in particular, knelt to lay his satchel on the floor…

And the room shook with the sound of manmade thunder as he rose, SPAS-15 semi-automatic shotgun in hand. The weapon fired, belching a veritable cloud of buckshot into the ceiling. Bits of stone scattered, leaving pockmarks on the ceiling and across some of the statues. Bell hoped they could be restored, but he wasn't about to let fear of damaging the artifacts stop him. Not when faced with her.

The cloak of shadows that had rendered the dark-haired woman invisible to normal sight evaporated as she dove from the corner—where tendrils of shadow had held her several feet above the floor—and away from the stinging metal cloud. She hit the carpet in a roll and was on her feet faster than a human could have blinked. Her hands rose in a defensive posture, darkness swirling about her arms and body, making it difficult to draw a bead on any specific part of her.

"Honored to meet you, Archon Bell."

"Drop dead, Archbishop."

Lucita cursed internally, though no sign of it appeared on her face, as she dove once more from the path of the buckshot Bell sent hurtling in her direction. She knew of the archon by reputation—the so-called "Killa-B" was notorious through the ranks of the American Sabbat, and word of his prowess had spread even as far as Aragon. Still, she was fairly certain he should not have been able to detect her, concealed as she was. It could only be another sign of her abilities proving inconsistent, like her failing control over shadow. Bell was good for his age—possibly the best—but she'd seen almost six times as many years as he had. At her best, she had no doubt that, while it would *not* be an easy fight, she could take him. As things stood now, however, she was in a great deal of trouble.

Bell, for his own part, had heard too much about the dreaded Lucita to take even the smallest of chances now. Lucita was almost a legend among archons: an independent player in the sect wars and a stone-cold killer. Now that she'd thrown in her lot with the Sabbat, that respect was tinged with no small amount of hatred—and fear. Bell knew that if he gave her even a moment to take the advantage, he was dead. He knew, too, that his shotgun wouldn't be nearly enough to destroy the Lasombra, though a chest- or head-full of buckshot would slow *anyone* down. Even as he fired a third shot at the swift-moving patch of darkness that was all he could see of the archbishop, he was racing and diving his own way through the room, the power of his blood accelerating him to speeds unimaginable to mortals. Lucita was nearly as fast, however, and one of the pedestals behind her practically disintegrated as the shotgun blast struck it.

Bell spun about for a fourth shot, but Lucita was suddenly *above* him, held aloft once more on limbs of shadow. A tendril lashed out, wrapping itself about the shotgun. The sound of fatigued metal echoed through the room as the weapon began to compress, to bend in the center. "Let us see how you do without your toys, Archon Bell."

"Okay." Even at rest, Theo Bell was several times as strong as any mortal. Now, engaged in combat and with blood flowing through his limbs, he was stronger still. Without so much as tensing to warn her of his intention, Bell yanked on the gun, drawing it—and Lucita, still attached to it by a tendril she could not release fast enough—toward him. With the strength of a piston he slammed a fist upward, connecting with his opponent's skull.

Even through the preternatural resilience of Lucita's undead body, bone cracked. The world around her seemed to spin, to strobe as though God were turning the lights off and on in rapid succession. She felt the floor beneath her back as she landed, felt her control over the shadows slip and the tentacles vanish. The last time she'd been struck that hard, it had been by Leviathan, a creature of the Abyss who had laired beneath the haven of her sire, Cardinal Monçada. She wasn't certain any other vampire had ever hit her with that sort of force.

But Lucita was far too experienced, far too well trained, to let even this degree of pain and confusion disorient her. As the archon loomed over her, one shard of the wooden pedestal in his hand, she rolled back, kicking up into Bell's chin with both feet and flipping upright in the same movement. She landed in a wide stance, hands raised before her. Bell, staggered by a kick nearly as powerful as one of his own, nonetheless recovered just as swiftly as she had and stood before her, stake and fist both held ready.

Lucita began to move forward—and abruptly stopped, assailed by a sudden wave of nausea, something she hadn't felt since her mortal days. It passed almost as swiftly as it came, but it frightened her more than anything Bell himself might have done. If her own ailment, whatever it was, was worsening—if it could flare up so suddenly in the midst of battle—she simply couldn't afford to fight so skilled a foe as the archon. Not at least until she had a better handle on what was happening to her.

It was time for Lucita to employ an unusual tactic: the truth.

"Bell, listen to me. This isn't necessary. I'm not here as your enemy tonight."

"Right. Best assassin in the Sabbat just happens to show up in the city of the man they consider their biggest traitor. Dunno what you've heard of me, but I ain't *that* stupid."

Before the sentence was even concluded, Bell lunged forward, leading with a roundhouse punch to Lucita's head. It wasn't intended to land. Had she blocked it, as many fighters instinctively would have, she'd have left her chest open for the stake, which he thrust forward at almost the same instant.

But Lucita *was* one of the best, and she'd seen the feint coming almost before Bell launched it. Instead of blocking, she dropped beneath both strikes and spun in a leg sweep. Bell landed hard on his back, but scrambled up an instant later in a move less graceful than Lucita's, but no less efficient. He expected to have to ward off an attack even as he rose, and was surprised to find that Lucita hadn't moved in to press her advantage. In fact, she'd taken a few steps *back*.

"Bell, listen to me. I'm not here for Giangaleazzo." Which was true, so far as it went. The execution of the traitor prince was not her primary objective in Milan. She'd seriously considered killing him while she was here as something of a fringe benefit to the trip, but she wasn't about to mention that.

If it had just been a matter of taking Lucita's word, Bell would already have launched another attack. But he hadn't missed the fact that the fight was going a little too well for him. Lucita had been at this for nigh on a thousand years, if he remembered right (and he did)—he should be hurting by now, but wasn't. And if that meant what Bell thought it might, it was suddenly vital he learn more. He didn't for one moment drop his guard, but he refrained from advancing. "All right. So why *are* you here?"

Lucita debated not telling him for an instant, but decided it couldn't do any harm. Even if he personally didn't already know what she was about to tell him, his superiors certainly did. Say what you wanted about the Camarilla, she knew their spies were efficient.

"Several Sabbat elders have vanished in recent weeks. Others have weakened, as though attacked from within. It was my thought that this might be the first stage of a Camarilla offensive, perhaps some damned Tremere ritual. And were that true, it was likely that your people would be in contact with Giangaleazzo, seeking his inside knowledge of European Sabbat strongholds. I'm here to gather intelligence, Bell, nothing more."

"And the mighty Archbishop of Aragon doesn't have minions she can send to do her legwork for her?"

"The mighty Archbishop of Aragon doesn't have minions she'd trust on matters this important—though your own superiors clearly don't feel the same way."

Bell scowled. He didn't really *want* to believe her. He wanted this to be another trick, for her to be covering the fact that the blood weakness affecting Camarilla elders was actually a Sabbat plot. But not only was Lucita claiming that Sabbat elders had contracted it, she seemed to be suffering some of its symptoms herself. Foreign as the concept was, he had the awful suspicion that Lucita was telling him the truth, or at least part of it. So if the Camarilla wasn't responsible—as he was fairly sure it wasn't—and if the Sabbat wasn't responsible—as now seemed to be the case—what did that leave?

Lucita's abilities were waning—but they were still formidable. More importantly, she still knew how to take advantage of an enemy's distraction. Even as Bell opened his mouth to ask another question, the shadows wrapped around Lucita like a curtain.

When they faded, Bell was left alone with a badly damaged museum and a lot of explaining to do.

Outside the Prehistoric Anthropology Museum Monaco

It only rained, on average, about sixty days out of the year in Monaco. Tonight wasn't average. Torrents of water fell from the skies, as though someone had turned the world on its side and the Mediterranean was now *above* the city, rather than below it. Pedestrians, largely tourists, but some natives as well, dashed toward hotels and homes, umbrellas and the ever-popular newspaper-above-the-head all proving more or less useless in the face of such a deluge.

Even now, over an hour after sunset, a few scattered people emerged from the museum—primarily staff, racing home after finishing up their evening duties. They were all of them unaware that they, not the relics to which they tended, were the exhibits.

Across the street, with beady, unblinking eyes watching those exiting the library, was a large black bat. It hung from a tree branch, remaining utterly motionless except for an occasional shimmy to shake at least some of the water from its fur.

It was times like these that Beckett wished vampires were as resistant to wet as they were to heat and cold. The fur helped, as did the fact that he couldn't feel the chill in the rain, but that didn't change the fact that he was borderline miserable. Under most circumstances, he'd long since have given up, decided to pursue the issue some other night.

But he and Kapaneus had been in Monaco for nearly two weeks now, chasing down leads and coming up largely empty-handed. Samir was nowhere to be found, either at his haven or at his favorite stomping grounds (or at least those of which Beckett was aware). Nor had Beckett so far had any luck in digging up any of Monaco's other Tremere. Granted, when he'd last spoken to Samir, there were only three Tremere in the country. But in a country smaller than most major cities, finding any one of three specific vampires should not have been impossible.

Finally, Beckett had run across another vampire who, in exchange for a few hundred in casino chips, had informed him that one of Monaco's other Tremere had a ghoul—last name of Rheveaux, didn't know the first—who worked in the Museum of Prehistoric Anthropology. If anyone in the country knew where to find the absent warlocks, and assuming the ghoul hadn't vanished with them, it'd be him.

So now Beckett the bat watched the staff of the museum leaving, their faces largely obscured by umbrellas and other forms of personal shelter. He was trying to find a man for whom he'd never even gotten a reliable physical description. Beckett entertained a sudden urge to flutter down there, transform in front of everyone, and announce, in his best Bela Lugosi, "I am here for Rheveaux." He chirped once, the chiropteran equivalent of a giggle.

And then, just like that, he was there, at the end of a small procession of staff leaving the museum. Rheveaux was utterly average: limp brown hair plastered to his head by the rain, glasses, a cheap off-the-rack suit. Beckett would never have noticed him at all, if it hadn't been for his posture, and the furtive, desperate look in his eyes. They darted back and forth as though seeking escape, narrowed against the wind and rain, bloodshot. His stance was sunken, his gait shuffling, as though he were recovering from a virus. It could just be that the man was sick, but Beckett didn't think so. He looked like a man in withdrawal, and not just from nicotine or smack.

Beckett followed him, flitting through the night sky. The rain made it difficult, interfering with his echolocation and weighing down his wings, but fortunately the man didn't have far to go. Only a handful of blocks, and he was turning into a cheap (for Monaco, anyway) apartment building. Two minutes later, the lights clicked on in one of the fourth-floor units.

The windows were sealed up tight against the rain, with no room at all for a bat to climb in. But then, Beckett wasn't so limited in his choice of shapes. He fluttered his way over to one of the other windows, one that opened into a room still dark, and concentrated. The effort it required to take this particular shape, as fast as he did, took a lot out of him. He'd have sweated, if his final form was capable of sweating, and he knew he'd have to feed before another night had passed. The world went gray, then faded to nothingness as Beckett's sight was replaced by a less sensitive, more tactile sense.

Settled in a large recliner with the television turned to some random commercial, Rheveaux was unaware of the bank of mist that flowed unnaturally through the window into his bedroom. Nor did he hear Beckett's soft footsteps on the carpet behind him. It was only when he felt razor-sharp talons pressed to his throat that he became aware that he was not alone.

"Evening," Beckett said to him in flawless French. "Where's the chantry?"

On the Boulevard des Moulins
Monte Carlo, Monaco

Having retrieved his satchel from the hotel room, and now fully sated on the blood of the ghoul, Beckett stood outside a large but plain-looking house on the outskirts of Monte Carlo. The gate to the property stood open, and not a single light shone in any of the windows. The rain had died down to an irritating drizzle, but lightning and thunder still split the skies on a regular basis.

Of course, Beckett thought. *Can't have an abandoned house of magic without the "dark and stormy night" to go with it, can we?*

He gave brief thanks that the Tremere had several hedges growing near the fence line. It would allow him to set up shop on the lawn with little fear of being seen from the street. He fully expected the chantry to have a number of sorcerous defenses set up, and he wasn't nearly stupid enough to just waltz in without trying to take them down first.

Except that closer examination revealed no such defenses. He observed the house with all his heightened senses, even with his ability to read auras. He took a few moments to search the grounds for mystic markings, glyphs, any symbol or anything out of place that might suggest a ward. Finally he just stood for minutes on end, motionless as any statue, and simply stared at the house before him. Either the ghoul had lied to him about the chantry's location—unlikely, given his desperation for even a *taste* of Kindred vitae, which Beckett had offered—or the Tremere had left the place defenseless.

That, or someone else had been here already to clean up.

Beckett cursed himself, loudly. Why the *hell* hadn't he thought of that? The Camarilla knew the Tremere had vanished—Hardestadt was the one who'd let on, for fuck's sake! How could he not have realized they were going to come through and clean up any evidence the warlocks might have left, before the Sabbat—or worse yet, some intrepid mortals—could do so?

The chances of him finding anything inside to suggest where Samir or the other Tremere had gone were practically nil at this point. Still, it was the best lead he had. He might as well at least follow it through.

Tentatively, eyes unblinking, sniffing the air for any traces of company, Beckett approached the front door of the house. He experienced one brief moment of near panic where he believed he might have triggered some mystical defense or ward that he hadn't detected. His hands began itching horribly all over, and he ripped his gloves off expecting to find them burned, or discolored, or rotting away, or *something*. They looked perfectly normal, however—well, normal as fur-covered clawed hands *could* look, at any rate—and the itching subsided almost as swiftly as it had begun. When several minutes passed without a repeat of the sensation, Beckett gave a mental shrug and continued.

The front door was locked with a simple latch, one that took Beckett and his lock picks barely a minute to bypass. Pretty shoddy security. He could only assume the Tremere had much more potent defenses up when they dwelt here. Still, it surprised him that a Camarilla clean-up team left the house so easily accessed, when there was always the chance they'd missed something they wouldn't want others to find. Something about all this was very, very wrong.

The door drifted open with a faint squeak of its hinges, allowing access to a tight, narrow entryway. It was uncarpeted, the walls undecorated except for a single abstract painting. The shapes were almost hypnotic, and Beckett realized that when looked at from the corner of one's eye, rather than directly, the strange colors and forms blended into the triangle-and-squared-circle sigil that was the mark of Clan Tremere. Cute.

Doorways stood on both the right and left sides of the hall, but not for a ways down. Beckett could only assume the construction was intended to provide a means of defense, a short, cramped area in which an intruder couldn't move well while the defenders—

DOWN!!

Beckett had long since learned to trust his instincts. Sharp as they were, augmented by his undead abilities, they often warned him of dangers that even his night-vision and heightened senses were unable to detect. So when everything inside shrieked at him that the floor was the best place to be, he didn't hesitate.

Even as Beckett was eating tile, the hallway shook with a loud roar, and *something* flashed by over his head to blow a hole in the door behind him. Eyes blazing even more brightly than usual, Beckett looked up.

"Bell." It had been quite some time since he'd met the archon, and then only briefly, but the guy was *not* easy to forget.

Theo Bell, now clad in his traditional baseball cap and leather jacket, swung the barrel of the twelve-gauge pump down for a second shot. Beckett neither knew nor cared that Bell was carrying a pump because he'd been unable to repair the one damaged by Lucita. From the business end, the weapon looked menacing enough.

A number of different thoughts danced around one another in Beckett's head in the span of a split second. One: Apparently Hardestadt had decided he was too great a threat after all, though whether it was because of what he knew or what he might yet learn, Beckett wasn't sure. Two: if Bell had already opened fire, it meant he'd discounted any possibility of simply capturing Beckett —probably a wise decision, given Beckett's own abilities. And three…

Three was that Beckett had nowhere to go. He couldn't run; even if he somehow avoided catching a shotgun blast or three in the back on his way to the door, he had little doubt that Bell was faster than he. He still hadn't reached the doors beside which the archon stood, so neither side was an option.

That left forward. *Damn, this is going to hurt…*

His blood pumping through his limbs, granting what extra speed and agility it could, Beckett shot to his feet and lunged. Rather than moving in a straight line, he actually hurled himself against the left wall as he moved, allowing the momentum to bounce him into the right.

As he'd hoped, Bell's first shot ploughed a deep hole in the left wall where Beckett had been a moment earlier. The second, unfortunately, caught Beckett square in the left shoulder.

This wasn't the first time Beckett had been shot, but with so powerful a weapon at such close range, even his toughened hide couldn't just shrug it off. The pain of the metal fragments tearing into his flesh caused his teeth to clench, the Beast to rise from the depths of his soul. The urge to flee the agony nearly overpowered him—he felt his legs quiver as he moved—but the need to rend the source of that pain limb from limb was stronger even than that. A deep, bestial growl emerged from Beckett's throat, and at some point his talons had torn through the fingers of his gloves. Archon or no, how *dare* this arrogant creature threaten him? *Him!* An elder twice Bell's age!

Even as he struggled to keep the Beast at least somewhat in check—against a foe like Theo Bell, he was going to need his wits about him—Beckett leaped forward. The shotgun discharged again, just to the left of where he'd been, and then Beckett plowed into the archon. He heard a clatter as the shotgun fell to the ground and skidded across the floor, and then he saw nothing, heard nothing, but the foe before him.

Fast as he was, Bell was nearly able to avoid the attack completely. He backpedaled, and talons that might well have torn his heart out instead traced a line of blood down his chest. Beckett knew the wound had to hurt like hell—but if it did, the archon wasn't showing a trace of it. Bell began throwing devastating but lightning-swift punches, elbows and knees. He was indeed much faster than Beckett, and stronger, but Beckett could take an unholy amount of punishment. Hell, the shoulder-shot alone would temporarily put down many Kindred by itself. Beckett knew it was a race, now, to see if he could land a telling shot with his claws before Bell pummeled him into unconsciousness, torpor, or worse.

It was like being caught in a hailstorm—with hailstones the size of dumpsters. His entire body shook, his bones cried out in protest, as the archon delivered blow after blow with a speed that Beckett couldn't hope to block or avoid. All he could do was keep his arms up to shield his chest and face, until he spotted an opening.

He thought once more of fleeing, but between the Beast within and the pummeling from without, he simply couldn't muster the concentration necessary to change his shape into something more appropriate to flight. Instead he twisted suddenly and slammed his uninjured shoulder into Bell, throwing off the other's rhythm. He'd hoped that would give him a moment to launch an attack of his own, but even as Bell staggered he grabbed Beckett—one hand around his throat, the other at his belt—and slammed him up into the ceiling. Pieces of sheetrock and fiberglass, and splinters of a support beam, rained down around them. Beckett felt the archon's grip on his neck tightening, and wondered if Bell actually had the strength to rip his head from his body, or if he was merely planning to break Beckett over his knee.

He wasn't about to wait and find out. Beckett reached down and grabbed both of Bell's arms—talons first. His thumbs and forefingers actually *met* between the bones of Bell's forearms.

The archon screamed, then, and hurled Beckett away down the corridor, no thought in his mind but the Beast's need to stop the pain of those unnatural claws digging into his flesh. Beckett hit the floor with a painful thump and skidded most of the way to the door. Even as he landed, his hand lashed out. If he'd only judged properly where it had fallen…

Bell was already moving down the corridor toward him, murder in his eyes and the Beast evident in his face. Beckett half rolled into a sitting position and scooped up the shotgun from where it had fallen. Rather than taking the time and concentration to retract his talons, Beckett simply snapped the trigger guard off the weapon, took a brief instant to enjoy the sudden widening of Bell's eyes when he saw his own shotgun pointed at him, and then fired. And again. And again, as fast as he could pump the weapon.

In truth, Beckett wasn't the world's best shot. He tended to use guns only when faced with large numbers of mortals, preferring his innate weapons when faced with Kindred foes. Still, in such close quarters, and allowing for the spread of the buckshot, even Bell would find it difficult dodging a single blast, let alone a barrage. The archon fell to one knee as a portion of his left thigh disintegrated under the hail of lead.

Using the shotgun almost as a cane, Beckett struggled to his feet. His entire body quivered, his talons twitched with the urge to rip through his enemy's flesh, to drench themselves in his blood.

But Beckett, for all that he saw himself as a predator, was determined to remain more than a tool of the Beast. Further, while he knew that if Hardestadt wanted him dead, he couldn't be in *too* much more trouble, dusting an archon certainly wouldn't help.

"I don't want to finish you, Bell," he said, his voice low, despite the fact that a large part of him did. "But I swear if you…"

Beckett trailed off as Bell raised his head to glare at him, and he had to fight a very human urge to swallow. There was nothing sentient remaining in Bell's features. The eyes were narrowed, and Beckett could swear he almost saw a gleam like that of his own eyes in the archon's sockets. The jaw was open, fangs protruding. A deep bass rumble sounded from Bell's chest and throat. And slowly, as though the pain were a mere inconvenience, rather than the agony Beckett knew it must be, Bell rose.

"Oh, shit."

All right, reason was no longer an option, and there was no *way* he was taking on a vampire as powerful as Bell in the midst of a frenzy. For a split second, Beckett fingered the gun he held—at this range, a shotgun blast to the head might just be enough to finish even a vampire as tough as Theo Bell. Then, with a soft curse, Beckett emptied the last few shells into the rising archon's wounded leg instead—it just might slow him down even further—hurled the empty shotgun at Bell's feet and ran. Bell wasn't feeling pain right now, but the sheer damage to his leg should prevent him running at his full speed for a few minutes, no matter how much blood he pumped into it. Beckett, on the other hand, was in a *lot* of pain—his shoulder burned like it was on fire— but his legs worked just fine. Now that the shotgun was out of the picture, he just had to get far enough away that Bell couldn't grab him during his transformation into a bat, and he was *gone*.

His footsteps sounding not unlike a machinegun, so fast did they strike the ground. Beckett tore through the front lawn of the property and out the main gate, not caring for the moment what sort of spectacle he made. He could hear the archon roaring in rage behind him, knew he hadn't yet gained enough distance. He turned, dashing along the sidewalk, swerving to avoid the few late-night pedestrians who stared after them in shock, praying he wouldn't slip in a puddle left by the fading drizzle…

A sudden whine sounded in the street behind him, the sickly-sounding siren used by police cars across Europe. The tiny car came barreling around a corner and pulled up onto the sidewalk in the vampires' path. "All right, now!" one of the officers shouted in French as they both left the vehicle. "Someone care to tell me what's—"

Bell tore into the first officer with a scream of primal rage, one that almost drowned out the man's own cry of pain and terror. The other officer, eyes wide, grabbed for his weapon even as he moved around the car. For a moment, all eyes were off Beckett, and a moment was all he needed.

He could have stepped in. Maybe he *should* have stepped in. Maybe he should have just put a round through Bell's head when he'd had the chance.

He hadn't then—and he didn't now. Ignoring the pain in his shoulder—and, with greater difficulty, the screams of the officers—he leaped the nearest wall, a stone barrier surrounding another small property, and was gone. If anybody had been watching, they'd have seen a large bat fluttering away from the yard, its flight path erratic as it favored its left wing.

On the Boulevard Princesse Charlotte
Monte Carlo, Monaco

Slowly, the sensation of warm blood in his throat and the first twinges of healing brought Bell back to his senses. His vision swam slowly into focus, and the pounding in his skull lessened until he was once more capable of rational thought. His eyes seemed unwilling to focus, and he kept seeing flashes. It took him a moment to realize this was because he was staring into the lights atop a police car.

"Oh, fuck."

Bell glanced downward. He was absolutely covered in blood. A police officer, his neck mangled down to his now visible spine, dangled from his arms. A second lay, limbs obviously broken, at the curb. Pain shot through Bell, from his lacerated arms and his mangled leg, but for at least a few minutes, he could ignore it.

This—this was wrong. Bell had more self-control than most of his fellow short-tempered Brujah, but he still experienced his share of frenzies, of maddened, violent rages. But this? Never before had he experienced a frenzy so severe that he'd not only been unable to control himself, but had been completely unaware of what he was doing. He had only brief flashes of memory from the moment Beckett shot him until now. He didn't remember how he got here, and he had only bloody images of his massacre of the cops.

Something was very wrong with him, and he wasn't about to go after someone as dangerous as Beckett again until he found out what.

By the time more police arrived, accompanied by paramedics who had precious little to do but clean up, Bell and the original police car were gone. The Monaco police found the car abandoned several blocks away, but though they kept up the manhunt for months, they never did find the cop-killer.

The Thompson Plantation
Outside Savannah, Georgia

Even through the floor and thick carpeting, they could hear the sounds of many Kindred milling about the dining room, waiting for them to make their appearance. A local conclave called by Hardestadt personally, it was made up of nearly every powerful or important Camarilla vampire within a five-hundred-mile radius. None of them knew precisely what they were here to discuss, though theories ranged from a new offensive against the Sabbat—Savannah had repelled a Sabbat incursion last year and many saw it as a staging-ground for retaking Atlanta—to a discussion of the blood sickness—the "withering," as many were calling it—making its way through the ranks.

The latter theories were pretty much on target. Hardestadt did indeed intend to update them on current events. Several cities—London, Houston, Glasgow, Nice and others—had come across a single solution to both the withering and the problem of Gehenna-spouting troublemakers, one that Hardestadt intended to implement, with the help of archons and local sheriffs, as official Camarilla policy.

But all this was for discussion later. Right now, Hardestadt had other matters on his mind.

He was not alone in the room, the same office where he'd spoken with Beckett weeks earlier. Before him, sitting in one of the cushioned chairs, was the house's owner Victoria Ash, now clad in a simple black dress as befitted the seriousness of the gathering.

"What happened when you met, Miss Ash?" Hardestadt asked.

Victoria turned her attention from contemplating the upcoming meeting back to the questions at hand. "I purchased the relics, as we agreed, and he left. It would have been the last I saw of him if you hadn't chosen to use my manor as a meeting place."

"And that was all?" Hardestadt looked skeptical. "He didn't try to explain what meaning the relics had, or how they related to Kindred lore or mythology?"

Ash frowned. "As I understand it, Hardestadt, they *didn't* relate to our lore or mythology. That's why he was willing to sell them."

"That may be true," Hardestadt muttered, as though speaking to himself, but Ash wasn't fooled; if he spoke aloud in her presence, he wanted her to hear. "Beckett wouldn't likely part with anything he thought might contain any of his precious answers. That does not mean he wouldn't have someone he trusted hold important items for him, though."

"Oh, really. I don't even know the man that well. He had some baubles to sell, I liked them, I purchased them. Not even *we* could be so paranoid as to turn that into some sort of conspiracy."

Hardestadt nodded. "You're correct, of course. Come, we should keep our guests waiting no longer." But despite his acquiescence, suspicion lingered in his eyes.

Victoria Ash shuddered once at the notion of Hardestadt becoming an enemy, and wondered once more what Beckett could have done in mere weeks to make him so dangerous to the Ventrue Founder.

Hotel de Paris
Monte Carlo, Monaco

Kapaneus glanced up as a bat fluttered awkwardly in through the open window, transforming into a battered and burned Beckett even as it dropped toward the floor. "Are we departing?" he asked blandly.

"Kapaneus, you have *no idea* how much we're departing." Clearly favoring his left shoulder, he began tossing his few possessions onto the bed. Abruptly he froze.

"Shit!" Beckett sat down abruptly on the bed, not caring that he knocked half of what he'd just put there off onto the floor. "I left my satchel."

Kapaneus looked concerned. "Are there materials we require in there?"

"No, just some basic thaumaturgic components. I can replace them. I just liked the damn satchel." Oh, well. He'd pick up another on the way out tomorrow night. He thought about running out and feeding, but realized—oddly enough, given the amount of blood he'd burned that night—that he wasn't particularly hungry. He felt almost like his Beast itself was somehow languid, uninterested even in the basic necessities.

Before he could ponder the phenomenon any further, his train of thought was interrupted.

"Beckett, where are we going?"

That was the question, wasn't it? He had the first inklings of an idea forming, but he really, *really* didn't like where it was leading him. Rather than answer Kapaneus directly, he first checked his watch—yes, it was late enough that the sun should have set where he was calling—and picked up his satellite phone.

"Beckett," Okulos' voice greeted him after only a few rings. "How are things working out?"

"Lousy doesn't begin to cover it, Okulos. What about on your end?"

"It's getting bad, Beckett. This disease, or curse, or whatever it is, it's spreading. The Camarilla's calling conclaves about it."

"Damn."

"That's one way to put it. It's gotten unpredictable. A few victims report getting *stronger* for a while before they began weakening, but it's always temporary. It's not just hitting the really old anymore, either. Even a few ancillae are falling victim now. Meanwhile, every second vampire from Paris to Poughkeepsie has his own theory about what's causing it. You can bet the Tremere are at the top of everyone's suspect list, but Gehenna is right there in second place. Rumor is the Sabbat has begun opening every ritual with a quote from one of the prophecies. 'Where is your pride, where is your strength, where is the wrath that should endure?' That sort of crap."

"For Christ's sake, Okulos. This is not Gehenna. How gullible *are* these people?"

"Hey, don't ask me. I'm not the one spouting Noddist sound bites. A lot of neonates are starting to listen, though. The Camarilla's going nuts trying to keep a lid on it."

Beckett tensed. Given his friend's penchant for understatement… "Okulos, what are they doing?"

"Well… you understand these are rumors only, Beckett. But a lot of the most vocal proponents of the Gehenna theory are going away. Suddenly."

"Executed?"

"Maybe worse. Rumors abound that Kindred blood temporarily alleviates the affliction, Beckett. Doesn't cure it, but it replenishes the lost strength. Nobody who actually knows anything is talking, but I'm starting to hear whispers of warehouses and old office buildings converted to internment centers—and buffets. And the level of violence at the street level is skyrocketing."

Holy shit. Beckett had no doubt the rumors were exaggerated—they always were—but for such stories even to have begun making the rounds meant *something* big was going on. He had to get a move on.

"What about the search I asked for? Found anything?"

"That depends. I have found a great deal of confusion, more than a bit of consternation, and a trace of befuddlement."

"If you meant 'no,' you could damn well have said 'no.'"

"I'm sorry, Beckett. I've looked everywhere I know to look. I've called every contact I have, and every contact *they* have. Every chantry is empty, every haven abandoned. If I hadn't met some personally in my years, I'd wonder if the Tremere ever existed at all."

Beckett cursed, multiple times, in several dead languages. "I *have* to talk to the warlocks, Okulos. Blood weakness, strange events, apocalyptic portents… This all just *screams* Tremere."

"Surely there are other mystics you could discuss this with."

Were there? Beckett knew his fair share of practitioners of the magic arts. Some were Kindred who, like him, had developed some skills with thaumaturgy outside the Tremere aegis. Several other clans had their own forms of blood magic that, while often less malleable than thaumaturgy, were no less potent. He even had multiple contacts among mortal magicians, such as Nola Spier in Los Angeles or Josef Ravid in Tel Aviv.

But no, he didn't believe offhand that any of them could provide the necessary information. Nobody had the sheer faculty with blood magic—and, more importantly, the in-depth records and studies—the Tremere did. Besides, if the Tremere *were* responsible, nobody else would be able to confirm that fact. If Beckett *had* to seek out lesser resources, he would, but not until he'd exhausted his final option.

However much he *really* didn't want to do it.

"Okulos," he said after a moment's silence, "I don't have access to a computer just now." Time for him to quit stalling and obtain a laptop. Something else he'd have to do on the way out tomorrow night. "Could I impose on you to check some train schedules for me?"

"Of course." Beckett's hypersensitive ears easily picked up the clacking sounds of a keyboard over the connection. "Where do wish to go?"

Beckett closed his eyes. "Vienna."

Atop the Sanwa Bank Building
Los Angeles, California

The night air blew in a steady wind past Prince Tara's face. From the high rooftop of one of downtown LA's many skyscrapers, she stared out over the city she intended—and, for the moment, failed—to pacify. Fully recovered from the wounds she'd sustained at the hands of Jenna Cross and her flunkies, the prince had nonetheless laid low, observing events as they transpired.

It was not good. In what was rapidly becoming a guerilla war the equal of any Sabbat crusade, several elders were fighting from various hidden havens, but most of the primogen and the rest of the city's elite had been massacred, cornered in their havens or run to ground like dogs. Night after night, thin-blooded Kindred arrived from elsewhere in the country, apparently drawn by the notion of an entire faction of their own kind. Los Angeles was already home to more vampires than Tara had ever seen gathered in one place, and she wasn't certain how well the human population would support such an influx of predators. Under other circumstances, it might have been an interesting sociological experiment, but right now it was just a nuisance.

Her initial plan had to been to band together with the city's other elders, but they no longer remained in sufficient numbers to fight off the growing horde. She had called for help from neighboring princes and the Camarilla as a whole. *Now* they were sending aid—given the "current environment," they couldn't allow an entire city to be wrested from their grasp—but she had no idea how much or how soon. Nor was she certain if the arriving forces were going to allow her to play any major role in retaking her city, and if they did not, if she ultimately failed here, she wasn't sure how long she could maintain her San Diego princedom. The Kindred, by and large, didn't allow failures to remain in power very long.

Her one point of consolation was that Cross and the MacNeils were still fighting each other as viciously as ever. Apparently, the older anarchs were no more welcoming of thin-bloods than anyone else. But while they might weaken each other, the two factions weren't likely to destroy one another without help. So, though it had caused her pride to twist and strike at her gut from within like she'd swallowed a viper, she'd called on the only other force she thought might prove able to help her.

"Thank you for coming," she said over her shoulder, unable to turn and face the man—the *thing*—standing behind her.

Four Winds Conspire, member in good standing of the New Promise Mandarinate, bowed, though she couldn't see it. "I am honored to be of service." He was a tall man—almost abnormally so—and thin. He was clean-shaven, and wore a navy blue pinstriped Armani that really didn't suit him at all. If he'd been mortal, Tara would have placed his age at about forty, give or take. As one of the Cathayans (Kuei-jin, they called themselves), creatures similar but not truly kin to the Kindred, he could be practically any age at all.

"Has the Mandarinate considered my offer? I know most of your kinsmen have departed Los Angeles, but any *one* of you is still more than a match for any three anarchs." She'd reluctantly agreed to double the initially agreed upon tribute—despite that ten million dollars was not an amount she could just brush off—if the Cathayans would aid her in retaking her city.

"They have."

"And what was their decision?"

"Alas, Prince Tara, it was decided that, as we will most likely be joining our brethren back home before long, we are better off accepting five million to do nothing than ten million to engage in yet another conflict."

Tara's eyes narrowed, and she spun, her rage boiling up. "You fucking idiot! If I don't retake this city, you won't be getting any tribute at all! You…"

And then she understood. Four Winds Conspire grinned a grin far wider than any human (or Kindred) could have managed as the stairwell door behind him opened, and that bitch Cross—and at least a dozen of her people—emerged onto the roof.

"You son of a bitch!"

Four Winds Conspire merely shrugged, bowed once to Jenna Cross, and descended the stairs out of sight.

Well, she'd taken the bastards on once already, and that was when she had no room to maneuver. Let them see what an elder could *really* do! Prince Tara began to run, to dodge at unbelievable speeds. She allowed her power and her rage to flow from her, generating an emotional force that should have driven the younger Kindred to their knees.

After her first four steps, she grew puzzled. She didn't seem to be moving as fast as she should be…

On her seventh, the first bullet caught her shoulder, spinning her around. The next several dozen punched through her face, her throat, her ribs, her pelvis, each wound a trail of pain that she should never have felt.

Strangely, Prince Tara's last thought was completely calm, completely rational. *How odd*, she noted, *that I was so strong the last time I faced them, and so weak tonight. This illness makes no sense.*

And then the barrage forced her over the edge. Seconds passed, and then Prince Tara thought nothing at all.

Atop the Sanwa Bank Building
Los Angeles, California

Jenna Cross leaned out over the edge, fighting a brief flash of vertigo. "I don't think even an elder could survive that," she said to the others behind her, "but call down and have Toby and Chris take a look at the remains just to be sure. Hurry, before we start gathering a crowd down there."

Most of her people began filtering back down the stairs, until Cross was left with just two other companions on the roof. Both wore beards, but were otherwise hardly mistakable. The first could have been a powerful figure—broad shouldered, sharp featured, with long black hair and a thick but well-maintained beard to match. He had, in fact, been such a powerful figure before, when he was a force for change and anarchy among the Kindred, a legend in his own time. Now he dressed in ragged pants and an itchy wool tunic stained with the blood of numerous feedings, the modern equivalent of ashes and sackcloth. It wasn't that he couldn't take care of himself. He was just more concerned with other issues than his physical appearance.

The second wore a neater beard, boots, and a flannel shirt. His name was Samuel, and he had known Jenna rather longer than Jenna had known him.

"Well shit, daughter," the more unkempt of the pair said. "You did it. Fucked up another one who might have called down the end on us."

Jenna scowled. "I'm not your daughter, Uncle Jack. I've asked you not to call me that."

"Might as well ask the sun not to rise, sweet-cheeks. Don't mean it'll happen that way."

This time it was a sigh. "Come on, Uncle. We don't want to get left behind."

"No. No, we wouldn't want that at all."

Jenna Cross, the newest thorn in the Camarilla's side, and the man called Smiling Jack, former anarch leader turned prophet of the coming Gehenna, left the rooftop together. Samuel watched them go, and then slowly followed behind.

An outlying home
Ciudad Juarez, Mexico

Lucita slipped out of the house on the edge of town—it would be some time before anyone found the owners—and walked at a deceptively casual pace down the rough and broken road. The sounds of daytime in the city hadn't yet faded, less than an hour after sunset. She'd forced herself to rise this early, to start her search as swiftly as possible.

Her Giangaleazzo theory hadn't held up (and had almost gotten her killed, for that matter). Neither had any of the leads she'd chased down in the weeks since. Lucita was patient—it was something she'd learned in her many centuries of tracking down targets others wanted eliminated—but she was still unaccustomed to this degree of failure. She had nothing but her initial conclusions, and a better idea of what the blood weakness and the violence *weren't*.

She'd finally decided to try once more to follow her earlier instincts, to speak with Aajav Khan, the current supreme Seraph of the Black Hand. The Hand was more than just a military arm of the Sabbat. They were fanatics, Gehenna cultists even in a sect partially founded to avoid or survive Gehenna, and they did not necessarily march to the beat of the Sabbat's drummers. Lucita didn't think they could, or would, be responsible for the curse (or what have you), but excessive violence and strange disappearances? Those were definitely in the Black Hand's purview.

So, if nobody was going to help her contact Jalan-Aajav by phone, she'd have to pay him a personal visit. And if that meant searching all of Juarez building by building—since all she knew was that he made his normal haven and headquarters somewhere in this city—well, she wasn't getting any older.

Tonight was merely the beginning, a night for scouting and reconnaissance. She would locate at least a few of the other Cainites of the city, make it known who she was and what she sought. One of them would talk to her, tell her what she wanted to know, or else the Hand would come to her. Either way, she—

"I knew you would come here eventually, Lucita."

Lucita was an elder, not all that far shy of a thousand years old. She had abandoned any semblance of humanity several years back, and prided herself on her progress along the so-called Path of Night. Yet it was all she could do to stifle a very human gasp of surprise at the sound of a voice—*that* voice—that she had never thought to hear again.

"Fatima…"

The Assamite stepped lithely from the shadows, and beckoned Lucita to join her in a wide alleyway between two rundown houses. Eyes alert for some sort of trap, though she didn't really expect one, Lucita followed.

She hadn't the first notion what to make of this meeting. Through the years, she and Fatima had been close, in one way or another. They had been friends. They had been enemies. They had loved one another as two undying beings laboring under the same curse, not in any fashion that mortals, encumbered with their various lusts, could comprehend.

When they had last parted four years ago, it had been in Fatima's hidden haven in the deserts northwest of Medina, Saudi Arabia. And it had not been on particularly good terms.

"You have changed, Lucita, since last we spoke. This—this is not you."

The archbishop's surprise gave way abruptly to disdain, even anger. "This *is* me. For the first time since that bastard brought me into his world, this is me! And what would you know of it anyway? Last we spoke, you were pushing me to involve myself, to decide what I stood for, who I stood with, while you sat around on sand and rocks awaiting some great message from Allah before you'd get out and do anything!"

"I merely observe, Lucita. I do not judge. You could grant me the courtesy of doing the same."

Lucita snarled, and began to push past the Assamite. "Get out of my way, Fatima."

"No. What's past is past, and may be irreparable. Nevertheless, in memory of what we were, I'm here to warn you. The Black Hand will not help you, Lucita. Do not seek them out."

Lucita stepped back, and only a fighter as experienced as Fatima could sense the slight tension in her muscles. "And you know this? Allah came to you in the desert and told you"—even as she spoke, Lucita dropped and aimed a sweep at Fatima's ankles; the Assamite easily jumped over it, throwing a spinning kick at Lucita's head for good measure; Lucita rolled backwards and rose to her feet—"that I was wasting my time?"

"After you left my home," Fatima explained, launching a series of punches and elbow strikes that would have devastated most opponents, "I realized that your arrival itself was the sign for which I waited. It was time for me to emerge into the world once more."

Lucita ducked two of the punches, blocked the elbows with a series of swift arm movements—"making boxes," she'd once heard it jokingly referred to—and then grabbed Fatima's extended arm on the next punch, twisted, and flipped the Assamite over her shoulder. "*I'm* a sign from God?" she scoffed even as she moved. "That's priceless, Fatima. The desert heat has cooked your brain."

Fatima stuck one leg out beneath her, catching herself before she could slam into the concrete. The other leg lashed out in a kick, striking Lucita in the forehead. The archbishop staggered back, and Fatima—from what appeared to be an absolutely impossible angle—righted herself.

"Has it? Does not your own Path of Night teach that you serve a specific role in God's design?"

"How could you know—"

"Since departing the desert," Fatima continued, idly stepping over a tiny tendril of shadow that tried to grab her ankles from behind, "I have made substantial efforts to increase my contact and interaction with those who might prove allies against the might of Alamut." Fatima was one of those Assamites who had chosen to go her own way, rather than abandon her faith at the orders of Ur-Shulgi. She paused, waiting, and this time it was Lucita who attacked, gliding in low, striking at the head with her hands, the ankles and knees with a series of swift kicks. Unable to block them all, Fatima found herself retreating.

"You are *not* about to tell me you joined the Black Hand, Fatima. You—" The rest of Lucita's comment was lost as the Assamite abruptly leaned forward into her assault, taking a heavy blow to the shoulder in the process, and delivered a stiff-fingered strike up into Lucita's solar plexus. Pain shot through the archbishop's chest, and the air she'd inhaled for speech was driven from her lungs in a loud grunt.

"No, of course I did not—" She staggered back as Lucita, who had been leaning forward with the pain of Fatima's strike, turned the sudden movement into a head-butt that landed solidly on the Assamite's chin. She paused a moment, working her jaw back and forth to be sure it still worked. "But I have been in contact with them," she continued around a mouthful of her own blood. "I have aided them on certain matters, just as I have the Camarilla. I require allies, Lucita, havens to which I might retreat on short notice if Ur-Shulgi sends others after me."

"The Black Hand doesn't trust outsiders."

Fatima caught Lucita's punch in one hand, grabbed her wrist in the other. "In these tumultuous nights, they sometimes prefer honest outsiders to traitors within the Sabbat—traitors they must deal with before the end."

Lucita rolled back, drawing the Assamite with her by her own grasp, and kicked. Fatima landed, hard, on the pavement, and Lucita kicked up to her feet once more. "Are you telling me the Black Hand is responsible for the disappearance of the elders?"

Fatima twisted her legs about like a corkscrew, and was also on her feet, her stance wide. "Some of them. Some have indeed disappeared thanks to—other forces. But when this blood weakness began to spread, several Sabbat elders feared Gehenna had come, and decided to attempt to locate and bargain with agents of the rising ancients, rather than battle them. These elders had to be removed for the good of the sect."

"And why would the Hand be unwilling to tell me this themselves, or aid me in hunting down the source of the weakness and those who truly *are* missing?"

"Simply, Lucita, they do not trust you. You have been Sabbat for but a few years, an avowed enemy of the sect for centuries. The Hand does not know if you are loyal, or will turn coat at the first opportunity." At the spasm of rage that crossed Lucita's face, Fatima added quickly, "Their doubts, not mine."

"I will just have to convince Aajav Khan, then," Lucita said, the last word punctuated with a kick to Fatima's midsection.

Fatima blocked the blow. "Jalan Aajav has gone missing as well, Lucita."

With a slight grunt, Lucita straightened up, dropping her hands to her sides. Fatima did the same, and for a moment, they stared at one another.

"Were we fighting?" Lucita asked then. "Or sparring?"

"I'm not certain. If I'd given you a lethal opening, would you have taken it?"

Lucita couldn't answer, and Fatima didn't really seem to expect her to.

Instead, she merely continued. "The Black Hand would not have seen you if they could avoid it, would not have helped you if they could not, and if you had pressed the issue, might well have decided to treat you as a threat. With their high seraph vanished, they are more paranoid than ever.

"I can tell you, however, that their advice would serve you poorly. They have their theories, but they are no more certain as to the reasons for recent events than you are."

"And you? What do you believe?"

Fatima frowned, and Lucita was startled to see traces of fear in her eyes. "Something has awakened, Lucita. I have felt it moving about the world for weeks now, and everywhere it goes, death follows for our kind. I cannot say if it is some great Methuselah, like Ur-Shulgi. I cannot say if it is something other than Cainite. Allah preserve us, I cannot even say if it is one of the Third Generation, come to herald the end of nights. I know only that it is here. That I have some connection to it, though I know not why. And that it, and other events, have frightened even the mighty Black Hand.

"And I know," she said, stepping closer, "that I do not wish to see you fall to it, or to those who would fight it." She stopped only when she stood directly before her old companion. Either of them could kill from this distance with a single movement, even an opponent so resilient as a vampire. Neither moved.

"So you came to warn me?"

"I came to say farewell, Lucita. I think it unlikely that we can both hope to survive what is to come. And no matter what you—or I—have become, or will be in the future, I could not allow our previous parting to be our last."

Lucita, the conflicting emotions within her paralyzing her as efficiently as any stake, could only stare as Fatima leaned in and kissed her once upon her forehead. "Farewell, Lucita of Aragon, childe and conqueror of Monçada. You always were more than your father's daughter."

And with that, Fatima was gone once more into the darkness.

An anonymous alley
Ciudad Juarez, Mexico

For many long minutes, Lucita stared, unseeing, in the shadows of the alleys, determined to squelch not only the bloody tears that wanted to well up within her, but the emotions that spawned them.

You are not some weak-willed mortal pining for a lost love! You are Cainite! You are vampire! You walk the Path of Night, and this does not become you!

In the end, she triumphed, pushing her feelings down into an abyss deeper than that from which she drew the shadows she manipulated. She wondered, briefly, if this was a good thing.

It galled her to admit it, but she was going to need help. Normally even asking for assistance would be a violation of her new (and still somewhat shaky) moral code, but she could justify it—barely—as she was asking for the sake of her sect, not herself.

But whom to approach? The Black Hand wouldn't help her. And Fatima obviously wasn't prepared to travel with her, or she'd have stayed. Probably just as well, given the rather volatile nature of the relationship. Nor could she turn to others in the Sabbat, if there were traitors within. Besides, she was still a new enough convert, as Fatima had pointed out, that few of the Sabbat would willingly aid her. She could call Bishop Andrew and his pack from Aragon, but that would leave nobody to manage her domain while she was away.

All right then. If she couldn't find allies within the sect, she'd simply have to go outside it. And she realized, with a sudden ironic chuckle, that she knew exactly whom to ask.

The Mission Inn
Riverside, California

Theo Bell wasn't even remotely surprised that the Kindred spearheading the growing Camarilla effort to retake Los Angeles had chosen this place as their central headquarters. Less than sixty miles from LA proper, substantially less to many of the city's outlying suburban areas, it was near enough for close observation and direction of tactics—and even, should the need arise, for those orchestrating the assault to move in and take part personally—but far enough that they were out of the main line of fire.

Further, the Mission Inn itself would likely make most of the elders feel at home. An enormous structure that occupied an entire city block, it was built, at least partially, in the style of an old Spanish fort. That alone would convey a sufficiently martial atmosphere to the Kindred within, and its hundreds of rooms allowed them to occupy several adjoining suites where they could communicate and plan without anyone the wiser.

Bell himself had precious little interest in being here. He'd done the whole city siege thing once already in the last few years, and the taking of New York left him with more than enough of that particular experience. Sure, if ordered to participate in the coming conflict with the thin-bloods—and where the fuck had they all come from all of a sudden, anyway?— he would, but he didn't especially want to.

Bell had other concerns. The journey back from Monaco had allowed him substantial time for introspection, but he still couldn't figure out what was wrong with him. He'd never really lost control like that, not to such an extent. Was he losing his grip on humanity? On sanity? Or was this a symptom of whatever was afflicting elders, finally making its way down to one who hadn't yet celebrated his bicentennial? He was hoping that Hardestadt, who was assuredly not happy about Bell's failure to kill Beckett, would at least remain willing to listen to his reasons, maybe answer some questions.

The room he entered was a study in controlled chaos. A large suite, it was occupied by half a dozen Kindred and at least twice that number of kine (Bell assumed ghouls). Most of the ghouls sat at computers, telephones, radios or televisions, constantly relaying orders or taking reports. The vampires—Hardestadt among them, his suit still somewhat rumpled from several hours spent on a plane—took in the reports as they stood over an outspread map of the Los Angeles metropolitan area. A small stack of papers lay beside it. Bell knew from experience that those would be reports on Jenna Cross and any other thin-blood leaders the Camarilla knew by name, as well as members of the other anarch faction, the MacNeils. He was surprised to see the name Smiling Jack atop the thin-blood stack, not the other.

The vampires turned to face him as he approached, and he nodded his head in respect. In addition to Hardestadt, he recognized the archon Federico di Padua—a quick smile conveyed Bell's congratulations that the other archon had managed to survive his travails in the Lone Star State. If anything, di Padua seemed healthier than Bell remembered him being when they had served together in the assault against the Sabbat in New York several years previously. Like all his clanmates, Federico had a twisted and downright repulsive countenance, but tonight he wore it with something akin to class. He seemed just plain ugly, rather than outright diseased. Bell shrugged. The Nosferatu often masked themselves in illusory countenances. That's probably what di Padua was doing now. A look at another of the vampires at the table confirmed that impression, when Bell a recognized one of the Nosferatu justicar Cock Robin's favorite illusory masks. He nodded again, a sign of true respect for his own boss' brethren.

As he approached, one of the ghouls turned from his radio and announced, "Police reports coming in of, and I quote, 'some sort of gang-related disturbance' in the downtown area."

Di Padua acknowledged the report, waited for a specific street address which came a moment later, and placed a red marker—the sign for active engagement—on the map. Bell noted several of those on the map. So far, only one green marker—"acquired territory"—stuck up, and he was surprised to see that it marked the airport.

"Gas leak and a fire in the kitchen forced an evacuation of the Hilton around ten in the morning," di Padua explained, seeing Bell's expression. "Between the repair crews and our own ghouls, none of Cross's people who might have been havening in Tara's old Elysium survived the sunlight."

"Nice job. Still, I'm surprised not to see more green on the map."

"We had less time to coordinate this than we did New York, Bell, and there are a *lot* more thin-bloods here than there were Sabbat there. Besides, we were supposed to have some of our people follow up a drug raid on one of Cross's suspected havens, but an 'accident' on US-101 kept us from arriving on time."

"You don't think it was really an accident?"

"Damn convenient for Cross if it was."

Hardestadt abruptly rose. "You are not here to discuss our tactics, Archon Bell. You are here to answer for your failure to complete your assigned duties."

Bell glanced around. "We doing this in front of the help?" he asked sarcastically, waving a hand at the ghouls.

"Kindly explain," Hardestadt continued, sitting back in his chair and steepling his fingers before him, "what happened."

With a mental shrug, Bell did so. He'd already called in a report about the events at Sforzesco Castle, so he bypassed that and jumped straight into events in Monaco. He left nothing out.

"Are you telling us, Archon Bell," Justicar Robin piped in, his voice slurred by the deformity of his mouth, "that you failed to pursue because you were afraid of hurting *kine?*"

"No. I failed to pursue because by the time I recovered, I'd lost him. And mostly because I wasn't about to take on someone as dangerous as Beckett when I wasn't in full control of myself.

"And in case I didn't make myself clear," he continued, even as Hardestadt opened his mouth to speak, "this wasn't just some temper tantrum like you people seem to expect from us Brujah. This was complete and total madness. Beast in your head, blood in your eyes, go through anything that looks at you cross-eyed, bug-fuck frenzy. Only time I've ever seen anything like it is hunting down a werewolf, and I sure as hell haven't fallen *that* far yet."

"No," Hardestadt said, though clearly unhappy about being interrupted, "you have not." As though Bell were no longer present, he turned to the others. "What do you think?"

"Could be a symptom," di Padua said thoughtfully. "I didn't feel enraged myself, just weak. But we've seen that this illness affects different Kindred and even different clans in different ways."

"Or it could be an excuse," Robin added, "to justify the failure of a simple assignment." He glared at Bell. "I wouldn't take such pretexts from one of *my* archons!"

Bell's jaw clenched, but he bit down hard on any comment that might want to emerge. Mouthing off to a justicar was fairly high on the list of Things Not to Do, Ever. Di Padua caught his eye and gave a minuscule shrug, as though apologizing for his superior's attitude.

"All right," Hardestadt said finally. "If Archon Bell *has* fallen prey to the growing malady, we'll not hold that against him."

Gee, thank you so fucking much. But Bell, again, knew better than to give voice to such thoughts.

"Nigel?" Hardestadt waived one of the ghouls over. "Show Bell to the detention area, and allow him his choice of remedies." He turned back to Bell. "Once you're more yourself, come back here and we'll discuss your next attempt."

Bell blinked. *Detention area? Remedies?* Even as he nodded and turned to follow the mortal from the room, he began to experience a sudden sinking sensation.

Just outside city limits
Riverside, California

It was worse than he thought. The stench of blood, both fresh and dried, struck him as the ghoul opened the side door to the garage. From outside, it looked like any house in any suburban neighborhood. And inside the house itself, all seemed normal (if one could ignore the complete absence of any mortal inhabitants). But inside the two-car garage, its walls padded by towels and blankets to aid in suppressing sounds...

Eleven vampires waited within, watched over by two others equipped with heavy pistols and what looked like a fire ax. Some lay on the floor, staked and dropped to lie however they fell; one had apparently landed badly on the broken bat that pierced his heart and had torn a gaping hole in his chest. Others hung from the ceiling, some by their wrists, some by nooses around their necks. These last weren't staked; their bodies' attempts to heal their cracked spines, while the nooses continued to press on the breaks, kept them helpless enough.

"What the *fuck* is this?" Bell asked, his voice literally quivering, the Beast once more threatening to burst forth.

"Prisoners of war," the ghoul told him. "Agents and spies of the LA anarchs and thin-blooded."

Yeah, right. Bullshit. Bell had heard it before. This one's a spy. That one's an agitator. He'd heard rumors of young Kindred disappearing off the streets these past few weeks, and he'd known that some of it had to do with the Camarilla's efforts at silencing the rumors of Gehenna. But he'd never imagined something like *this*!

"What, only eleven spies?" The sarcasm in his voice was so thick it very nearly dribbled to the floor to pool along with the blood. "I'm surprised there aren't more. You people must be slipping."

"Oh, there are more. We just didn't want to overload any one area. We've got two other houses, and there's a warehouse in downtown that—"

Bell bellowed once, the call of an enraged animal. Depending on the efficiency of the makeshift soundproofing, the neighbors might or might not have heard the sound of screams, shotgun rounds exploding, bones crunching beneath the blade of an ax. It was violent, it was brutal, but it was no frenzy like the one he'd experienced in Monaco. Bell knew exactly what he was doing. He relished it.

When it was over, a dead ghoul lay beside two piles of rapidly decomposing flesh that would be naught but ash in a matter of minutes. On the other side of the room, a pile of stakes and severed rope lay in the corner, and eleven badly injured neonates stared up at the hulking Brujah, fear, confusion and the faintest traces of hope warring in their eyes.

"Get the hell out of here," Bell told them, his voice hard. "I don't mean the garage, I mean out of this damned city. It's more than your asses are worth to be in Riverside when the sun sets tomorrow."

They didn't need to be told twice. Those who could, ran; those who couldn't, limped. But they *all* fled, leaving Bell to stand alone in the midst of the carnage.

He stared around him, at the bloodstained floor, the stakes, the rope. "This," he snarled to the empty room, "is *not* what I signed up for. No fucking way."

What the hell was the Camarilla becoming? Is this what lay ahead of them? Elders keeping younger vampires in pens, as food, to grant them temporary respite from a malady they couldn't even identify? For fuck's sake, they ought to be devoting their efforts to finding the *cause* of this weakness, or disease, or curse, or whatever, not just to regaining their own strength and squelching rumors of the end of the world!

But then, that's all elders ever did, wasn't it? Worry about themselves, worry about keeping what they had at the expense of everyone else. Well, it wasn't going to happen! Bell wasn't about to let the ordered society he'd always fought to protect— hideously flawed as it was—tear itself apart in a frenzy of self-cannibalization. *Someone* had to do something, and if the elders wouldn't do it, he damn well would.

Still, he couldn't do it alone. He was going to need help— help from outside Camarilla ranks, since he was going to be fugitive number one soon as word of what happened here got out. So who…?

Bell laughed suddenly. Yeah, it was fitting somehow, all things considered. Now all he had to do was find her.

Aboard a train
Just outside Vienna, Austria

It had taken a number of days—which were spent packed away in cramped cargo crates—and several changes of trains, but they were finally almost there. They could easily have made the journey in a few hours by plane, but Beckett didn't want any record of their arrival in Vienna, and while he didn't *think* anyone among the Kindred had connected the ID numbers of his Gulfstream with him, he wasn't about to take the risk.

Besides, he'd been hoping the extra few nights would allow either Okulos or himself to come up with some alternative to what Beckett had in mind. It didn't, they hadn't, and there was nothing for it now.

Beckett sat atop an open cargo crate and furiously scratched at his right hand, ignoring the moonlit scenery as it raced past. This was the third or fourth time since the incident in Monaco that one or both of his hands had begun to itch like he'd just plunged them into poison ivy. At first, he'd attributed it to the lingering remains of some thaumaturgic ward, but now... Now he was worried. He scratched so hard he gouged several tufts of hair from his skin. He couldn't *see* any problem with his hands, though—they looked the same as ever, save for the furrows he'd just made in the thick fur. Slowly, of its own accord, the itch faded. It always did, after a few minutes.

Beckett rose, contemplating whether to tell Kapaneus about it, and decided instead to walk about the train, stretch his legs a bit.

Kapaneus was waiting for him just outside the door. "Look there," he said by way of greeting, pointing over the heads of the seated passengers toward the front of the car.

Beckett saw only a man—or possibly a vampire; it was hard to tell from this distance—with thick brown hair and a beard just turning to gray, vaguely scruffy looking, wearing a flannel shirt. The man glanced casually at Beckett, and then moved to the next car.

"Problem, Kapaneus?"

"That man has been watching the entrance to the baggage vehicle for some time now. I believe I observed him watching us last night as well."

"All right then. Let's go."

Beckett and Kapaneus wandered the train from the engine to the baggage car and back again, until the first rays of dawn threatened in the eastern sky, but they found no trace of the bearded man.

"We should have just enough time to feed before sunrise," Kapaneus noted as they returned toward the baggage car. "It will require some care, but I believe I can ensure that nobody remembers—"

"You go ahead, Kapaneus. I'm not especially hungry."

The elder stopped. "Beckett, when was the last time you fed?"

Beckett stopped, considering. "Oh, it was only…" His eyes widened as he mentally counted nights. "So why the hell am I not ravenous? I mean, I'm not about to starve, but I rarely go this long… What does it mean?"

Kapaneus opened his mouth as if to answer, but Beckett cut him off.

"No. Don't even say it."

The elder quirked an eyebrow. "Beckett, Kindred are growing weak, the sects are in chaos, and now even you are having some unusual experiences. Shouldn't you at least consider—"

"It's not Gehenna."

"Why are you so certain?"

"Because Gehenna's a myth."

"Why," Kapaneus asked again, in exactly the same tone, "are you so certain?"

Beckett almost told him. *Because I have to be. Because if I'm wrong, if Gehenna and the Book of Nod and everything else is real, it means that not only have I not found the answers I seek, but everything I've done, everything I believe in, is a lie. It's bad enough not finding the answers. I refuse to accept that, for almost three hundred years, I've been asking the wrong questions.*

But he didn't say it. Some things Beckett could barely admit to himself, let alone a relatively recent acquaintance. Instead he simply walked away and returned to his crate for yet another oblivious day.

Outside the Fortschritt Library
Public facade of the Tremere Fatherhouse
Vienna, Austria

It was now the night after their arrival, and Beckett and Kapaneus found themselves near the portion of old Vienna called the Mölker-Bastei, at an edifice that could only be described as imposing. Originally intended to become a church, it was bought and completed as the Fortschritt library in the mid-nineteenth century. Tall steeples, gothic arches and stained glass still stared out over the streets of Vienna. Numerous gargoyles—after a quick examination, Beckett determined they were of the normal, stone variety, not the more ambulatory sort employed by some Tremere as soldiers and guardians—occupied many a ledge. The stairs leading to the entrance angled down from ground level to a sunken doorway. Two particularly large and imposing gargoyles, their eyes reflecting in the moonlight, stood eternal sentry on either side of the stairs.

Oddly enough, the street directly before Fortschritt was blocked off by wooden police barriers, and a bit of stone rubble lay about within them. Beckett briefly questioned a lone passerby (who provided some much-needed sustenance, as well as answers), who told him the street had been closed off for almost two days now, the result of a collapse of the pinnacle of one of the steeples.

"Natural wear, perhaps?" Kapaneus had asked, his voice not especially hopeful.

"Not a chance. The Tremere would have so many preservation spells wrapped up in this place it would probably survive Gehenna itself. No, if it's falling apart, it means something's wrong with the magics within, and that's not a good sign however you read it."

The pair, after one last quick scan for further pedestrians, edged their way around the barriers and descended to the front door. For just an instant, Beckett thought he saw a bearded face staring at them from around a corner down the block, but it was gone before he could even hope to go investigate.

Well, screw it. If the man from the train was spying on them, so be it. Let him follow into the depths of Fortschritt, if he had the stones.

Beckett half-expected to face some sort of ward or defense that would prevent them from entering, but the door was sealed by nothing more arcane than a good lock. He removed his picks from his new satchel and made short work of it. He glanced at the large iron ring and thought briefly of knocking, but decided against it. The Tremere wouldn't appreciate unannounced company, but if there was anything *else* here, Beckett didn't want it to know they were coming.

"I've been here before," he told Kapaneus, one hand on the door handle, "but it was a long time ago, and I never saw much more than the public areas. This place is supposed to have a number of subterranean levels, but we may have to search them out if we can't find anyone to answer our questions."

Beckett pushed the door open—and froze.

The entryway of the Fortschritt library was a wide, high-ceilinged hallway that led directly into the massive chamber that had probably originally been meant as a church's nave. It was carpeted, and the walls were adorned with beautiful murals of religious significance.

Tonight, it was also adorned with gore, enough to make even a predator like Beckett blanch. Blood stained the murals, not in streaks but in literal spatters. Several outfits, reeking of stale blood and progressive rot, lay about the hall. A quick examination showed Beckett that the remains of their occupants were still inside them, but these were not Kindred remains as Beckett had ever seen them. Rather than decaying to ash, the victims had left strange pools of liquefied viscera in some cases, desiccated and mummified strips of flesh in others. Beckett found a few intact limbs. Some were pulpy, liquefying even as he touched them, while others were mummified and completely absent of any blood or liquids at all. One in particular, a disembodied arm, appeared mutated, its fingers curling back in on themselves, an extra joint present a few inches above the wrist.

"Well," Beckett said slowly, revulsion evident in his tone, "we know where at least some of the Tremere went…"

"What *is* this deviltry?" It was the first time Beckett could remember Kapaneus sounding truly shaken, and that worried him as much as anything else.

"I don't know. It looks like these poor bastards either burst or were sucked dry."

"Could it be the result of this blood magic you spoke about? Tremere thaumaturgy?"

"It could. A ritual gone wrong, or some sort of Kindred poison, maybe…" But his eyes kept drifting back to the mutated arm, and something about his theories didn't sound right. He took a moment to examine the warped limb further still. "This looks like something the Tzimisce might have done," he muttered, referring both to that clan's hideous flesh-shaping abilities and their longstanding hatred of the Tremere, "but there's no way I'll believe they managed to attack the fatherhouse itself."

With no answers forthcoming, the pair proceeded further into the church-turned-library. The nave had been transformed into a repository of books the likes of which could never have been imagined when the place was first built. Pews, the altar, everything had been replaced by chairs, tables and shelf after shelf after shelf of books. They stretched nearly to the peaked ceiling in many places, requiring rolling ladders to reach the highest tomes. This room, too, was scattered with remains, the last lingering shreds of Kindred who appeared to have been slaughtered or corrupted from within. The stench was so overwhelming, Beckett's eyes would have watered if they were capable. Beckett wondered if the entire clan lay dead, scattered throughout their fatherhouse, but decided it was unlikely. He'd seen several dozen bodies, true, but not nearly enough to account for an entire clan. On the other hand, the remains—what little could still be determined of them, at any rate—suggested people from cultures and countries across the globe. Clearly, a great many Tremere had all gathered at Fortschritt, presumably summoned by the Council of Seven, the warlocks at the peak of the clan's pyramidal hierarchy. Was the entire clan accounted for, hidden somewhere nearby? What had killed so many of them, and what had become of the rest, Beckett didn't know. Was it related to the blood-weakness? Had it *caused* it?

Beckett felt conflicted. He knew that here, in the public portions of the chantry, the odds of him finding any information on either the fate of the Tremere or the origins of the spreading malady were almost nil. Still, part of him rebelled at the notion of turning his backs on all these books without at least making an effort to look through them. He compromised with himself by deciding that he would come back and check these if his searches in the depths uncovered nothing. He—

"Beckett, *move!!*"

He didn't question; he merely dove. His ears filled with the sound of cracking stone, and even as he slid across the floor and under a table, he looked back to see an enormous chunk of the ceiling, chandelier still attached, plummet into the spot he'd just vacated. Glass and stone splinters flew in all directions, and Beckett threw an arm over his eyes to protect them. When he looked once more, he could see nothing but a massive cloud of dust kicked up by the impact. Slowly, Beckett climbed out from under his makeshift shelter and rose to his feet, waiting for the dust to clear…

Which it did, revealing an undamaged floor and no trace of rubble at all. Staring upward, Beckett saw a perfectly intact ceiling, without so much as a crack to indicate structural weakness.

"I don't think I care for this place," he muttered grimly.

"Beckett, if the magics that permeate this structure are breaking down, as you suggest, perhaps some degree of speed is in order."

So they searched, seeking any means of entrance to the hidden rooms and lower levels that Beckett knew existed. They combed the library, examining every nook and cranny, even peeking behind bookcases that stood against the walls.

They searched the offices and reading rooms—former priest's chambers and vestment rooms. Hours passed, and Beckett grew evermore grateful they'd decided on an early start. He didn't relish the idea of sleeping the day away down here.

Damn it! Beckett couldn't understand it. He knew all the techniques, all the tricks for both hiding and locating secret passages. Not only that, he'd *been* here, been in at least one chamber he could no longer find. What the hell was going on?

He calculated time zones briefly, and pulled his satellite phone from his satchel. "Okulos? Beckett. I need some help…"

Time passed. Kapaneus wandered the library idly, glancing at books. Beckett merely slumped against a wall. Every few moments, he'd ask a question of the phone, never receiving an answer he liked.

"I'm not sure what you want from me, Beckett," Okulos finally told him. "None of my contacts know Fortschritt any better than you do, and it's not as though the Tremere uploaded the blueprints for the chantry to the Internet. I've got the floor plan of the church itself, the public parts of the library, but I'm afraid none of them have 'secret entrance' marked on them. Are you sure you've looked everywhere?"

Beckett grunted an affirmative. He heard keys clicking as Okulos brought what images he had up onto his computer screen.

"You've got the entry hall, you obviously came through there. You've searched all the walls and the floor of the cathedral?"

"Yes."

"The individual reading rooms on the left? The offices on the right?"

"Yes."

"What about the small book restoration room behind the altar?"

"Well, no. The door's marked 'private.'"

There was a long moment of silence from the other end of the line.

"Okulos? You still there?"

"Beckett... Please repeat to me what you just said."

"I said I hadn't gone in. The door's marked 'private.'"

"So ancient curses, religious prohibitions and nearly certain Final Death don't dissuade you, but a 'private' sign does?"

Beckett felt something give in his mind, not entirely unlike feeling an ear pop during a pressure change. If he still possessed mortal reactions, he'd have blushed.

"I've been affected by some sort of aversion spell or ward, haven't I?"

"Unless you've suddenly developed a remarkable obsession with other people's privacy, I should say so."

Beckett sighed. "Thank you, Okulos. We'll negotiate later what it's going to cost me to keep this quiet."

"Just bring your checkbook."

Beckett hung up and proceeded toward the door at the far end of the chamber. Even now, knowing about the spell that must have certainly been cast on it, he wanted to turn away, to search somewhere else. It required an act of will even to put his hand on the latch, but as soon as he did, the sensation vanished.

He glanced back at Kapaneus. "Why didn't you point out that we hadn't searched here?"

The elder raised an eyebrow. "You made such an obvious point of avoiding it, I assumed you had a good reason."

"Kapaneus... Next time, ask."

Beckett pushed the door open.

Fortschritt, the Tremere Fatherhouse
Vienna, Austria

Beckett hated to admit it, but Fortschritt was proving to be rather boring.

The alleged book-restoration room had indeed been a passage down, shallow steps leading into the depths of the earth, littered with the remains of several more Tremere. From there, Beckett and Kapaneus had emerged into a large library ringed by various mezzanines and other balconies. Beckett recognized it as one of the few inner chambers he'd seen the last time he was here. The room's only other exit led to a small but somehow confusing complex of stone rooms and passages.

Of course, navigating those passages hadn't been *entirely* uneventful.

"Kapaneus," Beckett had asked his companion softly at one point, as they reached a four-way intersection of hallways. "Didn't we just pass that painting a few moments ago?" He pointed to a dark frame, in which sat a dark oil painting of a window overlooking a windswept moor.

The elder's eyes narrowed. "It must have been one just like it, Beckett. We haven't turned from the hall."

Beckett approached the painting. "No, it's the same one. I recognize this scratch in the frame."

"Beckett, that would mean that the hallway we are in just intersected itself—without turning."

"It would. I really hate this place."

He'd turned then, took a step back toward Kapaneus, and the ground beneath his feet simply wasn't solid any more. No trapdoor, no sliding panel—the floor had simply ceased to be.

Beckett would have plunged to whatever fate awaited below—he was fairly certain it was nothing so prosaic as the next level downward—were it not for reflexes honed over centuries of exploration. Before he'd even realized he'd sprouted his talons, he'd sunk them into the nearest wall, clinging by his fingertips.

It was at that moment that his hands had begun once more to itch, worse than they ever had before. Beckett felt his fingers spasm, felt himself slip…

And then a crushing but comforting grip on his wrists as Kapaneus had hauled him up to solid footing. Beckett found himself standing beside his companion, literally shaking as the Beast flailed about within him, anxious to flee.

But why? Beckett had been closer to death than that glorified pit-trap. Was the unnatural nature of this place affecting the Beast itself? Or was it something more, something related to the itch in his hands, to his lack of hunger?

Beckett, eyes slightly wild, had decided he very much didn't want to think about that. He nodded his thanks to Kapaneus and—with some trepidation—they proceeded onward.

This and a few other events of similar strangeness were the highlights of a slow search that took up at least half the night. None of the various chambers, laboratories, cells or libraries held anything of use. Despite their early start, dawn was only a couple of hours off.

They now stood in a large octagonal chamber. The air within was substantially warmer than the surrounding halls, to the point where even vampires like Beckett and Kapaneus were moderately uncomfortable. The walls were papered, floor to high ceiling, in lengthy strips of parchment, each covered with hundreds of lines of writing. Most were Latin or Ancient Greek, but some were written in even more esoteric tongues: Sanskrit, Babylonian, Enochian, even something Beckett recognized as Minoan Linear A. Beckett was making his third circuit of the room, holding his phone out before him and taking frequent snapshots with the camera inside. Kapaneus stood off to the side, watching silently.

"You get all that?" Beckett asked Okulos after bringing the phone back to his ear.

"I believe so. I'm rather surprised you need translation help, though."

Beckett shrugged, even though Okulos couldn't see it. "I've no problem with the Sanskrit or the Enochian, but I'm a little rusty on Minoan."

"Ah."

More silence, punctuated by typing. Beckett leaned against the wall, his hand—itching again, damn it!—occupying the thin space between parchments. Christ, but it was hot in here!

"Just more of the same, I'm afraid," Okulos reported a moment later. "Like the Latin, it consists almost solely of Hermetic texts and theories. Some fascinating thaumaturgic principals, but nothing immediately relevant to your situation."

"That's what I was afraid of. Have to keep going I…guess…" Beckett felt a wet sensation on his fingers, moved the phone away from his head, and stared at his knuckles. Blood. He felt his face with his other hand, and it came away reddened as well. He was sweating, and that wasn't a vampiric response to heat, no matter how high. "Kapaneus," he began, fighting sudden panic…

And then there was *pain*. Beckett felt like someone had ignited a flame within him, a raging inferno that would consume him from the inside out. The Beast howled in his mind, terrified of this strange torment. The Red Fear washed over him, and it was all he could do not to run screaming from the room. Surely his blood itself must be boiling….

Of course.

"Kapaneus!" Beckett yelled again, a part of him morbidly fascinated by the pink-tinted steam that emerged from his mouth as he spoke, "Get out of the room!"

He didn't have to tell the elder twice. Kapaneus lunged through the door before Beckett had even finished speaking. Beckett himself followed a second later.

The instant his feet hit the floor of the hallway, his blood began to cool. In a matter of seconds he felt better, though he was certain he would be sore for nights to come. He looked back into the octagonal room in time to see the corners of the parchment smolder and ignite; he watched, helpless, as thin lines of flame ate their way upwards, destroying irreplaceable secrets of ancient magics.

"Beckett?! *Beckett!!*"

He finally heard the tinny voice coming from his phone, realized that Okulos must have been shouting at him for some time. "I'm here," he answered, surprised at how rough his voice sounded, at how much his hand shook.

"What happened?"

Beckett snarled once, punching an angry fist into the nearest wall. "Thaumaturgic trap," he rasped. "The warlocks attached a fucking blood-boiling enchantment to the room!" He shook his head at the cinders still drifting to the floor. "Looks like it got out of control, since I seriously doubt the magic was intended to destroy the writings. Do you have any idea how important those pages could have been? The *history* of them?!"

"That's a shame. Are you sure you're all right?"

"No, but we'll manage. I'll be in touch." Beckett closed the connection before Okulos could protest. He glanced at Kapaneus, shook his head once more, and continued down the corridor.

He didn't have far to go. It soon opened up into a chamber,

narrow at this end but widening towards the other, where a pair of doors waited. It appeared to be an antechamber or foyer of some sort. Several chairs and even a sofa occupied the room, as did a table with a small stack of books.

At the far end, between two of the doors, a large suit of fourteenth-century plate armor stood on a raised pedestal, an ancient bastard sword clasped in its gauntlets. The visor was shaped much like the face of the gargoyles outside the main entrance.

"Oh boy, here we go."

Kapaneus looked puzzled. "What do you mean?"

"The Tremere love their clichés, so long as they work. Soon as we step into this room, that suit of armor's going to animate and come after us. I'd bet you almost anything."

"We should take care then. I will go one way, you the other."

"Sensible."

Beckett, talons raised before him, stepped swiftly to the left as he entered; Kapaneus went right. Warily, slowly, they edged their way around the room, hugging the walls, moving toward the far end.

The armor remained motionless.

When they'd reached the halfway point, and still nothing happened, Kapaneus threw Beckett a wry glance. "I am grateful you told me of the danger here, Beckett. Otherwise I might feel a bit foolish."

Beckett didn't answer. The creeping pair reached the far wall and began converging on the doorways. Still nothing.

Scowling, Beckett walked over to the armor and rapped the breastplate with his knuckles.

"Well," he said, after yet another moment of silence. "I'm almost disappointed."

"I'm not. Which door?"

Beckett pondered their course so far, but couldn't make out anything resembling a pattern. "Beats me. Pick one."

Kapaneus yanked open the left door. Inside was a cloakroom. Pegs lined the walls, mostly empty. Ceremonial robes hung from the remainder. A brief search was sufficient to convince Beckett that the room was what it appeared to be.

The right door opened into a short but wide hall, both

walls covered in murals depicting scenes from Tremere history. The one on the right portrayed a tall, regal man staring down into a sarcophagus. The left showed several warlocks atop a hill, directing a flock of gargoyles against an unseen opponent. The door at the end of the hall was carved in an intricate abstract pattern which, when viewed up close, was made up of constant repetitions of the squared-circle symbol of House and Clan Tremere.

"Now, I think, we're getting somewhere," Beckett said, reaching out to yank the door open. "We've got to be close to the center and—*Jesus Christ!!*"

A second suit of armor stood beside the doorway. It was no more mobile than the first had been, but a pair of tiny eyes peeked out of *each* of the slots in the helm.

The visor snapped open and, with a high-pitched squeal loud enough to hurt the ears, a veritable torrent of tiny homunculi poured from the armor. The size of small rats, each of the little constructs resembled a man in general form, but lacked detail, as though sculpted from clay. They swarmed over the intruders' feet and legs, their touch the faint brush of a roach's legs or a snake's tongue. Even through his thick pants, Beckett's undead skin twitched, as though trying to pull away.

And they bit, bit with teeth that were most certainly *not* made of clay. Beckett kicked, squashing the first one against the wall, but a dozen more waited to take its place. Fighting them wasn't an option, even assuming Beckett could overcome his revulsion enough to do so. The pain in his leg suggested that their fangs and claws, though smaller than Beckett's own, were no less potent; the wounds they left stung far out of proportion to their size. They might be easy to kill, but they were fast and many, and he didn't think he could squash enough of them before they did some real damage. The notion of being swarmed under, of being drowned in a tide of these hideous vermin and eaten bite by tiny bite, was enough to make him physically shudder. He could turn into a bat and fly above them, but he wouldn't be able to open doors or search books that way. If they followed him...

Wait. Maybe...

"Kapaneus!" Beckett called, not even looking to see how

his companion fared against the horde. "Come on!" And he ran back the way they'd come, in his haste knocking over the suit of armor beside the door with a deafening clatter. He ran, and he heard both the loud footsteps of Kapaneus and the chittering squeals of the homunculi at his heels.

In the antechamber, he turned suddenly and shoved Kapaneus into the cloakroom, slamming the door behind him. "Stay in there!" he called, and was off again. He didn't think the tiny creatures could open the door, which meant they'd all be after him…

Bracing himself, Beckett dove back into the octagonal room. The ashes that were all that remained of the writings swirled about his feet. Instantly he began to feel warm once more, but he forced himself to wait, letting the homunculi pour into the room after him.

And then, though he could scarce afford the blood so swift a transformation would cost him, Beckett allowed himself to fade away, his body once more losing cohesion and drifting into a bank of fine mist. He felt better already, for this form had no blood to be boiled by the room's ward.

The homunculi, their tiny minds confused by the sudden disappearance of their prey, hesitated, looking around. Though Beckett could not see in this form, he could feel—and he felt the tiny moving shapes around and within him suddenly convulse, and then begin, one by one, to collapse into puddles of bubbling ooze. The room smelled oddly of both blood and baked clay. The few that remained outside the room when he drifted out into the hall and resumed his physical form were not at all difficult to dispatch.

Hungry, tired, sore, but smiling, Beckett went to let Kapaneus out of the cloakroom. They still had a ways to go.

Fortschritt, the Tremere Fatherhouse
Vienna, Austria

Or perhaps not *that* far of a ways.

Beckett stared around him at the thaumaturgic laboratory. Tables of beakers and burners straight out of a mad scientist's wet dream stood side by side with incense braziers, summoning circles, alchemical formulae carved in stone, and cages that had once held live animals and people. Even now, God knew how long after it was last used, the place smelled vaguely of chemicals and brimstone.

It also lacked any means of egress but the door through which they'd entered.

"This can't be right," Beckett commented, not for the first time. "There's more to this place; there has to be. We've missed a door or a stairway somewhere." He began pacing the walls, knocking on the stone, examining the room's fixtures.

"Beckett," Kapaneus said, trying to calm his frustrated companion, "if there *is* a hidden passage, I rather doubt it will be here, where those who would use it must interrupt their brethren's work to access it."

Beckett stopped, frowning. The elder was probably right—hell, Beckett figured he'd have thought of it himself, if he wasn't so exhausted and sore—but it still went against his instincts to backtrack without searching.

"Fucking warlocks. Why the hell did they feel the need to make this place so difficult, anyway? It's not like an invader could ever have gotten this far when all their wards and defenses were active." Still muttering, Beckett stepped out of the laboratory and back into the hall, Kapaneus following behind.

The walls *rippled*.

Beckett stared, eyes widening, as both sides of the hall began to move slowly, like the surface of a lake. Drops of what used to be solid stone suddenly stained the carpet. Was this another sign of the chantry's magics breaking down, or was it another eldritch trap?

And frankly, what the hell did it matter? Beckett and Kapaneus ran, even as the walls collapsed behind them in a loud splash and began to flow, viscous and inexorable, after them. The hallway was already full of liquid stone to ankle height, slowing the running vampires dramatically as they had to force and struggle through the heavy substance. Several bones and a yellowed skull flowed past them in the rising tide of liquid rock, one skeletal hand almost seeming to grasp at them as it was washed by. Beckett could only pity the poor souls who had been trapped in this hideous deluge, even as he suspected that he was about to join them.

They were barely a step ahead of the rising flood, a lead they couldn't maintain for long. As they approached one of the doors through which they'd come, Kapaneus leaped, propelled by a strength far greater than Beckett's. He slammed into his companion from behind, lifting him out of the clinging stone and through the doorway. The pressure of the stone itself slammed the door shut behind them.

Beckett, ribs and back aching from Kapaneus' impact, offered a single nod of thanks, and then there was nothing to do but wait. They took the opportunity to scrape the liquid stone from their feet and ankles as best they could before it dried, and listened to the sounds of sloshing behind the door.

"I *did* mention how much I hate this place, didn't I?" Beckett commented.

"Indeed. I cannot imagine why."

Several minutes after the sounds behind the door finally stopped, Beckett decided they had to see what was happening. The door wouldn't open due to the stone behind it, so Beckett clawed through the upper portions of the wood.

The hallway behind the door was filled to about three feet high with stone that had solidified in strange, wave-like patterns. Various bits of furniture protruded here and there, as did some of the bones they had seen earlier. With a shrug, Beckett began to scramble over the stone on his hands and knees, always alert for the slightest sign that it was softening once more.

Some distance down the hall, they came across various pieces of equipment they recognized from the laboratory. Clearly the liquid walls had, like so many other wards in these strange nights, gone out of control. Beckett doubted the stone was supposed to spread beyond the initial hallway.

In the end, however, it proved a boon, for the hall in which it had all started was utterly stripped of the stone that had made up its walls—and even, in some small portions, its floor. It would be a tight squeeze, but the explorers could use the largest of those holes to drop to the level below, without having to find the "proper" route at all.

Beckett landed first, and stood before a huge open doorway, over twice the width of the hall he'd just exited.

He did *not* see the runes carved into the floor beneath him. He didn't feel the arcane energies building up within it, never knew how close he was, at that moment, to Final Death.

Kapaneus dropped down behind Beckett, his eyes narrowed. Behind his companion's back, he raised a hand briefly, as though waving away a horsefly.

"All right," Beckett said, glancing back, "we—Jesus!" He stared down at the ward he'd missed, paler even than usual. "It's a damn good thing that one wasn't active, Kapaneus. It would have completely baked both of us."

"Truly?" Kapaneus said, his tone neutral. "A good thing indeed, then."

Beckett paused at the doorway, suddenly reluctant to enter. "Kapaneus," he said softly, "if this *is* the heart of Fortschritt…"

"Yes?"

"Legend has it Tremere himself sleeps down here."

For a long moment, neither spoke. Then, Kapaneus said, "You knew this before we arrived, did you not?"

"Well, yes, but—"

"So nothing has changed. We came this far, knowing what you know. Why turn back now?"

"I can think of any number of reasons," Beckett muttered. Nevertheless, he stepped through the doorway—and knew, beyond any doubt, that he was indeed standing in the heart of the Fortschritt chantry.

The chamber was enormous, with a domed ceiling that must have risen up behind the laboratory, for it was clearly taller than the height of the next level up. Dozens or even hundreds of sigils and runes so intricate that Beckett couldn't follow any one of them intertwined with one another across the entire floor. Several shelves lined the walls, some replete with musty tomes, others containing a bizarre assortment of items that Beckett could only assume were components for rituals. Many more of those warped remains littered the floor—hundreds, perhaps over a thousand. Beckett still wasn't entirely certain this could account for the whole clan, but then, he wasn't certain it could *not*, either. So where were the survivors, if any? And what the hell had they all been doing here?

The room was clearly set up for a ritual, but it was like none Beckett had ever heard of. A single massive symbol of deepest red and mind-bending complexity was painted on the ceiling, but that was the only "normal" element to the rite. On the rightmost wall was painted an enormous mural of the dawn, so realistic that Beckett flinched away from the sun peeking over the artificial horizon. In the center of the room stood a pair of tall torches, and the fact that they still burned was proof enough that the flame was unnatural. The far wall boasted a painting of a forest scene; the leaves were a deep green, flowers blossomed around their trunks, and sunlight filtered through the heavy canopy. Beckett turned to look behind him, and his eyes widened. By the door through which they'd entered lay a baby cradle on the left, a coffin on the right. The wall was occupied with a painting of an enormous crucifix, surrounded by a Star of David, a crescent moon, and dozens of other religious symbols from around the world. Lying beside the cradle, where it had clearly starved to death after the ritual was complete, was a dead sheep.

Only the leftmost wall was left unadorned, and that one boasted a single doorway—open—which showed a steep and winding staircase leading down. Even from where he stood, the aura from the depths gave Beckett the chills. Whether the legends of Tremere were accurate or not, *something* awful had slept at the base of those stairs. Shivering, he turned his attention back to the room.

"Beckett," Kapaneus asked slowly, "what happened here?"

"I don't know." Beckett made a casual circuit of the room. "The symbolism is unmistakable, though." He began to gesture. "Sun. Fire. Faith. Birth. Growth. Everything opposed or foreign to Kindred nature." He stopped at the animal carcass. "Even the sheep. Abel was a shepherd."

"So we are told, yes."

"Whatever the Tremere did here, it was a rite aimed at the very essence of what we are."

Kapaneus frowned. "Could this be the cause, then? Could this rite be responsible for the blood-weakness?"

Beckett knelt to examine the symbols on the floor. "Well," he said after a few moments of thought, "I don't think so. This ritual is *way* beyond me—hell, it's way beyond anyone I've ever heard of—but I recognize a few of the principles. The spell cast here was aimed at those *within* the chamber, not outside. Given what we've seen outside this room, I won't swear to anything—but I don't *think* this is the source."

"Protection from the weakness then?"

"Possible, but this seems more complex than a protection spell. Look at the symbolism again. They were trying to make some sort of fundamental change to their own natures, though I can't imagine what it might…" Beckett trailed off as he paced the room. A table beside the door contained several large tomes, but nothing that appeared immediately useful. The room offered only more questions, none of the answers they sought.

Slowly, his eyes met Kapaneus's own, and then both their gazes drifted to the staircase leading down.

"Whatever was down there," Beckett said softly, "is probably gone. I mean, everything else here is dead."

"Probably," Kapaneus agreed.

"So we should be perfectly safe exploring down there."

"As safe as the rest of this place has proved, at any rate."

"Great. You want to go first?"

The deepest chamber of Fortschritt, the Tremere Fatherhouse Vienna, Austria

The stone stairs leading down, and the chamber into which they led, were cold—not the cold of winter, but a cold rather like the one Beckett had experienced in Kaymakli. It also felt empty, though, in a way the ancient

Cappadocian city had not. Whatever spirits had haunted this place once were gone.

Still, Beckett couldn't contain a shudder of relief when they'd come to the bottom and found a large stone bier—empty, save for a broken black stake lying atop it.

Something had happened here, that was clear enough. Beckett could see silhouettes burned into the cave walls. They reminded him of pictures he'd seen of the aftermath of Hiroshima, though he knew that no natural or manmade energies had caused *these* figures to appear. The tang of burnt flesh lingered, ever so faintly, in the air. He was so busy studying the images, trying to make sense of them—he was fairly certain that some sort of conflict had taken place, to judge by the postures of the silhouettes—that he didn't notice his companion's activities until he heard his name called.

"Beckett," Kapaneus said softly, bending down to examine something on the floor, "look at this."

Beckett wandered over and glanced downward. Beside the bier, largely hidden in the shadows, was a book. Beckett's eyes widened as he recognized the personal sigil on the cover.

These were the writings of Etrius, highest of the Council of Seven and seneschal to Tremere himself.

Beckett flipped it open to the final page—written in Latin—and read.

…no longer hold out any doubt, or any hope, that our initial conclusions were mistaken. This is no illness we suffer, and be it a curse, it is one beyond any even our Father could bestow. What makes us Kindred is slowly being drawn from us, perhaps from the world entire, for this weakness is hardly limited to Clan Tremere. This, I fear, is why elders suffer it first, for they have further to fall, more power to lose. Our magics fail. Our very natures become corrupt.

Our diviners find signs and portents everywhere they look. The Red Star burns. Omens resonate across the world. Powers walk the Earth that should not be; we can feel them—and worse, we can feel our own strengths drawn toward them. Barriers weaken: between worlds, between creatures, between the nature of things.

And it is this weakening that may be our only hope, for if the line between what we are and what we were is blurred, it may yet be crossed once more. It is a foolish hope, a madman's dream, but we must try. The Father is great, but he is not as they. He cannot protect us. When they come, we must not be what they seek.

It is time. God, if your ears still hear the pitiable cries of one such as I, be merciful.

His hands shaking, Beckett placed the journal—perhaps "dropped" would be more accurate—on the bier. His stomach clenched, as it never had even as a mortal, and he fell to his knees, his body wracked with conflicting desires to sob or to vomit.

"Beckett?!" Kapaneus was standing beside him. "Beckett, what is it?"

"It's real. It's real. It's all real." He didn't seem to be answering Kapaneus, didn't seem even *aware* of the other vampire.

"What is real, Beckett?"

Barriers were failing… Dear God, is that why he'd been able to rescue Okulos? Had it begun even then?

"Ancients walk, stealing what makes us Kindred from us. What else could it be? Oh, God, not now. Not so soon, I don't *know* yet, I haven't *learned…*"

As they never had before, Beckett's hands began to itch. Furiously, he yanked the tattered remains of the gloves over his fingers. Like a tiny snow flurry, fur floated gently from the gloves to spread across the floor. He almost couldn't look down. He was already certain what he would see.

What makes us Kindred is slowly being drawn from us…

Beckett stared down at his hands. His absolutely normal, furless, clawless hands.

"Gehenna," Beckett whispered. "It's time. It's over—and I never found out why it started." Tears of blood streaked Beckett's face, but he wasn't aware enough to wipe them away.

"Beckett," Kapaneus began, placing a hand on the other's shoulder, "this may not be—"

Beckett's entire existence had turned upside down in the past ten minutes. He had wasted his entire unlife questing for answers he'd never find.

With a scream of pain, rage, and paralyzing despair, Beckett simply went away. Without conscious thought, blood flowed to Beckett's hands, and though the nails and fur had gone, they were still capable as ever of sprouting their deadly talons. And the Beast within him rose with a snarl and slashed at Kapaneus's throat.

Nuestra Señora de la Almudena Cathedral
Madrid, Spain

Begun in the sixteenth century, built bit by bit over the course of the next three hundred years, the Almudena didn't look that old, wasn't particularly impressive. It was a plain building, not fancy, hardly memorable at all—on the outside.

Within, it was an entirely different story. Scattered lamps illuminated the numerous paintings and statues that occupied alcoves along each wall, running the entire length of the basilica. Brighter lights shone on the statuary atop the altar, reflecting a golden glow throughout the chamber. Flying buttresses supported the high arched ceilings, tiled in white. Throughout its many years of use, the cathedral had absorbed the scent of worship, a distillation of candle smoke and the combined odor of thousands of people.

Below the cathedral was a catacomb of low vaulted chambers, many occupied by graves older than the Almudena. Here, cracks in the ceiling offered the first evidence that all was not right, though the damage had been largely repaired, at least at this level.

And beneath even the catacombs was the true rotted, withered, and finally deceased heart of a domain Lucifer would have been proud to claim as his own.

Here, where many passages had converged in a pattern fully known only to the cathedral's master, had been the lair of Archbishop Ambrosio Luis Monçada, ancient Cainite, sire to Lucita of Aragon, and paragon of faith among the Sabbat. A fanatic follower of his own brand of Christianity, maintaining that it was the duty of all Cainites to acknowledge, revel in, and earn the damnation already thrust upon them, Monçada had been a monster among monsters. Rarely if ever leaving his haven, he had ruled his domain to a degree few vampires in the modern world could claim, using proxies to give orders he knew the recipients would not dare disobey. Even some cardinals bowed to his experience, or came to him for confession, and it was said that Monçada represented the very soul—if such a thing existed—of the European Sabbat.

He might have been still, had his obsession with gaining complete control of his unruly and rebellious childe Lucita not occupied him for centuries, taken much of his energies that might better have been spent elsewhere. He had finally fallen several years gone, consumed by the Abyssal creature he had attempted to loose against his childe and her Assamite companion.

Since then, though violated by looters, pilgrims, and Lucita herself, his haven remained as it lay following his death. Rubble choked every corner of the room, blocked off most of the passages from the surface. Shards of glass, some the size of swords, lay everywhere, for Monçada, despite his lack of any reflection, had ever been fascinated with mirrors. Combined with bits of statues and splinters of toppled bookcases, the floor of the chamber was a veritable deathtrap, with a point or an edge at every angle. Dust and cobwebs covered the whole of it. It had been some time now since even the most desperate of the Sabbat's faithful, the most determined of Kindred historians, had set foot in this place.

In the emptiness, in the dark, something stirred.

It seemed to be nothing, had no substance. Merely shifting shadows, currents of darkness, a trick of the light—in a place where no light shone.

Somehow, in a room already black as pitch, a spot on the floor began to darken further still. Had any been present to observe, they might have noted that it appeared in the exact spot Leviathan had vanished back into the Abyss after claiming Monçada for its own. They might have noted that it spread in the direction of the archbishop's confessional, where he heard the sins of thousands of vampires, and exhorted them to more.

It did not slither like a snake, this tendril of shadow, so much as abruptly widen and lengthen like a crack in the world itself. Through it, a strange and alien wind began to blow. It was utterly silent, this wind, as though it somehow failed to disturb the air not already caught up in the gust. It carried with it no scent of any kind. Even the miasma of must and mold that filled the room faded away as it passed. It was cold—not the active, hammering cold of a blizzard or the burning cold of ice, but a complete and utter emptiness, a chill from a world where the very concept of warmth was foreign.

The rift widened further still. Bits of debris, broken stone and old tomes, tumbled in and were gone, lost to this reality. And within the endless darkness, something moved.

It emerged into the world slowly, tentatively, one bit at a time. A wisp of shadow, like a probing limb or the flickering tongue of a reptile tasting its environment, flickered upward. It was followed, moments later, by a large column of pure and utter darkness.

And followed. And *followed*. The former haven of Archbishop Monçada filled to the walls with a darkness heavier than night itself, and still it came, still it dragged more of its bulk—if bulk it could be said to have—from the Abyss.

A few years ago, a cabal of mystics had attempted to summon from the depths the essence of their founder, the Father of Night, the god who walked in a Kindred guise called Lasombra. They had, instead, called forth a creature of the Abyss shaped by their own thoughts, their own desires. Formed of shadow-stuff, it was nonetheless artificial, manmade.

This… This thing was not. No mortal or once-mortal imagining could have envisioned it; no living or unliving sight encompassed it. It was pure. It was nothing. It was Abyss.

And it had once had a name.

Darkness flowed upward through the passages of Almudena, through the doors and windows of the cathedral. It flinched from the stars, the moon, the streetlights around it, for it came from a home where light itself was an intruder.

It liked not these things—and so it dealt with them.

In a neighborhood in Madrid, on a night that would never be forgotten by any who lived it, the lights went out. The streetlamps died. The very moon and stars ceased to shine, all save a single red star that none of the city's inhabitants had ever before seen.

The darkness flowed, moving across Spain like a cloud,

leaving terrified mortals in its wake, giving thanks on their knees for the return of the light. It vanished, eventually, at the shore of the Mediterranean.

And behind it, now visible to Kindred and kine alike, the Red Star shone.

part two:
midnight

*There will come a time
when an Elder Darkness will stir
deep below a city which has forgotten
and will surprise the Elder, its children.*

*Of these signs, you will know,
the Dark Father, bastard of Caine,
will awaken, and drink deep of blood
sacrificed to it.*

—*The Book of Nod*, "The Chronicle of Secrets"

Somewhere beneath Mexico City, Mexico

The roaring bonfire, fueled by wooden furniture, irreplaceable copies of Sabbat declarations, and the clothes of those who had been hurled, screaming, into the flames, cast dancing shadows across the length of the massive stone chamber. The room was filling rapidly with smoke, which would have been a problem if the occupants of the room had needed to breathe. Most of those inhabitants danced around—and in some cases through—the fire, shrieking bloodthirsty paeans, goading one another on, and hurling insults at those the mob had taken prisoner. "Traitor!" "Collaborator!" "¡Cabrón!" Blood stained the stone floors, dried between the cracks like a layer of mortar.

Several of the prisoners were already ash, having been fed to the inferno. The others stood in line, some staked, some merely chained. The shuffling procession, guarded on all sides by young Cainites with naked blades and drawn pistols, moved ever closer, step by step, to the center of the room. There, where a podium had once stood for the cardinals of the Sabbat to address their brethren, a functioning guillotine—a true relic from, appropriately enough, the Reign of Terror—now loomed. The ash that covered the bench and the floor beside the device gave mute testament to the number of vampires who had already perished beneath its blade.

The Lasombra cardinal known only as Greyhound would be next, if something didn't change quickly. He had only a very little time to come up with some escape plan. He was third in line, behind a pair of Tzimisce who were arguing with each other in heated Spanish. The neonates would kill them, and he would be next if he didn't—

The first of the Tzimisce before him screamed, a high-pitched wail that sounded like nothing even remotely human. The second followed a second later, her shriek perhaps an octave higher than the first. They slumped together, collapsing as if their bones were no longer strong enough to support them, bending in spots where no joints could exist. Their flesh began to meld and to mix, and in a matter of seconds it was impossible to tell if they were one being or two. They swiftly collapsed into a viscous mess of unidentifiable liquids, strips of flesh, and the occasional limb warped and mutated almost beyond recognition. They had, or so it appeared, been cannibalized by their own flesh-shaping abilities, and these were hardly the first Tzimisce to fall victim to this particular aspect of the withering: in a matter of months, the clan had been reduced to barely a tenth of their previous number.

They had also, so far as Greyhound was concerned, picked a remarkably inconvenient time to die.

The cardinal—naked save for various trophies taken from his foes, as was his wont—found himself yanked forward as a young Cainite jerked on his chains. Once more, he strained to break the bonds, tried to hurl his will against his captors and smother their thoughts and urges with his own. And once again he failed, just like the last time, and the time before that. He was weak. Helpless. That thought galled him more than any consideration of his coming death.

But only a little more.

No charges were read. No opportunity given for defense, explanation, or appeal. Somewhere, the masses of the Sabbat had gotten it into their heads that some of their elders had betrayed the sect, turning to the Camarilla or other elders in the face of the spreading chaos and the coming of Gehenna. Perhaps some of them had, but by now hysteria had swept the Sword of Caine from top to bottom. With a few exceptions, no Cainite older than a few hundred years was safe. Terrified by the notion of what was to come, galvanized by signs that could only signal the coming end, the younger vampires had turned on *all* their elders, frantic to weed out any servants of the Antediluvians before those ancients arose themselves. Dozens of elders had met their Final Deaths in previous weeks, in scenes like this one played out across the globe, and many more were yet to come. It didn't help that still more elders had died, not at the hands of childer, but under the fangs of their brethren, as vampires across the world discovered that the blood of their own kind could alleviate the withering.

After feasting on blood as potent as Greyhound's, the neonates felt much better indeed.

A warehouse in Midtown
Houston, Texas

The cement floor was no longer empty; rows of heavy metal pylons had been driven into it. Thick wooden stakes protruded from those columns in all directions, and dozens of Kindred hung paralyzed from those stakes like slabs of beef. Narrow cages, with insufficient room even to turn around, lined the rear wall. The prisoners within were filthy, beaten, and preserved on a diet of dog and pig blood ladled into their bowls on a nightly basis. Atop the catwalk and wandering the rows between cages and pillars were a dozen ghouls, armed with high-powered firearms, broad-bladed knives and heavy stakes, and a smaller number of vampires, who oversaw the operation. Every few nights, one of Houston's elders would wander in, seeking relief from her mounting weakness. Accompanied by an armed guard, she would select one of the "cattle" held within to alleviate the problem.

It was hardly the only installation of its type. Across the globe in just about every Camarilla-held city, "incarceration centers" were becoming the norm. Officially, princes and archons maintained that they were necessary to stem the rising unrest, facilities intended only to hold those who would incite disobedience or otherwise disturb the peace.

In truth, they had become little better than concentration camps in a matter of weeks. Sheriffs and other enforcers snatched neonates and strangers off the streets with the slightest provocation, or often no provocation at all. Publicly, their mandate was to keep the peace, to ensure the continued smooth functioning of Camarilla society.

Privately, their mandate was far simpler: Keep the elders fed, keep them strong, and keep the incarceration centers full. No matter what it took.

Their preferred choices were newly Embraced neonates, Caitiff, thin-bloods, strangers and newcomers to the city and, of course, anyone actually guilty of a crime. Speaking publicly about Gehenna was the most frequent charge, and many of those in custody were indeed guilty of having loose lips. Still, any Kindred weak enough to be taken easily, and lacking powerful allies to notice his absence, was at risk. In some cases, the princes of larger domains had actually turned their people loose on neighboring communities, in essence conquering smaller domains purely for the additional fodder they might provide. Police forces across the world were reporting a substantial increase in crimes of passion, terrorist activities, gang wars, riots, and other violent incidents.

Some elders attempted to Embrace entire herds, to create their own supplies of fodder—only to discover that even the Embrace had grown unpredictable beneath the weight of the withering, that many of the attempts resulted in corpses rather than vampires.

Tonight, Prince Suadela herself had phoned ahead, informing Jack Fowler, the overseer of this particular center, that she would be arriving later in the evening. For an hour after her call, he had his guards scrambling about the place. Cleaning was of no concern—the elders knew, and even approved, of the squalor in which the detainees were kept— but all hell would break loose if Karen Suadela or any of her entourage discovered even the slightest hint of a lapse in security. Locks and bolts were checked over and over, the hanging vampires made secure on their stakes, video cameras realigned, weapons fully loaded.

All was in readiness when they heard the sound of an engine pull up to the loading dock at the back of the warehouse. A sycophantic smile of welcome on his scruffy, weasel-like visage, Fowler stepped outside.

He froze at the sight of the old red Chevy van idling outside. The prince always arrived in a Towncar limo.

To his credit, Fowler recognized immediately that something was very wrong. He hadn't been made the overseer of the detention center for nothing. He wasted no time wondering how the van had gotten through the perimeter checkpoints, or what had happened to the prince. Instantly he had his Glock in hand and was making a dive for the nearest of the many panic buttons they'd installed at all the doors and at various points within the facility.

He never made it. From the edge of the roof above, a curtain of darkness fell over him like a net, slowing his progress. Limbs of shadow within the darkness grappled with him, hurling him back. Fowler staggered out of the dark, back the way he'd come—and bumped into something large and unyielding.

Theo Bell didn't let him turn. He simply grabbed Fowler's head from behind and twisted, hard, with all his strength. Honestly, he wasn't certain if it was going to work. These nights, his physical prowess was unpredictable. He awoke some evenings stronger than ever, ready to take on the world single-handedly. Others, he felt not much stronger than he remembered from his mortal days.

Tonight, fortunately, was one of the former. Fowler's spine shattered like glass. Bell let the body drop, then casually crushed his skull with a heel-stomp to finish the job.

"That was thoughtless of you, Bell." Lucita slid down from the roof on a cable of shadow, her descent far shakier and less fluid than it would once have been. "I might have used him."

"Sorry, Lucita. Wasn't thinking. First lick we find inside's all yours."

The staccato thump of automatic fire sounded from the front of the warehouse.

"Assuming anyone's left," Bell added. Then, shouting back at the van, "Go!"

Half a dozen Kindred of all ages, creeds, and clans poured from the sliding door. Some were armed with guns, some with blades, but all had weapons in their hands and fire in their eyes. Every last one of them—the six in the van, and the eight more attacking from the front—had once been just like the prisoners inside, and any chance to strike back at the Camarilla was a welcome one. Bell, a new but already well-used SPAS-15 in hand, followed them in, breaking left and ducking as they hit the doorway. Lucita leaped and dove through an upper window, coming down on one of the guards within.

Ultimately, it didn't take long. Numbers were about the same on both sides, but the defenders were mostly ghouls—tough, but far more easily killed—and the Kindred within had already lost their leader. The attackers, on the other hand, were vampires to the last, and they included two of the best skirmish fighters the descendents of Caine had produced. Lucita neatly crushed the larynx of the man on whom she'd landed and rolled forward, tucking beneath the stream of bullets launched her way by another guard. A foot lashed up, knocking the gun from the guard's hands and snapping three of his fingers. The ghoul screamed, then crumpled as Lucita sank a powerful fist into his solar plexus. She snatched the weapon up from where it had fallen and calmly put two bullets through the head of a third guard, standing up on the catwalk. She took an instant to be grateful that her opponents were only ghouls—as slowly as she was moving tonight, anyone tougher might have been a problem—and slipped off in search of additional opponents.

For his own part, Bell simply laid into those about him, shotgun in one hand, the other clenched into a fist that—at least tonight—was powerful as ever. The SPAS-15 spat twice, taking the head completely off one of the few true vampires guarding the warehouse. Bell spun, wincing but not slowing as a bullet caught him in the hip, and shattered another ghoul's collarbone with an overhand blow. Then, drawn by the sound of gunfire, he charged into a small side room, shotgun already blasting away.

When the gunfire finally ceased, the smoke cleared, and the blood began to dry, only two of the attackers had fallen, and both were revivable with sufficient quantities of blood. Not a defender remained standing.

"All right, people, you know the drill!" Bell shouted. "Malik, take Azure and Ben, and start piling the bodies in the center of the room. Joseph, grab three pairs of eyes and get the hell on perimeter. Anyone shows up, I wanna know about it before they do. The rest of you, start opening cages and drag those kids down."

Bell and Lucita watched dispassionately as vampires who had been paralyzed for God-knew-how-long were dragged from the stakes and allowed to fall to the floor. Other prisoners scrambled out of their cages, crawling eagerly toward the blood-filled bodies, but a shout from Bell stopped them.

"You'll fucking wait until the others are movin'," he said, gesturing at the Kindred with holes in their chests, who were only starting to show signs of unlife. "I ain't gonna have them wake up with nothing to eat." That wasn't beneficence on Bell's part, just good sense. No point in freeing these people only to have to kill them in self-defense when they lapsed into hunger frenzy.

"All right, listen up!" he shouted again later, when all who were going to awaken had done so. They'd all taken at least the cutting edge off their hunger, feasting upon the bodies, but there wasn't enough to assuage them all, and they were already starting to eye one another with baleful and hungry glares. Well, time to put a stop to *that*.

"You all know what the Camarilla's turning into, you better'n anyone else." Bell told them. "We all know." He gestured at those with him. "We've all seen it. Most of us have been in it, same as you. And we're doing something about it."

Indeed, in the past months, even as the Camarilla had grown harder, more violent, more oppressive, several cells of what could only be termed a resistance had cropped up within it. Bell's and Lucita's group of rescued refugees was only one among several, but it was already one of the largest, with nearly a hundred members across the continental US and parts of Canada. It wasn't much, in the face of what was happening to both sects, but for the time being it was all they could think to do. Hardestadt's own childe Jan Pieterzoon was said to be gathering a more formal sect to oppose the Camarilla, but he was nowhere to be seen on the ground, as far as Theo could tell. Neither elder held any illusions that they could build a large enough force to take either sect on directly. Their only objective, at this point, was to assemble sufficient numbers to last until the sects either righted themselves, or toppled under their own weight. Assuming they survived that—and, God help them, Gehenna itself, if that's really what was coming—they'd have the basis to start over.

Of course, Bell and Lucita had *vastly* different ideas on how to construct this fledgling society, if and when the time came, but unspoken agreement between them put off that particular reckoning until and unless it became necessary.

Bell didn't tell the newly freed prisoners that. He simply gave them a rousing, if less than eloquent, speech about the evils of the Camarilla in recent nights, how he himself—former champion of the sect—was now standing against them. Lucita was, frankly, a more eloquent speaker, but they'd decided at the beginning that a former Sabbat archbishop making these speeches wouldn't go over nearly as well. If and when they shifted operations into Sabbat territory, *then* maybe she'd do the talking.

As always, Bell ended with an invitation. And, as always, only about a quarter of the prisoners expressed any interest in joining, the rest taking off to go their own way as soon as they were certain Bell wouldn't stop them from doing so.

"Half'll be dead or prisoners again in a month," he muttered to Lucita as they fled. "Fucking idiots."

"They're free now. That's all we can do for them." Lucita scowled. It went against her instincts and her moral code to help people without expecting something substantial in return. She knew that, in the long run, she was doing what needed to be done, but she'd spent much of the last four years refining her grip on a belief that she was, at her core, an agent of damnation, not liberation. Yes, these raids served their purpose in disrupting her enemies' operations and creating new recruits, but Lucita was not comfortable with herself in the position of liberator or partner. She had learned to stand alone in this harsh world. To do otherwise now, to even think it was *possible* to do otherwise, implied regrets that could, if she let them, swallow her whole. If this went on for too long, they would do just that.

"We need to get gone," said one of the caged prisoners, a young Nosferatu who sported a thick Old-West style mustache over his gaunt, leathery, earth-brown features. "Them guards were scurrying all about, makin' ready for something. We're gonna have company, we tarry too long."

Bell thought briefly of waiting, of expressing some of his displeasure on whoever arrived, but decided it wasn't worth it. "All right, people," he announced, to those who were already his and those who were just now joining, "let's move. We've got a drive ahead of us, and the night ain't getting any fresher."

While the new recruits were escorted outside and loaded into the larger van, the one parked out front, Bell and a few of his soldiers took the time to plant a few charges, scatter some gasoline. A large portion of the building was cement, but they could at least *delay* any further use of it as a feeding camp.

By the time the first plumes of smoke rose into the night sky, they were gone.

Jenna Cross's haven in the San Fernando Valley Los Angeles, California

Jenna Cross, dressed as she was in a tank-top and denim shorts, combined with the shoulder holster she sported almost all the time now, had passed from pop-star wannabe to video-game knockoff in terms of her look. Still, the fact that she was still around and kicking—and, more importantly, that the greater portion of Los Angeles County was still hers, rather than the Camarilla's—earned her the respect her appearance and wardrobe did not. That, and the crescent moon on her shoulder. When she'd started this whole thing with a small coterie of thin-bloods and the support of a famous anarch leader, most of those who knew her had dismissed it. Now, with all she'd accomplished against the Camarilla and all the chaos in the world, her people—and indeed, thin-bloods across the world who had heard of her activities—were beginning to take it seriously. She couldn't count how many times *The Book of Nod*, and all its blather about orphans and thin-blooded ruling cities in the end times, had been quoted at her. It didn't make her feel any better. Frankly, given what she knew of vampire religion, it scared the unholy crap out of her.

She took a sip from her overly sweetened coffee—caffeine and sugar didn't do much of anything for her anymore, but unlike the "thick-blooded" vampires who wanted her truly and finally dead, she could still enjoy the taste—and scowled at those who sat around the table with her. For the most part, she wasn't liking what she was hearing.

"How did they find us out, Rob?"

"Don't have a clue. I just know that our people had barely set foot in Riverside when some of the Camarilla's hounds were all over them like flies on shit." He paused, and his lower lip quivered.

Oh, fuck. Jenna knew what that meant. "They didn't all get away?"

Rob shook his head. "We lost Moose and Laurence both."

"Oh, shit…"

"They took at least one archon with them, Jenna, and they bought everyone else time to get the hell out of Dodge. They didn't go easy."

"They shouldn't have 'gone' at all!" Jenna glanced at the wall, where she'd hurled her mug without even realizing it, letting the trickle of the coffee down the wallpaper sooth her. "All right, no more attempts at infiltrating Riverside for a while. How are we doing on defense?"

"That's a little better," one of the others at the table, a dark-haired woman named Tabitha, chimed in. "We still haven't managed to retake much of Pasadena, but so far we've held onto East LA proper. We burned down the motel they were assembling in, and we've managed to dig up one of their spies. Chris and Toby are chasing him down now. Won't be long."

"What about the firefights downtown?"

"The first was just an advance party, we think, mostly ghouls and some sewer-faced scouts. We lost some good people there, but we don't think the enemy actually acquired any territory.

"The second wasn't Camarilla related at all. We rounded up another batch of the MacNeils, but they didn't care to be disarmed. We dealt with it."

Jenna sighed. Basically, same as it had been yesterday. And last week. And last month. Every night, more thin-bloods arrived in LA from across the country and even other nations, having heard of her efforts to make the city a free haven for all their kind. But even with constant reinforcements, they never seemed to gain any additional advantage. They held the Camarilla now at more or less the same borders they'd held since the real assaults began. That they still held out at all was nothing shy of a miracle, attributable at least partially to the fact that the Camarilla had too much on its plate and couldn't devote the proper resources to this war. But a war of attrition wasn't going to cut it. If the thin-bloods couldn't win a decisive victory, prove to the Camarilla, as the Cathayans had done before them, that it was easier to tolerate them than to fight them, then it was only a matter of time before they *could* devote more attention to them. And when that happened, the near-infinite weight of the sect would crush the LA thin-bloods like an avalanche.

Then they had the damn MacNeils to deal with. Cross had hoped, now that the Camarilla were no longer the dominant force in LA, that she and the other anarchs could come to some sort of accord, but the MacNeils had made it quite clear they weren't about to let a no-name thin-blood take charge. To date they were more or less a nonentity in the conflict—they'd been severely weakened by the war with Prince Tara, and then by the Camarilla's initial offensive—but their habit of showing up at random intervals and shooting at any Kindred who weren't part of their social circle made an already chaotic situation even more maddening.

"Thanks, everyone," Jenna said finally. "Now go away."

Only when the room was empty, save for the so-called "Last Daughter" herself, did she hear the door to the basement open, and footsteps proceeding through the kitchen. She didn't even look up as Samuel pulled a chair out from the table and sat down.

"You heard?"

"I did. You've done well, keeping the Camarilla out for so long."

"Not well enough, Samuel. I haven't pushed them back, either."

The newcomer leaned forward. "You might try approaching the MacNeils again. Maybe if you didn't insist on remaining in charge—"

"Fuck *that*! I'm the one who put this whole thing together, I'm the one who took out Prince Tara, I'm the one my brothers and sisters are coming to LA for. Like hell I'm going to just hand all that over!"

"Commendable, Jenna. But don't forget, you've more to lose than the others. The Camarilla is a pragmatic entity. If they win here, they'll execute a few anarchs to make a point, but the rest will be allowed to remain so long as they swear allegiance. But you…" His eyes shifted noticeably to her shoulder, and the mark that adorned it. "The Camarilla may say Gehenna's a myth publicly, but a lot of the elders believe in it. Why do you think they're silencing anyone who speaks up about it? It's not just to prevent disorder, it's because they're scared. If *anyone* in the Camarilla decides you're really a part of the coming apocalypse, they'll spare no expense. They'll track you down, and if you're *lucky* they'll just kill you. If not, you'll be—studied."

Jenna shuddered, her skin crawling beneath the moon-shaped mark upon her shoulder. Over and over in her head, she heard Samuel quoting *The Book of Nod*, any one of dozens of passages, talking about the "Last Daughter," the woman with the crescent moon mark. Jenna, frankly, didn't *want* to be anybody's savior, except maybe her fellow thin-bloods. And she *sure* as hell didn't want to be caught up in any religion frenzy.

"I'm not the only one with the mark," she said. Some of her followers had made a gruesome hobby of finding children with crescent-shaped scars and birthmarks. So far, they'd found a dozen in LA alone.

"True," Samuel said, "but you're the only one who is full-grown, thin-blooded, and leading a revolt against Camarilla authority. I imagine anyone who cares will decide you're the Last Daughter."

"But—"

"Never forget," Samuel interrupted, "that your greatest enemies are those interested in what you represent to their ancient religion, not those who want your streets or your kine."

He didn't mention the name—not this time—but he'd also warned her, over and over, about who the worst of her hunters would be: *Beckett*.

She shuddered again just thinking it.

"That said," he continued, "I'll talk to my contacts among Hardestadt's people. We'll put out a rumor that you're close to making an alliance with the MacNeils, see if I can't focus the Camarilla's efforts there for a little while and give you a break."

For the first time that evening, Jenna Cross smiled. "Thank you, Samuel."

"As always, Jenna, you're welcome."

Fortschritt, the Tremere Fatherhouse
Vienna, Austria

"Beckett… You need to wake up, Beckett. Things to do, miles to go."

No. No, he wouldn't wake up. He liked it here. Quiet. Drifting. Uncomplicated. Out there—out there was bad.

"Yeah, it's bad. Going to get worse, too. You really want to miss all that?"

In the dream—if dream it was—Beckett opened his eyes. He was somehow not surprised to see the Malkavian's face, framed with unruly blond hair.

"So I'm truly dead, then?" Beckett pondered the notion. "It doesn't feel that bad."

"You're still kicking, I'm afraid. Though I've seen corpses that looked and smelled better."

"I'm dreaming then."

"Right. At midnight? Unless you've had a career change so dramatic you're working days now, that doesn't sound too likely."

Beckett frowned. "No, there was something…"

Flashes of memory, in reverse. He saw himself tearing madly down the corridors beneath Fortschritt, smashing furniture and shredding books until he collapsed. He saw himself fleeing the central chamber, where the Tremere ritual had taken place. He saw himself lunging at Kapaneus, saw the elder toss him across the room like he was a mewling infant. And he saw the journal before him, remembered the horrible revelations it contained.

"Oh, God…" Beckett squeezed his eyes shut once more. "Go away, Anatole."

"Can't. You need to wake up."

"I don't want to wake up! It's really Gehenna, Anatole! You were right all along. It's the end."

"Certainly getting there. Lion hasn't lain down with the sheep quite yet, but he's gotten her drunk and he's calling a cab."

Beckett's eyes popped open again. "Have I mentioned that you don't sound like you used to?"

"You'd be surprised what death can do for the sense of humor." Anatole knelt down beside him. "Beckett, listen to me. I gave my existence for answers, or so I thought. I remember sinking into the pulsating mass of the Cathedral of Flesh, and I welcomed it. But just at the end I felt—a call, I guess, though it was nothing so mundane as any noise. It was almost like a sudden yearning, a homesickness. I followed it, or part of me did.

"You've heard rumors of my clan, that we're all connected at a level below even the subconscious. It's true, Beckett. People dwell here—people and things, things even the maddest of us couldn't imagine. But it's home. That's where I am. I'm a part of it. That's why I seem different to you. I'm not just me anymore.

"There's enough of me left to remember who my friends were, Beckett. But I can't reach out to you for long. Right now, you're lying facedown in a stone hallway, where you've lain in torpor for almost three months. You can't stay here any longer."

"Even assuming I believe this is more than just some crazy dream—why not? Why does it matter if I stay here? If I die here?"

"Why does it matter? Isn't that what you've always wanted to know?"

Beckett blinked once in the dream—and slowly, in the real world, his eyes began to open. Anatole began to fade from sight, but he wasn't gone yet.

"Anatole, have you only appeared to me? Lucita would be delighted—"

"Lucita wouldn't want to see me anymore, Beckett. Watch out for her. You're going to meet with her before the end, and she's not who she was. Even I can't see which way she'll go; the darkness surrounding her is too thick."

The Malkavian was almost completely gone now, replaced by a blurry stone wall, torn carpeting, and a rough feeling against Beckett's cheek.

"Anatole… Thank you. For what it's worth, I'm sorry you died."

"I'm not. Are you kidding? I just have to float around in your head and be cryptic. You're the poor clown who has to deal with Gehenna."

And he was gone. Slowly, his limbs aching, Beckett pushed himself to his feet. He—

Hunger!

—doubled over as the need struck him. It felt as if the Beast itself were clawing at his insides. If he *had* been in torpor for months on end—had he collapsed of starvation, or had Kapaneus been forced to take him down?—it was amazing he had the strength to rise at all.

He'd intended to scour the place, see if Kapaneus had stuck around by some strange chance or if he'd done the smart thing and taken the hell off, but that would have to wait. He couldn't afford to run into the elder like this. Given the red haze already clouding his vision, he didn't think he could maintain control in the presence of a source of blood. And while he couldn't for the unlife of him remember *how* it had happened, Kapaneus had already dealt with him in frenzy once already.

Focusing as best he could past the pain, Beckett gathered what power he had and sent out a mental summons. Months ago, when it was still the domain of undead sorcerers of unequalled power, Fortschritt was no doubt empty of any animals or vermin the Tremere themselves didn't welcome. Now that the owners had vanished, Beckett could only pray that nature had reasserted itself…

Sure enough, the first of the rats arrived a moment later,

in answer to his call. Beckett, his entire body trembling with the need to keep still, allowed it draw closer, and closer still. He thought, briefly, that he could see himself through the rodent's eyes, and he struggled to blend into the wall, to send out soothing waves of calm.

The rat's blood was thin and unsatisfying, like a single cracker offered to a starving man. It trickled, hot and vaguely sour, down Beckett's throat, hardly making an impact in the raging fire of thirst that filled his belly and his soul. He called again. Not many rats seemed to live here—not for a complex of this size. Only a few dozen. Taken together, however, they were sufficient to curb the worst of his hunger, to still the Beast in his belly enough that he thought he could stand face to face with Kapaneus without going for his throat. Again.

Much to Beckett's surprise—and, though he'd never admit it, to his relief—he found the elder in the central chamber where the ritual had taken place. Kapaneus was seated comfortably in a chair he'd apparently dragged down from the public library portion above, and was idly flipping through one of a tall and teetering stack of tomes.

He smiled as Beckett entered, and rose to his feet. "I have been gathering these for you," was all he said. Beckett couldn't help but smile in return.

"You've been here all this time?"

"For the most part. I occasionally departed to find sustenance, of course. I would be happy to do so again, if you require some for yourself."

"I may take you up on that. No danger of us being found here, I take it?"

"None. The outer façade of the building has continued to collapse. Judging by signs posted on the doors it has been condemned, though condemned to *what* I am not certain.

"Your communication device," and here Kapaneus produced Beckett's satellite phone, "chimed frequently for the first few nights after your, ah, incident, but then it stopped."

"Battery's probably dead." Beckett glanced at the phone, and wondered if he could find an electric outlet down here. Well, in the meantime…

He walked over to his bag of equipment, which had been neatly placed in the corner, and removed his new laptop. A quick glance at the glowing light indicated that he still had battery power. Good thing it hadn't been left on these past months. Time to see what had happened in the world during his absence—right after he and Kapaneus went topside and found something a little more satisfying than rat.

Fortschritt, the Tremere Fatherhouse
Vienna, Austria

"Let me see if I understand," Kapaneus said, staring suspiciously at the laptop. "You can receive written messages on this device, from anyone else in the world who has a similar device."

"Well—for the most part, yes."

"And you say this involves no magic?"

"Nope. Mostly the same general principles as the phone."

"Fascinating." Kapaneus leaned in. "And they need merely know the name to which they must send their message?"

"Again, for the most part."

"This is truly an amazing world you've brought me into."

Unfortunately, from what Beckett read—mostly from Okulos, but from other contacts throughout the world as well—there was precious little else to recommend the modern era. Kindred scholars, occultists, and Noddists were disappearing at an alarming rate. Some had probably gone to ground in hopes of riding out the storm, but Beckett suspected that a number of them had fallen to the Inner Circle's iron gag order about Gehenna. The Sabbat was degenerating into a violent and unruly mob (not that it had far to go to begin with), while the Camarilla was beginning to resemble a Fourth Reich. The withering had spread through almost all levels of Kindred society to a greater or lesser extent, and strange occurrences were being reported from all over the world. The Masquerade was a soap bubble, ready to pop; any single catastrophic event at the wrong place or time could blow the whole thing wide open.

"You couldn't just let me sleep this out, could you, Anatole?" Beckett muttered.

Kapaneus looked equally concerned as Beckett summarized current events for him. "What do you plan to do?" the elder asked, after a long period of silence.

Beckett took a deep breath, though it was hardly necessary. "I'm going to keep going. My entire worldview has been—well, blown all to shit and back. But it doesn't change the bottom line. Our kind were born for a reason, Kapaneus. I'm more convinced of that now than I ever was. If we've got a set ending, we damn well had a set beginning. And I'm going to figure it out."

"An admirable goal, Beckett. But if this is truly is Gehenna, you've not much time."

"No." Beckett looked askance at his hands. After so many years of seeing them fur-clad, the smooth skin looked blatantly unnatural. "So we'd best begin."

Fortschritt, the Tremere Fatherhouse
Vienna, Austria

Beckett was an experienced researcher—as an explorer, an archeologist, a historian, and a scholar, he had to be— but Fortschritt held a *lot* of books. If he had to go through them all, it would take months, and he knew he no longer had the eternity he once counted on. Better to start at the center, then, and work out. He began by delving into Etrius' journal, staring with the most recent entries and working backward, while Kapaneus perused the other tomes that had already waited in the central chamber when they arrived.

Even in his own private journal, the Tremere's greatest magus was apparently unwilling to discuss the specific details of the so-called "Red Sign" rite—Beckett still wasn't entirely certain what it was intended to accomplish, though he had his suspicions—but it was clear the warlocks were frightened. Numerous references to signs and portents, to failures of once-reliable thaumaturgic rites, to the early stages of the blood-weakness, and to "Tzimisce taint," filled the latter entries. Clearly, whatever the ritual was intended to do, Etrius saw it as the final hope for his clan. He made it very clear that if it failed, the Tremere would perish, to the last. Beckett was intrigued at one particular line, which read, "At the very least, I have the gratification of knowing that whatever fate awaits us, should we fail, the same awaits the fiends as well." But he didn't go on to explain, and Beckett was soon caught up in reading about other things.

"Beckett," Kapaneus asked some hours later, glancing up from his own book. "You spoke of Cathayans."

Beckett thought back to the news and information he'd received from Okulos. Had there been—oh, right.

"Yes. Seems they've all but disappeared from the West Coast, and nobody knows why. Frankly, I'm just as happy to see them go."

"It appears that some of the Usurpers were studying them. Their mythology, their physicality."

"Interesting." Beckett pondered. "Were they planning to try to cast some rite on the Cathayans? Or was this part of their studies of Kindred nature, in preparation for the Red Sign ritual?"

"It does not say. But perhaps their activities are responsible for the Cathayan disappearance?"

Beckett acknowledged that it was possible, but that it didn't seem likely. Lacking any further answers, they moved on.

Fortschritt, the Tremere Fatherhouse
Vienna, Austria

Beckett finally closed Etrius's journal. He leaned back in the chair, idly picking at a spot of blood on the upholstery, and glanced sadly at the body of the kine that lay on the floor beside him. He hadn't meant to kill the man, he really hadn't. But after his long torpor, he was finding it difficult to control the hunger. Even worse, a part of him had to acknowledge that there was an upside to having drained the man dry—he wouldn't have to feed again for a while, could spend more time in research—and he felt a bit guilty for thinking of one of his accidental killings in such clinical terms. It was probably that guilt, he acknowledged to himself, that made him keep the body where he could see it, instead of hiding it away in some empty room.

Kapaneus looked up at the sound of the book closing. "Have you learned anything?"

"Maybe." Beckett's eyes remained unfocused for a moment, lost in thought. Then he blinked, looked at his companion.

"The Tremere weren't particularly interested in where or how Kindred came about. They were more concerned with manipulating our natures and abilities to their full potential. Still, there are a few things in here that might take us in the right direction. Are you aware of the Tremere efforts to destroy the Salubri?"

Kapaneus nodded. "Those efforts were underway well before I entered Kaymakli. The Usurpers hunted the Salubri down, called them demonic."

"Right. For the most part, they succeeded. Up until a few years ago, the Salubri population was in the double digits, or even less. But here," and Beckett thumped the journal once, "Etrius talks about a Salubri called Rayzeel, just recently emerged from torpor. A childe of Saulot himself."

"Indeed?"

"Indeed. Saulot was just about the greatest scholar of Kindred nature and prophet of Gehenna ever known, to say nothing of the fact that he was older than dirt. Rayzeel might be able to tell us a *great* deal about his studies. Hell, Saulot might have spoken to her about the beginning, and about Caine himself." Beckett had acknowledged, reluctantly, that if Gehenna was a fact, the Caine myth might be as well.

"And the Tremere did not set out to destroy her?"

Beckett cracked open the journal and read. "'In light of current events surrounding both the Father and the portents we have seen, I cannot allow so valuable a source of knowledge and information to be swept under by an ancient grudge—even if that grudge be our own. I shall not report this discovery to the Council, nor tell anyone where she may be found. This source of wisdom I will keep for my own, in hopes that it may yet save us.'"

"Then she survives!" Kapaneus smiled.

"Yeah, she survives—or at least if she doesn't, it wasn't the Tremere who did her in."

"Then why do you sound so despondent?"

"Because," Beckett replied, "Etrius didn't bother to write down how he found her, or where she might be."

"Ah." Kapaneus pondered. "Yes, that could prove a difficulty."

Beckett cursed, and his arm quivered as he fought the urge to hurl the book across the room. "This Rayzeel may be the best source of answers I've ever *heard* of. A childe of Saulot, for God's sake! And I don't have the first fucking clue where to look!"

"We can go through the other books here, Beckett. Surely somewhere—"

"No. No, if Etrius wanted something kept secret, he'd have made sure of it." Beckett sighed. "There's another lead in here. Not as promising, and a lot less appealing on a personal level, but…

"A while ago, I was in Los Angeles. Right before the Cathayans began to vanish, come to think. I was following up stories of Caine's coffin, of all things."

Kapaneus raised an eyebrow.

"Yeah, that's more or less what *I* thought. Turned out to be about as genuine as a Nosferatu's hairdo. Hell, I even heard some rumors of Caine sightings while I was there."

"This sounds less than promising, Beckett."

"Right, but listen. One of the people involved in this whole mess was an anarch leader called Smiling Jack. Now, according to this," and again he waved the journal, "Jack turned into a busy boy after I left. He's been having Kindred artifacts brought to him from all over the world—*real* ones, not fakes. And Jack's been acting weird recently, spending more time spouting Gehenna prophecies and quoting *The Book of Nod* than he has blowing things up."

"And you think this important?"

"Well, Jack's not the sort of guy I'd expect to find

religion. More to the point, though, Etrius had his people approach Jack, trying to acquire some of these artifacts. Jack wouldn't sell, and the Tremere found the answers they sought elsewhere, so they didn't press the issue. But Etrius was convinced Jack knew something, had somehow gained some insight into what was coming. That he wasn't just another born-again-Noddist. I'd like to know what his source is, and he's a lot easier to find than Rayzeel."

"Indeed. So we leave?"

Beckett nodded. "We'll take a few more nights—Cesare will need that long to fly the plane over here and prep it for another intercontinental flight. But if we don't dig up anything else in these books before that, we're going to LA."

The Thompson Plantation
Outside Savannah, Georgia

Victoria Ash, with only the faintest frown to indicate her annoyance at the interruption, laid the semi-conscious young woman down on the sheets, gently dabbed the blood from her lips with a handkerchief, and stepped over to the bedroom door.

"I believe I requested that we not be disturbed, Allan."

"My most sincere apologies, Mistress Ash. There's a Mr. Beckett here to see you. He claims that it's most urgent."

Beckett? *Here?!* Ash fought down a brief moment of panic. If Hardestadt found out…

But she couldn't just order him removed. Among other things, she doubted her guards were up to the challenge. Best to see what he wanted and usher him out as politely—but rapidly—as possible.

Pulling a flimsy silk robe on over her shoulders, Ash left the room and stepped over to the balcony that overlooked the first floor. There he was, wandering among the displayed items and sculptures, lingering—as she might have anticipated—over the historical curiosities. He glanced upward, as though sensing her presence.

"Hello again, Victoria," he called with a wave.

With a polite smile, she waved back.

"Very well, Allan," she said over her shoulder. "Have him wait in the office." Without waiting for a response, she returned to the bedroom and began to dress in something more substantial.

The Thompson Plantation
Outside Savannah, Georgia

Victoria stepped into the office, firmly closing the door behind her. "All right Beckett, what in Heaven's name are you doing…"

To most Kindred, and certainly to Ash's mortal guards, the man behind the desk looked like Beckett. He moved like Beckett, spoke like Beckett, and even smelled like Beckett. But weakened as Ash was by her own bout with the withering, her powers of perception were still second to none, and she knew Beckett personally, if not well. She'd missed it from the balcony, but standing this close, she recognized the illusory disguise for what it was, though she couldn't see through it.

"Who are you?" she asked, her voice hard, angry—the voice of an elder in her own haven, one who didn't take kindly to being surprised.

"Actually, I don't believe we've been formally introduced, Miss Ash." Beckett's form shifted, faded, revealing a burly man wearing flannel and a thick beard. "My name is Samuel. Sorry for the little charade." Samuel rose and came around the desk. "I just have a few questions about those relics you purchased from Beckett, and I thought that if you believed you were talking to him…"

"Oh, for Caine's sake! How do you know about those? Did Hardestadt send you? He and I have been through this already. I'd like for you—"

The blade slid effortlessly across Ash's throat, parting flesh and cartilage with a single stroke. It wasn't remotely sufficient to behead her, but it certainly prevented her from talking as the air in her lungs rushed futilely over severed vocal chords.

A mere few months ago, this would have been a minor inconvenience. Ash had crushed the will of vampires far older than she beneath the weight of her own emotions, her unnatural presence.

But now, weakened as she was, the blood responded sluggishly to her commands. She saw Samuel flinch, but he did not collapse in a gibbering heap as he should have. Instead the blade—a viciously hooked weapon, not entirely unlike those used for gutting fish—flicked out again, and again. And each time, Ash's concentration, already shaky, faltered just that much more.

And then Samuel *really* went to work. Other than the nights she'd spent as a prisoner of the Tzimisce during the Sabbat's East Coast offensive, she'd never experienced torture even remotely like this. Samuel removed strips of flesh from her body, inches at a time. He splattered blood across the four walls of the office, left her clothing in tatters. And only as her sight began to dim, as the world began to recede, did Ash realize what Samuel was doing.

Her last conscious thought was, *I hope Beckett guts you for this.*

Calmly, Samuel watched as the body quickly decayed, and a wide grin split his face. "Ash to ashes," he said snidely, and chuckled.

A quick look around showed the room looked just as he wanted it to. No body remained, of course, but the splattered blood and the shredded clothes certainly suggested a vicious assault. The hooked blade of the knife left tears that could easily be taken for claws. And the servants had all seen Beckett enter the building. Yes, that should do nicely.

Samuel slowly faded from sight—another application of his powers of disguise, misdirection, and obfuscation—and proceeded downstairs to steal the items Ash had purchased from Beckett three months before.

Gutierrez Textiles
Ciudad Juarez, Mexico

The door shattered inward, and Fatima stood in the open doorway, blades in hand, ready for bloodshed.

She needn't have bothered.

As with every previous occurrence, the room was full only of decaying vampires. The bodies lay on the floor, sat in chairs—they had died, all of them, before they even had time to rise to their feet. And Fatima's sensitive nose could detect the lingering odors of blood, and—strangely—of desert sands. The room was still faintly warm.

Much of the leadership of the Black Hand lay on the ground before her, their ashes already beginning to mix with the dust. Some may have survived, and Aajav Khan might still be out there, but the sect-within-a-sect that had terrified even the most monstrous of Caine's get was now gone.

As she did every time, Fatima knelt and began to pray. She asked Allah to give her strength, to grant her wisdom.

And she asked—if the strange force she followed, the creature to which she felt inextricably drawn, was what she thought it was—that Allah grant her the mercy of as quick a passage into true death as it offered its other victims.

Carver's Meat Packing and Storage
Riverside, California

The large chamber echoed the sound of their footsteps on the concrete floor, yet those same echoes sounded only briefly before they were absorbed and silenced by the rows of frozen flesh.

The vampires weren't interested in the dead cows, of course. Their objective was the second room, entered through the rear of the primary freezer.

"I want to know what happened," Hardestadt hissed angrily, not for the first time. "By all rights, I ought to have every one of her people staked out for the *dawn*." His voice, quivering with rage, remained barely low enough that the others, who walked several paces behind the arguing pair, wouldn't hear.

Federico di Padua, largely unmoved by the Founder's anger, merely shrugged. "While I certainly don't welcome the news of Miss Ash's death, Hardestadt, might it not be for the best? You yourself have said that you didn't ultimately expect Ash to go along with this." He stepped to the side and paused, allowing one of the ghouls—who also happened to be the night manager of the facility—to step forward with a key and unlock the door before them. "You said," he continued in a low whisper, "that she was too soft for it, that you expected her to wind up working against us. With the traitor Bell, perhaps, or with Beckett." Di Padua very deliberately did not mention Jan Pieterzoon or his nascent sect the Nephtali, who were said to work in partial cooperation with Bell's malcontents. Ash probably would have turned to Pieterzoon, with whom she'd shared a great deal in the past, but bringing up Hardestadt's wayward childe was not a good way to endear oneself to the Founder.

"So now you have two solutions in one. Ash is dealt with, and you've got a much stronger case to take to the justicars and the Inner Circle. Beckett's not just a potential threat anymore; he's murdered a respected Camarilla elder. He returned to the States, argued with his accomplice—probably over the relics he stole back from her as he left—and shredded the poor woman. You can have archons crawling all over his trail in a matter of nights, including myself, if you wish it—archons a lot more dependable than that traitor Bell."

The others stepped back once more, allowing Hardestadt and di Padua to enter the back room first.

The scent of Kindred vitae was overpowering, even dulled as it was by the cold bite of the refrigerated air. The sound of dripping blood, completely blocked out by the room's walls and the thick metal door, now filled their ears. The blood collected in drains that had been specially modified to catch the valuable fluids in reusable containers. Waste not, want not.

Kindred, mostly neonates, hung motionless from large metal hooks mounted to the walls. Wooden skewers protruded from their chests. Large plastic canisters hung from the ceiling beside them, equipped with drinking tubes; the blood in those containers was primarily a mix of pig and beef blood—easily obtained in a packing plant—with bits of rat, dog and human mixed in. Once every few nights, the stakes were briefly removed, allowing the prisoners to feed. To prevent escape, their feet dangled inches above the floor, ensuring they had no purchase, no leverage, even when they could move. Many also had their hands cuffed behind their backs or otherwise bound.

Numerous guards wandered the perimeter of the room, or stood watch by the only door. They were heavily armed, not that any potential escapee would have the strength to fight them off even if they weren't.

"It is not 'for the best,'" Hardestadt answered as he wandered through the hanging bodies, looking for all the world like he was idly browsing the wares in some boutique, "because Beckett *didn't* do this, and you and I both know that. I certainly do not object to using it against him, but I very much want to know who really did it, and why they went to so much trouble to implicate Beckett. Good for me or not, I dislike mysteries.

"Furthermore, did it ever occur to you," Hardestadt continued, "that I might not *want* archons crawling all over this?"

"How do you mean?"

Hardestadt stopped at a particular young Kindred, a neonate who'd had the audacity to slay his sire in self-defense when the older vampire had attempted to diablerize him as a means of overcoming the withering. The "crime" of destroying another Kindred was more than enough excuse to have him locked up as fodder. The Founder ran a hand across the dangling childe's back and neck. Even staked and paralyzed, the prisoner seemed to shudder.

"I mean, not all my archons are as loyal as you are. With so many of our kind seeking more powerful blood to overcome their growing weaknesses, too many archons might try to take Beckett alive. If they do *that*, he might be questioned, and too many of our kind have means of determining the truth of such questioning. It might come out that he did not kill Victoria Ash." *Other things,* he added silently, *might come out as well, things I do not need made public.*

"Sensible. Would you like me to go after him myself, then?"

Hardestadt looked at the archon. Despite the careful use of the criminals and their blood, di Padua was showing signs of weakness. Most remarkable, the repulsive countenance that he had inherited from his sire seemed to be fading—there were fewer folds, creases and sores on his twisted face than even a few weeks ago. Many Nosferatu defined themselves by their very ugliness, and Hardestadt wondered just what one would do if given the chance to lift that particular curse upon them. *If neonate blood has done this, would blood as potent as Beckett's do more? Is that what you wish to find out, Archon di Padua?*

"No," the Founder said, "I don't want you going anywhere near Beckett. Actually, I want you to try to find out who really killed Victoria, and bring your findings to me and me alone."

Hardestadt continued to poke and prod, as though he really were choosing a slab of beef. "This one should do," he said finally. "He'll make a nice change from the ordinary."

"All right, Archon di Padua," Hardestadt continued, stepping back so the plant workers could come and remove the chosen meal from the hook. The metal left the childe's flesh with a soggy tearing sound. "Are we certain Beckett *is* back in the United States?"

"Not certain, no, but fairly sure. My intelligence has him somewhere in Oregon, making inquiries about the current situation in Los Angeles. My guess is he's heading there next, though I couldn't say why."

"And you trust your source?"

"He's a clanmate of mine who's passed me information before. He's as reliable as any of our kind—that is, I trust him as long as nobody makes him a better offer."

"Very well."

Hardestadt knew he was going to have to find someone he could trust to kill Beckett, someone who would do the job properly. Since even the reliability of the archons was in doubt these nights, it would need to be someone outside the normal channels. Fortunately, reluctant as the Founder was to call on him, he had just the person.

That decision made, Hardestadt sank his fangs into the paralyzed neonate, dispassionately draining him of blood and soul, slowly, bit by measured bit. Not a drop of blood, not a single dribble of the childe's unlife and soul were spilled. Long after he'd consumed enough to replenish his strength for many nights to come, Hardestadt continued to drink, until he held nothing but dust in his arms and the burgeoning love of the slaughter in his heart.

Apple Valley Airport
Apple Valley, California

Though substantial danger and difficulty loomed in the immediate future, Beckett was exceedingly grateful that the flights, at least for a few nights, were coming to an end. For the entirety of the flight from Vienna to the States, the only peace Beckett had gotten was the slumber of day. Cesare, ever artificially loyal to his master, waxed eloquent (or something like it) for hours on end. How worried he had been when Beckett vanished for months in Vienna! How grateful he was to God that Signore had been returned to him! How concerned he was that Beckett's current activities might place his valuable person in danger once more! In English, in Italian, in Portuguese, he'd gone on, in person and even, at times, over the intercom.

Even worse, to Beckett's eyes, was the fact that Cesare's constant effusiveness served as a constant reminder that he'd enslaved the man's mind and emotions. Beckett—a world traveler, an independent Kindred, and a great believer in personal freedoms—always found that notion disturbing, no matter what sort of spin he tried to put on it.

Between soliloquies, on the flight overseas and during several nights spent in Lakeside, Oregon, Beckett and Kapaneus had discussed their current situation and planned as best they could. Often advised by Okulos via phone or e-mail, the pair had a fair idea what was facing them in Los Angeles. And it didn't look good.

"It's like the Sabbat offensive all over again," Okulos had told them at one point. "Actually, it's worse. At least then, you had the archons and princes running around trying to shore up the Masquerade, cleaning up after the various battles. This time, the Camarilla seems too focused on retaking LA and worrying about the withering to deal with anything else. So far, all the news reports are still stuck on riots, terrorism, and gang wars, but I don't know how long that's going to last. This entire thing's going to blow up on us but good, Beckett, and I'd as soon you not be there when it happens."

"Explain to me," Beckett had asked him, "how this thing's dragged on for over three months. The average siege is a matter of nights, maybe a few weeks. By then all the local sect leaders have either fled or been targeted."

"Numbers, my friend. The thin-bloods are somewhat more numerous than Sabbat crusaders."

"What kind of numbers are we talking about?"

Okulos had muttered something, almost too low for Beckett to catch.

"*How* many?!" Beckett had been stunned, certain he'd misheard his old friend, that the satellite connection must be faulty.

"Hundreds, Beckett," Okulos repeated more loudly. "Literally. They've come from all over the world, flocking to Cross's banner. I have no idea how LA's sustained them even *this* long without coming apart at the seams."

"Jesus…" The Camarilla was accustomed to thinking in terms of maybe a hundred combatants, tops, on both sides of a conflict. If LA was truly playing haven to hundreds of thin-bloods, it was no wonder the Inner Circle hadn't yet launched any major offensives on Cross's haven or the thin-bloods' other centers of power. They were fighting a war of attrition, trying to thin the numbers through skirmishes— fights where sheer numbers wouldn't overcome their own greater strengths and experience.

After learning *that*, Beckett had decided to land in Apple Valley, almost a hundred miles outside of LA. The Camarilla, the MacNeil anarchs, and Jenna Cross's thin-bloods would all be watching LAX and the other Los Angeles airports too closely, alert for any sign of enemy reinforcements. They'd have spies and maybe soldiers swarming all over a privately owned Gulfstream faster than you could say "customs inspection." Okulos arranged to have a rental car, acquired through so many layers that nobody would ever connect it to Beckett, waiting for them. It was nearly two hours' drive into LA proper—given that they planned to avoid any of the major highways and thoroughfares—but as long as they arrived sufficiently early in the evening, that shouldn't pose a problem. Cesare, to his chagrin, was ordered to wait in

Apple Valley, and keep the plane ready for quick takeoff. Beckett actually sighed in relief as the car door closed between him and his effusive ghoul.

"So," Kapaneus offered after much of the drive had passed, the silence broken only by the rumble of other engines on the highway and the sound of the radio, tuned to one of LA's all-news stations. "Have we anything resembling a plan?"

It was not an idle question. Beckett didn't know precisely where Smiling Jack could be found. What intelligence Okulos had been able to gather suggested that the anarch-cum-prophet had sided with the thin-bloods, strangely enough, and not the MacNeils, but that didn't really narrow things down. The thin-bloods still controlled the majority of LA, and they had dozens of staging areas and communal havens scattered throughout the city. The Camarilla—and Okulos's own Nosferatu contacts—had succeeded in locating most of them, but other than the occasional harassment by local police or other pawns, didn't have the manpower or firepower to take them on directly. And given the security those places must have—Cross would undoubtedly be worried about Camarilla assassins—Beckett didn't much relish the idea of trying to sneak in himself. Normally he'd just have made his presence known, asking around about Cross until she heard of his interests and found *him*, but he really didn't need to advertise his location to the Camarilla.

"Sure I have a plan," he told his companion after a moment's pondering. "I'm going to call Okulos and see if he can use any of his contacts to learn which of the thin-blood havens serves specifically as Cross's headquarters."

"You believe Okulos will be able to learn that when Hardestadt's archons cannot?"

"You'd be surprised what Okulos can do."

"All right. Assuming he can find out, what then?"

"Then I'm going to go knock on the door and ask to come in."

The elder stared. "I wish," he said after a brief pause, "that I believed you were jesting."

"So do I."

The San Fernando Valley
Los Angeles, California

Things didn't turn out to be *quite* that easy. Beckett and Kapaneus managed to avoid picking up any tails when they entered the city—even with their substantial numbers, the thin-bloods were too widely spread to watch every route into Los Angeles. As they approached the property an incredulous Okulos had indicated as Cross's home, however, two other vehicles appeared from the other direction and blocked the street. A third car blocked the street behind them. Three people emerged from each car, every one of them armed, while a fourth remained behind the wheel.

Beckett smiled his best smile as the first of the thin-bloods approached the car. "Efficient," he announced, rolling down the window. "Well organized. You're good."

"And you're stupid, if you thought you could just barge in here." He raised a pistol that, from Beckett's angle, appeared to be roughly the size of a howitzer, and gestured. "Get out of the car."

"Good to see you lot are more civilized than rumors have it," Beckett continued, opening his door and motioning for Kapaneus to do the same. "I half-expected you to just shoot up the car and call it done."

"Oh, not at all," the thin-blood replied with a smirk. "We're going to shoot you out *here*, and then behead your bodies. You have any idea how hard it is to move a car riddled with bullet holes without drawing attention?"

Beckett turned his gaze on the man before him, staring through his shades. "There's no call for that. We just want to speak with Jenna Cross. That's all."

"Right. *Sure* you do. And I'm going to believe you're not just another Camarilla hit man why?"

Beckett smiled—and then faded away. A thin stream of mist flowed down the road, vanishing into one of the gutters. A moment later it billowed up from a nearby manhole and was once more human in shape and form.

"Because," Beckett said, ignoring the panicked expressions and the numerous barrels pointed his way, "if

I'd really wanted to get into Cross's home without being stopped, I could have done so. But I *wanted* you to see me coming, to prove my intentions aren't hostile."

"We have ways of detecting things like that," the sentry scoffed. His worried voice, however, belied his words. No doubt he was either too young to have ever seen a vampire take the form of mist, or else he'd never seen it done so *fast*.

"I'm certain you do. Do you want to stand here and argue some more, son, or do you want to let us speak to your boss? We just have some questions, then we're gone. I don't give a rat's ass about who runs LA."

One of the other vampires stepped up beside the first one. For a moment she stared at Beckett, hard, examining him with more than human senses. Then she began speaking, her voice barely a whisper, but Beckett's sensitive hearing was more than able to pick out the words.

"I don't think he's bullshitting us, Mike. I could tell if he was afraid, and he's not."

"Just means he's a cold fish, is all. I don't like it."

"You don't have to like it," Beckett interjected calmly, as though they'd always intended to involve him in the conversation. "You just have to ask your boss about it."

The one called Mike scowled, but apparently decided the intruder was right. He reached into a pocket for a cell phone.

"Lizzie? Mike. Listen, there's someone here who wants to talk to Jenna. No, he's not one of us, but I don't think he's a Camarilla gun, either. What? Hold on." He lowered the phone slightly. "What's your name?"

"Beckett."

Jenna Cross's haven in the San Fernando Valley
Los Angeles, California

"He's *here*!" Jenna, pale even for a vampire, was practically whispering into her phone, her voice quivering with a fear that any experienced Kindred would recognize as unnatural. Her subordinates had pulled her out of an important meeting to tell her who was here, and she'd

182   GEHENNA: THE FINAL NIGHT

immediately called the only man she thought could help. "What the fuck is he doing *here*, Samuel?"

"I honestly have no idea, Jenna. That's why you're going to speak with him."

"What?! I'm going to have the bastard killed before he gets his claws on me—"

"Jenna, you called me for my advice, yes? I'm advising you not to be stupid. You don't know Beckett, for all I've told you about him. This isn't like your battles with the Camarilla. Beckett doesn't want your neighborhoods, and if he were here to kill you, he wouldn't have announced himself. He's not going to stand and fight, he's going to run, and the odds of your people killing him before he escapes are pretty much nil. Then he's going to know you're on to him, and he won't bother being subtle anymore."

Jenna began to pace nervously, a habit in which she'd never have indulged if any of her people could see her. "You told me he was the biggest name Noddist out there. That if he learned who I am," and here she absently rubbed the crescent mark on her shoulder with her other hand, "he'd either kill me, in hopes of somehow averting Gehenna, or he'd try to take me alive for study."

"Correct. But he doesn't yet know who you are. If he did, he'd have approached very differently. Find out what he wants and get him out of there swiftly, and you won't be at risk. After that, you can deal with him at your leisure, before he *does* become a threat."

Jenna sighed. She didn't like it, but Samuel hadn't steered her wrong yet. Of all the vampires she'd met since her own unorthodox entry into the society of the undead, he was one of the few she trusted. She'd talk to Beckett, find out what the hell he was doing here. And then—*then* she'd destroy him, before he had the chance to do the same to her.

Jenna Cross's haven in the San Fernando Valley
Los Angeles, California

Underground catacombs, cursed tombs, haunted caves—all these, Beckett could deal with. He was so accustomed to dealing with the abnormal, however, he'd practically forgotten that most vampires tried to make their surroundings as innocuous as possible.

The room was so blatantly suburban it could have come straight out of a sitcom or the pages of *Better Homes and Gardens*. The furniture, from the leather sofa to the brass-and-glass coffee table, were placed just so around the room. The windows boasted matching curtains and valances, and the lamp resembled less a source of light and more a piece of post-modern art. The carpet was sea-foam blue, and the various beverages on the table even sat on matching coasters.

None of it, however, masked the palpable sense of hostility Beckett felt as he was ushered alone into the room. Kapaneus had been asked to remain behind with the guards as a show of faith. It wasn't the two men who walked beside him, Berettas in hand. It wasn't the fact that the house was crawling with thin-bloods sufficiently armed to take on an entire drug cartel. It wasn't even the glares of suspicion he could feel pressing down on him as they moved through the hallways of the large house, hurled his way by those who had known only oppression from vampires of Beckett's age and power.

No, as the innocuous-looking Jenna Cross rose from her leather chair and met his eyes, Beckett knew that the sense of menace, the weighty hatred he could practically smell in the air, the threat that set the Beast within him pacing its spiritual cage, came from her. Beckett had no idea why, considering he'd never met the woman, but her utter hatred for him was unmistakable.

She wore thick-soled boots, a pair of jeans, and a long-sleeved sweatshirt that somehow didn't seem her style. Her hair was tied back in a simple tail and she clenched a Desert Eagle semi-automatic pistol in her right fist.

"My name is Beckett," he began, deciding to seize the initiative before it seized him. "You may have heard of me." A touch arrogant, perhaps, but Cross needed to learn from the get-go that, guns and guards aside, she was *not* in control here.

"I've heard of you." Cross scowled, and the click of her thumbing the pistol's safety on and off, on and off, served as a threatening harmony line to her words. "You're an elder. Just another fucking vampire."

"Like you?"

"No. I still remember what it means to be human."

Beckett felt his hackles rising, his anger mounting. He wanted to respond to the threat in her tone, to tear this arrogant upstart several new orifices. Given the number of guns in the room, however, and the number of angry thin-bloods holding them, he decided to forbear. More importantly, however, now that she was speaking, Beckett could pick up an undercurrent to her hostility. More than hating him, Jenna Cross was afraid of him.

Keeping his voice calm, he replied, "I'm nothing like your enemies, either. If you've heard of me, you know that I'm not one of Hardestadt's soldiers. I'm not here as your enemy, and I could give a fig who wins this little war you've got going."

"Right. So it's a coincidence you're here right in the middle of that war."

"Pretty much." Beckett took a single step forward—raising his hands, palms out, at the same time, in signal that he wasn't moving to attack. "Look, Cross, I don't know you, but I know you're not stupid. You couldn't have held out this long against the Camarilla if you were. So you know that something is happening to the Kindred everywhere. Strange omens, odd weaknesses. Some of us think Gehenna's here, and that would make your little insurrection pretty much a moot point anyway, wouldn't it?"

Cross growled low in her throat, and her hand clenched so hard the grip of her pistol cracked. Beckett, startled, actually retreated that step he'd just taken. He was used to strong reactions to the notion of the end of the world—it had sent him into months of despair after all—but he'd never seen such naked anger before.

"What the hell do I have to do with some mythical apocalypse?" Cross snapped at him.

"You? So far as I know, not a thing. I'm here to see Smiling Jack."

Whatever Cross was expecting from him, that clearly wasn't it. For the first time, Beckett saw not only anger but confusion flicker across her features. "What?"

"Smiling Jack. I know he's involved in what's going on here, and I know he sided with you, not the other anarchs, though I'll admit I'm not sure why. I have reason to believe he knows something about what's going on, and I want to speak with him about it." Beckett smiled, though if it was meant to be reassuring, it failed rather dramatically. "Honestly, Cross, this doesn't actually concern you at all. You're just the only person I knew about who could put us in touch, and you're easier to find—albeit marginally—than he is."

Cross's expression wavered—and then her jaw tightened. "No. This is bullshit." She raised her weapon, and Beckett didn't have to look behind him: he could hear the others in the room reacting the same way. "You went to all the trouble of tracking me down, just because you thought I could play matchmaker with Uncle Jack? I don't fucking think so."

Uncle Jack? Interesting.

Frankly, though, her choice of monikers was of secondary importance. For whatever reason, Cross clearly thought Beckett was here for some other reason, thought of him as the enemy, and apparently she wasn't inclined to let herself be talked out of said notion. Beckett tensed, his fingertips burning as his talons slid from their fleshy sheathes. If Cross thought a bunch of children with guns were going to be enough to take him down, she was about to make an enormous mistake.

"You," said a voice from the breakfast nook, a voice Beckett had never thought to hear again, "are about to make an enormous mistake."

All eyes in the room turned. There, in the doorway, stood a dark-haired woman, clad almost entirely in black.

"Well," Beckett said, straightening from the crouch he'd instinctively adopted in preparation for bloodshed, "I'll be damned."

"Lucita," Cross said, her voice quavering with rage even as she tried to remain polite. "I appreciate your advice—and your patience, in waiting for me while I deal with this other matter—but this isn't any of your concern. If you wish to discuss an alliance—"

"Then," Lucita interrupted, "it behooves me to ensure that my potential ally survives long enough to have such a discussion."

Cross allowed a single scoffing "Ha!" to escape her throat. Then, "Whoever Beckett is, he's not going to beat six of us with guns, Lucita."

"Yes he is."

It wasn't Lucita's words so much as her tone that stifled whatever further protest Cross might have made. The elder clearly believed what she was saying—and if she did, suddenly Cross had to wonder if she should too. Reluctantly, she lowered her pistol.

"I would take it as a personal favor," Lucita continued when things seemed well on their way to calming down, "if you would consider granting Beckett's request. It would form a solid basis of goodwill for our future negotiations."

"Whatever." Cross turned to her nearest companion. "Tabitha, go tell Uncle Jack he has a visitor." She turned once more to stare balefully at Beckett. "And tell him we've got *important* shit to worry about, so make it quick." And then she stormed from the room, leaving a puzzled Beckett to wonder just what the hell he'd walked into.

Jenna Cross's haven in the San Fernando Valley
Los Angeles, California

With a snarled "Wait here!" from a thin-blooded vampire who probably had no better reason to hate Beckett and Lucita than that they were elders, the door to the house slammed shut. The two Kindred found themselves alone on the back porch, looking out over a backyard garden that appeared to have been professionally landscaped and maintained.

"Well," Beckett commented, glancing around warily, "this is very suburban." He chuckled once, mirthlessly. "It appears Cross wasn't in the mood to finish your meeting right now…"

Lucita scowled. "These arrogant childer need to learn some respect for their elders."

"To be fair, Lucita, every elder they've ever met has wanted to either murder or oppress them. I'm not entirely thrilled with Cross's attitudes either, but it's understandable…"

"I have no interest in being fair, Beckett. I demand the respect I am due, and that's final. It was bad earlier. It got worse from the moment she received the phone call saying you were here."

Beckett glanced sidelong at Lucita. Once upon a time, Anatole, she and Beckett had been traveling companions, allies, even—perhaps—friends. "Yet you still stepped in to help me out. I appreciate that."

"I have no interest in your thanks either. We have assisted one another multiple times in the past. I simply wish to ensure no lingering debt remains between us—at least on my part."

"All right, listen." Beckett turned to face her, eyes narrowed. "I know we haven't spoken much since—well, in the last few years, but I don't think…"

And then Beckett looked at Lucita—*really* looked at her. He took in the sharp cast to her expression, the complete absence of any human movements or gestures, traits she'd once attempted to emulate as a means of linking herself to what she'd once been. He looked at her eyes, and saw no emotion save a burgeoning anger reflected in their depths.

And then he looked deeper still, rude as it might be, peering through dead flesh to the twisting colors of the emotions and the soul within.

"Oh, fuck me…"

Lucita growled. "I did *not* give you permission to read me, Beckett."

"The hell with your permission! Damn it, Lucita, what *happened* to you?! I heard rumors you'd joined the Sabbat, I figured you had your reasons… But *this*?! Your humanity was what separated you from your sire, Lucita, and you've fucking thrown it away! You're turning into *him*."

"Don't… you… *dare!*" The darkness around Lucita's feet began to thrash and tremble, shadows beginning to creep up toward the single outdoor floodlight that illuminated the garden. "Don't you *ever* compare me to Monçada! I am *not* as he was, and I never will be!

"What I *am*," she continued, just a bit more calmly, "is honest. I've had longer than you to examine our situation, Beckett. I've learned that any attempt to cling to the morality and the faith of what we were is doomed."

"Right, and those of our kind who have done so for longer than you've been around, they're what? All flukes? And even if they were, there are other paths, Lucita, other options that don't require you becoming what you've always fought against."

Lucita's eyes narrowed. "Beckett, as we were companions once, I'll explain this much to you. My constant opposition of my sire, Monçada, was an anchor about my soul. Even when the monster was dead, I was so determined not to become what he was, I became nothing at all. Now— now I have accepted what we all are, and it has allowed me to move on. And that, to be blunt, is all I care to tell you. I have left what I was behind, Beckett, and I do not particularly care if that offends you. I owe you no further explanation." She began to turn away.

"Really? What about Anatole, Lucita? Would you have explained to him? *Could* you have?"

Lucita spun back with a hiss somewhere between that of an angry cat and a striking viper. Her hands rose, the shadows stretched to claim Beckett, to rend him limb from limb. He tensed as well, prepared to leap, to try his hardest to rip out his old companion's throat before the Abyss could gain a grip on him.

"This is a serious downer, man. You gotta at least tell me what you wanted to see me for before you murder each other, okay?"

Both turned to see a man standing in the doorway. He wore ragged pants, sandals, a stained wool tunic. His hair and beard were matted with dirt and blood. He stepped out into the garden, putting himself between his two guests.

"Smiling Jack?" Beckett asked, more out of a sense of politeness than any uncertainty.

"Not smiling so much anymore, right?" The old anarch

chuckled. "But yeah, he's me. I'm he. Or something like that. And you're Beckett."

"Yes."

"You want to talk to me about Gehenna?"

"Among other things."

Lucita glanced from one to the other. "Beckett," she finally asked, "is it real? We've all seen the signs, we've all begun to suffer the withering, but there could be other explanations…"

"No, Lucita. It's real. It's started."

For a moment, Lucita fell silent. She'd known it to be so, but to hear it confirmed from the one individual she'd most hoped—despite herself—would provide an alternate explanation…

"Very well," she replied after a moment. "Then I will be part of this conversation as well. I would know all that is going on, Beckett."

Considering they'd been steps away from rending each other limb from limb, Beckett considered refusing, but decided it wasn't worth the effort—or inevitable violence.

"Walk with me," Jack told them, and began making his way through the yard.

And walk they did, through garden paths that took them through holes in fences. House after house had similar gardens, and Jack stopped and knelt to examine almost every single bush. Roses here, philodendrons there, lilies growing around a koi pond. All of them seemed in remarkable health, their stems or branches tall and thick, blossoms open and lush even at night.

"Been watering them myself," Jack explained, though nobody had asked a question. "My own blood, man, and some from Camarilla agents we capture in our territory. Makes 'em grow nice and strong, see?"

Lucita and Beckett exchanged glances. "And the neighbors do not object to you coming onto their properties and spilling blood?" she asked.

"Nah. We own half the block. Not on paper, course, but there's a whole metric shitload of ghouls living in this neighborhood now. Only way we could have a place for so many of us."

"Us," Beckett parroted back. "You're not thin-blooded, Jack. Why are you with them?"

"'Cuz it's the end, Beckett, like you said. And the thin-blooded are gonna come out on top. Ain't no good cause for the old folks to come after them. They ain't got thick enough blood to worry about. Why do you think the withering hasn't affected them, when it's got damn near everyone else over sixty pissin' their pants?"

Beckett frowned. Everyone? No, that couldn't be right. He himself had felt no weaker than he ever had. A little tired, maybe, but that could just as easily be attributed to the stress and frequent (even for him) travel. And there were his hands, of course, to suggest that he hadn't remained unscathed. But he certainly wasn't fading away, wasn't losing his strength.

He decided not to bring that up for the time being, however. No sense in showing everyone what might amount to an extra ace in his hand.

Jack stopped at the koi pond, thrust his hand in with lightning speed and came out with a thrashing fish. He licked it once, shrugged, and tossed it back in. "Been feeding on the blood-watered plants," he explained. "Wanted to see if any of the vitae's been passed along." And then, once more, they walked.

"Jack," Beckett finally interjected minutes later, "I don't mean to interrupt your gardening, but—"

"Caine came to me, you know."

Beckett blinked. "What?"

"Yeah. You were here, in town. I know you were. The whole bit with the coffin, that was fake. Hell, even after I spoke to Caine, I wasn't really sure he was the real deal. Might *not* have been, I guess. But there was *something* about the guy, something important." He glanced sidelong at Beckett. "Something similar about you, actually. You've been touched, if not by the Dark Father then by something almost as ancient."

Beckett wondered briefly if his time in Kaymakli had somehow marked him.

"Still, man, it was all just talk at first. I figured I could get everyone riled up about Gehenna, maybe get the anarchs moving again, you know? We'd pretty much been scattered by the Camarilla and the New Promise Whatever-the-Fuck, and I thought, shit, people think Gehenna's coming, maybe they'll get off their bloodless hemorrhoids and *do* something.

"And right about then I found Jenna Cross. Twenty-two-year-old college dropout, couldn't decide if she wanted to run away from daddy's money or blow it all on booze. And she had the birthmark..."

Beckett tensed. "The crescent moon? *You* found the Last Daughter?!"

"Almost. Took her to a tattoo guy I know to touch it up a little. But see, I figured—and I told her the same—that she was a prop. She'd help me make a good case for Gehenna. Like the coffin, and the other artifacts I'd been gathering."

Beckett began to feel a sinking feeling in his stomach.

"And then," Jack continued, his voice going soft, almost reverent, "she came to me one night—and she wasn't a ghoul no more. She was one of us. Thin-blooded, yeah, okay, but a fucking grade-A, all the way, ninety-nine and forty-four-one-hundredths-percent pure vampire."

"Someone had Embraced her without your permission?" Lucita asked.

"Nah, that's the whole point. *Nobody* Embraced her!"

Beckett and Lucita stopped walking. Jack continued for a moment before he realized he was alone, and stepped back to them.

"Yeah, it's something, ain't it?" he chuckled. "I mean, you've all heard about elders getting weak—or some of 'em getting stronger and weaker, like manic-depressives on PCP, right? Been doing that one myself. On good nights, it's a real rush, man. On others...

"But you ain't heard all of it, have you? Some really freaky shit going on, stuff the Inner Circumcision don't want people to know. Some old ghouls have just up and died, like the blood wasn't strong enough to keep 'em from decaying anymore. And a few other ghouls—like my Jenna—went the other way. It's like they just woke up and the blood had strengthened, so much that they weren't human no more. So far as I know, Jenna was the first." Jack leaned over and stuck his face in a rosebush, inhaling deeply to catch the scent. He didn't seem to notice or care about the thorns puncturing his nose, his cheek, his lips.

It was possible, outlandish as it sounded. Some of the rumors Beckett had picked up, from Okulos and others, suggested that some of what was happening was even stranger than the withering. At this point, Beckett wasn't willing to dismiss anything out of hand. A quick glance at Lucita's expression convinced him that she felt the same.

Beckett nodded for the old anarch to go on.

"So I realized that Caine put me on the path," Jack continued, rising to his feet, "even if I was too fuck-headed to see it at first." He reached into his back pocket, removed a BIC lighter and a bent cigarette, and lit it up, flinching slightly as he brought the flame near his face. "I been trying to tell everyone who'll listen what's coming, that they got to get ready to be judged. Jenna keeps me around to minister to the thin-bloods, and 'cuz she knows I been fighting the Camaretards a long time and know how to do it. She still don't really believe Gehenna's here, though. The idea scares her for some reason—I mean, more'n it scares anyone else."

"And your knowledge?" Beckett asked. "Your prophecies, your sermons? Where do they come from?"

"Here'n there, man. Gotta piece this all together, you know. Been having some old and moldy shit brought to me; told you that, right? Got some old relics with funky symbols on 'em. Even got me a few fragments of *The Book of Nod*. Hey, man, I bet you could get me the others. You gotta have like, what, every edition from Caine's himself to the King James, right?"

"Umm… Not with me."

"Yeah, course not. Wouldn't want *that* lost at customs. Hell, man, I even got me a few genuine prophets. Couple of Cross's thin-blood friends seem to have a serious knack for seeing what the Camarilla's going to do before they do it. Cross is usin' them tactically, but I've been trying to get Gehenna info out of them when I can."

Beckett almost felt like crying. All the way to LA, and what did Smiling Jack turn out to be? A half-mad second-rate street preacher who'd hallucinated a Caine sighting and gathered just enough information to sound convincing. A thin-blooded talent for prophecy was interesting, and under other circumstances, it might be worth looking into. But judging by his welcome, Beckett didn't think Jenna Cross would allow him to question her people, and Jack personally had no information he could use, no mysterious sources Beckett could tap into.

"I see," he said, after taking a moment to bring his emotions under control. "Well, thank you for your time, Jack. You've been most helpful. Do you suppose," he added, as though the idea had just occurred to him, "that you might petition Jenna to let me discuss all this with her? If she *is* the Last Daughter, she might know things—even if she herself isn't aware of it."

Jack frowned. "Well, I'll ask her. Us scholars gotta stick together, right? I dunno how likely it is though, Beckett. I couldn't begin to say why, but she really doesn't like you very much."

No kidding, Beckett thought. What he said, however, was, "I'll take my chances."

Jenna Cross's haven in the San Fernando Valley
Los Angeles, California

"He wants *what*?!" Jenna Cross drummed her fingers on the coffee table hard enough that the various mugs and glasses standing on it rattled.

Tabitha kept her gaze on her shoes—and the mud from the garden she'd tracked in with them. As soon as Jack had called her outside and passed along Beckett's request, she knew her leader wasn't going to like it. Cross seemed angry at just about everything these nights—understandable, given current circumstances—but she nursed a burning hatred for Beckett that infected the others, even if they still hadn't the first clue why.

"He wants to meet with you again," Tabitha repeated. "Something about this whole Gehenna nonsense."

Jenna felt her hand quiver, and she quickly lowered it below the table so Tabitha wouldn't see it trembling. He knew. It was the only explanation. She glanced at her own shoulder, somehow feeling she could see the crescent moon even through the thick material of her sweatshirt.

"What time is it?"

Tabitha blinked at the sudden topic change, but checked her watch. "Um, right about four-thirty."

"All right. Tell the bastard I don't have time to talk with him tonight, but I'll meet with him before midnight tomorrow."

"Okay, I—"

"I'm not done." Cross paused, thinking. As thin-blooded Kindred, she and her people had very few advantages over elder and more powerful vampires. They trained, regularly, to take advantage of those few they *did*. "Who's got our best record for staying awake after dawn?"

"Moose had almost two hours, but with him gone… I think Darryl's managed for over an hour, and Nicky for almost as long."

"All right. Tell them I want them to stay up late this morning. Beckett and the others will be in the guest rooms. Tell them to wait for half an hour after dawn, and then make sure Beckett doesn't wake up. Ever."

"Jenna, is this wise? He's got allies…"

"I'm not asking for opinions here, Tabitha. I'm giving orders. Better take care of his companion too. I don't need a vengeful elder running around the neighborhood."

"And Lucita?"

Cross frowned for an instant. "Better not. From what we saw, she knows Beckett, but they didn't seem all that close. I don't think she'll jeopardize our potential alliance by complaining. Don't hurt her unless you have to."

Tabitha nodded once, albeit reluctantly, and left to pass along her orders. Cross leaned back in her chair and smiled for the first time in many nights. This would be at least one weight off her shoulders. She debated calling Samuel again, running this past him, but decided rather petulantly not to bother. She was her own woman. She was the leader of an entire Kindred army. She could make her own decisions. Once it was done, she'd tell him. It's not like he was going to *complain* about her killing Beckett; he hated the bastard almost as much as she did, though she wasn't sure why.

Well, in a matter of hours, neither of them would have to worry about it anymore.

Jenna Cross's haven in the San Fernando Valley
Los Angeles, California

Tabitha stepped through the door and wandered away down the hallway. She didn't notice—nor did the two guards standing outside Cross's door—that she swerved once as she walked, as though stepping around an unseen obstacle.

The guards were two of the best Cross had. The thin-bloods had insisted she take precautions against Camarilla or MacNeil assassination attempts, and these two were that precaution. They were both some of the most highly trained, and most alert, of the LA thin-bloods. They both possessed powers of perception and observation not only beyond those of mortals, but beyond those of many more powerful Kindred.

It was unlikely in the extreme, however, that any intruder could even reach the guards. Further down, far enough that the guards themselves wouldn't trigger it, a state-of-the-art motion detector monitored the hall. Any motion in that portion of hallway larger than a roach and moving faster than a glacial crawl triggered a warning light, both in the hall itself and in Cross's meeting room.

Kapaneus stood in the hallway, arms crossed, head cocked to one side. Though he stood mere feet away from the guards, though Tabitha had brushed against him as she passed, nobody saw him. The motion detectors had remained quiescent as the elder approached, as they would when he left.

So, Cross was going to have him and Beckett killed, was she? Kapaneus felt a brief flash of anger, the prideful rage of a Beast he couldn't quite overcome even after centuries of solitude. A hand slowly reached out, hovered just before a thin-blood's ribcage. The guards in that hall were within inches of a swift and sudden end, one they would never even have seen coming.

But no, not like this. He'd attached himself to Beckett, had allowed the younger vampire to handle everything but those details he simply wasn't equipped to deal with. No sense in sowing any confusion in their working relationship at this stage.

Kapaneus lowered his arm and wandered back down the hallway. Let Beckett know of the situation, and handle it in his own way. Whatever he decided to do, it was sure to prove interesting.

The Mediterranean Coast
Western Turkey

Above, the Red Star shone.

Beneath, darkness rolled up from the waves like a second tide. It came ashore near the border with Syria, flooding over the beaches, over the sands, over the roads. City after city fell dark as it crawled north: Ceyhan, Kozan, Feke. Men, women and children rose shrieking from nightmares that rattled the soul, shattered sanity. Some few never woke at all, found dead beneath the blankets from causes no medical examiner could possibly determine. Fearing some new biological agent from the southeast, perhaps some remnant of the recent conflicts, soldiers moved across the border, clad in heavy protective gear, seeking any possible origin for the mysterious "cloud." Men died in accidental clashes and misunderstandings with Kurdish troops, but no trace of a rogue weapon or research facility was ever unearthed.

And the darkness continued north, snuffing all light in its path. Where it lingered, neither moon nor stars, fire nor electric light, shone. Where it passed, prayers of thanksgiving and cries of mourning sounded. When the sun rose, the darkness faded, dropping to earth and slowly dissipating as though sinking into the rocks and the ground, always rising again like a fog even as the last rays of daylight blinked out at the horizon. Villages evacuated where possible, for no matter the wind, no matter the terrain, the shadow's course remained steady, remained predictable.

North. Always and unerringly north.

Until, finally, it drifted to a halt. Not over any community, any village or city, but within a valley in the Taurus Mountains, south-southwest of Kayseri.

At the entrance to Kaymakli, on the very spot where Beckett had invoked his ritual and succeeded beyond his wildest dreams, the entity of shadow paused.

Tendrils of darkness flickered out, a tongue to scent the air and taste the earth. It dug into the sand, sensing the presence of the blood Beckett had spilt into the desert, no matter the months of evaporation and the many layers of sand blown across it.

Forward and back those tendrils moved, digging furrows in the sand, the gentle scrape of the grains the only sound to break the otherwise perfect stillness. They brushed against the stone of the cave and felt their way up and around the surface of the rock, outlining the passageway. Here they sensed the faint lingering traces of true power, the final signature of one nearly as ancient as the Abyssal thing itself. Here, weakened by the convergence of prophecy and by the illumination of an otherworldly red light, that power had shattered, rent asunder by one who should never have been capable of such a feat.

This was the center. This was the spot whence the call sounded, the long summoning that had drawn this thing from the depths of the Abyss, awakened other ancient powers from their own immeasurable slumber. Here it had begun, and the one who caused it had moved on, likely unaware of what had truly transpired.

And the thing thought, so far as its mind worked in ways humans might call "thinking." Was it a threat, this one? Did its presence here, at the beginning of the End, mark it as different, superior? Did it yet possess power, or had it merely been a catalyst, an insignificant spark to ignite a spreading inferno?

It had tasted him now, this thing of shadow had. Tasted

his presence, tasted his fear, tasted the power that had once infused this place and surely lingered still on he who had destroyed it. Let him run to the ends of the earth and beyond, let him hide in the deepest dark or brightest light. It mattered not.

As the sun rose, the darkness once more seeped into the ground to avoid the burning rays of a light even it could not snuff. Tomorrow night it would rise, and then it would travel north no more.

And above, in the growing light of dawn, the Red Star shone.

The Mission Inn
Riverside, California

The room was well away from the cluster of suites currently serving as the command center of the Camarilla's efforts in Los Angeles. According to the registry, a businessman from Portland named Robert Perkins occupied the room. Gossip among the staff had it that Perkins—a semi-regular at the Mission Inn—was spending most of his evenings in the company of his flavor-of-the-month mistress, and that was the reason the room was constantly off limits to cleaning staff.

In truth, Robert Perkins was currently on a well-earned vacation in Tahiti, and would have been rather surprised to learn that he was supposedly staying in Riverside. The staff of the Mission Inn would have been equally stunned to know he was in French Polynesia, since most of them remembered conversing with the man at various points throughout the last few days. The notion that those memories might have been implanted—as was the compulsion *never* to enter the room—would certainly never occur to them.

It was well known to the other high-ranking Kindred involved in the Camarilla efforts that this was where Hardestadt went to discuss matters not directly involved with the LA operations. They understood that, as the most active of the Inner Circle, the Ventrue Founder had far too many irons in the fire to focus solely on any one task, regardless of its import. Hardestadt was a leading strategist in the LA conflict, he was a prime shaper of the Camarilla's new direction and response to the withering, and he had God-only-knew-what-else going on as well. If he needed privacy to conduct some of that business, even the other elders, curious as they might be, were wise enough to give it to him.

Some of that respect for Hardestadt's privacy, of course, might have been inspired by the wards surrounding the room, preventing any Kindred or ghoul from entering without the Founder's express permission. He'd had it cast by several powerful Assamite sorcerers—the Camarilla's only reliable source of blood magics now that the Tremere had all up and vanished in a final paroxysm of melodramatic mystery.

In fact, those Assamite sorcerers had indirectly given him the idea he was now pursuing. Hardestadt sat in the room's only chair at the room's only desk. Normally, any visitor would be forced to sit on one of the beds, an informal and certainly undignified position intended to give Hardestadt a psychological edge in any conversations or negotiations.

His guest tonight simply remained standing, and Hardestadt was not about to take issue with that choice.

"I wish to thank you," Hardestadt began after the various niceties, formal greetings, and offers of refreshment had all been observed and exchanged, "for traveling so far on such short notice."

Tegyrius nodded once. His pointed beard—lightly streaked with gray, as was his dark hair—looked almost as if it was gesturing of its own accord. Beside revered al-Ashrad himself, Tegyrius was perhaps the most powerful of the so-called schismatics of Clan Assamite, those who had entered into alliance with the Camarilla rather than surrender to their mad elder Ur-Shulgi. "I was quite certain the Inner Circle would never make such a request of me without reason," he said.

"You mean you saw I needed a favor and jumped at the chance to hold a debt over me."

The Assamite smiled thinly. "That might play into it somewhat as well, yes."

"Fair enough. I have a problem I would like to go away. He is a threat to the Camarilla as a whole, but given the ongoing war and their efforts at rounding up insurgents, thin-bloods, and rogue Sabbat packs, no archons are currently available for reassignment."

In other words, Tegyrius knew but did not say, *he's more of a personal problem than a concern of the sect.* What he said instead was simply, "Who?"

"Beckett."

Tegyrius was not easily surprised, but that name raised an eyebrow. "Indeed. I've heard of this one."

"Good. Then I'll not have to tell you he's a dangerous one, and not to be toyed with."

"I do not toy, Hardestadt. Not with Beckett, and not with you. You want Beckett destroyed. I can have some of my clanmates take responsibility for seeing it happen. But Beckett is dangerous, these are troubled times, and most of my warriors are not as strong as once they were.

"It is no secret that the Camarilla is changing night by night, and that your hand is a leading one in that change. If I am to do this for you, I want nothing less than an equal position for my clan in the new order, with as loud a voice as any Toreador or Ventrue.

"Otherwise," Tegyrius continued even as Hardestadt opened his mouth to protest, "my clanmates will have to continue trading favors for influence. And I cannot guarantee that anything they learn from Beckett will remain secret."

Hardestadt slowly rose from his chair. "Are you attempting," he asked in a low growl, "to blackmail me with information you do not even *possess*?!"

"Not at all. I'm merely telling you the price of this particular contract, and to what desperate measures we might be forced—most reluctantly, I assure you—to resort if that price is not forthcoming."

The Ventrue glared a moment longer—and then suddenly, almost despite himself, he began to laugh. "I think you've been with the Camarilla too long already, Tegyrius. Your schemes are showing. All right. You solve this problem for me—and remain available for others down the road—and I will join my voice with yours when it comes time to formalize our new structure."

"Excellent. So... tell me what you can about Beckett."

Jenna Cross's haven in the San Fernando Valley
Los Angeles, California

When the smoke detector first began to shriek like a banshee in the predawn hour, Jenna Cross was absolutely positive it was a false alarm, a distraction arranged by Beckett or one of his companions for some nefarious purpose or other. Reacting swiftly, she snatched up a Glock, gathered half a dozen of her followers behind her, and marched directly toward the guest rooms the elders had been given. She wasn't worried about them escaping the house. Even if they knew they were in danger—and they couldn't possibly—every exit from the doors to the smallest windows to the mail slot was guarded. Her concern here was simply in seeing what sort of damage they might be doing.

She turned through the living room—and stopped dead in her tracks, jaws agape.

From the hallway before her rolled an enormous cloud of thick, jet-black smoke. It filled the doorway as it billowed through, immediately spreading out as though grateful to escape the confines of that small wing of the house. She couldn't hear the crackling of any flames over the piercing shriek of the smoke detector, but she had no doubt of their existence. Only a truly massive fire could generate volumes of smoke that large.

"Out!" she screamed, turning and dragging the first of her brethren back the way they'd come. "Get everyone *out!*"

They were in trouble. Dawn was less than an hour off, and they couldn't possibly extinguish a fire this size in that amount of time. Their best bet was to take shelter in the other houses occupied by their people, and to hope the fire department could bring this blaze under control before it spread to the surrounding buildings.

She had only two consolations, as she directed her people to evacuate in a swift but orderly fashion. One, as thin-bloods, she and her followers were more easily able to resist the instinctive fear all vampires felt in the face of fire, and thus able to avoid a complete panic that might well have caused further damage and injury. And two, whatever Beckett thought he might accomplish by setting such an enormous fire, he was either going to find himself trapped within it or faced by a mob of angry vampires when he fled from it. She had an overt excuse to have her people kill him now, and she wasn't about to waste it.

The smoke billowed out the front door as the thin-bloods—and, slowly but surely, other inhabitants of the neighborhood and passersby—gathered from directions to watch the house, and any who might come out of it. This first cloud drifted off over the lawn and faded away into the darkness.

And that was it. No fleeing prisoners. No roaring fire. Not even any more smoke.

"Shit!" Cross was racing back through the front door even as the first sirens sounded in the distance. It *was* a distraction—and apparently a damn good one. Nowhere during her brief, frantic search of the house could she find any sign of Beckett, Lucita or Kapaneus. And she didn't really have much time to search. The fire department was going to insist on looking the place over. She and her people had to take shelter in the other, nearby homes, as this would almost certainly take until well after dawn.

Cross, still seething, fell asleep that morning on the floor of a friend's bedroom with five other thin-bloods, growing ever more frightened of the man who'd escaped her—and wondering how the hell Beckett had done it.

The San Fernando Valley
Los Angeles, California

Some distance away, down on the bank of a small creek that served the neighborhood as a storm sewer, the cloud of smoke drifted. It moved slowly now, and any observers would have been puzzled to note it moving against the wind. Other than a few early-rising birds, however, and perhaps a number of frogs and lizards, no one was in a position to see it.

The air twisted briefly, almost seeming to wrinkle like stretched rubber or latex, and Kapaneus appeared from his cloak of obfuscation. He looked around him, listened to and scented the area, all with senses far more than human. They were alone.

"I believe it's safe," he announced in a loud voice.

The smoke roiled for a moment, and then came apart.

A bank of mist, the constant shift and flow of which had given the strange mass the illusion of rolling like smoke, now drifted away to hover over the grass. It left behind a core of absolute and utter darkness, an artificial shadow clearly unnatural in nature. Had Cross or her thin-bloods examined the smoke closely, they would likely have seen through the illusion, would have noticed that the shifting and rolling was a façade over a night-black center. But what vampire in her right mind would stay near a fire long enough to do that?

The mist gathered, twisted about itself until it formed a man-sized column, and solidified slowly until Beckett stood on the dew-wet grass. The darkness faded, revealing a haggard-looking Lucita ankle-deep in the creek.

"That," she wheezed as though short of breath, though that was clearly not the case, "was possibly the most idiotic thing I've done in many a century."

Beckett shrugged. "It worked, didn't it?"

"You and I both know from experience that success in an endeavor doesn't mean the endeavor wasn't asinine. You didn't know if you could concentrate your mist-form thickly enough to trigger the smoke alarm. I didn't know if I had the strength anymore to maintain an Abyssal cloud for so long. We should have set a real fire and been done with it."

"And risk being caught in the flames? To say nothing of destroying any hope of alliance between your resistance and the thin-bloods? I think not."

"Why," she retorted, "do you *care* about any alliances my organization makes? Or, for that matter, about the organization at all?"

"Because the more the Camarilla has to worry about you," he told her flatly, "the less they're focusing on me."

"Friends," Kapaneus interjected, "may I remind you that we no longer have eternity for discussion? The plan worked. We escaped the childer's haven without harming them. Can we worry now about finding shelter from the sun, and about what we're to do next, and less about whether the plan *should* have worked?"

Beckett and Lucita glanced at Kapaneus, then at each other, and nodded.

"How about there?" Beckett asked after a moment's contemplation. He pointed to a small concrete drain from which a trickle of water flowed to feed into the creek. "That should lead us far enough back to stay away from the sun."

Lucita scowled—it wasn't nearly as secure as she would have liked—but their options were precious few at this point. She acquiesced, as did Kapaneus.

"What of tomorrow?" Lucita asked, as they crawled their way through cold water, various molds and fungi, and other, unidentified substances. "You said you knew a way we might depart the city without encountering either the thin-bloods or Camarilla soldiers."

"Yeah," Beckett added, his tone not precisely encouraging. "A way we *might*. Ask me again in the evening."

Approaching Sewer Juncture 27-B
Beneath Los Angeles, California

The sewer systems of many European and American cities were far more elaborate and extensive than even planners and most sewer workers were aware. Through manipulation of city services and physical labor on their own part, the Nosferatu of these cities expanded chambers, connected passages, even added whole layers. They created vast underground networks, realms of their own where they might dwell with at least some measure of acceptance from those around them, rather than face the constant hatred and condescension that their inhuman appearance drew from most of those, Kindred and kine, who dwelt on the surface.

LA's warrens were somewhat less elaborate. It did appear, in many stretches, that the Nosferatu had once attempted to employ their traditional techniques, but the combination of California's tectonic instability, and the Kindred wars that raged in the city on and off for decades rendered much of that work futile. Here, a vaulted chamber with a single collapsed wall still saw use as a sanctuary or a crossroads; there, only a brief length of passage that ended in a concrete rockslide bore mute testament to the labyrinth that once honeycombed the earth.

The most modern portions of the sewer system had been built with various architectural and scientific techniques designed to make them quake resistant, and it was in these portions that the Nosferatu of Los Angeles spent most of their time. It was difficult to hide their presence from workers, true, and almost impossible to build more than the smallest of additions without being discovered, but they made do.

Only because these details conspired to make the LA sewers and warrens less complex than those of other, comparably sized cities could Beckett even *think* of doing what he was doing.

Okulos didn't have any real pull with the Nosferatu of LA, all of whom were either thin-bloods (who would attempt to stop Beckett on Cross's behalf), Camarilla infiltrators, saboteurs, sentries (who would attempt to stop Beckett on Hardestadt's behalf), or MacNeil anarchs (who would attempt to destroy any intruders in their domain out of fear and general territorial principle). Okulos was unable, despite his efforts, to arrange for a guide, or for any easy avenues of escape to be left unguarded. He did manage to e-mail a rough map of the sewer system, including at least some of the Nosferatu "improvements," and an even rougher schedule of Camarilla and thin-blood patrols near the borders.

That was a great deal more than many could have obtained, but it frustrated Beckett that the unnamed contacts Okulos had called on to find Jenna Cross and to guide him to her without incident, now seemed unwilling to provide any assistance. Beckett had made a mental note to ask about that, when he had the opportunity.

In any event, it wasn't the first time Beckett had picked his way through a hostile labyrinth, guided only by an inaccurate map. Most of said previous labyrinths had been located deep in ancient jungle ruins or beneath the shifting desert sands. Doing it while cars roared past far above him, while in constant danger of being drenched by some apartment-dweller's flushing toilet, was a new and not entirely welcome permutation.

He, Lucita and Kapaneus were now in the midst of their second night in the sewers, which they'd crawled to from the drainage pipe where they'd first sheltered. As risky a proposition as traveling by sewer might be, it was less dangerous than trying to make a break for it aboveground, where Cross and her thin-bloods were no doubt actively hunting for them and watching every possible thoroughfare.

They'd already slogged for hours tonight, through calf-deep sludge, feeding on slime-slick rats and dodging falling roaches. The scent was so overpowering that all three spoke as infrequently as possible, to avoid drawing breath, but the miasma of human waste invaded their nostrils regardless, refusing to be ignored. They couldn't afford to take what would otherwise have been the swiftest, most direct route: that would keep too close to Cross's center of power, where the searchers would be most numerous. Walking across half of LA was a time-consuming process, though, especially since Beckett's map didn't take into account any of the most recent damage caused by the ongoing three-way war. They'd lost upwards of three hours to backtracking and detours already, with no indication that the remainder of the journey would be any easier.

They were picking their way across a thin, slime-covered brick ledge, overlooking a ten-foot drop into deep sewage, and had just ducked beneath a stream of foul water flowing from a rusty grate, when Lucita placed a hand on Beckett's shoulder. "Stop," she hissed, her whisper barely audible over the rushing water. "Do you smell that?"

Beckett, who had received a face-full of filth, was trying hard not to smell anything at all. With Lucita's warning, however, he focused past the stench and took a deep breath.

He did indeed sense it, a fact he conveyed with a nod once the urge to retch had sufficiently passed. There, almost buried beneath the aroma of sewage, was the faintest tang of Kindred blood. Was someone injured down here, or...

Oh, shit.

Beckett moved forward, edging his way around an upcoming corner. As he moved, he felt a sudden pressure on his foot. Glancing down, he had to suppress a shudder as a cockroach the length of a hot dog crawled across him. He could actually feel the weight of its legs through his boot. That alone was sufficient confirmation. He knew what he would see even before he'd made it completely around the turn.

There, around the bend, a trio of walkways came together around a raised cistern, kept separate from the surrounding sewage. The water in the cistern apparently came from curbside gutters above, and consisted largely of rainwater and whatever detritus happened to wash down with it. Hardly appetizing, but for those animals living down here, a source of drinkable water.

It was from that cistern that the smell of Kindred blood emerged, and in a Nosferatu warren, that could mean only one thing: a spawning pool. Commonly found in larger warrens, Nosferatu created spawning pools by spilling bits of their blood into a local water source. The animals who drank regularly from it not only grew loyal to the Nosferatu, but they often mutated, growing larger, stronger, fiercer.

Beckett opened his mouth to warn his companions— and was struck from a nearby passage by what felt like a car doing eighty-five. Beckett slid several yards back across the slimy stones until he fetched up against his companion's legs. Instantly he was on his feet, his talons sliding from his fingertips, staring at the thing that had struck him.

It had, at one point, been a rottweiler, to judge by the shape of the head, the tone of the growl, and the color of what little fur wasn't coated by filth and slime. It was easily the size of a small horse, and its jaws were distended by oversized teeth. Those jaws, Beckett realized, had already failed once to penetrate his jacket and toughened skin. They were already gaping open again as the dog-thing leaped once more for his throat.

Beckett swiftly shoved his left forearm deep into the dog's mouth, preventing it either from ripping his throat out or from closing its teeth completely around his arm. Still, the pain of those rear teeth tearing into his flesh was substantial. The dog was clearly strong enough to overcome a large portion of Beckett's preternatural resilience. His other hand clutched the dog around the ribs, claws digging into its side, spilling copious amounts of blood.

Unfortunately, Beckett could do nothing to counter the momentum of being struck by a creature that outweighed him by nearly two to one. The struggling pair toppled backwards even as they fought. Beckett experienced an instant of freefall before his back hit the sewage below with a heavy splash and he sank beneath layers of scum-covered refuse and was caught in a slow-moving but powerful current.

Drainage Chamber 13
Beneath Los Angeles, California

Some minutes later and some indeterminate distance away, Beckett found himself falling once more. He and the now-motionless dog shot from a drainage tube high on the wall of a large collection chamber. Beckett had a brief flash of a circular room, numerous tubes all around the room flushing water into the central pool where it in turn flowed out through various floor-level tunnels, before he hit the water yet again. Fortunately he landed near a small raised floor, one of several areas designed for repair crews to stand and evaluate the flow of sewage. Digging his claws deep into the stone, he paused long enough to shake the dead dog off his shredded arm. Then, as the body slowly sank out of sight, he hauled himself out of the muck, spitting raw sewage from his mouth and throat. Ignoring the stinging pain in his arm, he rose to his feet and looked around him.

In the confusion of the battle, he hadn't really noticed which of the various sluice gates he'd fallen through. Still, with his sense of direction, it shouldn't be *too* hard to backtrack and find his companions. It was just a matter of—

"Have you any idea," came a rodent-like, high-pitched shriek, "how long it took to grow him to that size?! And now you've *ruined* him! I'll have to start over!"

Beckett looked up, and up. There, near the ceiling, a small passage with a broken grate opened onto a thin metal platform that had once been part of a catwalk now long gone. Standing atop that platform was a gnarled, hunched figure no more than four feet in height. His features, so far as Beckett could see from this distance, were distorted and distended, as though his face were a balloon filled beyond safe capacity. Standing behind was a second rottweiler, not quite so large as the one that lay dead beside Beckett, but still large enough to tear a man to shreds in a matter of instants.

"You should be more careful who you sic your pets on then, shouldn't you?" Beckett called up, hands quivering with anger. The Beast paced within him, wanting nothing so much as to sink its claws into the Nosferatu's heart.

"You'll pay for this! All of you, you and the ones who arrived with you!" The strange little vampire seemed almost to dance back and forth across the broken catwalk, so wild was his rage. "I'll feed you to my pets! I'll saturate their pool with your blood! I'll—"

Beckett dropped his inner guard, allowing the Beast to rise up within him. His vision went red, and he felt his lips curling back in a snarl. The world seemed to recede before the Beast's ascendance.

But frenzy here, with the Nosferatu so far out of reach, would do him no good. That was not why he allowed his bestial nature to emerge. Just before Beckett would have lost control, would have ceased really to be Beckett, he clamped his will down hard on the Beast and pushed out and up. In a show of willpower and a familiarity with the Beast that few other Kindred possessed, he transferred his fury and his hate into someone else.

Or, in this particular case, some*thing*.

The Nosferatu was still ranting and raving when his

second rottweiler struck him from behind like a freight train, cracking bone, sinking canines into sagging flesh, and carrying both Nosferatu and canine off the catwalk in an echo of Beckett's own experience moments earlier. The vampire's tirade blurred into a single high-pitched squeal as he fell, to vanish utterly when they hit the murky water.

Instantly Beckett dove after them, his preternatural senses allowing him to home in on the thrashing pair as easily as a shark on a thrashing seal. He sank his talons into the Nosferatu's back, filling the water around him with blood. Beckett's Beast fled from the rottweiler and reasserted its place in the vampire's own soul, but he forced it to remain quiescent, denied its urge to bite the Nosferatu and drain him dry. Instead, lifting with his uninjured arm, Beckett dragged his foe from the sewage and laid him out flat atop the nearby stones. The dog, frightened and confused by the power and rage of Beckett's Beast, fled into the tunnels the instant it was free.

"Now," Beckett growled, a talon held just over the soft flesh where the Nosferatu's left eyelid joined his face, "I'm going to ask you some questions." His other hand clutched the side of the Nosferatu's head, the claws hovering about—and in some cases just within—his distended ear. "How many senses you lose depends entirely on how quickly and thoroughly you answer. Since I wouldn't recommend nodding at the moment, tell me if you understand."

"I understand!" The Nosferatu's voice was loud, piercing. "I understand, I understand!"

"Good. Let's get started."

Sewer Juncture 27-B
Beneath Los Angeles, California

"His name was Roger, or so he told me. He was one of the MacNeil anarchs," Beckett explained to his companions after the Nosferatu's terrified directions had led him back to the tunnel in which they'd first been attacked. Lucita and Kapaneus were both covered in a myriad of small wounds where others of the Nosferatu's ghoul menagerie had attacked them, but they'd apparently come through their own conflict not really any worse for wear. They'd still been debating whether to go in search of Beckett or to wait for him to return when he found them. "He was told we were coming. And he was waiting for us—or, more specifically, for me."

"Why?" Lucita asked, her mouth quirked in an expression of revulsion as she drank the remaining blood from a rat—one they'd taken far, far from the spawning pool. "Who wants you dead?"

"Who doesn't?" Beckett rejoined bitterly. "Right now I've managed to piss off both Hardestadt the Founder *and* Jenna Cross, to say nothing of any of the other enemies I've accumulated over the years. I'm not sure why either of them would resort to making deals with the MacNeils when they've got their own people, though. According to Roger, the order came from a higher-up in the MacNeil organization. He doesn't know why."

"That," Kapaneus interjected thoughtfully, "does not concern me nearly so much as the fact that this Nosferatu was waiting for us here specifically. Whoever our enemy in this instance may be, he knows that we are in the sewers."

"Probably," Lucita said thoughtfully. "It could just be a fortunate guess—our options were somewhat limited, after all—but I'd hate to rely on that."

"Whichever the case," Beckett told them, "this wasn't a total waste of time. Our rat-like friend was only too happy to direct me on the fastest way out of here. We should be outside LA city limits by tomorrow night."

"You're certain he told you truth?" Kapaneus asked.

"Oh, quite certain. He'd lied to me once already, and he knew *very* well not to do it again."

"What did you do?" Lucita asked him.

Beckett shrugged. "I gave him an earful."

He pretended not to notice the looks his companions gave him at that comment, a comment intended to hide the revulsion that filled him to the core of his being. He felt like something unclean had crawled inside him and died. A predator he had always been, but never casually cruel. When he'd finally slain the helpless Nosferatu, it was an act of mercy as much as self-preservation. What he'd done to Roger was necessary—he *had* to have his answers—but Beckett knew he'd feel filthy long after the last of the sewage was washed from his skin.

Drainage Chamber 13
Beneath Los Angeles, California

Some time after the echoes of the fugitives' footsteps had receded into the distance, a figure appeared in the central drainage chamber. Samuel, his flannel shirt soaked in sewage, emerged from one of the tunnels, picking his way carefully over pockets of sludge and other flotsam. He stepped silently over several sections of broken stone, made jagged and loose by the last quake, until he stood at the spot where the Nosferatu had died. Bits of sodden ash clung to the slime in a pattern that, if one looked hard enough, still suggested a human shape.

He crouched by the remains of the corpse, careful not to get any of his cat's-paw's remains on him, and shook his head. He hadn't expected this little exercise to result in Beckett's death—frankly, he'd have been disappointed if it had—but he'd hoped for a longer delay than this. As it was, they'd likely be out of the sewers in another day. Sure, he still had time to put the next phase into motion, but Beckett, despite all obstacles, was proceeding at a rapid pace. *That* wouldn't do at all. It was time to start sharing some more information.

Samuel stood, then, and proceeded toward the nearest manhole. As he climbed, his visage and outfit blurred briefly, shifted, just in case any of Roger's allies happened to be nearby. The figure that appeared on the street looked very much like Calvin Roper, a member in good standing of the MacNeil anarchs—and, not incidentally, the man who'd told Roger to wait for Beckett in the sewers. He opened a small cellular phone, dialed a number from memory, and waited patiently as it rang.

"I need to speak to Jenna Cross," he announced in a voice that didn't match his new appearance. "Tell her it's Samuel. Tell her I have some information for her about Beckett—and his means of transportation."

Somewhere over the Western United States

With the Nosferatu's more immediate knowledge of the tunnels added to the map and the information provided by Okulos, the rest had been easy, if not precisely pleasant. They'd avoided no fewer than three coteries of thin-bloods, and at least one group of Camarilla infiltrators, and emerged the following night into another drainage ditch outside the LA city limits. Then it was simply a matter of hiking to the nearest convenient spot—a convenience store and gas station, as it turned out—and acquiring a vehicle. (Kapaneus and Lucita, who hadn't really had the stomach to drink their fill of the Nosferatu's animals, had been as happy with the driver as Beckett had with the car.) Kapaneus had also detected a few more of Cross's thin-bloods at the airport in Apple Valley, but they didn't seem especially alert. Beckett felt it probable that Cross was watching *all* regional airports, as opposed to her having learned anything specific about Beckett's location. Since they knew the spies were there, it was a simple matter of avoiding them long enough to board the plane and for Cesare to obtain clearance for takeoff. Now they were headed for Dallas, but whether they were picking up or dropping off wasn't entirely clear yet.

Beckett sat at the desk that occupied the better part of one wall of the cabin. Kapaneus, in a very un-elder-like pose, was sprawled out across his sleeping bag, and Lucita perched on the edge of Beckett's coffin. Though they'd spent nights together picking their way through the sewers, they'd done little real talking. It hadn't seemed appropriate, somehow.

"Beckett," Lucita finally asked him after several moments of uncomfortable silence, "how certain are you? Truthfully."

He didn't have to ask what she meant. "Utterly," he told her, his voice neutral. "As certain as I've ever been of anything, Lucita. The withering, the disappearance of entire clans, what I found in Etrius's journal… I fought against it for a long time, but I can't hide anymore. This isn't some blood curse. It's not a disease. Gehenna really is upon us."

"I thought you didn't believe in Gehenna."

"I didn't."

More silence then.

"And you truly believed Smiling Jack might be able to help you?"

"It seemed a good idea at the time." Beckett frowned. "My only other lead is a Salubri named Rayzeel who supposedly awakened some years ago. She's supposed to be a childe of Saulot himself. But I'll be buggered if I know where to look for her." He felt the urge to break something rise within him. "Damn it, if only I had more *time*! For all the myths and legends, we know so little… I don't even know how long Gehenna is supposed to take."

"Well, then," Lucita asked, "what do you propose to do about it?"

"I'm more determined than ever to find my answers," Beckett began. "Whatever else, this proves to me that we, as Kindred, have—or at least *had*—some purpose to our existence, and I'm going to learn—"

"Yes, yes, that's nice. I meant what are you going to do about Gehenna itself?"

Beckett blinked. She couldn't be asking what he thought she was asking.

"Do?"

"Yes. How do you plan to stop it?"

"Lucita…" Beckett shook his head. "This is *Gehenna*. It can't *be* stopped. As soon stop the sun from rising or the tide from coming in."

"Nonsense." Lucita rose to her feet and began to pace, so far as the size of the cabin would allow. Even only taking a couple of steps in each direction, Beckett was astounded at the grace of her movements. Lucita might be weaker than she'd been in centuries, but she didn't show it in her poise.

"I've spent a thousand years fighting that which supposedly could not be fought," she continued. "I broke free of Monçada, a power that everyone said could never be deterred. For centuries I opposed the entire Sabbat, and they never defeated me. In fact they welcomed me when I *chose* to join them. I do not believe any fight is hopeless, if you approach it properly."

"Is that why you abandoned the fight to hold to your humanity?" Beckett asked, a trace of bitterness in his voice.

Lucita actually smiled. "You don't understand. I didn't abandon the fight to maintain my humanity. I *won* the battle to figure out what I am."

"And is it what you want to be?"

Now she scowled. "As I said, I need not explain myself to you."

"Not at all. You just need to explain yourself to *you*, and I don't think you've really done that yet."

The tension in the air grew so thick, Beckett was surprised it didn't blow out the windows. He wondered, briefly, if he'd made a mistake; if he might have made Lucita angry enough to attack him even here, in such a confined— and fragile—environment. Kapaneus propped himself up on an elbow, watching the dark-haired woman intently.

Instead, however, she merely clenched her fists so hard Beckett could hear the knuckles crack. "Are you going to help me stop this?" she asked gruffly.

For a brief instant, Beckett wavered. What if they could? What if they really could halt, or at least postpone, the coming destruction? After all, he still didn't know why he seemed less affected by the withering than others of his age. Perhaps he *could* do something?

No. No, it wouldn't work. Beckett had gained a newfound respect for the ancient myths in the past weeks— and every one of those myths, every legend he'd ever heard, stated with absolute certainty that this could not be changed, that it must run its course. If his unusual resilience to the withering suggested anything, it was that he was being granted more time to find his answers. He wouldn't waste that tilting at windmills. He had his own answers to find, and he wouldn't gamble them on the futile hope that every recognized source was wrong.

"I can't," he said simply. "And frankly, I don't think you can either. You would be better off completing any unfinished business you may yet have, Lucita. Surely you, of all Cainites, know how to face death when it finally comes." He paused, thought for a moment.

Why don't you and your allies come with me? he almost asked. *With greater numbers, we stand a better chance of finding our answers; you'd at least know why it's all happened.*

But he didn't ask. Even as he opened his mouth, he could have sworn he heard a voice—Anatole's voice—saying, "I wouldn't. You can't trust her anymore, Beckett. She's not who she was."

It was almost certainly a hallucination, perhaps a lingering echo of his dreams. Yet despite himself, he obeyed. Instead, he said, "Is there someplace we can take you and your people before we leave the States?"

"What if I asked you to take us with you?" Lucita asked. She clearly meant it as a challenge, not an offer.

"Can't do it. Look around you, Lucita. It's hard enough getting a private plane through customs these days, especially with some of the unusual living conditions back here. To say nothing of damn expensive, between legal permits and bribes. No way in hell I could smuggle an entire hold full of undocumented passengers—or apparent corpses, if it happens to be daylight out."

"Ah, Beckett. Always an excuse why you *can't* do it." Lucita turned and opened the door to the chamber. "I believe I'll spend the remainder of the flight in the cockpit, with Cesare." As she left, she called back, "Just drop me off near Dallas, as we'd discussed. I'll rejoin my people there, and we'll continue to fight as best we can. You go search for your precious answers." The door didn't quite slam—that would be beneath Lucita—but it closed with a definite firmness.

"Is Cesare safe with her?" Kapaneus asked.

"Oh yeah. Lucita may be angry, but she's not suicidal, and she doesn't know how to fly one of these things any more than I do."

And with that, there was nothing at all to do but wait.

Braque et Chabrol Textiles
Lille, France

Though a substantial portion of those who held seats at this council were unable to attend due to their duties elsewhere in the world, the assembly still represented an enormous portion of the Camarilla's highest. Princes and justicars, Inner Circle members and sect Founders, all sat or stood around the massive basement chamber beneath the textiles plant. Various neonates, "criminals" often guilty of no crime greater than ill luck, lay staked about the perimeter of the room, where attendees could easily access them to slake their thirst.

Several devices recorded the proceedings, for later review by those—such as Hardestadt himself, many of the world's most powerful princes, and several of the justicars and Inner Councilors—who could not attend. The data was, as always, heavily encrypted and sent via multiple secured lines.

"The point I was *attempting* to make," Prince Voorhies of Amsterdam announced with an irritated glance at Carlak of Prague, "is that at least in my own city, and elsewhere too as I understand it, force is proving insufficient to maintain order. This is *not*, as some would have it, a failure of my rule." He glared around at several others who had spoken. "As the withering grows stronger, and more and more neonates experience what we have dealt with for months, they seek reasons. We cannot allow them to dwell upon Gehenna as an explanation, obviously, but neither can we simply continue incarcerating those who suggest it. We require an explanation to feed them, and it must be consistent."

"Agreed." Madame Guil, Justicar of the Clan Toreador, rose to her feet. Normally, she would have been heavily involved in Hardestadt's efforts to retake Los Angeles, for the Western United States was one of her primary arenas of operation. She was here now simply because she found herself at loose ends; Hardestadt had steadfastly refused to work with her, owing to some past conflict or other. "Our protestations of diseases and curses grow pathetically thin. We cannot continue telling our childer what the withering *may* be. We must tell them what it *is*."

"Thank you," Voorhies said in acknowledgment of the justicar's support. "We need not worry as to whether our explanation is true or not. It must simply be believable, and universal."

"Oh, I don't know," Prince Nicholas of Kent spoke up. "I, for one, would very *much* like to know the truth of what's happening. Several of us have already mentioned our suspicions regarding the timing of the Tremere disappearance. Surely we should be looking very closely into the notion that it's more than coincidence."

On the other side of the room, another vampire rose to her feet. Short of stature as she was, Queen Anne of London radiated an aura of confidence and control unmatched by most of those present, even those far older than she. "I agree," she announced in a clear and regal voice. "But I also maintain, as have many others, that we must control the damage to our society before we can move onward. That said, I maintain that the Tremere have handed us our solution on a silver platter. The timing of their disappearance works well for us, regardless of their true guilt or innocence. Why not simply place the blame for the withering upon their heads publicly and openly? Such would not only give the neonates somewhere to focus their anger, we might also distract them by employing them in a search for the missing Tremere."

"The esteemed Queen Anne," Guil offered, "has succeeded admirably in keeping her own city calm, but I believe this has led her to underestimate the mood beyond her walls. Her suggestion is noted, and it would be a good one, save that the fear and anger of the neonates is beyond any phantom enemy. Were we to hand them the Tremere as a scapegoat, when no Tremere remain to be had, to suffer the vengeance of the masses, they would not believe."

"True." Jaroslav Pascek, the deceptively delicate-looking Brujah justicar, carried less weight in these councils than once he had. The defection of Theo Bell, long something of a mascot for Camarilla supporters, had seriously marred the reputation of the justicar under whom he had worked. Still, Pascek held the office, and his voice would be heard. "What we need, then, is an enemy the neonates can see. One they can fight—ostensibly, anyway."

Francois Villon, Prince of Paris, raised an eyebrow. "Whom do you propose?"

"The Assamites."

The uproar that swept the chamber took several minutes, and a substantial amount of shouting by all the justicars present, to quell. When it finally died down, it was the voice of Prince McTiernan of Indianapolis that uttered what most in the room were thinking.

"You're mad! Now, of all times, we cannot afford to alienate our newest allies! We *need* the Assamites, need the skill at battle, at espionage—and now, with the Tremere absent, at blood sorcery—they provide! You would throw away one of our greatest assets!"

"I would do no such thing." Pascek glanced around, his unblinking gaze steady enough, piercing enough, to cow even elders into looking away. "What I propose would, if anything, draw the Assamites to us ever more firmly.

"We blame the withering on the blood sorcerers of the Alamut loyalists. It is both an attack on Camarilla sovereignty and a punishment levied against those of their own clan who had the enlightenment to join us. This not only provides our own masses with an enemy on whom to focus, it will inspire those Assamites who wish to prove their loyalty to us to hunt down their brethren. Surely they will expect suspicion to fall on them as well, and they will seek to do all they can to turn it aside."

"And if any of our own discover that the Assamites too suffer from the withering?" Prince Villon asked. "What then?"

"Really, Villon," Voorhies interjected. "Camarilla Assamites are hardly likely to spread word of that fact even if they learn of it; they'd be too concerned that they wouldn't be believed, that it would be seen as a ploy to protect their clanmates. And who else is likely to have opportunity to observe or speak to a loyalist Assamite for long enough to make any such discovery?"

Again, muttering rolled through the room like a wave, but it was softer this time, less angry. Clearly a number of those present were at least considering the merits of the justicar's plan.

"We have a proposal," Madame Guil announced, bringing the discussion once more to a halt. "Is it seconded?"

Prince Voorhies rose to his feet once more and nodded. "It seems sound. It not only provides a solution to our immediate problem, but allows us time to hunt for the *true* source of the withering, be it the Tremere or something else. I second."

"Then, as this is not an issue even the Inner Circle of the justicars should decide on their own, let us vote on it. All in favor, raise…"

The Toreador justicar trailed off in confusion as a warm breeze swept through the room. She felt it on her skin—as did the others, clearly, for they all looked around them, perhaps seeking an open window despite the fact they were in a basement—yet it did not ruffle her hair, nor her clothes.

Rather than fade, as would be expected of a fluke gust, the wind increased. It carried along its forward edge the tang of blood, and oddly, the dry taste of sand.

Guil peered around alertly, drawing upon senses and powers of observation that would make even one such as Beckett seem blind in comparison. She saw the source of the desert wind.

Madame Guil's deafening scream, the pitiable cry of a four-hundred-year-old child, echoed through the chamber, piercing the ears of those nearest her like needles. The justicar collapsed to her knees, hands clutching at a face suddenly covered in blood. Almost as one, the assembly was on its feet, confusion and a growing fear evident in their eyes and on their faces.

The tang of blood grew thicker, the roar of the wind grew stronger still, and Jaroslav Pascek was the first to be slain. He simply blinked once, as though confused by a sudden thought, and crumbled into dust, drained instantly of blood and soul and everything that he was. In the chaos, it took a few moments for anyone to notice.

The destruction of Prince Voorhies of Amsterdam, who had seconded Pascek's movement, and of Prince Villon, who had already begun to raise his hand as Guil called for the vote, was somewhat more obvious. The pair had sat near the center of the room, arranged on either side of Prince Kleist of Berlin. Half the eyes in the chamber were upon Kleist, then, when he was suddenly showered in ash from both sides as Voorhies and Villon both died and decomposed where they stood.

And just like that, it was over. The wind faded away and was gone, the scent of blood vanished beneath the normal city smells of exhaust and mortal sweat that filtered down from above. In the center of the room, Madame Guil curled about herself, shrieking in a voice that grew swiftly hoarse. Her blood seeped freely from between lids that covered split and useless eyes.

Though all their instinct told them to flee, every vampire in the chamber seemed rooted to the spot. Though the Beast demanded flight, their higher brains simply could not process what had just happened. Minutes passed, and Guil's screams slowly faded into unintelligible rasps. Finally, her hands visibly shaking in her first show of overt fear in many a century, Queen Anne of London stepped forward.

"All in support?" she asked, her voice almost quivering. No response. "All opposed?"

Every hand in the room shot upward as if trying to escape the arms to which they were attached.

"Motion defeated. Meeting adjourned."

Anne was the first one out the door.

Beginning descent into Dallas/Fort Worth International Airport
Dallas, Texas

"All right," Beckett said, resting his elbows on the platter-sized café table. "Now I know I'm crazy."

"Why is that?" Anatole asked him, idly stirring non-dairy

creamer into a mug full of blood.

"Because it's the middle of the night. If it's the middle of the night, I can't be dreaming. If I'm not dreaming, this is a hallucination. Ergo, I'm crazy."

Anatole sighed. "Either that, or this really is a visitation, and I'm really speaking to you."

Beckett glanced around. The table at which they sat was the same one from Anatole's first visit. Rather than sitting on a Paris street, however, it was now surrounded by utter darkness. The bizarre chewing noises Beckett had heard the first time still sounded in the distance, as if they were moving away.

"If it is, you sure have a strange taste in meeting places."

"Thus proving that I'm in fact the crazy one, not you. Therefore, this really must be me, mustn't it?"

Beckett's head hurt even trying to follow that logic, so he gave up.

"The clock is ticking, Beckett," Anatole continued. "The sands are running out, you're on the last lap, the two minute warning has sounded, the sixth seal is breaking. You don't have a lot of time."

"Believe it or not, I'm aware of that." Beckett shook his head. "I don't know what to do, Anatole. I couldn't find the answers I'm looking for in the past three centuries. What makes me think I can do it in months, or weeks?"

"Nothing more or less than the fact that you must. Necessity is the best motivator. Believe me, I know."

"The damn thing of it is," Beckett explained, his voice suddenly tired, "I have a lead. Possibly the best I've ever had. But I don't know how to follow it up! I know who I have to find, but I don't have the first clue where she is!"

"My, yes, that must be frustrating." Anatole pointedly stirred his beverage. "It's a shame you don't know of any Noddist scholar and lore-keeper who's been gathering knowledge since the Middle Ages and keeps all that information in a big private library."

Beckett's jaw dropped. "No. No way. You can't believe I'm insane enough to go there."

"Hey," Anatole said with a shrug, "this is your hallucination, remember? You're obviously crazy enough." He smiled, showing perfectly white teeth unstained by the blood he sipped.

Beckett blinked and looked around the cabin in some confusion. Kapaneus was staring at him, concern evident in his face. "Are you well, Beckett?"

"I'm..." Beckett shook his head. "I'm fine, I think. What happened?"

"I'm not certain. I thought at first you were merely lost in thought, but you went utterly still, for several minutes straight. I initially feared you had somehow entered torpor."

"Odd." Beckett gave some brief thought to telling his companion about his vision, or dream, or hallucination, or whatever, but decided against it. No reason to panic the elder by letting him know he was traveling with a crazy person.

"Lucita still up front?" he asked.

"Indeed. Your ghoul informs us that we shall be landing momentarily."

"We won't be staying. We're dropping Lucita off and that's it. I think I know where we need to go next."

Dallas/Forth Worth International Airport
Dallas, Texas

Theo Bell walked at a steady pace across the open grass between the security fence and the distant runway. He wasn't supposed to be here, but he'd always been of the impression that any security system not good enough to keep him out wasn't even worth acknowledging. Besides, he had things to do.

Lucita's phone call had been brief. She hadn't told him how things went in LA, or what she suggested for their next step. He knew only that she was arriving on a private jet, and that she'd appreciate it if he would meet her there.

This late at night, it was unusual even for an airport as large as DFW to make use of these most distant runways. Even more so when the plane in question was a private one, rather than an airliner. Apparently, either Lucita or whoever was with her had arranged some sort of "special consideration." Bell wondered idly what the dollar value of that consideration had been.

His eyes narrowed as he approached the runway. He could already see the blinking lights of the plane in the distance—or at least he assumed it was the plane he was waiting for, since it seemed to be coming almost straight at him. What concerned him, however, were the three individuals lurking near the hanger. Bell was certain they weren't an airport maintenance crew, unless DFW had begun issuing uniform trench coats.

He shook his head. Trench coats. Yeah, *those* were inconspicuous. Idly carrying his SPAS-15 over his right shoulder, Bell sauntered up to the skulking trio.

"I'm terribly sorry," he said as he approached, "but I think you wanted baggage carousel C. That's over in the terminal, that way."

All three spun to face him, hands darting inside coats to reach for weapons they probably thought were well concealed. Bell had already counted and identified them.

"You got one chance to leave," one of them snarled at Bell in a voice that was intended to sound gruff. "We're not here for you."

"Good for you." Bell glanced to the left. The plane would be touching down any second, reach the end of the runway in just a minute or two. "But since you're probably here for the same people I am, that ain't going to cut it. So I'll make you the same offer. *You* get one chance. Fuck off, before this gets ugly."

The spokesman for the trio scowled. "All right, asshole, you had your—"

Without lifting it from his shoulder, Bell fired the shotgun, wincing slightly as the blast sounded right in his ear. He heard a splattering sound from behind him, followed by a loud thump. Three pairs of eyes grew suddenly very wide as they stared at him.

"Did you *really* think I didn't hear him coming?" Bell asked. "Motherfucker stomps like a damn rhino."

The lurkers immediately drew pistols and opened fire—not that it mattered, since Bell wasn't where they were aiming anymore, anyway.

When it was over, Bell was fairly disgusted at how long

it took. He hadn't weakened nearly as much as Lucita, given that he was far younger, but his periods of strength were growing less frequent, and his periods of weakness growing longer. He wasn't as fast as he should be, or as strong. Still, he had more than he needed to take out a trio of inexperienced fuck-ups like these, but it shouldn't have taken him a full two minutes to do it. By the time he looked up from the slowly decomposing corpses scattered about him, the plane had not only landed, but taken off once more.

"Huh," he commented.

"Nice job, Bell."

"Jesus!" Bell spun, shotgun leveled, as Lucita slipped from the darkness beside him. "Fuck, Lucita, don't *do* that!"

"I'm sorry," she told him in a tone of voice that clearly indicated she was nothing of the sort. "Did I startle you?"

"Startle?! If my colon still worked, I'd have shit my drawers!"

"My, how colorful."

As the pair began a leisurely stroll back toward the edge of the airport property, Bell gestured with the barrel of his gun at those he'd just slain. "These fools barely knew one end of a gun from the other. No way they were a Camarilla hit team. I'm gonna guess your negotiations with Cross didn't go so well."

She told him, as they walked, recounting everything that had occurred during her trip to LA. Bell listened intently, interrupting her only once as she was in the midst of describing their escape from Cross's home.

"How do you know this guy, this Kapainus—"

"Kapaneus," she corrected.

"Whatever. How do you know this Kapaneus guy told you the truth? You only had his word he overheard Cross planning to smoke the lot of you. How do you know he wasn't just trying to fuck up our discussions with them for his own purposes?"

Lucita frowned, her brow furrowed. "No," she said finally, thoughtfully, "I don't believe so. Considering how hostile Cross was to Beckett, I'd actually find it more suspicious if she *hadn't* tried something."

Still, Lucita was concerned. It wasn't that she thought Bell was right, so much that the possibility had never even occurred to her. She'd simply trusted the strange elder's word instinctively, and Lucita had survived far too long to trust anyone without very good reason.

Well, it was done now, whatever the case. And there were larger issues to worry about. Moving on, she finished her recounting at about the time she and Bell reached the airport fence line.

"Gehenna, huh?" Bell bent down to give the weakened Lasombra a boost over the fence, then stepped back and made a running leap over the razor wire. He landed with a muffled thump and an impact that would have driven the breath from anything that still needed breath to begin with. "Beckett's sure about that?"

"He is. And you cannot expect me to believe you hadn't considered it yourself, for all that we've spent months talking around the subject."

"Lucita," he told her as they once more resumed walking, this time toward the van he'd stashed some ways away, "from the night I was Embraced, I was brought up to believe Gehenna was a myth, a bunch of bullshit mysticism laid down by elders to justify their own positions and perversions." He shook his head. "I'd be an idiot to deny what I'm seeing, but it ain't easy to accept."

"Good. Because we're not going to accept it."

Bell stopped in his track, and turned. "Sorry, say that again in my *good* ear."

"Beckett's given up already. He doesn't believe this can be stopped. I do. So we're going to."

"Uh-huh. And how we going to do that?"

Lucita smiled. "Beckett mentioned a Salubri called Rayzeel, a childe of Saulot and a scholar of old who'd recently awakened. He didn't know how to find her."

"And you do?"

"Not personally, no. But I've had some dealings with the new line of Salubri who are now part of the Sabbat, and a number of them are determined to find every last connection they can back to their deceased patriarch. If anyone knows where to find this Rayzeel, one of them will. And it's a resource Beckett doesn't have.

"We're going to find Rayzeel before he does, Bell. And we're going to make her help us figure out how to stop this."

"And if Beckett gets in the way of that?"

Lucita shrugged. "I have hopes that once he sees what we're accomplishing, he'll realize his error and decide to help. If he doesn't—well, you already came near to killing him once."

Bell didn't look particularly happy at *that* prospect, but he nodded.

Jenna Cross's haven in the San Fernando Valley
Los Angeles, California

"No, *you* don't understand," Jenna Cross was practically snarling into her phone, her patience with the man on the other end long since run out. "I don't *care* what it costs. I don't *care* how hard it is. I don't *care* what you have to do to get it. Somewhere in that damn system is the flight plan and destination for Beckett's plane, and I do not want to fucking hear from you again until you have it!" She viciously stabbed the disconnect button on the phone, briefly regretting that she wasn't using a land line—it was always so much more satisfying to slam those down than to just punch a key.

"Still don't know where the man's going?" Smiling Jack asked from the doorway to the small study. His fingers and knees were filthy with potting soil, his shoes stained with grass, and an unlit cigarette hung, apparently forgotten, from the corner of his mouth.

Cross scowled. "I thought it would be easy once Samuel called me with the ID numbers of Beckett's private plane."

"Right. I heard about the pooch-screw at DFW."

"Not my fault. I didn't have time to get my own people over there. Had to rely on some of the locals who wanted to get in good with me." Her tone quivered just a bit there. Despite her wishes, her fears, her people were indeed beginning to see her as some sort of savior for the thin-bloods throughout the world. It scared her almost as much as the idea of the elders turning against her as an omen of the coming Gehenna. "They weren't exactly the most competent people I've dealt with."

"So what now? You dig until you find a destination where you can catch up with him, keep throwing people at him until he's dead?"

"Something like that."

"Jenna…" Jack pulled an old, practically empty BIC lighter from a pocket, held the cigarette well away from his face as he lit it, and took a long drag off it once it was burning. "This ain't the way."

"Oh, God, not again, Uncle Jack."

"No, damn it, you listen to me!" The old anarch stalked into the room and practically shoved his face in hers. A tiny spark of the Red Fear flashed through her soul, and she had to recoil from the lit cigarette. "You're something special. You got the mark—"

"Which you put on me," she reminded him.

"Don't matter. You got it. You were a ghoul who became a vampire without being Embraced. There's like, what, less than a dozen of those worldwide since this whole mess started?"

"That we've heard of, anyway."

"Thin-bloods everywhere are looking to you to help 'em through what's coming, Jenna. Hell, even some regular-Joe vampires are starting to talk, to think that maybe what you're building is a better option than the crumbling Sabbat or the Camarilla Nazis. You got important things ahead of you, big things. And you ain't gonna see a one of them if you piss Beckett off enough to kill you."

"Beckett," she told him through gritted teeth, "will be dead long before he's that pissed."

"Okay. So what? How many of your people you going to sacrifice to do it? How's *that* going to make you look to your people? And what about the *next* elder who connects you with the Last Daughter? You been using your mark as a recruiting tool, but that means word gets out. Others might not have the reputation in the field Beckett does, but enough of them start shouting about you, they're gonna be believed."

Jenna wanted to scream at him, to tell Jack that she didn't *want* to be the leader of some great thin-blood movement, and if her people lost some respect for her because too many of them died killing Beckett, well, she wouldn't object. But she couldn't. She'd seen how they looked at her, seen the hope in their face when she spoke of great plans and promises that she knew she probably couldn't deliver. She didn't want this damn job—but she wanted even less to see what would happen if she laid it down.

And she knew that Jack didn't—couldn't—understand her fear. She knew the elders, not just a scattered few here and there, but those who mattered, would eventually identify her as the Last Daughter. She knew, too, that as things got worse around the world, more and more of those elders would start to believe in the old legends again, would believe Gehenna was upon them. Once that happened, it was only a matter of time before they came after her. She wasn't all *that* scared of truly dying; she was *terrified* of being captured by the Camarilla or the Sabbat and subject to whatever tests and examinations they might have in mind for one such as she. And Beckett, while not the only one who could draw all those threads tight into a net around her, was certainly the most likely to do so. She knew, because Samuel had told her so.

If it were just her, she'd have gone into hiding long ago, left LA and the Camarilla as far behind her as she could. But it wasn't just about her. She really didn't know how it happened, but a great many people had come to count on her in the past months. She resented them for it, at times even hated them—but she wouldn't let them down.

She couldn't explain any of this Jack him, though. He couldn't get it, no matter how hard he tried. Jack had always battled "the Establishment" for his own sake, not for those who fought beside him. And he *certainly* couldn't understand her fear, since he rarely felt any himself. In his way, though, his concern was genuine, so she forced a smile as she rose to her feet. "I'll consider it, Uncle Jack. Promise. But right now, as you pointed out, I've got people to look after. If anyone calls back with info on Beckett and I'm not here, have Jacob take it down. I'll decide what to do with it then."

Jack held his own smile until she had been gone from the room for at least a full two minutes. Then he stubbed the cigarette out in a small potted plant on her desk and said, "You can come out."

A bearded figure stepped from the shadows. "I was wondering if you knew I was there."

"I been seeing a lot more clearly since Caine came to me, Samuel."

"Right. Your fabled visitation."

Jack shrugged. "Most people don't believe. Ain't no reason you should." He paused a moment. "Maybe I haven't been seeing clear as I thought, though." He glanced sidelong at Samuel. "It's all you, ain't it?"

"What's all me?"

"This whole Beckett mess. You're the one been advising her for the past few months, you with your 'connections' to the Camarilla and the elders. Nobody else who could've put that notion in her head."

Samuel shrugged. "The fear was there already, Jack, waiting to be exploited. You've no idea the pressures on that girl. I just gave it a direction, a nudge."

"Whatever you got against him, you too much of a coward to kill Beckett yourself? You have to torment Jenna to do it?"

"It's more complicated than that, Jack. I'd explain it to you, if I had the time. Or if you did."

"Ah, right. But I'm too dangerous, now, since I'm trying to talk her out of pursuing this dumbass vendetta." Smiling Jack took a single step back from the desk, his eyes beginning to smolder. "You think you can handle me, Samuel? I've faced a *lot* of folks tougher'n you, and I'm the one here."

"Oh, I know. You're a legend among the anarchs. I might be able to take you, or I might not. And either way, it'd be long, loud, and noisy enough to draw every thin-blood on the block into this room. But… how devoted are you to Jenna Cross and her cause, Jack?"

"Huh? What the hell do you—"

"I've left a message with some of my Camarilla contacts. Along with instructions to deliver it to Hardestadt directly."

Jack felt the bottom drop out of his stomach. "What kind of message?"

"One that explains everything I know about Cross and the thin-bloods. Names. Patterns. Locations. Strengths. Weaknesses. Names of mortal friends and family. Patrol routes. Emergency havens. The works."

The old anarch felt like he was on fire. The Beast roared in his head so loudly he was certain Samuel could hear it. Only with the greatest effort of will he'd ever made could he force it down.

"I thought you wanted to help us…"

Samuel shrugged. "I want this more. What do you think the Camarilla could do with that kind of info? They may know some of the generalities, but they don't know where Jenna sleeps during the day, or where she'd likely to go if *that* place is compromised. They don't know the precise strategies the thin-bloods are using for patrols, information gathering and such. Even if you killed me and warned her, she wouldn't have time to change enough of it to matter. Hardestadt would know who, where, and how to strike. He'd be able to take out your patrols, pick off Jenna's people one by one. They might even be able to launch an attack right here, despite the thin-bloods' numbers in these houses.

"All that happens in…" Samuel checked his watch. "Three hours. Unless I get back to Riverside in time to retrieve the package before Hardestadt gets it."

Jack's shoulders slumped. "How do I know you won't deliver it anyway?"

"Jack, as you pointed out, I've helped Cross this far. And she's still pretty important to my plans for Beckett, though I can do without her if I have to. I've got no *reason* to destroy what she's got going here—unless you force me to."

Smiling Jack, anarch leader turned Gehenna prophet, walked over until he stood practically nose to nose with Samuel. The intruder didn't flinch. "Whatever you're planning for Beckett," Jack told him, "I hope he fucks you over."

"I'll keep that in mind."

Jack turned away. The sound of a long knife leaving its sheath was the last sound he'd ever hear.

part three:
the witching hour

Hearken to the word of the scholar, for whom knowledge is a curse
And ancient horrors are but dreams of things to come.
From them shall come warning.
From them shall come wisdom.
From them shall come slaughter.

—*The Erciyes Fragments*, "Prophecies"

Sforzesco Castle
Milan, Italy

Those who knew him could no longer believe this was the same Giangaleazzo. The Giangaleazzo who had attended the Convention of Thorns, participated in the Anarch Revolt, risen to great prominence within the Sabbat and mercilessly purged his own people when handing Milan over to the Camarilla—this was a creature strong in his convictions, mighty of will.

The Giangaleazzo who now idly wandered the halls of Sforza, taking in the images and relics of bygone nights and wishing he might be back there, was something else entirely. He had turned the night-to-night governance of Milan over to his primogen, ordering only that he be consulted on the most major deliberations. When not meandering through the past as he was tonight, he spent most of his time locked in one of his various havens, doors and windows bolted and mystically sealed with what little tangible darkness he could still call upon.

Worse, the Prince of Milan muttered, speaking to himself. He wasn't even truly aware of the habit. He did it alone and in the presence of others with equal frequency. Those few who had overheard him were stunned to find him speaking in turns of his own death, the deaths of those he knew, and his mortal life. In fact, what none knew was that Giangaleazzo had not slept a full day through in weeks, that every afternoon he was awakened by intense dreams of either his sire or his mortal parents.

He was weak, far weaker than even the withering alone could account for. For months, his strength and his faculty with the stuff of shadows had ebbed, but his recent lack of sleep and constant fear rendered him a pale reflection of what he should yet have been. He'd not had the strength to attend the recent conclave in Lille, France, despite an invitation that was as near an order as any powerful prince was likely to receive. Nor did he really care.

Giangaleazzo wandered past the room of sculptures, where he'd had his conversation with Archon Bell—now declared traitor by worldwide decree of the justicars and the Inner Circle—some months ago. Even then, he had known what was coming, known that Gehenna was upon the Kindred and the world, but nobody had heard his warnings. Even now, horrific as events had become, the Camarilla refused to acknowledge the truth that lay plain before them, even going so far as to punish those who dared suggest it. Giangaleazzo had refrained from crawling back to the Sabbat, not only due to the tattered remains of his pride and the near certainty that they would kill him for his treachery, but also because of his knowledge that the Sword of Caine was collapsing from within. He'd heard of the sect's purge of elders, knew that it was little more than a ravening collection of frightened and bloodthirsty neonates. If only he'd acted sooner! Perhaps he might have done something to prevent this from coming to pass, might not have had to pass his last nights as some helpless old—

The lights of Milan, streaming in the window some distance down the hall, abruptly winked out, as though someone had simply turned the entire city off. No, worse, for no trace of the moon or stars shone through either. Sforza Castle was encased in a blackness as absolute as Giangaleazzo, despite his years-long familiarity with the Abyss, had ever seen. The screams of terrified mortals, trapped in the darkness, floated in through the windows. They were muffled, distant, eclipsed by a darkness that was not merely an absence of light but a physical impediment. Even the squeal of stressed metal and the shattering of glass, as suddenly blinded drivers ran into walls, trees and each other, wasn't as sharp as it should have been.

And then he heard the voice. Unlike the others, it was close indeed. It seemed to come from just over his shoulder. He could almost feel the speaker's warm breath on his ear.

"Giangaleazzo…"

Was it his sire's voice? Or his mortal father's? He suddenly could not remember, could not tell the difference. He spun about, but there, as before him, was nothing but shadow.

It began to speak, rapidly but at length. The words were gibberish. Even those that came from languages Giangaleazzo knew seemed chosen at random. It was the babble of madness he heard—or worse, the twisted mutterings of a being to which speech itself was an utterly alien concept.

The pressure of words mounted, pounding within Giangaleazzo's mind, imprinted directly onto his thoughts. The echo of each utterance melded into the next, until it was a stream of sounds from which he could no longer even pick individual words, individual syllables. It came from all directions, first behind, then from the left, as though the speaker moved around him. The entity surrounded him on all sides now, and still it gibbered in the voice of his fathers.

And Giangaleazzo knew the shadow for what it was. His eyes squeezed shut, unaware of the trickle of blood from his ears and nose. He abased himself before it, fell to his knees, placed his forehead and his palms upon the floor.

The darkness roiled, shifted—and Giangaleazzo screamed.

He spasmed, limbs jerking in all directions at once as he rose into the air, lifted by tangible shadows that invaded his body through ears, mouth, eyes, anus, even the pores of his skin. It flowed like a viscous liquid, filling Giangaleazzo from within. Blood fountained from those same orifices, expelled by the pressure of the growing darkness. Giangaleazzo thrashed, muscles contracting of their own accord, out of sequence with one another, until they tore loose from bone and tendon, or else bent his limbs in angles sharp enough to shatter joints.

For a brief instant, Giangaleazzo screamed—and then the shadow reached his brain, and he could no longer even find a voice. His jaw gaped open but no sound emerged, save the faint gurgling noise of the blood flowing in ever-larger gouts from his throat.

The darkness moved, not merely through his head but through his thoughts, through his memories. Where it went, darkness followed. In mere moments, what had been Giangaleazzo was gone, blacked out by this alien presence. All that he had been was now in *it*.

It knew—to the extent that it could understand the world through human or Kindred senses—all that

Giangaleazzo had known. It now possessed half a millennium of new experiences. And buried in that avalanche of knowledge, a tiny kernel of information, something Giangaleazzo himself had learned only in the very recent past, had practically forgotten in the face of its relative unimportance. After all, with his power slipping away, with Gehenna upon the world, what matter the news that Hardestadt of the Inner Circle was seeking a single fugitive?

But to the darkness, to the thing from the Abyss, this was not unimportant. For the name resonated through the entity's being, echoed the presence it had detected at the site of the broken ritual. It already had a trail, though it wasn't yet following it directly. Now it had a name.

Even better, with the name came further knowledge still, knowledge of one who often accompanied the fugitive, one whom the entity had long considered lost.

The thing gibbered and whispered still, though Giangaleazzo could no longer hear it. And as it babbled, two new words could be heard in the stream of sounds.

"Beckett…"

"Lucita…"

With a final shriek, Giangaleazzo was torn apart from the inside. Shreds of flesh and viscera fell toward the floor, only to vanish before they struck, consumed utterly by the darkness. With a final wail of endless despair, the soul of the great Lasombra prince followed.

The darkness moved across Milan, heading east.

A hidden library
Miskolc, Hungary

"How about this one?" Kapaneus asked, hefting a large tome and blowing the dust off its pages. "The passage is rather rambling, but it speaks of a journey through South America, and the author mentions 'that Noddist fraud' on multiple occasions."

Beckett put his own book down to shuffle over, and glanced at the pages. After a moment, he shook his head.

"No, I heard about that encounter from the other side. It's talking about Aristotle de Laurent, a former companion of mine. Not Rayzeel."

"Ah." Kapaneus went back to searching.

Beckett looked around him angrily. The cave was illuminated by a number of candles in an overhead chandelier, candles that had lit themselves when the two vampires entered the chamber. He stood alongside Kapaneus, multiple bookcases, two tables and a handful of chairs, within an echoing, limestone cave. It would, under normal circumstances, have been the worst place in the world to store books and papers, but the expected water dripping down the walls and the scent of must were utterly absent; something unnatural kept the moisture from leeching in from the rest of the complex, rendering this one small cluster of caves completely safe for even the most sensitive of ancient papers.

Beckett experienced a quick shudder of revulsion—far from his first—as his eyes swept over the furniture. The bookcases, the tables, the chairs, the chandeliers—everything was sculpted with meticulous care from the flesh and bones of living and unliving things. It was even remotely possible, though he didn't want to think on it, that some of them were in a fashion living still, trapped in an eternity of torment. He and Kapaneus had agreed to make no use of the furniture when they'd first discovered its awful nature, and Beckett was torn by conflicting desires, his yearning to preserve the assembled knowledge here for possible future use warring with his need to set the place alight as soon as they were finished, to destroy these abominations and possibly end their suffering.

Unfortunately, it was beginning to appear that all that assembled knowledge might prove useless. After several nights of searching, digging through various and sundry books in a fairly accurate reflection of their time in Fortschritt, they'd found nothing even remotely helpful.

Was this, then, all they had come to Miskolc for? If it was, they'd wasted large amounts of precious time they simply didn't have. He and Kapaneus had spent five weeks in Eastern Europe—starting in the Baltic States and moving south—tracking down every connection Beckett had in the region. It had taken them less than a month to learn that Miskolc was the city they needed, the site of the largest of their quarry's libraries—and in all that time, they'd seen neither hide nor hair of any opposition.

Their quarry. Such a neat, simple concept to encompass someone so utterly monstrous and unpredictable as Sascha Vykos.

Noddist, scholar of Kindred lore, and perhaps the single greatest monster either the Sabbat or the Tzimisce clan had ever produced, Vykos was perhaps the last person, Kindred, mortal, or other, that Beckett would ever have wanted to involve in this mess. Beckett had hated it—terms such as "him" and "her" could no longer be applied to a creature as physically warped as Vykos—for centuries. But he also knew that Vykos, who had collected volumes of vampiric myth and lore for longer than Beckett had walked the earth, almost certainly kept tabs on others who shared its interests, even if only so it could steal from and eliminate the competition.

Rumors Beckett had picked up during the weeks of searching for this place suggested that the Tzimisce clan had largely vanished, corrupted from within in a manner very much like the dead Tremere he'd seen in Vienna. For one thing, that certainly seemed to confirm the whispers Beckett had heard over the years, which claimed the Tremere had used Tzimisce blood to create the ritual that turned the Tremere from mortal magi to unliving blood sorcerers. More to the point, though, it suggested that Vykos was probably well and truly dead. Beckett found it difficult to keep from grinning broadly at that thought, though he wished he'd been able to see it firsthand.

Still, he'd been surprised to discover that the guardians of Vykos's repository had apparently gone the way of their master. He'd anticipated at least some of the twisted and reshaped servants Vykos was known to use. Hell, he wouldn't have been surprised to find some of the original Obertus Order—the monastic order Vykos originally made responsible for assembling all this esoteric knowledge—still alive and laboring for their master.

He and Kapaneus found none of that. They'd located the entrance to the library, hidden within a large manor near the edge of town. They'd found a staircase leading down from the basement, one that brought them into limestone caves that were almost certainly an extension of the famous Baradla cave complex. In that complex, they'd found these specially appointed—and very well hidden—library chambers. But they'd found nary a trace of inhabitants— vampire, ghoul or otherwise. Beckett had thought that meant their search was almost over.

Shaking his head to clear it of mental cobwebs, Beckett reached out and lifted yet another book from yet another shelf, flipped through it—and then, with a snarl of frustration, jabbed a hand's-worth of talons through it and ripped it in two.

"Nothing!"

Kapaneus watched the flurry of papers fall around Beckett's feet like large snowflakes and refrained from comment.

"It's that bastard's Goddamn system!" Beckett railed at his companion, for the third time in as many hours. "Ancient tomes, comments on ancient tomes, books by other people, books by Vykos, comments on other people's books by Vykos…" He shook his head, sheepishly allowing his talons to slide once more into their fleshy sheaths.

"Kapaneus," he said more calmly, "The notion that the information we seek isn't here actually scares me less than the notion that it's here but we're going to miss it. Vykos didn't think like a human any more than it looked like one, and it was certifiably paranoid to boot. If there *is* a system here, it's not by date, topic, or anything else I can figure out. All these books, all this information…" Beckett gestured at the many shelves surrounding them, at the doorways that led to at least four other caves of similar size, equally stalked with material. "All this, and no way to find what we're looking for."

The elder nodded his agreement and understanding— there were no words of comfort and encouragement to offer he had not uttered already. With a heavy sigh, Beckett returned to searching, pulling book after book off the shelf and flipping through it, for he had no other, more efficient means at his disposal.

Sometimes sheer determination is enough.

He almost missed it. His eyes skimmed over the text, and recognizing it as a bit of prophecy he'd read before, he almost put the book down.

As the Father is destroyed, and the Prodigals buried, and the Cousins rotted away, one Angel survives to hold the last Light of her True Clan. And when Darkness falls, and Blackness snuffs the Angel's Light, so passes another Barrier, and the Final Nights draw ever closer.

It was one of Saulot's prophecies; the patriarch of the now largely extinct Salubri clan was known for them. This wasn't one of his better-known predictions, but Beckett had seen a third-hand copy of the tablet on which it was written.

What drew his eyes back to the page, however, was the note that someone—Beckett assumed it was Vykos itself—had scribbled in the margin.

"According to Milivoje, Rayzeel attests that her sire was misquoted in this particular passage. 'Angel' is apparently a poor interpretation; the original word more accurately translates as 'little god.' Must address this further when circumstances allow. If true, it could suggest the passage refers not to the passing of the Cappadocians, as is widely accepted, but possibly to the Ravnos instead. 'Little god' is a title more in keeping with their Hindu origins than the Cappadocians' Christian ones, and the clan has been dying out of late."

"Kapaneus!" Beckett shot to his feet. "Come look at this."

After more hours of searching, it was Kapaneus who turned up another reference to this "Milivoje." Apparently Vykos had been referring to Milivoje Dobrosavic, a Serbian Tzimisce who fled the NATO bombing in '99 and had temporarily taken shelter with Sascha Vykos. What he might have offered in exchange wasn't clear, though Beckett believed information must have made up a large portion of the payment.

"All right," Beckett said thoughtfully after a few moments of pondering. "This Milivoje claimed to have spoken directly with Rayzeel, or at least to have had *some* sort of contact with her. No chance in hell that Vykos wouldn't press him for more info on that. The bastard would certainly recognize Rayzeel as a potential resource. All we have to do now is locate that information—"

"Assuming," Kapaneus interjected, "that Vykos wrote it down."

"Don't be a downer, Kapaneus."

Unfortunately, at least in the short run, the elder's pessimism was well founded. They found nothing more that night, and Beckett went to sleep for the day burning with frustration. He *knew* the information was here, if he could only *find* it!

The next night didn't show any more promise. Their first hour and a half of searching had uncovered no further mention of Milivoje, and the only other reference to Rayzeel barely mentioned her in passing, in relation to a discussion that had occurred in 1044. Beckett had just opened his mouth to ask Kapaneus (not for the first time) if he could remember anything useful from the period when he realized something was *very* wrong.

Thick as the walls were, Beckett's superior hearing could still detect sounds from out in the Baradla cave complex: the faint dripping of water that continuously built up the stalactite and stalagmite formations for which the caves were famous; the chirping and chittering of bats leaving or returning to their homes after hunting; the scrabbling feet of rats. It was all faint, even to his ears, but omnipresent nonetheless.

Until that moment, when it abruptly and completely stopped. It didn't fade away, didn't taper off. It was simply present one instant and absent the next.

Beckett's hair stood on end. He couldn't even hear the dull thump as Kapaneus lay his book down on the table, also glancing around in confusion as he realized something was amiss.

Only one thing Beckett knew of could possibly cause such a complete cessation of sound; only one clan possessed such an insidious ability. Slowly, acting as casually as he could under the circumstances, fighting every primitive instinct that screamed *run!* at him, Beckett rose to his feet and turned to the bookcase standing behind him, as if preparing to place the tome he held upon it. Then, abruptly sliding his fingers between the bookcase and the wall, he heaved it over, allowing dozens of books and the heavy bone-sculpted case itself to topple to the floor.

Or almost to the floor. As he'd expected, a figure invisible even to his heightened senses broke the bookcase's fall. Beckett didn't even stop to glance at the pinned figure. The Assamite was almost certainly uninjured, but it would take him a moment to free himself, and that was all the time Beckett and Kapaneus needed to flee for their unlives, heading up the stairs and into the house proper.

Beckett knew that he probably couldn't outrun the Assamites, but if he could stay ahead of them long enough to shift into one of his other forms, he could effectively hide from them. Unfortunately, that still left Kapaneus. Beckett had no doubt the elder could take care of himself, but these were some *serious* opponents.

Assamites, for Caine's sake! Beckett shook his head. *Hardestadt must really be pulling out all the stops to take me down.*

He and Kapaneus tore through the front door of the manor and dashed toward the road, their heels kicking up clumps of wet lawn. He was just considering where to go next, wondering if there were some way to lose their pursuers on the streets of Miskolc *without* shifting into a bat or mist—and effectively abandoning Kapaneus—when the two of them burst through the front gate at the edge of the property...

And came face to face with half a dozen young-looking men and women carrying pistols and other, even less friendly weapons. Judging by their dress, their bearing, and their general movements, these could only be more of Cross's thin-bloods.

Oh, wonderful. Their timing just couldn't be better.

Beckett hurled himself backward, allowing the stream of bullets to tear chunks out of the pavement before him. Splinters of shattered stone tore through his shirt and jeans, but if any of them penetrated his unnaturally resilient flesh, he didn't feel them. He landed hard on his back, rolled swiftly to his feet, and found himself pressed against the wrought-iron fence that surrounded the house. He crouched, talons raised before him. Kapaneus, he noted, stood beside him, a bit dirty from his own dive for cover but not obviously bloodied. Beckett flinched aside as a brick, of all things, hurtled past his head and careened loudly against a fencepost.

"Kapaneus," he asked, eyes darting back and forth as he carefully watched the advancing enemy for any sign of the next attack, "did we have a Plan B?"

"I don't believe so, no."

"Any idea where we can get one at this hour?"

The thin-bloods stopped their advance perhaps twenty feet away, and four of the six leveled pistols at the cornered pair. The others carried melee weapons at the ready—one a baseball bat (it was this guy who'd thrown the brick), the other a knife so large Beckett wasn't sure it didn't actually qualify as a sword—just in case their prey managed to close in.

Tough as he was, Beckett didn't think he was prepared to risk the eight or a dozen bullets he'd almost certainly take if he made a straight charge at them. He had no doubt that, under normal circumstances, he and Kapaneus could deal with six thin-bloods, though they might get bloody in the process. At this moment, however, God-knew how many Assamites were likely to materialize from behind them at any second. He was sure the only reason they hadn't appeared already was that they were being cautious, alert for ambush in the halls of the house. The thin-bloods might not be able to kill Beckett and Kapaneus, but they could delay them long enough for someone else to finish the job.

Something twisted inside his gut, as Beckett realized he was left with few choices but to abandon his companion. Kapaneus had stood by him, done everything a Kindred was capable of doing to qualify for the title "friend." Beckett would fight for him, but he just wasn't prepared to die for him, not with his answers so close.

Still, he determined to do all he could, to wait until the last possible moment. If they could take the thin-bloods down *quick*, there was still a chance. And if not, he could still escape later, especially if the Assamites and thin-bloods distracted each other.

Beckett abruptly crouched and snatched something from his inside jacket pocket. Even as the first of the bullets flew his way, he leapt to the right, yanked a small piece off the item in his hand, and then tossed the device into the midst of the thin-bloods.

Three of them immediately hurled themselves away, arms coming up to protect their faces. To their credit, the other three merely flinched, but took a split second to examine what exactly it was they were fleeing from. Still, though it took them only an instant to realize that Beckett had simply thrown his cell phone at them after yanking the antenna off like a pin, that instant was all Beckett needed to close the distance between them.

The first two thin-bloods were dead before they even realized what was happening, one beheaded, the other eviscerated by Beckett's razor-sharp claws. The third brought her revolver to bear and fired. The sound was nearly deafening at such close range, particularly to Beckett's sensitive ears, but he managed to knock the woman's arm aside so that the bullet flew harmlessly past him and struck a wall halfway down the block. Continuing the turning motion begun when he struck her arm, Beckett spun completely around and dropped into a crouch as he did so. He cupped his hands, claws outward. Denim shredded as he gauged both the thin-blood's kneecaps from her legs with a sharp crack.

Beckett rose partially from his crouch and caught the woman even as she collapsed. Her shrieking didn't last long; Beckett spun her about with him, using her to catch the nine-millimeter barrage sent his way by one of the two enemies still standing. He charged the one with the revolver, using the now silent body in his arms as a battering ram. All three went down. Beckett's talons flashed once more, and only he rose. His eyes were wide, his skin flushed, and he felt the Beast's delight at the kill. It was a primal response, one that didn't bother him nearly as much as it would have mere months before. That fact might have disturbed him, if he'd noticed.

He turned just in time to see Kapaneus lift the last of his foes off the ground and literally wring the man's head from his body with sheer brute strength.

"Good," Beckett said, turning away. "Now let's get the hell out—"

As before, it was his heightened senses that saved him. This time it was the smell, the tang of protective oils that no mortal senses could possibly have detected. Beckett dove forward, and the tip of the blade cut through his jacket and shallowly into the flesh below his neck, rather than beheading him. The aroma of his own blood mixed oddly with that of the oil on the blade, creating a strange, surreal sort of scent in the air around him. He spun to face his attacker, already certain what he'd see.

God damn it! Couldn't you have waited another thirty seconds?!

The figure who had attacked Beckett looked to be a young woman, perhaps in her twenties. She had long hair, braided back, and her skin was a dark tone, not the hue of African or Middle Eastern descent, but almost black as though dusted with charcoal.

Only the Assamites grew *darker* as they aged. If the supernatural silence from earlier hadn't proved who was after them, this certainly did.

Several others spread out across the street, presumably having come from the house along with the first. Beckett had no illusions about his abilities. He knew he was tough, good in a scrap. None of these Assamites was jet black, meaning none could be older than he was. Despite their training, despite their skills, despite the strange abilities the clan possessed, Beckett was certain he could have taken on any one of them.

He wasn't *about* to challenge four.

There was simply no possible way for him to punch through the Assamites to reach his companion. Well, Kapaneus was old enough to take care of himself—and was probably smart enough to run. Either way, there was nothing else Beckett could do for him. He took off at a sprint for the nearest side street.

Under most circumstances, the average Kindred wouldn't have a chance in hell of outrunning an Assamite warrior. The eastern clan boasted among their talents a superhuman speed, comparable to that possessed by many Brujah. Even as Beckett's feet hit the ground, he heard a rapid-fire pounding behind him, knew that the enemy was closing on him *fast*.

All right, so they could run faster than any human, and while Beckett could increase his own speed by pumping blood through his legs to increase their strength, he couldn't possibly match their ability.

So he simply wouldn't be human anymore. He briefly considered shifting to mist, but that form, while immune to harm, was relatively slow. Better, if possible, to evade the Assamites completely, rather than allow them the chance, however slight it might be, to follow him even in his hazy form and ambush him when he resumed his natural shape. He could fly as a bat, but as small as he was in that guise, a single good shot before he escaped might cripple him.

Beckett dove forward, as though leaping for cover. By the time his hands hit the ground, however, they weren't hands anymore. They were paws.

Enhanced by the power of vampiric *vitae* within, a great white wolf loped through the streets of Miskolc at over forty miles per hour. It passed cars cruising along the city's smaller streets. Where it passed, people screamed, pointed, leapt out of the way. Sirens sounded, but it was always gone before the authorities could arrive.

More importantly, it left behind its pursuers, at least for a moment. Some of the Assamites could run even faster than the wolf, but they weren't able to maintain such speeds for long; the cost in blood was too high. Further, with the senses of the wolf— heightened beyond his usual inhuman levels—Beckett would easily sense the approach even of vampires able to mask themselves from sight. A single thrown knife struck his flank as he escaped, but as it largely failed even to penetrate his hide, he was able to shrug it off.

After nearly an hour of zigzagging through Miskolc, determined to avoid not only the pursuing Assamites but also the local authorities and any further thin-blood ambushes, Beckett found himself lurking under a large bridge. The water that flowed beside him, a tributary of the Sajo River, probably served the city as a storm sewer, and he took a moment to idly wonder how many of the damn things he was going to find himself in. He glanced upward, sending a swift mental impulse to calm the bats lairing underneath the bridge so they wouldn't flee from his presence. He contemplated shifting back to his natural form and calling Cesare, to find out if the plane was under surveillance, but remembered abruptly that he no longer had his phone. Then, deciding to take a few moments to rest and regain his bearings, he curled up on the muddy earth beside the stream and placed his tail over his nose.

He spent several hours lying there, certain he should be doing something but not at all clear on what it was. He was still worrying at the problem—chewing at a mental bur, as it were—when his canine sense of smell picked up a dangerous, disturbing scent. The hair on the wolf's back and neck stood up, and Beckett had to fight with himself not to let loose with a low growl. Damn it all, they'd tracked him, despite all his efforts! Beckett rose to his paws, prepared to flee in either direction…

Both of which were cut off. Several Assamites—he recognized the one who'd nearly struck his head from his shoulders—appeared at *both* sides of the bridge. The assassins weren't even bothering to use their powers of silence, as they had earlier. They knew he was trapped, knew he could smell them coming. They weren't converging quite yet—a wise choice, since the cramped quarters on the bank meant they could only come at him one or two at a time. They were hoping he'd panic, try to run, and in the process, move onto more open ground where they had the advantage of numbers.

Like they bloody well needed any more advantages, Beckett thought grimly. Then, abruptly, he smiled—or performed the wolfish equivalent, allowing his muzzle to gape open and his tongue to loll out. Actually, *he* had *them* outnumbered. So best give them what they wanted.

Beckett rose to his hind legs, which swiftly became his *only* legs, and looked around him. Then hands half-raised as though attempting surrender (as hopeless a prospect as that might be with Assamite assassins), he carefully picked his way toward the nearest group.

The Assamites weren't stupid. Though confident of victory, they kept their eyes on the approaching figure, their hands on their weapons, fully expecting a trick or a deception of some sort.

Well, wouldn't want to disappoint them.

Beckett raised his hands further—and then called out in a voice the Kindred could not hear, beckoning his allies to come to his aid.

With an almost deafening sound, hundreds of wings began to flap madly at once, and a veritable tide of bats dropped from the underside of the bridge to rush past Beckett and out into the open air. For an instant the Assamites recoiled, expecting the tiny animals to attack, but the bats simply fluttered past them and up into the sky.

By the time they realized what was happening, it was too late even for them to react swiftly enough.

Beckett, the bats fluttering past him so closely they made his jacket flap in mockery of their own wings, seemed to shrink in on himself. From the observers' point of view, it must have looked as though each passing bat nipped off a piece of him, causing him to deflate. And then he simply vanished into the midst of the swarm, just another bat swiftly climbing toward the clouds.

His hearing was good enough, especially in this form, that he heard the Assamites cursing long and loud in both Arabic and Farsi as he fluttered his way toward safety.

A downtown traffic circle
Miskolc, Hungary

Many blocks away, a small stone fountain stood in the midst of a large traffic circle. It was shut off, and the still waters in its basin reflected the dull black hue of the statue that rose in its center. Precious little traffic drove through at this late hour. Even less tonight than normal, as the police had cordoned off some nearby streets in response to a shootout near the iron mill and reported sightings of a wolf loping down the boulevard.

The lack of traffic, however, did not mean the intersection remained empty.

Kapaneus stood just beside the fountain's basin, eyes almost casually drifting left to right as he watched the three Assamites who approached him from different angles. These were vampires trained nearly from the moment of Embrace to destroy their own kind, killers that an entire race of predators feared. Their darkened skin suggested that they had decades, if not centuries, of violence to their credit.

Kapaneus knew full well that he hadn't gained any particular enemies during the months he'd been free from Kaymakli. Their instructions must have been to kill not only Beckett, but anyone traveling with him.

How inconvenient.

They *certainly* weren't amateurish enough to risk attacking an unknown foe one by one. Two of them abruptly lunged from opposite sides, determined to hit him in tandem so he could not respond to both, while the third waited just a step or two back, prepared to strike at any exposed opening.

Kapaneus relaxed, and let them come.

Miskolc Regional Airfield
Miskolc, Hungary

For the third time that night, Cesare thumbed his cell phone off after receiving nothing but a generic voicemail message from Signore Beckett's line. Something was definitely wrong. Beckett was most assuredly not at his ghoul's beck and call, but he usually made a point about checking in not long after Cesare left him a message. And this was important. Some of the thin-bloods (or at least Cesare assumed that's who they were) were not only watching the plane, they'd once or twice made as if to board, dissuaded only when Cesare made his presence known. They probably weren't worried too much about drawing official attention—the airport was tiny, largely closed for the night, and anyway Beckett's plane sat on the most distant runway. Presumably they held off only because they didn't know how much resistance the ghoul could put up, or whether he was alone, and Cesare wasn't certain how long that reticence would last. He really needed Beckett's advice, yet his master was nowhere to be—

Cesare turned, and practically leapt out of his skin at the sight of the large black bat hanging upside-down from the fluorescent light in the cabin behind him. As it was, he couldn't quite suppress an abrupt, high-pitched shriek.

The bat dropped from its perch, and had two human feet to stand on by the time it landed. Scowling, Beckett painfully rubbed his ears.

"Was that really necessary, Cesare? I was a *bat*, for God's sake! That was *loud*."

"Sorry, Signore Beckett. You startled me."

"No. Really?"

"We have a problem here, Signore Beckett."

Beckett listened intently as Cesare described the situation for him. Then, "I doubt they'll do anything precipitous tonight, Cesare. It's too close to dawn. As soon as the sun comes up, I want you go shopping to replace your cell phone. Then have the plane fueled up and ready to take off. If it looks like they're about to attack you in force, get out of here. Land at the nearest available airport, and be ready to be airborne again to come pick us up at a moment's notice."

"You are not staying in the plane tonight, Signore? I get the impression from looking at you that the library is not safe either."

"No, it's not, but I can find shelter if I have to. I'm going to see if I can find Kapaneus before dawn."

"Signore, I cannot abandon you to—"

"You're not going to do me any good if you get killed, Cesare. Stay if you can. Leave only if you must."

"Very well. I…" Something his master had just said finally penetrated the ghoul's skull. "Replace my cell phone?"

Beckett reached out, removed Cesare's phone from the clip at his belt, and stuck it in his own pocket. "Right now, I need this more than you do. If you *must* reach me between now and dawn, use the laptop and send me a text message."

"Understood, Signore. Ah—may I ask what happened to yours?"

"I'll tell you sometime. It's funny, if you weren't there." Beckett turned and wandered back to the safe room with the refrigerator. He hated to tap into his emergency supply, especially since he didn't have the contacts in this region's medical community to replenish it, but he simply had no time to hunt. He could feed from Cesare, of course, but he wanted the ghoul at full alertness, in case the thin-bloods *did* attack the plane.

God damn them, anyway! Hardestadt's animosity he could at least understand. What the *hell* did Jenna Cross have against him?

Beckett choked down two plastic bags of blood—damn, but he hated to drink the stuff cold—poked his head out of the plane's door to be sure he wasn't being watched at that exact moment, and concentrated once more. An instant later, a thin stream of mist flowed down the stairs and onto the runway, where it mixed invisibly with the rising fog that signaled the eventual approach of dawn.

A downtown traffic circle
Miskolc, Hungary

He found Kapaneus still sitting by the fountain, one of the various landmarks they'd previously agreed upon as a meeting point if they were separated. The agreement also stipulated that they would remain at such a prearranged spot only if they were quite certain they had not been followed. Still, Beckett made a brief circuit of the intersection, feeling about him with what few senses he maintained as mist, before accumulating in the air beside his companion and resuming his normal form. If Kapaneus was startled to see Beckett materialize out of the fog, he did a far better job than Cesare of hiding it.

"It is good to see that you survived, Beckett," the elder said in greeting. "I had begun to worry."

"You've got reason to worry, Kapaneus. But yeah, I'm still here, more or less. Did you have any trouble?"

"None to speak of. The Assamites pursued me briefly after you fled, but they gave up in short order. My assumption would be that you, not I, are their target, and they have little interest in me beyond the fact that I travel with you."

"Lucky for you. Let's get out of sight. No reason to push it."

Kapaneus nodded once and rose to his feet. "Where do we go? I'm certain the library will be watched, if not actually occupied."

"Most likely." Beckett looked around. "It's probably safe for us to find a hotel room for the day. The Assamites and thin-bloods can't be watching *all* of them. Tomorrow night— well, we'll see."

The pair of vampires carefully made their way up the street, toward the edge of town. Beckett never noticed the light dusting of ash that floated atop the water in the basin.

Hotel Baradla
Miskolc, Hungary

"I just don't understand it," Beckett complained once they'd made it to the hotel they'd chosen. "I'd barely even *heard* of Jenna Cross before this whole mess started. I've certainly never *done* anything to her that I know of." His voice was so low, no mortal could have heard him even from six inches away. Kapaneus, however, made his words out clearly enough.

"When you dig deeply enough into the root," the elder replied, equally as softly, "only two reasons exist for hatred of this magnitude. Either you are somehow in her way, keeping her from something she wants, or she fears you, fears you so greatly she can overcome it only by destroying you."

"I can't think of a damn thing I have she could want."

"Precisely. Consider it, Beckett. She was prepared to risk killing you—and me—in her own home, despite what such a rash move might do to her alliance with Lucita's people. This woman has waged war against the Camarilla for months, and prevented them from retaking Los Angeles. This is not someone prone to rash moves—except, it seems, where you are concerned."

"She's afraid of me, then. Big time."

"It would appear so. Perhaps unnaturally so."

A police car cruised by, and the pair crouched deep in the shadows, postponing any response Beckett might have made. Only when the taillights had fully faded in the distance did they continue.

"You think someone else is using her against me?"

"She obviously believes you are her enemy. *Someone* gave her that idea."

Save for the loud barking of a dog when they passed through the animals' property—barking that Beckett swiftly silenced with a sharp command—the next few minutes of the walk passed quietly.

"You know both the Assamites and the thin-bloods are going to keep watch on the house and the plane, Beckett," Kapaneus said finally. "We are not going to be able to do much research."

"I was just thinking about that." Beckett glanced at the eastern sky, then checked the time on his cell phone. "I think I have an idea about that, actually. It's risky, bordering on stupid, but that combination seems to have worked pretty well for us recently. And if it works, it should buy us at least a couple of nights."

"Fantastic. Two nights to locate what we couldn't find in four. Perhaps, Beckett, we should leave Miskolc and come back later? We can attempt to acquire information elsewhere, and—"

Beckett froze in his tracks. "Acquire information…" he repeated, almost as though entranced. "A later date." His eyes widened and he grinned fiercely. "Kapaneus, I could hug you."

"I'd as soon you did not. What have you realized?"

"Only how Vykos organized its library. Kapaneus, it *did* file the books by date—not the date they were written or the date of the events described in them, but by the date it *acquired* them!"

"Are you certain?"

"Well, no, not until I'm back in the library. It makes sense, though. It's something only it would know, a filing system nobody else could easily decipher."

"Can you?"

"We'll see, won't we? First, we have a few unwelcome tagalongs to deal with."

The next evening, immediately after awakening in the old but scrupulously clean rented room, Beckett spun to face Kapaneus. The elder actually took a step back. "I do not trust that grin, Beckett."

If anything, Beckett's smile widened further. "Kapaneus, I've seen you vanish from sight more than once. Would I be correct in assuming you can also take on the appearance of others?"

"It's not a skill I practice regularly but yes, I can do so."

"Good. Here's what we're going to do…"

Downtown
Miskolc, Hungary

Yet again, the white wolf loped through the streets of Miskolc, leaving a trail of panicked pedestrians in its wake. Its left flank was marred with a wet crimson stain, and it ran with a notable limp in its back leg. It was sufficient to slow the wolf down—and that meant the coterie of Assamites in pursuit were doing a much better job of keeping up than they had the previous night. They had detected him, scouting the streets near Vykos's manor, and were determined that he would not escape them yet again. They weren't yet catching up to Beckett, but he couldn't seem to shake them either. Still he ran, for he knew exactly what fate lay in store for him if they caught him.

The Assamites were clearly out for blood—and not merely as a means of fulfilling their assignment. Several of their companions had failed to return last night, and that could only mean they were either incapacitated or dead. They were uncertain how even prey as dangerous as Beckett could have slain three of their brethren with only a singe wound to show for it, but they weren't about to let him get away with it.

The wolf was heading for the airport—of that they had no doubt. Whether they could catch him before he reached the plane was an open question; every time they seemed about to close the gap between them, Beckett put on another burst of speed and pulled just slightly ahead once more. They were certain, however, that once on the tarmac, they could easily board the plane before it could take off, or at the very least damage it sufficiently to prevent it from leaving.

The wolf ran on, knocking slow pedestrians aside, sometimes leaping atop and over slow-moving cars in its haste to escape. Sirens sounded behind them, and the wolf darted down alleys too small for police cars to follow. It was a move even the Assamites appreciated; better not to involve the mortal authorities in this, however it turned out.

Until finally, with one last fence leapt, four paws pounded across the tarmac, multiple sets of human footsteps behind. As Beckett approached the hangar in which, presumably, his plane waited, he finally slowed just a bit, as though his wound were finally catching up with him, allowing the Assamites to do likewise.

The leader was a mere step away from bringing his blade to bear when the first shot cracked out from behind the hangar to strike the Assamite square in the chest. Even as he fell backward and staggered back to his feet, his companions were diving for cover as bullet followed bullet in a slow but constant barrage.

Half a dozen men and women emerged from behind the hangar. The man who had fired held his jaw clenched, his face twisted in anger and hatred. It seemed strange, then, that his companions all looked shocked, apparently confused by his behavior. The lead Assamite, his chest wound throbbing, wondered briefly if the trigger-happy fellow had jumped the gun (so to speak), launching his ambush before he was supposed to. He didn't know who these people were, wasn't familiar with the thin-bloods pursuing Beckett, and frankly didn't care.

The Assamites closed in quickly, negating whatever slight advantage the firearms might have given their attackers. Fear now replacing the shock on their faces, the others backpedaled, trying to keep sufficient distance to continue firing. The lead attacker, the one who had opened fire, leapt aside as the Assamites advanced and rolled behind an equipment shed.

It was short, bloody, and brutal. Had it been a simple straight-up fight, it would have been a massacre. Cross's thin-bloods, however, expected to be fighting Beckett, a vampire known for his resilience to physical harm, and—unlike their companions whom Beckett had battled outside the manor—had the opportunity to stockpile the appropriate weapons. High-powered rifles, heavy pistols, and even a few explosives that they'd intended to use to ambush Beckett on his way to the plane were instead turned against the eastern assassins. Fast as the Assamites were, few of the shots fired actually landed, but those that did were devastating.

In the end, a single thin-blood survived to flee back into the darkness of Miskolc. One of the Assamites who still stood made his way behind the shed, determined to express his displeasure on the one who had launched the attack—and found no trace of him. He was simply gone, as though he had never existed. The Assamite turned, his face angry, ready to rejoin his companions…

And Beckett, in human form and with talons extended, dropped on him from atop the shed. His clothes were red where the blood on the wolf's pelt had been—blood that came not from any real wound, but from rats' blood Kapaneus had splashed on him, to make the Assamites believe Beckett was injured and explain his apparent slowness. In a reversal of the usual circumstances surrounding the Assamites, the assassin died without a sound.

If the three remaining Assamites had yet been at full strength, Beckett would have considered a frontal attack to be suicide. One was unconscious, however, possibly in torpor; and of the two still standing, one was seriously injured, several large entrance and exit wounds still gaping in his body. When Beckett came around the shed with blood on his talons, with Kapaneus—still wrapped in the image of the thin-blood who'd started the battle—approaching from behind them, and Cesare in the doorway of the plane with pistol in hand, the Assamites decided they'd had enough. The warmth of the dead assassin's blood on his hands, Beckett, perhaps against his better judgment, let them go.

"At least a few nights to heal," he told Kapaneus as the elder resumed his normal appearance. "Longer if they have to wait for reinforcements."

"Then we'd better get back to the library and get started, hadn't we?"

"In just one minute." Beckett turned to face the field beside the tarmac, raised his hands and his voice both.

"I know you're out there!" he shouted. "You're hanging around to see what happened to your friends, and to me! Well, take a good fucking look!" Beckett flicked his hands, sending the Assamite's blood spattering across the ground. "I'm sick of this! I've killed more people in the past few months than I have in *years*, and it's your God damned fault! I'm not going to let you do this to me any more!

"How many of your people am I going to have to go through?! You weren't my enemy; nor was Jenna Cross, until you came at me. I want you to bring her a message. You tell her it stops, now. You people leave me alone from this point, and I won't hold a grudge. You don't, and Jenna really *is* going to be on my shit list. Whatever it is she *thinks* I'm planning to do to her, remind her that I've had several hundred more years than she has to hone my imagination."

Beckett knelt, scraped the remainder of the blood off his hands in the grass, and stalked into the darkness.

Cesare watched his master and the other vampire depart, and then set about cleaning up the mess, collecting shell casings and setting fire to those Kindred corpses not old enough to swiftly decompose on their own. He knew the Miskolc police were still dealing with the panic the wolf had caused downtown; he knew as well that, way out here on the private tarmac this late at night, it was possible nobody had heard the battle, noisy as it was. In neither case was he willing to take the risk. If the police *did* come around here, he wasn't going to make it easy for them to find anything. Whistling to himself, he went to get the hose the airport provided for cleaning the plane and turned it instead on the tarmac and surrounding grasses.

Behind him, a figure invisible to most mortal and undead eyes alike crept onto the plane. It crawled below, making itself as comfortable as possible in the maintenance crawlway for the landing gear, clicked open a laptop with a satellite modem, and settled in for what might prove to be a long wait.

The private library of Sascha Vykos
Miskolc, Hungary

"Looks like I was right," Beckett explained early the next night after they had finally made their way back to the library. As best they could determine, the house was no longer watched. "Filed roughly by the date Vykos got them, as best I can determine." He picked up a tome and flipped through it as he spoke, though his gestures were meant more for emphasis than any actual search.

"I see. And its own books? The ones it wrote?"

"That's part of what threw me. Look." Beckett began gesturing at various tomes on the shelves. "The books it wrote from its own knowledge, it stored in the order they were written, yes. But the notes it wrote about other books… It didn't keep those in the order it wrote them, it kept them in the order it received the *original* texts on which it was commenting."

"Ah." For a moment, Kapaneus fell silent. Then, "Forgive me, Beckett, but I do not see how this helps us."

"Sascha Vykos is—was," he amended with a grin, "—paranoid and selfish enough to make the rest of us look trusting as choirboys. There's no way it would have let Milivoje stay here without some sort of payment. I'm betting Vykos' guest brought it some books, or at least some knowledge it would want to record. We know when Milivoje arrived. So we should be able to locate anything Vykos wrote about those books—and, with any luck, about the Kindred who delivered them."

It wasn't *quite* that simple in execution; the task still required hours of searching to locate the appropriate texts, and to skim through them in desperate quest for anything relevant. Finally, in Vykos' handwritten scrawl, Beckett found it.

It turned out to be little more than a passing comment, as the most important revelations so often are. It was the first line of a passage in which Vykos recorded one of Milivoje's experiences with Rayzeel—yet another discussion about prophecy, as it happened. The beginning of the narration, apparently copied verbatim from Milivoje's own words, turned out to be far more valuable to Beckett than anything that might have followed.

We sat in her haven, tucked away in the shadow of her sire's greatest mistake, where none would think to look for her.

"My God." Beckett straightened up, closed the book with a dull snap. "If I'm interpreting this properly… She was right. It's a perfect hiding place. Who the hell would look *there* for a Salubri?"

"Beckett?" Kapaneus sounded puzzled. "Would you care to explain?"

"Have you ever heard of a Kindred sect called the Baali?"

The elder's mouth turned down in a sneer, perhaps the most extreme expression Beckett had ever seen from him. "Yes. A loathsome line of depraved demon-worshippers. They were considered the greatest of anathema in my time. Multiple attempts were made to wipe their stain from the Earth."

"Some almost succeeded. They haven't existed in any great number since the Middle Ages, and I haven't heard peep one from them in the last five years or so. Maybe someone finally stamped them out.

"In any event, I've looked into them—not personally, I assure you, just historically—a time or three. They had a very different view of Kindred nature, and I was curious about it, if only so I could safely rule it out of my own studies. In those investigations, I came across a small handful of myths about where they might have come from."

Beckett began to pace the chamber, dredging up old memories. "Though they disagree on many details, most of those legends claim they crawled from a pit of filth and carnage in a place called Ash-Sharqab."

Kapaneus blinked. "The City of Ashur?"

"The Kindred once called it that, yes. In modern geography, it's a small city called Qalat'at Sherqat, in the nation of Iraq." Beckett frowned. "Not the easiest or safest place to travel, these nights."

"What has this to do with Rayzeel or her sire?"

Beckett frowned. "It was never proven, mind you," he said slowly, "and the Salubri of the time made a concerted effort to cover it up, but while the legends cannot agree on who spawned the Baali, one of the suspects to arise in multiple myths is Saulot himself."

"Truly?" Kapaneus seemed honestly taken aback. "I would never have thought... How certain are you it is to this site the Tzimisce refers?"

"Not completely. Saulot made other mistakes in his day. For that matter, one could say that letting himself be sucked dry by Tremere was a mistake. But this is the only one I can think of that is both arguably the *worst* mistake, and wouldn't put Rayzeel smack in the middle of enemy territory. If any clan can be called dominant in Iraq, it would be the Assamites, and they would have nothing against her if they discovered her. Hell, they even share a common enemy in the Tremere."

Beckett shrugged and placed the book back on the shelf after skimming it for any further references. "It's not flawless reasoning, Kapaneus, I know that. And we'll keep looking as long as we can. But it's the best we've got so far, and it certainly *feels* feasible."

Feasible or not, however, it was the last piece of relevant information they found. As the clock ticked past midnight on the third night following the encounter at the plane, Beckett and Kapaneus reluctantly agreed that they simply couldn't afford to take any more time.

"If it proves to be a false lead," Beckett told him resignedly, "we can always come back."

"Can we?" Kapaneus gestured at the foul and unnatural accoutrements of the chamber. "Should we not destroy these abominations, free any souls who may yet be trapped within?"

Beckett stopped, glanced around him, fought with himself—and finally shook his head. "No. I'm sorry. I know we should. But I can't risk destroying answers I might need later. I swear to you, when this is done, if we can we'll come back here and do it then."

Kapaneus frowned, but followed Beckett out of the cavern. He wasn't certain which was darker, the empty cave behind him, or the eyes of the Kindred who walked before him.

Taking off from Miskolc Regional Airfield Miskolc, Hungary

"Beckett," Kapaneus asked suddenly as the plane lifted into the air, "do you feel any different?"

"Different? What do you mean?"

"Remove your sunglasses, please."

Beckett blinked, and did so. Kapaneus sighed. "I don't believe you'll be needing those anymore."

"My eyes?"

"Normal, now. Just like your hands."

"Huh." Then he shrugged. "I'll worry about it later. Right now, I'm a bit more concerned about—"

"Signore Beckett?" Cesare called from the cockpit.

"About that," Beckett concluded, and wandered forward, Kapaneus trailing behind. "Yes, Cesare?"

"As you expected, it was simply impossible to obtain flight clearance into Iraq. We'll be landing at Diyarbakir airport. I'm afraid will have to make the rest of the journey on the ground."

Beckett almost had to laugh. Turkey again. It wasn't just a feeling of frustration. He really *was* going in circles!

But then, it was no laughing matter. Turkey was home to more than a few Assamites. They were going to have to watch their backs even more closely than before.

"Well, it'll do, Cesare. Thank—"

"Signore, there is more. In your haste to get us airborne, I did not have the opportunity to tell you."

"Oh?"

"As you requested, I have been checking for email and other messages from Okulos during the day here. He left one not long ago, sounding rather frantic. He said he has been hearing reports of select elders simply collapsing in mid-speech. Some appear to have fallen into torpor, others have begun instantly to decay."

"The withering?"

Cesare nodded, though the gesture was almost invisible from behind him. "Okulos believes so. It has begun to kill."

Beckett sighed, slumping against the wall and sinking into a half-crouch. "We don't have a lot of time, Kapaneus. I don't know why I haven't weakened yet—or why you haven't, for that matter—but it's going to happen. My hands, that odd stretch in Europe when I was never hungry, now my eyes… It's only a question of time before the withering hits me, and hard."

Slowly, he rose once more to his feet. "I'm going in back to clean up. Cesare, let me know if anything changes. Kapaneus…" Beckett frowned for a moment. "If you're a religious man, I wouldn't take it amiss if you'd start to pray for me."

Kapaneus smiled sadly. "With all I've seen, Beckett, God and I no longer get along as we once did. You don't need my prayers."

Beckett looked at the elder for a long moment, then nodded and closed the door to the cabin.

Jenna Cross's haven in the San Fernando Valley
Los Angeles, California,

Cross sat at the table, her friends and lieutenants gathered in the room around her. It was by now a familiar scene, even routine. These briefings and strategy sessions were practically a nightly occurrence at this point.

As it had for weeks now, the chair directly to her right sat empty. Despite all her efforts, and the methodical searches of her best people, she'd been unable to locate even a single trace of Smiling Jack since his disappearance last month. The waxen pallor of her face, more wan now than many vampires several times her age, attested to her inability to sleep; so worried was she, even the rising dawn held only moderate power over her anymore. Had she been able to do so without burning to a crisp, she'd have kept the search up twenty-four hours a day.

Unfortunately, the rest of the world wasn't accommodating her need to find her absent mentor.

"...with minimal casualties," Tabitha was reporting. "With the absence of Prince Tara and the help of the thin-blooded already residing in the city, our people were able to eliminate the primogen and other elders without much trouble." With a broad smile and a wave of her hand that bordered on the melodramatic, she concluded, "Jenna, you can add San Diego to the list of cities we've liberated from Camarilla domination."

Cross could barely force a shallow smile as the room around her erupted in cheers. It was good news, no doubt of that. In the past months, other thin-bloods, inspired by Cross's successes in Los Angels, had risen up in her name—and often with the assistance of those who answered directly to her—to fight back against the ever-more-fascist oppression of the elders. In several cities, such as Dallas and Cincinnati, the thin-bloods had found themselves fighting alongside cells of resistance fighters tied back to Lucita and Theo Bell, despite the lack of any formal alliance between them. She'd never admit it, but Cross was actually glad she'd failed to kill Lucita when she tried.

In half a dozen major cities, and several times that number of smaller towns, thin-bloods clearly outnumbered the more "pure" vampires and were either one of the major powers or were running the vampiric show outright. Even Cross herself had been shocked to discover just how many thin-blooded vampires existed in the world. No doubt the Camarilla and surviving Sabbat officials were utterly stunned. Between those she commanded directly and those who fought under her banner and would certainly jump if she sent them a request, Cross had literally hundreds of vampires at her command, with more appearing every night. Further, that her people were fighting for more than one city forced the Camarilla to split its attention and its resources, making the battle for each individual city that much easier.

All of which meant, of course, that it was time for the other shoe to drop.

"I—" Toby began from across the table. He stopped briefly, cleared his throat, waited for the cheering and mutual congratulations to subside, and began again. "I'm sorry to bring the mood down, Jenna. But…"

She nodded in encouragement as he trailed off. "Report."

"Hardestadt's people have moved into Alhambra, East LA, Compton and Hawthorne. And they've retaken LAX."

The room fell utterly silent.

LAX was not, in and of itself, a surprise. The thin-bloods and the Camarilla had passed the airport back and forth like a football since the conflict began. Cross had taken it when she and her people had killed Tara, the Camarilla had wrested it away with their gas leak, and since then it had changed hands again at least three more times. When they'd last taken the area, however, Cross had been certain that their grip was unbreakable, their position unassailable.

Then again, she'd also been sure that East LA and Compton were firmly defended as well.

"How?" a young thin-blood named David asked, his voice shaking.

Toby frowned as he spoke. "Combination of factors. The usual police raids and other municipal pawns the

Camarilla loves so much served as a distraction. Our own ghouls were busy dealing with them when…" The thin-blood's shoulders slumped. "I take it none of you have turned on the news tonight, have you?"

Cross's eyes flickered around the table, then she shook her head. "We pretty much came straight here from waking up, Toby."

"Fire, Jenna, and more than a few explosives. I don't just mean a bit of arson here and there, I mean big time. Firebombs, Molotov cocktails—it looked like what I've heard of a Sabbat siege, not a Camarilla operation.

"The authorities are calling it a series of coordinated terrorist attacks. Forty-six people—kine—were killed, almost three times that injured. Property damage is estimated in the tens of millions."

"It's not just here," Steve added from the back of the room, his eyes glued to his laptop. "San Francisco, Las Vegas, Sacramento… And we're starting to see signs elsewhere, like Dallas/Ft. Worth. Those fuckers in Riverside have really pulled out all the stops. As of last night, we're losing territory big-time, Jenna."

Cross slumped forward, her face in her hands, and tried desperately not to cry in front of her people.

Dear God, this wasn't how it was supposed to go! This was a *Kindred* war. For everything she'd done, all the violence she'd arranged, she'd done her damnedest to keep the mortal population out of it. Maybe the Camarilla elders had been vampires long enough that they saw the masses of humanity as nothing more than food, but Jenna didn't have that luxury. She and most of her brethren weren't that long past the mortal coil. To her, people were still—well, people.

And now the Camarilla had apparently decided that squashing her was more important than—what? Keeping the cities they wanted in good condition? Than the Masquerade itself? Dozens, maybe hundreds of mortals were dying, and God only knew how many thin-bloods had been slain in these latest attacks.

To say nothing of the fact that she still hadn't heard from—

"Cross?" Another of her people stuck his head in the door. "Jacob's on the phone from Miskolc."

She was on her feet instantly. It wasn't merely that she'd been waiting for word for nights, that she knew whatever he had to say would be important. She also had to consider it was nearly dawn where he was, and they only had a few minutes to talk.

When she returned to the room, none of the assembled vampires had to ask if the news was good or bad; the look on her face was answer enough.

"The team's dead," she announced in a dull voice after a drawn-out moment of silence. "Everyone but Jacob. And he's pretty sure he survived only because Beckett wanted him to deliver a message to me."

"Fucker!" Toby spoke, but the sentiment was clearly shared by everyone in the room. "God *damn* him! We're going to track him down, and tear his ass a new—"

"No."

Jenna could literally feel all eyes in the room boring into her. "No?" Tabitha asked, clearly disbelieving. "What the hell do you mean, 'no'?"

The leader of the thin-bloods, of perhaps the largest faction of non-Camarilla and non-Sabbat vampires assembled since the Convention of Thorns, took a deep and totally unnecessary breath. She swore she could almost see Jack standing beside her, looking over her shoulder and smiling gently in approval. On the other hand, she didn't even want to picture Samuel's reaction; the mere thought of his displeasure made her ache inside, though she'd never been sure *why* his approval meant so much to her.

Still, some things were more important even than him.

"We're through with Beckett for now." It was like pulling her own teeth, forcing those words from her throat. All her friends he'd killed, the horrible fear that coiled in her gut of what could happen to her if he said just the right word in just the right ear, and the angry stares of her companions all screamed at her to bite her tongue rather than give voice to such a thought.

But she'd received Beckett's message clear enough—and though it galled her to admit it, at least part of it was accurate enough. Whatever he *might* do to her, it was *she* who had launched the first attack, she who kept sending her people after him—to their deaths, apparently. No more, at least for now. She was going to lose enough friends, enough soldiers, to the Camarilla. She wouldn't sacrifice any more to assuage her own fears. If Beckett proved a threat to her, she would deal with it herself. Until then…

Until then, if she *must* send friends to their deaths, let them die for a reason. No, Samuel wouldn't be happy about it—might even refuse to help her any further—but then, she hadn't been able to reach him for several nights anyway. She felt a swift flare of concern for his advisor, but she just filed it away with all the other hardships she'd had to endure for the sake of her people.

Jenna Cross pushed Beckett as far as she could from her mind, and turned her attention to planning her desperate defense against a Camarilla that seemed to have totally abandoned any semblance of following the rules.

The Mission Inn
Riverside, California

> "All in support?"
> "All opposed?"
> "Motion defeated. Meeting adjourned."

Hardestadt leaned back in the thick leather sofa, his chin in one hand, the other clutching the remote. Again, he rewound the recording for several seconds; again, he watched a trio of elders slain by a force they—and he—could not even see.

"As you will note," he said dryly to those occupying the room behind him, "we have yet another problem." Hardestadt rose and turned about, allowing the tape to play once more on the large-screen television, focusing instead on the other faces.

Federico di Padua, his face now as repulsive as ever thanks to scars from his latest encounter with Cross's thin-bloods, seemed unable to do more than shake his head in disbelief. Tegyrius stood with his hands clenched so tightly on the back of a chair that the wood had long since splintered. Cock Robin and Hardestadt's various lieutenants in the LA war displayed similar signs of consternation and dismay. Finally, the Ventrue Justicar Lucinde, who was in Riverside only briefly in her service as one of the Inner Circle's greatest (and busiest) surviving field agents, lifted a thoughtful eyebrow but otherwise showed little reaction at all.

Hardestadt frowned as his eyes swept the assembled Kindred, noting the exhaustion and injuries that marred them all. Cross's thin-bloods were doing too well. He wondered, not for the first time, if someone was feeding them information. Yet something *else* he had to deal with.

"We would be foolish," Lucinde commented, brushing her brown hair from her eyes in a gesture more appropriate to the innocent young woman she appeared to be than to the ancient and remorseless creature she truly was, "to ignore the timing of these events. Whatever struck the conclave in Lille, it clearly reacted violently to Pascek's proposal." She turned her intense gaze to Tegyrius, who still stared, fascinated, at the TV screen.

"How about it, Tegyrius?" Hardestadt asked. "Could your former brothers be responsible for this?"

"I do not see how," the Assamite offered, pulling his attention from the screen. "Even Ur-Shulgi himself is not so swift and so stealthy that he would be capable of invading an entire conclave of powerful elders and killing several without being detected."

"Still, sudden assassination is more your area of expertise than ours," Cock Robin offered in his strangely slurred voice. "Have you any idea what might have caused this?"

"None. I'm sorry."

Hardestadt could tell without even looking that at least half of those present didn't believe Tegyrius's claims of ignorance. Tense as the situation was, they wanted someone to blame, and they resented the Assamite for not providing one.

They were scared, the lot of them. Even in his pride, Hardestadt was forced to admit it. The withering was killing now, and no elder could be certain of safety. They'd even gone so far as to bring several staked neonates into the suite next door—constantly guarded, of course—in case any of the ancients present felt a sudden wave of weakness coming over them. The various internment facilities across all known Camarilla territories were as full as the authorities could make them, but it still wasn't going to be enough. Hardestadt knew—they all did—that as the withering grew stronger and the Kindred weaker, they would eventually run out of younger vampires on which to feed. Less than one Embrace in five was now successful. Hardestadt felt himself growing panicked and forced it down, along with a sudden craving for one of the childer in the next room. He couldn't afford to indulge his hunger until it grew truly overwhelming. The Kindred were going to have to ration their supplies, as it were, until this was over.

One way or the other.

"It could be some sort of blood magic, some thaumaturgic manifestation," di Padua commented. "Yes, the Tremere seem to have vanished, but are they truly gone? Even if they are, could this be an after-effect of whatever they might have done to cause the withering?"

"Nor need it be the Tremere to be blood magic," Lucinde put in softly. "It could be the Tzimisce, though they seem to have disappeared as well. The Giovanni. The Harbingers." She didn't include the Assamites, but her swift sidelong glance at Tegyrius left no doubt that she still considered them viable suspects, his protestations notwithstanding. He scowled back at her.

"This," Hardestadt told them, "is a perfect example of why I have chosen to alter my strategies when it comes to the swift conquest of Cross and her vermin."

He began to pace, at least so far as the confines of the room allowed, addressing the assembled Kindred like a general before his troops. "We are facing perhaps our greatest challenge since the Anarch Revolt and the formation of the Camarilla itself. The withering strikes us down from within.

Strange entities appear among us. We are dealing with at least two: the presence at the conclave, and the mysterious darkness that overwhelmed Milan when Prince Giangaleazzo disappeared."

A few of those present muttered a bit at that one. A small but vocal minority of Camarilla officials believed Giangaleazzo's disappearance amidst an Abyssal darkness indicated that he had turned coat once more, fled back to the Sabbat. Given the current status of the Sword of Caine, however, Hardestadt knew they were unlikely to welcome a new elder into their ranks, especially one long thought a traitor to their cause. Giangaleazzo was many things, but Hardestadt knew he was not stupid. No, something had happened to him, and this entity of shadow—possibly sent by the Sabbat Lasombra—was involved.

"Many of our brothers and sisters in the Camarilla," Hardestadt continued, "have taken all these signs to mean Gehenna is upon us. Not merely the neonates, now, but many who should know better. Anarchy and disorder spread like wildfire, and like flame they will consume us all if we let them.

"And now we must deal with this growing thin-blooded pestilence as well? We have, quite simply, too many items on our plate. Our attention is divided, our forces unable to cover all fronts. It is *vital* that we overcome the first of these hurdles as swiftly and decisively as possible, so that we may focus on the others. Thus, Cross must be crushed immediately.

"We have no more time for games, no more time for small skirmishes, lone infiltrations, subtle maneuvering. Though it galls me to admit it, though it goes against every instinct I possess, we must borrow a page from our greatest enemy. We must lay siege to LA, and the other thin-blood strongholds, as the Sabbat would do to us."

"Can we?" Lucinde asked her clanmate almost casually. Even Hardestadt couldn't be certain if she was honestly objecting, or simply playing devil's advocate. "Have we the resources? The thin-bloods outnumber us, Hardestadt, and we are not at our strongest just now."

"The thin-bloods themselves will provide our strength,

as we feed on those we do not slay outright. They may boast numbers, but we have resources. We know where they are, where their leaders meet, where they lair." A fire seemed to smolder behind the Founder's eyes as he spoke. Though many a century had passed, the Beast within him had not forgotten that he was once a warlord and the son of a warlord. War was not new to him, was not his enemy. "Cross and her people have a vested interest in causing minimal damage to their territory, but that is a concern we can no longer afford."

"More bombs?" di Padua asked, his voice troubled. "More fire? More accidents? What of the Masquerade?"

"What of it?" Hardestadt glared at the archon. "We will attract attention, true, but the mortals will not know they are in the midst of anything but a conflict among their own kind. Given events of the past few years, I doubt they'll even be all that surprised at the notion of further 'terrorist attacks.'" The Founder turned to Tegyrius. "If you or your brethren have any ghouls native to your homeland, we may have to borrow them, perhaps even allow one or two to be killed and found by authorities. You will, of course, be compensated."

The Assamite's jaw clenched tight enough to make his teeth ache, but he said nothing. Instead, as Hardestadt's planning session of horrors moved into details, into a discussion of how best to strike at specific targets, he rose and excused himself from the proceedings. As Tegyrius was not directly involved in the LA war, Hardestadt allowed him to go.

Tegyrius hovered at the door to the neighboring suite for a moment, warring against the temptation. But no, while a good meal would make him feel better, he didn't *need* it, and he, like Hardestadt, recognized the need for restraint. Soon it would be better. Soon they would have plenty of thin-blooded captives on which to slake their thirst. Until then, moderation in all things. Tegyrius stepped away from the door and returned to the room Hardestadt had provided him for the duration of his stay in Riverside. He passed several of the hotel staff—all now thoroughly and firmly under the influence of the occupying Kindred—and closed the door to his haven.

He froze.

Something was in the room with him. Tegyrius couldn't see it, couldn't hear it, but he could *sense* it. It resonated in his soul, connected to him in ways he'd never before acknowledged, but always felt.

A hot wind swept through the hotel room, overturning papers, rustling curtains. Tegyrius nearly grew heady with the powerful scent of blood that accompanied it. This, then, was the same intruder that had interrupted the conclave, the merciless killer whose work had appeared on Hardestadt's video even if it itself had not.

And Tegyrius recognized it for what it was.

He did not flee, this powerful Assamite elder. He did not raise his hands to fight against the inevitable. He did not scream.

Tegyrius knelt in the center of his hotel room, his head deeply bowed. In Ancient Arabic, he spoke his final words.

"I have disappointed you. I have shamed you, and your name. Forgive me."

For an instant, the wind blew fiercely, loudly. Then it was gone, leaving a silent room, empty but for a heap of ash that lay on the floor in the shape of a man.

Diyarbakir International Airport
Diyarbakir, Turkey

"Signore Beckett," Cesare suddenly said as the vampires were gathering supplies for the long walk, "let me accompany you."

"What?" Beckett blinked, so thoroughly thrown it took him a moment to be sure he'd understood his ghoul properly. "Cesare, you're a pilot. I need you with the plane."

"Under most circumstances, yes, of course you do, Signore. But this time, what use could I possibly be here? No matter what trouble you might encounter, I cannot come to get you. I could never obtain clearance to fly over the border, and it would do neither of us any good for me to be shot down. Further, the Assamites are quite prevalent here, in Turkey. I could not possibly defend myself against them, should they decide to eliminate your ability to escape. With you, I could at least be another pair of eyes—eyes that, I remind you, may remain open during daylight—and perhaps another weapon should you encounter danger. Further, I myself am *less* vulnerable to attack with you than on my own."

"He may have a point, Beckett," Kapaneus offered when Beckett continued to scowl. "If nothing else, he'll be available to feed from in an emergency."

"Umm—yes, of course." Cesare's face seemed to fall a bit at that notion.

For long moments, Beckett continued to scowl, trying stubbornly to find some good reason to object. He didn't *like* Cesare, didn't like that the ghoul reminded him that, when he had to, he'd play with mortals' lives like any other Kindred. In the end, though, he acquiesced. If nothing else, it would prevent the ghoul from coming after them on his own. *That* would almost certainly get him killed. "But you're going to have to carry the provisions," he warned his ghoul, his voice angry. "If I'm going to have to watch out for you, you're at least going to make yourself useful."

Mere minutes after they departed, a faint thump sounded as the invisible figure dropped from the landing gear bay. This was even better than he'd hoped! The presence of the ghoul might well provide him all sorts of interesting opportunities....

He couldn't keep up with them, of course. He'd have to acquire a vehicle, even as he knew they were going to do, and he couldn't stay close enough to risk them spotting him. That was all right, though.

He knew exactly where they were going.

The Southeastern Taurus Mountains
Near Sirnak, Turkey

So they traveled, Beckett carrying a new satchel with all his standard supplies, Cesare carrying a soft cooler containing several bottles of water, jerky and dried fruit, and a handful of plasma bags from inside the plane's refrigerator.

As they'd anticipated, it was easy enough to acquire a truck—not quite as good as the jeep Beckett had obtained last year, but it didn't have to carry them as far. In fact, it only had to take them about as far south as Sirnak. In quieter times, they could have driven, or maybe taken the train, from there into Iraq. As things stood now, however, travel over the border was *tightly* restricted. Sirnak was on the eastern slope of the Tigris Valley, surrounded by the Taurus Mountains and a stone's throw from both Iraq and Syria. Three armies and several militias stared uneasily at one another across the tripartite border here. They would have to cross on foot, eschewing the closely guarded Habur border crossing. Fortunately, Beckett didn't think it would prove too hard to find alternate means of transportation once in Iraq itself; he did *not* relish the notion of walking about a hundred miles from the border to Qalat'at Sherqat.

Once on foot, they used highways and the railroad tracks as guides, paralleling but never actually using them, traveling southeast from Sirnak. Beckett could have made the trip far more quickly and easily as a bat or a wolf, but he wasn't going to leave Kapaneus behind at this stage. The elder had proven an invaluable and—far more remarkably—loyal companion. He deserved to see this through to the end if at all possible. And there was Cesare to consider.

Their travel was slowed even further by the need to hide from patrols. The jeep that drove past on the highway just a few dozen yards to their left was very much like the one Beckett had used to reach Kaymakli months before, when he was a much more ignorant but also more content vampire. *Unlike* the one Beckett had driven, however, this one was full of Turkish soldiers, all of whom were armed with very large weapons. The same was true of the jeep after that, the jeep after that, and the various trucks that followed. The roar of the convoy was practically deafening, and the earth shook ever so slightly with its movements.

Beckett and his companions stayed low, crouched among the rocks. He wasn't sure if this detachment of soldiers was equipped with night-vision goggles, but he wasn't about to take the risk. The military patrols watching southern Turkey for either renegade Iraqi or Kurdish incursion were a nervous, high-strung bunch—for good reason—and Beckett didn't particularly feel like getting shot tonight.

Though the terrain in this particular area was not especially mountainous—not as compared to other parts of Turkey, anyway—it boasted sufficient peaks and smaller hills that Beckett had no doubt they'd be able to find shelter from the sun. In fact, his biggest gripe at this point was that the group lost over an hour of travel every night because they had to begin searching for a cave or other haven well before dawn, just to be certain they located one in time.

After several nights of travel, they found themselves briefly stymied by the actual border fence line, which had been rather dramatically beefed up during and after the recent hostilities. Beckett knew he could easily make his way either over or through the concertina wire barriers with ease, and Kapaneus had displayed sufficient strength and resilience that he could probably climb it without getting too sliced up. As Beckett had expected, however, Cesare was going to prove a problem.

In the end, after several minutes of debate, Beckett fluttered overhead as a bat, made his way to the nearest military checkpoint, and set a truck on fire. The distraction drew the attention of the roving patrols long enough for him to return, in human form, to the spot along the fence opposite his companions. There, Kapaneus tensed and bodily hurled the ghoul over the razor wire. Beckett squelched a sudden temptation to let Cesare take a face-plant in the sand as an object lesson and caught him. Kapaneus followed a moment later, moving in absolute silence despite the shifting and tensing of the fence beneath his weight. He had, when he was done, not a single cut on him. By the time the Kurdish and American patrols returned to their rounds—alert for saboteurs now, since they couldn't be certain yet how the fire started—Beckett and the others were long gone.

So was an old pickup truck, confiscated during the war, but the soldiers didn't notice that until several days later.

The Tigris Valley
Northwest of Qalat'at Sherqat, Iraq

All things considered, this cave was the best Beckett could hope for. Still, he felt uneasy. Kapaneus, Cesare and he were hunkered down and safe from the sun for now, only an hour before dawn and a few more nights' walk from Qalat'at Sherqat. Things were going as close to plan as Beckett could hope and some instinct told him that was a bad sign.

The trip from the border had gone as expected. Other than the change in uniforms and languages, the soldiers on one side of the border seemed very much like those on the other, as far as Beckett and his companions were concerned: obstacles to avoid. Unfortunately, that hadn't always been possible—traveling by truck required that they stick to the roads and on three separate occasions, men with very large weapons had flagged them down. At the first two stops, Beckett and his companions had been able to talk themselves through—civilian travel in the region was not actually unusual, and people associated with the reconstruction of local oil pipelines and other pieces of the national infrastructure were doing a brisk, if risky business. A certain amount of US currency also helped relax security precautions.

The third stop, unfortunately, had been a more formal checkpoint and the soldiers had insisted on seeing some form of documentation. Kapaneus was able to cloud the minds of the soldiers standing beside the car, but he couldn't do the same for the remainder a few yards down the road. The trio had fled into the desert, leaving the truck behind. They'd then proceeded to Mosul on foot, taking the time to hunt there and replenish what supplies they could. Since then, they'd been following the Tigris. Finding shelter had grown progressively harder as the terrain grew less hilly, but they'd managed. Still, Beckett was worried.

For the past several nights, that worry had become focused on Cesare. The ghoul seemed to be holding up quite well to the physical hardships of the journey, but he'd fallen largely silent, speaking to Beckett and the others only when directly addressed.

Further, he tended to hang back while traveling, keeping at least a few yards between him and the rest of the group. When Beckett had questioned him on it, Cesare had replied, "You cannot afford to give of your blood right now, Signore. So I stay back, where it does not call to me or tempt me." Frankly, Beckett wasn't convinced that was all of it—he was convinced something else was bothering the ghoul—but he just didn't have it in him to worry about it right now.

Beckett was debating asking Kapaneus if he'd noticed anything wrong with the ghoul, when the elder, reclining against a wall, abruptly rose, head cocked as though listening. He sniffed twice. Beckett watched him for a moment, then also rose. "Problem?"

"What?" Kapaneus blinked. "Oh, no, not at all. I just— recognized this place. I have been here before, many centuries ago."

"Here, in this region? Or you actually mean here in this cave?"

"Definitely this area. I am not certain…" Kapaneus abruptly turned toward the exit. "I believe I will look around, see if anything else is familiar. I shall return before dawn, worry not."

"Why don't I go with—"

"Beckett," Kapaneus said with a smile, "for the first time since you freed me from Kaymakli, I may have found something I know. Allow me a bit of time for nostalgia on my own. Please."

Beckett glanced at Cesare, who merely shrugged, and then nodded. "All right, Kapaneus. Be careful, though. We've still got people after us, and for all we know some of the area out there is mined."

"I will. Watch for me within the hour." Then the elder was gone, leaving a vaguely puzzled Beckett behind him.

The Tigris Valley
Northwest of Qalat'at Sherqat, Iraq

Out in the desert, some yards away from the main road that paralleled the Tigris in this area, a manmade eyesore marred the pristine expanse of desert. A blackened husk that had once been an Iraqi tank lay scorched and shattered on the sands. A truly sensitive vampire might well have been able to smell the lingering blood of the men who died within and around it, no matter that it happened some time ago.

None of these vampires was particularly concerned with the tank, however. They simply happened to be passing it.

Over half a dozen of them slipped silently across the sands. Their stealth was not born of the supernatural, though it certainly could have been, but simply by year after year of training and experience. They were almost invisible as well, again not due to any gifts of the blood, but merely to the knowledge of how to use the shadows of the night around them. That most of them were dark enough of skin that they largely disappeared from sight against the nighttime horizon certainly didn't hurt their efforts any, either. The desert predators, snakes and scorpions, fled from their path. They knew the greater hunters when they saw them.

Had Beckett been present, he might have recognized several of the Assamites from Miskolc. They had followed all the way from Hungary, picking up additional reinforcements on the way. Unlike the thin-bloods who had pursued Beckett, they did not rely on intelligence regarding their prey's plane or destination. They tracked through mystical means, guided by their clan's sorcerers who, now that the Tremere had gone, were very likely the greatest remaining in the world. Thanks to talismans granted them by those blood magicians, they knew both direction and distance to their quarry. Beckett was less than an hour away, and had ceased to move. Sheltered for the coming day, no doubt. The Assamites would reach him moments before dawn. He would be unable to flee and, cornered, would die. They would take advantage of the shelter he so conveniently located for them, and depart the following night. They had so far been unable to reach Tegyrius to report, but he would no doubt be pleased once they finally contacted him.

The leader of the Assamite coterie was the first around the burned-out husk. And there, on the other side, someone was waiting for him.

For a long minute the assassins froze, assessing the situation. Clearly, for all their stealth, they'd been detected. Yet the waiting figure hadn't launched an attack the instant they appeared. With a few subtle hand gestures, the leader gave his orders. His companions fanned out to approach the newcomer from multiple angles while the leader himself stepped forward.

"I am impressed," he said in heavily accented English, choosing that language because it was one he knew the other spoke. "Few indeed could detect us coming at all, let alone from so great a distance."

Kapaneus nodded. "I, too, am impressed. Few would have the ability or the tenacity to follow us all over the world like this." He glanced, idly, at the Assamites moving to surround him. "You attempted to kill me in Miskolc."

"We did. We failed, which is not something to which we are accustomed." The leader began to pace slightly—a calculated move, intended to keep Kapaneus's eyes drawn to him so that he could not so easily keep track of the others. "Still, you are not our target. Should you choose to leave now, we will permit you to go. I cannot promise you that you will find shelter before the sun rises, but you stand a better chance searching than you do attempting to stop us."

"Indeed." Kapaneus sounded remarkably unconcerned. "Let me inform you, Khalid, of what will shortly happen."

"How did you know my—"

"You and your brethren," Kapaneus continued, refusing to be interrupted, "are going to leave. You will turn back, you will depart Iraq, and you will cease any further attempts to slay Beckett and his companions."

"Indeed?" The Assamite leader, Khalid, raised his hand in preparation to signal the attack. "And why are we going to do this?"

Kapaneus smiled. "I am delighted you asked."

For long minutes the desert went deathly silent, broken only by Kapaneus' words, no longer speaking English but an ancient tongue the Assamites should not have known, but somehow dimly understood. The words seemed to be directed not at the Assamites themselves, but at their Beasts—and the Beasts cringed in terror. Even the wind was deathly still, as though the world itself strained to hear the elder's voice.

And as Kapaneus spoke, he somehow subtly changed. It was not a physical transformation. Rather, he revealed just enough of his true self to support his words.

Beneath their age-darkened skin, merciless Assamite assassins paled. When the elder finally ceased speaking, they turned as one and fled back into the desert whence they came. There would be no more attempts on Beckett's unlife, at least not from any Camarilla-aligned Assamite.

With a quirk of his lip that might have been a grin, Kapaneus turned and made his way back toward the cave.

Qalat'at Sherqat, Iraq
Former site of the City of Ashur

The last two days had been utterly miserable. Unable to find caves in which to shelter, Kapaneus was forced to bury himself in the sand. Cesare covered himself with his companion's shirts, in order to avoid the direct rays of the pounding sun. Beckett, thanks to his gifts as a Gangrel, was able simply to meld with the earth, but that didn't make things any easier on his companions. By the time they saw the first traces of Qalat'at Sherqat before them, they were all grateful to be out of the barren expanse.

The city itself, home to perhaps forty thousand souls, looked very much like any other desert community. Even after nightfall, people clad in everything from T-shirts and khakis to black chadors wandered the streets on this errand or that. Many had harried, frightened looks on their faces, and they skirted out of the way of strangers—including Becket and his companions.

Most of the city was made up of homes built of stone. Some sat on streets that were actually paved, but others—particularly toward the outskirts of town—were lined up along roads of dirt. Other buildings, offices and businesses, punctuated the houses here and there, and many were gathered in a central area that hardly rated the term "downtown."

Many sections of the city were also in ruins, blackened craters and piles of rubble where people had once lived and worked. Qalat'at Sherqat was not a military target, but it had been hit several times during the war due to an alleged special weapons factory hidden within. Beckett had long since stopped paying attention to most human wars, but had followed the course of this one out of concern for the historical areas within the country. He didn't know if that factory had truly existed or not, but if it had, it was certainly gone now.

Qalat'at Sherqat no longer possessed any real remnants of its former glory. Attacked and rebuilt and excavated multiple times throughout the millennia, beginning as early as the seventh century BC, any ancient structures or historical landmarks and monuments were long gone.

But *somewhere* within the buildings or the wreckage was a pit, a pit that reportedly led not merely into the depths of the earth but in some ways into the depths of depravity itself, the depths of Hell. And if Beckett were truly lucky, somewhere nearby was the woman he had come so far to find.

Now all they had to do was figure out where the hell it was. Odds were, no native vampires existed to ask. A town this size might, under normal conditions, boast no Kindred at all—at most one or two. And any sane vampire would have fled Qalat'at Sherqat in advance of the American bombs. Even if Rayzeel was here, it was highly unlikely any other Kindred were.

Beckett, fluent in Arabic, began to ask around. He explained that he was an anthropologist, hoping to preserve the local culture, to ensure it was not lost in the effort to rebuild. And right now, he said, he was studying superstition and local myth. Was there, he asked, any part of town considered bad luck? Anyplace that people would not go unless they were forced to do so?

He received few answers at first. Most of the people here, for rather obvious reasons, were nervous around strangers. Nor did most of them have large amounts of free time for speaking about unimportant matters.

Still, in the end, though it required him to part with some American currency and several bottles of Cesare's water, Beckett learned what he needed to know.

There was such a part of town, a place rumored from the days of antiquity to be haunted by the *djinn* or other malicious spirits, a place where few worked and only the poorest lived.

And if Beckett had really thought about it, he'd probably have guessed where it was. It all made perfect sense.

Beckett, Kapaneus and Cesare stood at the very edge of the worst of the destruction, staring at a pile of rubble nearly the size of a city block. This was ground zero, as it were, the spot where warplanes had dropped a two-ton bomb on a reputed weapons plant. Beckett knew, however, that something far worse than any factory had been buried in the debris.

It couldn't possibly be coincidence. Surely the foul nature of the pit itself had drawn the violence to it. Surely none the generals who planned to destroy the area, the pilots who carried it out, or—if they were real—the men who chose the spot for the construction of hideous weapons, had realized they were driven by instinct as much as military proficiency. Darkness called to darkness, and this place that spawned the Baali would draw both the foulest urges and the most intense hatred from humanity.

"You don't suppose, Signore Beckett," Cesare asked as the trio stared helplessly at the various heaps of rubble that had once been a number of homes and buildings, "that the woman lies buried beneath all this?"

That had, of course, been Beckett's first thought. He needed a moment to calm down, to silence the Beast that craved to howl in frustration and fury, to feed on all those near it, before he could answer.

A few seconds' rational thought did the trick.

"I don't think so, Cesare. She'd want to be close, where none would think to look for her, but she wouldn't want to be right on top of it. Even assuming the place itself didn't have some sort of corruptive influence, it's an ugly memory she wouldn't want to wake up to every night. No, she's somewhere near here. All we have to do is find her."

"Assuming," Kapaneus pointed out softly, "that she didn't leave here long ago. The Tzimisce's account *was* several years old."

"Don't even start with me, Kapaneus. I'll burn that bridge when I come to it." He glanced around warily, ignoring the stares directed at him by the poorest of the poor from several nearby windows. "Come on, it's getting toward dawn, and we've got a long night ahead of us tomorrow." He waved about in a gesture that encompassed the entire block. "There are enough abandoned buildings around here; I'm sure one of them has a cellar or a contained room we can use.

"Cesare, sleep as long as you need, but try to get out at least once during the day, see if you can find out anything."

"Signore, I speak no Arabic."

"For God's sake, enough people here speak English, Cesare. I'm not asking you to deliver Rayzeel wrapped in a big pink bow. Just see if you can learn *something* useful."

"Of course, Signore. I will do what I can."

"Good. Now let's find a cellar before we start tanning."

An abandoned house
Qalat'at Sherqat, Iraq

"Beckett? Beckett!"

He didn't want to open his eyes. The light would hurt them. "Go 'way. Sleeping."

Though he couldn't see, he somehow knew the figure he felt kneeling down beside him was Anatole.

"Beckett, you need to wake up."

"Don't you have anyone else you can haunt?" Beckett muttered irritably, cracking his eyes just enough to see the Malkavian's face, ringed with blond hair. He couldn't clearly make out his old companion's features. The light shining from behind him was too bright. "Surely you have other friends who also sleep occasionally?"

"Beckett, this is a bad place."

*"Well of course it's a bad place. That's why we're here.
It—"*

*"Beckett, this is a bad place for you. And you need to wake
up!"*

"Anatole, it's still light, I—"

"WAKE UP!!"

Startled and more than a little frightened by the
inhumanly loud scream and the distended shape of Anatole's
jaw, Beckett forced his eyes fully open. He felt slow, sluggish,
as though he were trying to move through half-dried cement.
His head pounded, the Beast curled and whimpered in his
gut. He couldn't do it, couldn't stay awake during the day.
He felt his eyelids beginning to droop…

And then, just before he faded into oblivion once more,
he felt flesh tear beneath his fangs, tasted the coppery flavor
of blood on his tongue.

Beckett came suddenly and completely awake, staring
in horror at the woman—barely more than a girl—he
clutched in his arms. At this angle he couldn't see her face,
just her hair, her ear, her neck…

The Beast rose from cowed to controlling in an instant.
Beckett felt like a puppet with twisted strings—his arms
refused to obey his commands to let go, his mouth and throat
continued to swallow of their own accord. He literally
trembled with exertion, but he simply lacked the willpower
to stop. Only when he found himself sucking the strangely
scented air that was all that remained in emptied veins could
he hurl the body away from himself with an angry shout.
The girl's body flew with the force of his anger to slam dully
against the far wall.

Around him, littering the floor, was the remainder of
the girl's family: an older woman; a man with an injured leg,
probably from fighting in the war; a little boy, probably her
brother. They were dead, all of them, drained of more blood
than Beckett could possibly have needed even in the throes
of frenzy. They must have wandered into the building for
some reason. Perhaps they were homeless, accustomed to

sheltering here from the heat of the day. But how had he…?

Beckett looked around him at the grim tableau, and realized with a sudden shock of horror that he was standing mere feet from the front door to the building. Sheer luck and boards over the windows were all that currently stood between him and the waning—but still quite lethal—sun.

He hadn't merely grabbed passersby in his sleep and fed on them. He had come upstairs from the basement, opened at least one door, moved down a short hallway…

And if his dream hadn't awakened him, what then? In his somnambulant state, would he have followed the scent of blood any further? Would he have opened that door and immolated himself without ever fully waking up?

It had to be the pit, of that he had no doubt at all. Even now, buried beneath tons of debris, the foul emanations of that unholy place twisted and writhed in his mind like a poison. That it was still mystically active didn't surprise him, but that it could hold such power over a newcomer, that it could affect him so swiftly, was not merely shocking; it was terrifying.

Beckett raced back down the stairs. What of the others? Had they…

No, Kapaneus lay in the corner he had chosen, dead to any examination mortals could concoct. Whether due to more potent blood or stronger will than Beckett's own, he remained unaffected by the pit, at least so far. Cesare sat bleary-eyed against the wall, the strain of the journey clearly showing on his sweat-soaked face.

With a brief nod to his ghoul, Beckett sat down opposite Kapaneus, and for an hour and a half stared unseeing into the darkness, his mind and soul wracked with images of the family of corpses above. He did not sleep again that day.

An abandoned house
Qalat'at Sherqat, Iraq

Beckett had just about finished telling Kapaneus what had happened, when Cesare returned, perhaps an hour after sundown. He appeared somewhat haggard, and when questioned would only say that despite his best efforts, he'd been able to learn nothing of any value. Already feeling deeply frustrated, and determined not to spend another day in this Godforsaken place, Beckett wandered outside, followed by his companions.

"This is unbelievable," he muttered to Kapaneus as they stood on the street, watching sporadic pedestrians pass them by. "We know she's in the city. Hell, we know she's probably in the neighborhood. But we don't know how to find her!"

"This is a woman who does not wish to be found, Beckett. She's not going to make it easy for us. I am certain we can locate her eventually, but that's going to require staying here for many nights. I don't believe we can afford to do that."

But Beckett had stopped listening after the first sentence. Instead, with a gleam in his eyes that almost matched the red glow that had recently faded, Beckett stepped out into the middle of the street.

"I," Kapaneus said softly to Cesare, "do not trust that expression."

The ghoul nodded sadly. "I fear Signore Beckett is about to do something patently unwise."

"*Rayzeel!*" Both Kapaneus and Cesare jumped slightly at the volume of Beckett's shout. "Rayzeel, I know you're here! We just want to talk!"

Before the echoes faded, Beckett's companions were with him in the street. "What are you *doing*?!" Kapaneus whispered at him. "Have you gone mad?"

"You said it yourself, Kapaneus. This is a woman who doesn't want to be found. So she's got good reason to come out and shut me up, doesn't she? *Rayzeel!*" Beckett began meandering slowly down the street, ignoring the shocked stares of passersby. "We mean no harm, Rayzeel! We need to speak with you!"

"Did it occur to you," Kapaneus continued, stalking along beside Beckett, "that she might well choose less friendly methods than speech to silence you?"

Beckett shrugged. "She's still got to show herself to do it. *Rayzeel!*"

Despite Kapaneus' protests, this continued for several minutes, and down multiple streets. Finally, as the trio passed a narrow alley between houses, just when Beckett was drawing breath to shout once more, a voice hissed at him from the shadows. "Enough!"

A trio of figures emerged from the alley. The first was clad entirely in a burqa; Beckett could make out nothing save her deep brown eyes. The two Kindred with her, however, were all too familiar.

"I really should have expected this," Beckett snarled, hands clenched into fists so tight they trembled. "I'm surprised she's still alive; you must not have been here very long."

"They are not here to harm me," the burqa-clad woman explained in heavily accented English. "They sought only to speak with me—as you do, or so you have told everyone with ears."

"Really, Beckett," Lucita chided, her narrowed eyes indicating that she found this no more amusing than he did. "Shouting in the streets? Even *you* are capable of more subtlety than *that*."

"You knew where she was?" Beckett growled, eyes locked on his former companion. "When we talked on the plane, you knew?" He took a step forward, hands now open, talons sprouting from his fingertips.

"Back off, Beckett," Theo Bell warned, also taking a step forward.

"No, Beckett, I didn't know," Lucita told him. "But I had an *idea* how to find her."

"And you said *nothing*, you bitch!"

"Why would I care to help *you*? You've no interest in stopping this, in saving everything we've worked for! You just want your precious enlightenment! I had more important uses for the information than helping you justify your useless existence!"

"Damn you, you've cost me weeks, maybe months!" The Beast rejoiced at the anger in Beckett's voice, added to it with its own. "Give me one reason I should let you walk away from here to fuck me over again!"

"You're welcome to try to stop me!" Lucita snapped, her own eyes blazing. The darkness around her feet began to swirl.

"My friends," Rayzeel began, "please…"

But Beckett and Lucita were both beyond listening, and it was all Bell could do to hurl himself aside as Beckett's claws flashed through the space he'd occupied on their way toward Lucita's flesh. A thin tendril of shadow rose up and parried, striking aside Beckett's hand mere inches from the Lasombra's chest. Beckett spun with the momentum, launching a spinning kick, but it was a move he'd learned from Lucita herself. She easily leaped over it, kicked him once in the head from the air, landed in a low crouch and knocked Beckett's remaining leg out from under him with a second swift kick. He hit the ground with a heavy thud. Lucita moved in to keep him down, and barely leapt back swiftly enough to avoid a swipe that would have removed at least one of her feet at the ankles. Beckett rolled upright, and the pair faced off once more, hands raised.

"Beckett," Kapaneus called, trying to get through, "this isn't helping!" At the same moment, Bell shouted to his own companion, "Lucita, stop!" Rayzeel merely shook her head sadly, despairing that nothing about the Kindred had changed in her many centuries of torpor.

But Beckett and Lucita didn't get the chance to attack each other again. Even as they tensed, each preparing to make the next move, a sudden high-pitched shriek, like a rusty dentist's drill, split the night. Across the length and breadth of Qalat'at Sherqat, men and women looked in horror toward the center of town, from where the hideous sound came. The vampires, so near the source, were practically deafened by the sound.

Lucita first recognized it, not as the scream of any living thing, but as the roar of an Abyssal wind, a force that had no corollary in the physical world. She had heard them before, though never one that sounded precisely like this.

From three blocks over, from the darkest of the dark places, from the pit buried beneath layer upon layer of rubble, darkness erupted like a geyser into the desert night. Bits of stone and old bones were tossed aside as a force greater than any the Baali could ever have hoped to summon tore through their place of birth and destroyed it like a child's toy. A column of shadow rose up like some unholy tree, its canopy expanding to blot out the moon, the stars, the entirety of the night sky. Tendrils of darkness whipped this way and that. Where they landed, buildings crumbled. Where they landed, people died.

The shadow towered over Qalat'at Sherqat, and specifically over the vampires gathered on the street.

And in the darkness obscuring the sky, where no natural light could penetrate, the Red Star shone.

Islamic Center of El Paso mosque
El Paso, Texas

Fatima knelt on both knees, facing east, and prayed. Slowly, she lowered her forehead to the rug, all the while praising the name of Allah. She sought guidance. She sought protection. But most of all, she sought the courage to face what she knew was coming.

For hours she had prayed, as she had for many previous nights. She knew she'd not be interrupted. This late at night, the facility was empty save for a small janitorial staff, and she'd come to something of an understanding with them when she'd first arrived in El Paso.

The presence she'd felt for so long weighed heavily on her mind. It had traveled temporarily beyond her ability to follow it. This she knew, without knowing *how* she knew. So rather than chase it around the globe, she had chosen to wait.

It took weeks, but she'd finally sensed it nearing once more. She had begun to pursue it, traveling north into the United States, and then thought better of it. While in El Paso, she had stumbled quite by accident across the Islamic Center. Further, the weight of the presence in her mind, and on her soul, was growing steadily greater. She knew she was no longer pursuing it. It was coming for her. And if

Allah had led her to this holy place, then this was where she would stand.

So she had waited, praying night after night after night.

She knew, even before the wind began to blow, that she would wait no longer.

A hot wind swept the room, ruffling her hair, displacing some of the carpets and hanging decorations of the mosque. Fatima smelled the scent of blood, strong as any fresh kill. Staring straight ahead, unwilling to futilely chase the wind around the chamber, she rose to her feet.

"All I have done," she began, softly but firmly in Arabic, "I have done in Allah's name, but also, where possible, in yours. All for His glory, but for yours as well." She felt her voice shake. The deadly Assamite killer had not been truly frightened in she couldn't recall how long. Well, if the one to whom she spoke would hold that against her, so be it. She'd be a fool *not* to fear.

"I have loved my brethren, loved my clan, from my youngest nights. I would gladly have sacrificed my existence for them a thousand times over, died a new death for every night I have walked this Earth. I loved you.

"But I would not, could not, betray my God, even at the demand of Ur-Shulgi, your herald. Nor, I think, would your ancient teachings have truly required me to. Loyalists to Ur-Shulgi call me traitor. I say that by remaining true to Allah, and to myself, I have remained true to our clan.

"Punish me as you will. But I do not apologize."

In perhaps the greatest act of courage she had ever committed, Fatima fought back the instinct of both body and Beast to close her eyes. She would see it coming. She would look death in the face, as she had always done, one last time.

The hot wind blew…

And faded.

Fatima al-Faqadi had been judged, as had so many before her. And she alone stood.

Tears of blood fell from a Kindred who did not cry. They were tears of relief, yes, but primarily tears of joy. Any doubt she ever felt was stripped away in that final gust of desert wind, for the greatest of all judges but Allah Himself had declared her worthy. Let her death or even Gehenna come tomorrow, and she would face it with a smile.

"Thank you, Grandfather Haqim," Fatima whispered softly into the darkness. Then, like a phantom, she was gone.

Amidst the chaos
Qalat'at Sherqat, Iraq

Terrified mortals ran screaming or stood rock-still, petrified by fear, as the stars above simply winked out of existence, as lights on the street and even in their homes faded, guttered and died. Beckett and the others hurled themselves at the nearest shelter, ending up inside several rooms already occupied by horrified kine. Beckett practically leapt over one young boy in his way and landed in the center of the room standing beside Kapaneus and Lucita. Where the others might have ended up, he wasn't certain.

A strange scent filled the air. No, not a smell, but a *lack* of smell. The odor of sweat from the mortals around him, the blood pounding through their veins, the dust and stone that made up the city—all of it was simply *gone*.

Darkness flowed in from the street outside. Parts of it seemed solid, pouring in through open windows, under doors. Other bits of the great shadow seemed insubstantial however, appearing through the very walls as if they were naught but illusion.

Those mortals who fled from the encroaching shadow were ignored; those who froze were consumed, their bodies and souls swallowed by a darkness far worse than anything darkness might conceal. It rose both above the city and against the roof over Beckett's head, waves and tendrils and abstract shapes of blackness, a Rorschach writ large across the face of the world.

In all his years, Beckett had seen nothing even remotely like it. Lucita had, and the fearless predator of predators shook violently with the horror of what she faced. She had confronted Abyssal nightmares before, but never one this large, never one that exuded so much sheer power. And worse, in ways that even her sire Monçada never had, it felt connected to her.

It felt paternal.

As if to confirm her dreadful realization, Lucita felt what strength she had left drain from her body as if someone had literally pulled a plug. Her muscles went flaccid, her blood thinned, even her flesh seemed suddenly to shrink against her bones, leaving her an emaciated parody of what she had been. Her knees buckled, and it was only Kapaneus' quick reflexes that kept her from slumping to the floor.

But it was not Lucita for whom the shadow hungered. Twitching like the poison tendrils of a jellyfish, strands of darkness reached out for Beckett.

Limbs of shadow with the physical strength to shatter buildings and the mystical power to shame the greatest blood magicians remaining in the world struck outward and downward, and even had they not struck with the speed of lightning, Beckett had nowhere to go. He could do nothing at all save flinch aside as the tentacles lashed toward him…

And passed directly through him as though he were a ghost. He felt a strange, painful chill run through his soul, and he felt the Beast cringe within him, but no harm came to him.

For a long and potentially fatal moment, Beckett could do nothing, so shocked was he to still be in one piece. With wide eyes he glanced around him, meeting Kapaneus' equally intense stare. If Lucita, clutched in the elder's grasp, had seen what happened, she lacked even the strength to react.

The shadow reared up like a startled horse, passing partially through the ceiling. Again and again the tendrils struck, and each time they passed through Beckett, or broke up around him like wisps of smoke.

"Lucita?! Beckett?!" The call came from outside, seconds before the door shattered beneath a booted foot. Bell stood in the doorway, shotgun in hand. "You all right? We didn't know where you'd gone and *holy fucking shit!!*" Bell leaped aside as a stray tendril, aimed almost negligently in his direction, slammed down in the spot he'd occupied.

It was enough to shake Beckett out of his stunned stupor. "Kapaneus, move!" Even as he shouted he was sprinting for the door, snagging Bell's shirt and dragging him behind him as he passed through. Kapaneus, Lucita thrown over his shoulder in a fireman's carry, was only steps behind. Rayzeel and Cesare waited in a doorway across the road, staring upward at the roiling darkness that was now the entirety of the night sky.

"God *damn* it!" Beckett was so maddeningly furious as he skidded out onto the street with the others, it temporarily overcame his fear. "Why is everyone trying to kill *me*?! Why the fuck is it after me?!"

"Perhaps," Rayzeel suggested softly, "we should concern ourselves with that at a later date, and in some alternate location?"

"I'm with her," Bell announced.

"Yeah," Beckett answered, "except that for whatever reason, it doesn't seem to be able to hurt me. Wish I knew why, but it means that all it can really do is try to scare me to—"

The portion of the shadow that had attacked Beckett burst from the building, a great whale breaching a surface of stone. Enormous chunks of rock and concrete, pieces of furniture, and parts of bodies sailed out into the night sky and rained down over the city of Qalat'at Sherqat. Even the bombs that had fallen on the city during the war were less frightening, for those at least were not so completely random, nor so unexplained. Tons of debris landed on buildings, on homes, on cars. Dozens died in the deluge, hundreds were injured.

Beckett hauled himself from beneath an old bathtub, wincing as his left arm bent somewhere between the elbow and the wrist as he used it to brace himself against a nearby slab of concrete. He ignored the pain, forced his body to pump just enough blood to the wound to strengthen the arm and no more. He could heal it fully later—right now, he expected he'd need his strength for other things.

Kapaneus knelt beneath the shelter of the doorway across the street, Rayzeel beside him, Lucita still over his shoulder. How he'd gotten there so fast, Beckett didn't know. Cesare lay in the street moaning, blood on his scalp and a painful-looking gash across his belly, but apparently in no immediate need of aid.

A large chunk of rubble shifted and Theo Bell, blood running down his face and murder in his eyes, rose out of the wreckage. "I think," he snapped in Beckett's direction, "that this thing sure as shit *can* hurt you."

"Beckett," Kapaneus called from the doorway, his voice deceptively calm, "I think I have that Plan B you asked about in Miskolc."

"Run like it's dawn and we're facing west?"

"That would be it, yes."

"Way ahead of you." Beckett glanced up at the hovering darkness, which seemed to have ceased doing much of anything after obliterating the building in which they'd taken shelter. "Let's get out of here before this thing figures out that it's got another weapon in its arsenal and—"

With a shriek of stressed metal and a shattering of stone, the top two floors of a nearby structure simply disintegrated into a hail of deadly projectiles as a tendril of shadow thicker around the middle than a city bus slammed through it. Again metal and rock and glass and bodies—some of which screamed until the moment they struck the ground—rained down on Beckett. This time, however, it was no accidental fallout from a random and chaotic act. This time, it was aimed. Beckett felt a painful gash open in his left side, his right leg shatter at the knee and in at least two other spots, and his right shoulder dislocated before his vision was eclipsed by the hurtling screen of an old television. Then there was impact, and then a blackness nearly as complete as the entity of darkness took him.

The Tigris Valley
West of Qalat'at Sherqat, Iraq

Beckett came to abruptly. It was one aspect of the Kindred condition he could sometimes have done without, the abrupt shift from oblivion to consciousness. Were he awake during the day, he might have been groggy, half-awake—and might have had the time to slowly assimilate everything going on around him. At night, a vampire was either fully awake or unconscious. Barring drug-tainted blood or some form of supernatural influence, no middle ground existed.

The pain hit him first—a sharp ache in his right leg, both arms, his chest, his head. It all had the familiar feel of injuries only partially healed through the body's instinctive application of blood. He could move, could probably even run for short distances if he had to, but it wouldn't be fun.

Beckett kept his eyes closed, reaching out with his other senses to determine what was happening. A wind blew across his face. Slightly warm, rough, smelled of rock and sand. Desert, definitely. The roar from just ahead of him and the fact that he was bumped and jostled suggested a car, and by the strength of the wind, one moving at high speed.

And blood. Even within the case Cesare carried, even wrapped in plastic, he could smell the blood. Beckett opened his eyes.

He lay unceremoniously sprawled in the back of a beat-up old orange pickup. Lucita lay alongside him, looking worse than he felt. If he didn't know better he'd have mistaken her for a real corpse, so gaunt had she become. Cesare sat beside them, his knees tucked to his chest and his arms wrapped around them. Kapaneus too was in the back, resting on his knees by the tailgate, staring out behind them. That probably put Bell at the wheel and Rayzeel in the seat beside him, assuming everyone was still together. Beckett rose painfully to a sitting position to see…

And saw what was behind them. He promptly forgot about checking the cab.

In the distance, he could still see Qalat'at Sherqat, plumes of dust and smoke rising into the night sky where multiple buildings—far more than the two he had experienced while conscious—had been simply obliterated, wiped from the city like a frustrated child's model. The rocky desert bumped and rolled by beneath them as the small truck gasped and wheezed its way across terrain it simply wasn't equipped to handle.

And in the air behind them seethed a cloud of pure shadow. It stretched almost from the city itself and rolled across the sky like a storm front. Tendrils lanced out and down like lightning, tearing chunks of sand and stone from the desert floor. The sky ahead of them was full of stars and a brightly gleaming moon; the sky behind, a featureless expanse of black.

Worse, shadows lashed out from ahead of and beside the truck as well, seeking to snare the wheels or otherwise halt the vehicle. The great Abyssal force behind them didn't stretch that far. For the darkness ahead to strike at them as well meant the thing wasn't merely of the Abyss, it could *control* the Abyss like the Lasombra themselves.

Beckett lunged across the bed of the truck, drawing a sharp startled yelp from Cesare, and yanked away the cooler. Like an animal he dug into it until he found the few remaining bags of blood. He drained one in an instant, squeezing the bag to force the blood out faster. The second he drank a bit more slowly; the third and final he left for whatever might come.

"Beckett," Kapaneus shouted over the roar of the wind and the engine, "are you well? You were badly—"

"Later!" Beckett worked his way forward, made certain he had a good grip on the cab, and leaned forward so his face was beside the driver's side window. Sure enough, Bell was at the wheel, Rayzeel, her head still largely covered, beside him. Even from his angle, Beckett could see wires hanging from under the dashboard where someone—either Bell or Cesare, almost certainly—had hotwired the truck.

"You back among the living?" Bell asked, his eyes focused on the desert ahead of them.

"Cute. We're not going to outrun this thing, Bell."

"Noticed that, did you? You got a better idea, though? We can't fight it. Showed us *that* well enough back in the city."

"Sure we can. Head for as empty an area as you can find, and here's what we're going to do…"

When he was through, Bell actually *did* take his eyes off what passed for a road. He stared as though Beckett had grown a second head. "You're fucking nuts."

"Probably. You have a better idea, now is well past time."

Bell shook his head and gritted his teeth. "Just say when."

Beckett pulled himself back to look at those in the bed of the truck. The darkness was only a few dozen yards behind them now. "Everyone, when I say so—jump."

His reward was two more incredulous stares. Even Lucita, who hadn't moved in some time now, managed to flick her eyes in his direction.

"I'm sorry," Kapaneus said, "would you repeat that?"

"When I give the word, jump. Out of the truck. Kapaneus, you'll have to carry Lucita again."

Cesare's eyes grew wider still. "Signore, what are we—"

"Shut up and do what I tell you." Beckett slid to the back of the bed, both hands tightly gripping the tailgate, and watched nervously as the darkness grew nearer.

And nearer.

The aroma of the desert faded, replaced by the complete absence of scent that presaged the coming of the shadow. The wind that blew past them changed direction, as the frigid Abyssal winds grew stronger than the forward motion of the truck. Beckett, his undead body normally unbothered by extremes of temperature, shivered violently in the unnatural, soul-numbing cold.

And then it was upon them. A tendril lashed out from the darkness and did not fall short. It wrapped around the right rear tire and popped it like grape. The truck lurched, skewing wildly for an instant until Bell could regain control. Lucita slammed hard against the side of the bed with a bone-crunching impact. Cesare toppled head over heels to land beside her, and only Beckett's quick instincts allowed him to avoid being tossed from the bed by sinking his talons into the metal. Only Kapaneus, predictably, seemed to have no difficulty keeping his balance.

The second tendril wrapped around the entire truck, just behind the cab. It tensed, somehow reminding Beckett of an industrial cable, and began to lift. The truck immediately tilted forward, unbalanced by the weight of the engine, as it rose above the desert floor.

"Now!" Beckett shouted—not that he really needed to. He'd have been hard pressed to *keep* his companions from abandoning the truck at that point.

Cesare vaulted over the edge of the truck bed, while Kapaneus scooped up Lucita and leapt well clear. Beckett heard but did not see both doors fly open, and he knew he had to throw himself clear before Bell carried out part two of this lunatic plan.

Beckett tensed to leap—and the world turned inside out. He felt nauseated, sicker than he'd ever been as a mortal, let alone since his Embrace. A quiver ran through his limbs as his muscles all contracted against one another and slowly released, leaving behind a dull ache. Even his heart, dead for centuries, beat once and once only, that flaccid muscle giving one last spasm along with the rest of him. His vision blurred briefly, realigned itself, blurred again, cleared again, all in a span of instants. The strength seemed to drain from his legs. He didn't grow weak exactly; he was still far more fit than most mortals, and many other Kindred. But he felt worn, felt that a small but significant portion of his own vitality had been sucked out of him. His leap faltered, and he slammed his ribs into the side of the bed and fell back into the truck.

Now, of all possible times, Beckett had lost his advantage, lost whatever blessing had kept his safe. Now, finally, the withering had him too.

Lying right in the angle where the bed met the cab, Beckett looked up into pure, unbroken darkness. Even as he drew near to oblivion, he faintly heard multiple cracks from Bell's shotgun below. The former archon was following the plan; he either didn't know Beckett had failed to leap free, or he was—wisely—not allowing it to stop him.

"Piss off," Beckett spat at the shadow looming above him even as the truck shuddered with the first impact. Then, mustering every last bit of strength he had remaining, Beckett scrabbled awkwardly to his feet—an impressive accomplishment, given the constant shifting and bobbing of the truck—and jumped once more.

The gas tank blew even as Beckett's feet left the metal.

The desert sky was abruptly lit, the air shattered by a sound that hadn't been heard in the region since the bombing had finally ceased. Temporarily blinded, deafened and burned, Beckett felt himself hurtling through the air far farther than any leap of his could possibly have carried him. The ground rose up to meet him and he hit hard, digging a furrow in the coarse desert sand.

Painfully, blinking his eyes clear, Beckett rolled onto his back and looked back at the conflagration. Tendrils of shadow writhed in agony as the husk of the pickup continued to burn. A loud keening pierced his ears—no, not his ears, the scream sounded directly in his mind. The creature of shadow hurled this source of pain with all its might; still burning, the truck sailed into the darkness and vanished behind a sand dune.

Beckett slowly rose to his feet even as his companions assembled around him, all of them staring at the Abyssal beast. They had stung it, perhaps, but that was all. If the eruption of flame had done it any lasting harm, they certainly couldn't see it.

"Nice try, Beckett," Bell said softly. "But I think that was all we had."

"Everybody back away."

"What?"

Beckett scowled. "I said everybody back away. Now."

Hesitantly, they obeyed, moving perhaps a dozen yards off. Beckett stood alone in the empty desert as the darkness gathered around him.

"I don't know what you are," Beckett said, his voice just shy of a shout. Actually, that was only partially true; Beckett had a pretty good idea what this thing *might* be, and the notion terrified him like nothing before ever had. If he gave in, even for an instant, the Beast within would have him in headlong flight—and that way lay suicide.

Not that trying to shout the thing down offered much better odds, but it was about all he had left in him to try.

The Tigris Valley
West of Qalat'at Sherqat, Iraq

The creature was yelling at the darkness, and the darkness recognized it. *This* was the one. It was on this tiny, pitiful entity that the darkness could sense the taint of the energies that awakened it, the energies released when the barrier was torn down. It had been like this pathetic creature once, when it had a name that shook the pillars of the world whenever it was spoken. Now, now it was something else; now it was not of this world. Things of matter, things of light, these were painful. This tiny creature had brought it back into this painful world and it would destroy him first.

"I don't really even know if you can understand me," the tiny thing continued, "but I know you're smarter than you look. So listen up! I don't know why you want to kill me. Right now, I don't care. For whatever reason, you can't hurt me directly. We saw that back in Qalat'at Sherqat. Well, we're out in the middle of nowhere now. Iraqi desert plains. What are you going to do, throw pebbles at me? You could go grab a boulder somewhere, but I'll be mist or melded with the earth before you get back."

Above Beckett, the darkness writhed. The tiny entity was standing before it, as though offering itself. Frustration made the tendrils of shadow quiver, made them thrum like violin strings. It had the creature at its mercy, but it couldn't touch it! Something—something more than the tainted energies, something truly powerful—protected it. For all its power, the shadow could not touch the tiny entity so long as it was warded.

But there were others here, others it *could* touch. Others it *knew*. Slowly, like thick batter poured from a bowl, portions of the darkness began to pile up on the ground behind the entity that continued to jabber on, unaware of what was happening between it and its companions.

"We have a standoff here," Beckett was saying. "Given your reaction to the fire, I'm going to bet that you don't like the sun any more than I do. I can meld into the earth at my feet. Can you? And if so, then what? You just going to hover around out here in the desert until I decide to come out? You have nothing better to do, nowhere else you need to be?"

It *could* wait, of course. The tiny entity before it didn't understand. It thought it knew patience, thought it knew immortality, but it knew nothing of true eternity. The thing from the Abyss could wait as long as it needed to wait, and longer.

But why should it? Why wait, when it had other, more immediate options?

The shadow on the ground behind Beckett rose, and as it did so it began to take on form. Darkness poured upon darkness, creating folds and bulges that quickly took on the appearance of rolls of human fat. At the base of the shape it split apart, until it appeared to stand on two human legs. More shadow trickled down from the top and hung, forming arms. And at the top, like a growing pustule, the darkness extruded a shape that swiftly formed a head.

Still the darkness twisted, warped and shaped itself, until what stood between Beckett and his allies was the perfect silhouette of a man.

Or a vampire. A particularly obese vampire.

And Lucita, for the first time since this last great weakness had swept over her, reacted: She screamed, as though her soul had been rent apart from within.

The Tigris Valley
West of Qalat'at Sherqat, Iraq

Beckett spun, the shriek from behind his first warning that something was happening. Even from the back, even with no details but the silhouette, he recognized immediately what was happening, what this thing of shadow had done.

"Oh my *God*…"

Ignoring Beckett, ignoring all present but Lucita herself, the figure stepped forward, waddling with the strange side-to-side shuffle of the morbidly obese. And impossibly, the shadow spoke.

"It has been too long, my daughter. I have missed our conversations."

To Beckett's ears, the voice had a strange, double-layered quality to it—as if it echoed at the same moment it first sounded. The primary voice was normal, physical, tinged with a slight Spanish accent. The other was inhuman, otherworldly, and reverberated in the minds of the listeners even as the first sounded in their ears.

"You're gone…" Lucita sobbed, slumped in Kapaneus' grasp, hanging limply from his arm. "You're gone!"

Though still largely featureless, the shadow that bore the shape and the voice of Ambrosio Luis Monçada smiled. The watchers could tell simply by the flexing of its cheeks and jaw. "My beautiful daughter, I taught you better than that. Surely you did not think I could be taken from this world so easily? I, who know God's plan and my own place within it? I told you we had purpose in the divine order, Lucita. Clearly you did not believe. But you believe now."

Again the figure stepped nearer, until it was within fifteen feet or so of Lucita and the others. Bell, with a snarled "Fuck *this*!" opened fire on the approaching darkness. The rounds passed through the phantom Monçada as though he was nothing more than the shadow of which he was made, and Beckett had to hurl himself aside to avoid them. Picking himself up, he saw the greater body of the Abyssal creature hovering motionless, its attention apparently devoted entirely to the puppet show playing out before it.

"Lucita!" Beckett lifted himself to his feet, grimacing as he wiped sand from the burns inflicted by the exploding truck. "Lucita! It's not Monçada! It's not your sire! It can't be!"

"Can I not be?" Monçada loomed over his daughter, and slowly facial features began to appear in the formerly empty darkness. "Did you not see me taken below, consumed by the Abyss, there to join with all our brethren who had come before? And have we not now, all of us, risen again from depths of darkness to resume our place in God's creation?"

"No… no…" Lucita wept tears of blood she could not spare, unable to meet the thing's gaze. She pressed her hands to her ears, but its voice continued in her mind.

"Still you doubt, dear Lucita. Let me show you, in ways I never could before when I was merely Monçada, what you have to gain by accepting your rightful place."

The cold wind blew from the darkness, and Lucita shuddered as though struck by a powerful shock. Strength flooded her body, strength she hadn't felt in months. Her flesh instantly lost much of its pallor and filled out once again. She felt her connection to the Abyss grow strong, stronger than it had ever been. All she had lost to the withering returned, and more beside.

Lucita pulled away from Kapaneus to stand on her own. Where she looked, the shadows danced at her merest thoughts and whims, requiring no concentration at all. She spun about to watch them, and her speed kicked up a storm of sand. She vanished utterly from sight, reappeared seconds later a dozen yards away, returned just as quickly. If she strained, she could hear the thump of each individual grain of sand as it fell back to earth. In wonder and not a little fear she stared up at the thing that claimed to be her sire.

"You are not Monçada," she insisted, but even now, stronger than she had ever been, her voice quivered.

"You know better than that. I am Monçada, for I am all that have come before. You know me, Lucita. Now serve me, as you were always meant to. Only submission to your role will bring you the happiness and the contentment you have sought."

Like a burrowing worm, the voice insinuated itself into Lucita's soul, wrapped around her brain as though it were a physical thing. She had taken three steps toward her "sire" before she was even aware of her movement. "What…" She stopped, cleared her throat of dust and sand. "What would you have me do?"

Monçada very deliberately turned his head to stare in turn at each of her companions, lingering longest on Beckett. That he had to turn his head completely around to do so seemed not to bother him in the slightest.

"No." Lucita drew herself up. "I will not."

"My dear, I would not ask you to slay your old companion. Not at first. We will work up to it, start with one of the others. They are nothing to you, after all."

"I won't."

"You stupid child!" Monçada's voice rocked the night sky, reverberated miles through the desert. Beckett, Rayzeel and Bell dropped to their knees, clutching their heads in pain. Cesare fell to his back in the sand and writhed. Lucita would have joined them, but tendrils of darkness held her upright. "Have you truly forgotten *everything*?!

"They are nothing, my daughter. *You* are nothing, and ever shall be nothing without me. I define you, Lucita. I always have, whether by your resistance or by your submission. But the time for childish games is over. Take your rightful place, Lucita. Return to me—and bring the dark one's head with you."

Lucita could not see the desert for the shadow that filled her eyes. She could not hear her companions for the phantom's voice in her ears. She could not feel anything, think anything, for her sire had taken hold in her soul. There was nothing left to the world. Monçada was all. No desert existed, no Beckett, no Bell.

No Lucita.

Eyes blank and unseeing, she turned toward the huddled form of Theo Bell, who was still trying to shake the pain from his head. She stood above him, and the shadows came at her call, forming a blade that hovered over the Brujah's exposed neck...

And Beckett, his entire body shaking with the pain, blood trickling from his left ear, rose to his feet. "Lucita!"

She turned instinctively at the sound of her name.

"Ignore him, child!" Monçada commanded. "Do as I have instructed!"

"How many times, Lucita," Beckett asked, "did you seek comfort, solace, and enlightenment in Anatole's teachings? How many times would you have returned to Monçada without his support?"

"Silence him, my daughter!" Tree-sized tentacles of shadow writhed in the night sky, but Beckett refused to turn around.

"If you do this, Lucita, you make Monçada right. Everything you fought for was a lie. *Everything Anatole ever told you was a lie!*" Beckett stared at her, meeting her empty eyes. "Did you truly hate Anatole that much, that you'd wipe his influence from your existence in one fell swoop?"

And for an instant—just a single, fleeting moment—Lucita's eyes cleared.

She screamed once more, no bleat of fear this time but a primal shriek of rage the likes of which even most vampires were incapable. In a fraction of a second Lucita was behind Beckett and leaping, not at the dark reflection of Monçada but at the heart of the shadow that spawned it. As she hurtled at it her skin seemed to melt away as she called upon her returned mastery of the Abyss to take on a shadow form. Wings of darkness propelled her into the center of the thing from the depths, claws of darkness sliced at its substance in a way no material weapon could.

"Lucita!" Monçada's voice echoed in her mind, but it felt distant now, far away. "Lucita, stop this at once!"

"No one owns me!" Her response was mental, emotional, not physical, but she knew he heard. Thrashing about, she tore chunks of darkness from the surrounding shade. "Not Monçada! No one!"

This time, when the voice came, it sounded not as a pair of tones but as a thousand, all reverberating within her head.

I OWN YOU! FOR YOU ARE OF ME, AS MONÇADA WAS. I AM THE ONE WHO WAS AND THE ONE WHO WILL BE! AND YOU CANNOT DISOBEY!

Though she had no features remaining to show it, Lucita smiled. "Watch me, you bastard."

The shadow that was Lucita lashed out in all directions. Wings, claws, fangs—anything she could strike with, she did. Bits of darkness fell away, only to be consumed immediately by the greater whole. If the dark was what it claimed to be—and she knew, in what remained of her soul, that it was—she could not destroy it. But damn it, she would try.

And she *would not yield.*

Not even to Lasombra himself.

Pressure pounded on her mind as the thing sought to reassert control, but whether it was Lucita's force of will or simply the madness of a frenzy she hadn't even realized she'd entered, it could not force her to stop. She felt herself lifted, supported, as though someone else were holding her aloft and offering her the strength to resist just a few moments more. The mind of an ancient washed over her like a tide, but it could not take hold of her own thoughts.

Her newfound strength drained from her like blood from a wound. Between one second and the next she found herself physical once more, unable to maintain the transformation into shadow. Still she lashed out, but it was an exercise in pure futility. Even had she strength to strike with any force—strength she was rapidly losing—her solid form was simply incapable of damaging the darkness.

Her strength faded until she had none left to give, and still the drain did not stop. Her vision—what little of it existed in the midst of this darkness—blurred. Her racing thoughts began to slow. Even her pain, her last anchor to unlife, faded away.

Here, at the end, she would lose her independence before death. She would be absorbed into this monstrous thing, and she lacked any remaining strength to stop it. She—

"Hello, Lucita."

With her last bit of mobility, Lucita turned her head to stare in shocked recognition at the sound of that voice. She stared up, not into darkness but into a blond-framed face surrounded by light, and wept her final tears. And they were tears of joy, for she had won.

Lucita reached out to take Anatole's hand, leaving her body behind to be absorbed by the shadow that could no longer hurt her, and was gone.

The Tigris Valley
West of Qalat'at Sherqat, Iraq

The Abyssal entity hovered over the desert. For a time, it simply ceased to move at all. Tentacles and limbs of shadow hung motionless, dragging on the sands. The stars remained blotted out, but the darkness ceased to expand, ceased to move.

For the darkness didn't understand. In that portion of its mind still capable of confusion, it pondered what had just occurred. It was inconceivable. The thing of shadow could no more accept it than a human might have understood if one of its own limbs had turned against it.

It contemplated for only a brief time before it dismissed its concerns entirely and turned its attention back to the matter at hand. But a "moment" for an entity that was undying even before it became one with the darkness below is long, and when it was once more aware of its surroundings, the desert was empty. Still, it felt the pull of the one it sought, back in the direction from which they had come.

It also felt the growing weight of the sky, and knew the bright was not far away.

Slowly, the shadow sank into the sands. Tomorrow night, it would catch the elusive creature once more. And then it would move on, for there was still much to do before the others awoke…

A disused house
Qalat'at Sherqat, Iraq

The night after Lucita's death, Beckett woke on a cot in a disused house on the outskirts of the city. Battered, beaten, weary and shocked to the depths of their souls by Lucita's sacrifice, he and the others had fled the scene the instant the great shadow ceased moving, and reached the outskirts of Qalat'at Sherqat barely an hour before sunrise. The city had been bustling with grim activity: rescue teams and concerned civilians digging through rubble with insufficient tools and bloody hands to rescue any who were trapped within; poorly equipped firefighters struggling to contain the various blazes that had flared up in the midst of the devastation; paramedics carrying the wounded to hospitals that barely had the requisite supplies to care for them.

Beckett and the others had ignored it all, seeking only shelter from the fast approaching sun. Thankfully Rayzeel had led them to an area on the outskirts where they were likely to find several houses abandoned by those displaced during the war. Beckett had stumbled, weak and wounded, into one, taken a few deep breaths, and determined from the scent that no mortal had been inside in months. He and his companions had then stumbled into the basement and collapsed into slumber as the dawn broke.

Now, Beckett painfully cracked his eyelids open and saw Rayzeel bustling about the room around him. Cesare and Kapaneus stood against the wall, watching warily. Bell was nowhere to be seen, and Beckett figured (correctly, as it happened) that the Brujah was out scouting.

Rayzeel had removed her burqa and wore only in a simple skirt and blouse. Beckett, for the first time, got a good look at her. She was beautiful, in a strange, slightly off-kilter way. Her features were sharp, her hair a rich coffee brown. She definitely had the look of someone from a prior age, though Beckett couldn't have said precisely *what* about her features marked her as a walking relic. He also noted, and he couldn't quite repress a shudder even though he'd expected it, the third eye that stared, rarely blinking, from the center of her forehead. She saw his movement, knew he was awake, and sat down gently beside him on the cot.

"Rest," she told him. "You will be weary for a few moments yet."

"Weary? Why?" Or at least, he *tried* to ask. He was startled to hear the words come out slurred, to realize that he was practically weighted down to the cot with an exhaustion that far surpassed the weakness he'd experienced as the withering finally took hold.

"What…" He tried again, speaking each word deliberately and slowly. "What did you do to me?"

"Do not be angry at Rayzeel," Kapaneus said, stepping forward. "We all agreed it was necessary."

"Kapaneus," Beckett said, the words coming faster and easier as he continued to speak, "I'm going to drag myself off this cot and start breaking necks if someone doesn't tell me *what the hell you're talking about*!!"

"I cleansed you," Rayzeel said softly, her third eye glowing ever so faintly.

And Beckett's horrified look, Kapaneus nodded. "You remained in slumber later than we, due most likely to your wounds." Something in his look told Beckett that he knew it was more than that. Kapaneus knew the withering had finally claimed Beckett as well. Out of respect, perhaps, he said nothing about it to the others. "We knew that the great darkness would be on us once again, and we knew it was after you. Rayzeel and I examined your aura, closely, and we found your soul tainted."

"We believed," the Salubri picked up where Kapaneus stopped, "that it was this taint that drew the shadow to you. I thought I might be able to wipe the taint away, to protect you—all of us. But I could not wait until you awakened to ask permission."

Beckett drew himself upright and glared at the woman. He knew just enough of the Salubri to know what that process must have required. "So without asking, you just sucked my damn soul from my body and fiddled around with it?! What *else* did you do to me, you God damn—"

"*Beckett!*" Kapaneus' voice thundered through the room. Cesare jumped, Beckett cringed back against the wall, and even Rayzeel seemed shocked. Beckett was actually surprised to see the elder's shout hadn't shaken dust from the walls. "You of all people know better than to fall prey to silly superstitious prattle. If Rayzeel had 'fiddled' with your soul, you wouldn't be capable of questioning her. This woman—who you have spent months trying to find, I might remind you—may well have saved you."

Beckett nodded once, slowly, and turned back to Rayzeel. "I apologize," he said, and if there was still anger in his eyes, he kept it out of his voice. "I'm a bit—harried, right now."

"I understand. My people are accustomed to the fear of others."

Beckett wondered if it would make her feel any better to know the Tremere—the scourge of the Salubri and the source of most of the hatred that had fallen upon them over the centuries—had apparently disappeared. He decided that, at least right now, it probably wouldn't.

"So," he said instead, "how do we know if it—"

"Heads up!" They heard the shout, and heavy steps on the floor above them and the stairs leading down, before Bell burst into the room, shotgun held at the ready. "It's back!"

"...worked?" Beckett finished flatly.

Rayzeel stared at him with all three eyes. "We wait."

For several minutes, silence fell. Then, filtering down from the streets above, they heard screams, and more screams. At first they were screams of fear, as the rolling darkness approached. Then the ground shook and the air was shattered with constant roars as limbs of shadow smashed flat building after building. Then they were not merely screams of fear but of pain. The sounds came first from this direction, then from that, with no apparent rhyme or reason.

"It's striking at random!" Beckett hissed.

And then, just like that, the sounds and the shaking passed them by and were gone.

This time when Beckett turned to Rayzeel, his anger was well and truly gone. "Thank you," he whispered.

The Salubri smiled. "You're welcome. But I think this was not why you sought me out."

Beckett curled around until he was sitting cross-legged on the cot. Rayzeel stood near the door, Kapaneus opposite her against the wall. Bell and Cesare left the room to keep an eye topside, just in case.

"Kapaneus told me a bit of your search," Rayzeel told him. "Though frankly, he hardly needed to. Given Lucita's quest, I guessed yours to be similar."

"Not precisely. Lucita wanted to stop Gehenna. She..." His voice trailed off. "I can't believe what she did."

Kapaneus nodded slowly. "I pride myself on my ability to judge others, and it surprised me as well, Beckett. She did not do it for us, you understand."

"I know. Her need to be free. Still... I don't know if I could have done that."

For a long time, no one in the room had anything to add.

Along a ruined street
Qalat'at Sherqat, Iraq

Cesare stood staring at an enormous pile of rubble that had once been a building—a building where people lived, laughed. Now it was a tomb, a monument to monsters. The ghoul loved his master, could have done no less, but at times, he resented Beckett as well, resented him for showing Cesare the world as it truly was.

He was grateful, really, that Bell had suggested splitting up to cover more ground, had gone a different way. Cesare really didn't want to be around vampires right now.

Unfortunately, he wasn't given the option.

Powerful hands, far too strong even for the powerful ghoul to fight off, wrapped around him from behind and efficiently snapped his neck. Cesare, his head wrenched almost completely around, died with the sight of his own assassin filling his vision.

An assassin who wore a face that looked exactly like Cesare's own.

Bell, after a brief circuit of the area, had taken it upon himself to guard the entrance to the house in which his companions recovered. He watched with unblinking eyes as smoke drifted into the night sky from the fires blazing across Qalat'at Sherqat, watched as those few people still dwelling in this part of town did what they could to fish survivors from the rubble.

When Cesare appeared from down the street and brushed past the former archon with a brief nod of greeting, Bell barely even noticed him.

A disused house
Qalat'at Sherqat, Iraq

Below, the silence dragged on, neither Rayzeel nor Kapaneus willing to disturb Beckett's ruminations. Finally, as though he'd never stopped, he said, "So, she wanted to stop Gehenna, but I don't believe that can be done. I just want to understand the Kindred's purpose before the end."

The Salubri laughed, but it was a light laughter with no mockery in it. "You don't ask much, do you?"

Beckett smiled wanly. "The world's about to end, or at least ours is. No reason not to go for the gusto."

"And why do you believe I can aid you in this?"

"Mostly because of your sire, I suppose. Saulot is said to have been the wisest and most enlightened of the Antediluvians. His writings are known throughout the world as the most precise and greatest of Gehenna prophecy. And it is said by some that he was favored of all Caine's children. I suppose I just figured that if *anyone* could help me find my answers, it'd be him—and, by proxy, his childe."

"I see." Rayzeel seemed to ponder this for a moment. "I cannot give you any specific answers."

Beckett felt his unbeating heart sink.

"I do not know God's thoughts, or Caine's, any more than you. But I *can* speak with you on these matters to the extent my father discussed them with me. Perhaps, from Saulot's knowledge, you may draw your own answers."

Beckett couldn't help it. He laughed.

Rayzeel blinked. "This is funny?"

"No, not at all. I'm sorry. It's just—you tell me that you offer me Saulot's insights as though it were some minor gift. It's not, Rayzeel. My God, you might just be offering me the knowledge to make my entire existence mean something."

"And you think your existence had no meaning before now, Beckett? I find that hard to believe. But if it's this important to you…"

"It is."

"Then I am delighted to help." Rayzeel smiled once more as she spoke, and her eyes seemed to light up.

And then they really *did* light up.

A sudden sizzling sound filled the chamber, followed rapidly by a sodden thump. Red-tinted light streamed from Rayzeel's open mouth, her eyes, even her nostrils, and smoke burst from the back of her head. Beckett's horrified gaze met hers, and she seemed slightly puzzled, as though she'd lost her train of thought.

And then Saulot's daughter, who had carried the lore and the love of her sire for well over a thousand years, dropped in a heap to the floor, her ancient body decaying to ash even before it landed. Rayzeel perished, and with her all the wisdom she might have bestowed.

Beckett could only stare. His mind simply refused to register what had just happened. Even Kapaneus, normally unflappable, seemed shocked at the suddenness of what had just happened.

In the doorway, behind the spot where Rayzeel had stood, Cesare stood crouched, with one foot on the stairs. In his left hand was a heavy pistol; in his right, a spent flare gun. He idly tossed it aside.

"That," he said in a voice that sounded nothing like Cesare's, "should just about do it."

"Who… who are you?" Beckett found that even speaking was an effort. "You're not Cesare."

"No, I'm not." The image of Beckett's ghoul shimmered briefly, like a heat mirage, and then someone else stood in his place. He was not tall, but he was broad of shoulder. He wore a flannel shirt, and his face was covered in a thick growth of beard. He was, Beckett realized, the man he'd seen on the train and in the streets of Vienna.

"I'm called Samuel." He grinned. "Pleasure for you to meet me."

"I don't know you." Beckett's entire world seemed tilted forty-five degrees to the left. "Why would you do this to me? Or to her?"

"You don't know me, no. But *I* know *you*, Beckett."

"Cesare?"

Samuel gestured to the smoldering ash. "Like her. Well, minus the rapid decay, of course. I—"

Beckett shrieked once, and deliberately called the Beast to the fore. Had he been at his best, he'd have been across the room with his claws in Samuel's gut before the other could likely have moved. Wounded as he was, and caught in the early stages of the withering, it took him just an instant longer to cross the distance.

An instant was all Samuel needed. His pistol fired three

times in rapid succession, knocking Beckett back and off his feet. He rolled back up, prepared to charge again—just in time to see Samuel fade from sight.

When Bell finally arrived, drawn by Beckett's scream and the sound of gunfire, he found the Gangrel curled in the center of the room, sobbing over a pile of ash—ash that represented not only the death of Rayzeel, but of Beckett's final chance.

Wexler & Sons Warehousing
Long Beach, California

The warehouse was partially burnt out, having been the victim several months ago of a fire started by two careless employees and a lit cigarette. The building itself was still structurally sound, but the loss of the merchandise within had caused the owners to fold up their business and flee town before their creditors came clamoring for reimbursement. The warehouse had lain abandoned, until its current tenants—a far cry from the previous owners—moved in.

In an office upstairs, at a heavy desk that had survived the blaze with only minimal damage, Jenna Cross sat with her head in her hands. How things had gone so bad so swiftly she still didn't know. Her mind was spinning from the events of the previous weeks.

It was unbelievable. Throughout the world, vampires were weakening, even dying. The withering was now affecting just about the entire Kindred population except the thin-bloods, and there was no guarantee they wouldn't be next. Strange, unexplained phenomenon cropped up all over. She'd heard tales of a hot wind that destroyed those over whom it passed, of a rolling cloud of darkness that left panic and corpses behind it, And she heard other, less wide-ranging but no less disturbing rumors: something strange had risen from the old sewers of London and eaten all the Nosferatu; a mass of corpse flesh had risen ad writhed through Midtown Manhattan; something else was causing all the Kindred of Cairo to flee or go mad. It was enough to make even Cross, who had always dismissed Jack's prophecies as lunatic ravings (and damn, she missed him now!), wonder if perhaps there was more to this Gehenna stuff than she'd thought.

And despite all this, with all the world crashing down around them, the Camarilla continued to focus on her thin-bloods!

They'd gone stark-raving insane, Hardestadt and the others. It was the only possible explanation. In the past weeks, the Camarilla's storm troopers had tossed away any pretense at secrecy. Oh, they still paid lip service the Masquerade, but any notion of "covert" warfare was gone. Cross still remembered with a shudder the blast that had shaken the walls and rattled her teeth one morning just before dawn. She remembered taking shelter in the trunk of a car as the dawn approached, watching through bloody tears as her home burned to cinders, along with every other thin-blood-held house on the block. She hadn't just lost a house that morning. She'd lost friends, people who'd either been unable to escape the conflagration or who hadn't managed to find shelter in the minutes they had before the sun rose.

The thin-bloods' superior numbers had meant nothing in the face of an enemy who simply stopped following the rules. There was nothing they could do, nowhere they might strike back. Cross wasn't prepared to destroy her own city to hold onto it, but the Camarilla apparently had no such compunctions. After the third straight night of firebombing, the government had taken a hand. Police and military units patrolled the streets day and night, and hundreds if not thousands of people were taken in for questioning based on no stronger criteria than proximity to the attacks or descent from the wrong parents. And still the attacks had continued, for Hardestadt and the other Camarilla leaders had sufficient ears in the government and military to keep track of the patrols and strike while they were elsewhere. LA burned, entire neighborhoods were evacuated, people huddled terrified in their homes, and still it continued.

And Cross lost, as she knew from the moment it started that she must.

In mere weeks, she and her people had lost nearly all the gains they'd made in months of struggle. Some few pockets of thin-blood resistance remained in Los Angeles, but most of her people had fallen back to smaller, surrounding cities. Her current "headquarters," this decrepit old warehouse in Long Beach, was her third since the destruction of her house. It probably wouldn't be the last, either, but for at least a few nights she ought to be safe.

Allowing herself the luxury only because she knew none of her people were upstairs with her, Jenna wept for lost friends and lost dreams.

"Believe me or not," a gruff but soft voice said from behind her, "I understand."

Cross was on her feet, Glock in hand, before the last tear struck the desk. Three quick steps back took her out of range of whoever might be standing there—not that she hadn't recognized the voice—and in position to dive either for the door or behind the desk.

"Beckett," she snarled. Then she blinked. "You look like hell."

Beckett nodded once. His eyes were sunken, his skin pale. He looked as though he hadn't fed in nights. His clothes were disheveled, and he bore the scars of several burns that hadn't quite healed yet. That he'd abandoned his sunglasses somewhere along the way was lost on Cross; she'd only seen him once, and had never known *why* he wore the shades at the time. "You're not looking especially shipshape yourself."

"You here to take advantage of that?" she demanded with something of her old fire. "Here to finish the job after all?"

Beckett sighed and sat down on one corner of the desk. "Cross, you *did* get my message, right?"

"Yeah. Delivered by the only one of my people you *didn't* kill in Miskolc."

"People you sent to kill *me*, as I recall. Don't expect any apologies for that." Then, shaking his head, he continued, "Cross, I didn't come here as your enemy. If I had, I'd have taken your head off from behind without ever revealing I was here. I'm weaker than I was," he admitted, seeing as how he couldn't precisely hide the fact, "but I'm still more than fast enough and strong enough for that."

Cross scowled, but she did lower the pistol. "How did you get in here, anyway? Once we figured out your stunt at the house, we installed smoke detectors at or near just about every door or window in every building we've taken. You shouldn't be able to sneak in as mist."

"I'm not entirely convinced that would work, Cross. I had to really make an effort to hover around the detector long enough to set it off." Beckett shrugged. "But as it happens, I just turned into a bat and hitched a ride in the satchel one of your boys uses to carry his AK around. Then I just waited until he got inside and I snuck up here."

"All right, so why? If you're not here to kill me—and I don't entirely accept that, yet, by the way—why *are* you here?"

"Uh-uh. Your turn first. How did you track me to Miskolc?"

Cross debated refusing to answer, or lying, and then mentally shrugged. Why bother? "Got your plane's ID numbers from a contact."

Beckett nodded. "This contact, he wouldn't perchance be the same guy who's been poisoning you against me, would he?"

"Poisoning? Give it a rest, Beckett. He told me *everything* about you. I know precisely what you'd do to me to learn more about your precious Gehenna—or what others would do, if you even implied to them I was who you think I am."

"I don't give a damn who you are. Was it the same man?"

She crossed her arms and said nothing.

"Bearded fellow?" Beckett pressed. "Flannel shirt? Calls himself Samuel?"

The defiance drained from Cross's face. "How did you…?"

"You've been played, Jenna. From the very beginning. If it makes you feel better, so have I."

For long minutes Beckett spoke. At the start, Cross interrupted frequently, questioning this assertion or challenging that. By the end, however, she had slumped back into her chair, shaking her head not in denial but in despair and a mounting anger.

"I'm an idiot," she said at last.

"Could be," Beckett answered noncommittally. Then, in response to the woman's glare, he added, "Or it could be something more than that. Cross, why did you believe this man?"

"He's an ally. A friend. He's advised me on the Camarilla, on Prince Tara. He's never steered me wrong."

"Except when it came to me. Why did you believe him?"

"I…" Cross actually struggled with the words. "I'm not sure," she admitted finally.

Another nod from Beckett. "Conditioning. I'm guessing you haven't seen him in a while, or it'd be a lot stronger. You're lucky all he did was make you gullible."

Cross glared at him. "All right, Beckett. Assuming you're right—why come to me with this?"

"Because I've had a shitty month, I'm running out of time, and I've got to start completely over from square one. I have neither the time nor the energy to keep dodging your people or the Camarilla's."

"Well, you won't have to worry about us much longer," Cross told him, and Beckett could almost hear her voice break. "We're just waiting out the clock now. The Camarilla's more or less crushed us."

She tried to look away, to hide the emotion in her eyes, but Beckett's gaze held hers. "Don't you dare give up now."

Cross blinked. "Why the fuck do *you* care?"

"Cross, what do you think the withering is?"

"I—hadn't thought about it, I suppose."

"I don't know precisely either, but it's something to do with the end. Maybe it's the Antediluvians themselves, draining the strength and life from their progeny. They're supposed to rise and feed at Gehenna. Maybe this is how."

"You believe in them?"

"Cross, I've *seen* one of them. Anyway, the point is, whatever's happening, it started at the top—at the ancients—and worked its way down. The only Kindred unaffected so far are thin-bloods. You and yours.

"I don't know if any of us are going to survive Gehenna, Cross. Probably not, to be honest. But if *anyone* does, it's going to be you. And that means it'll be up to you to recreate."

"Oh, gosh, no pressure there."

"Don't get worked up. You'll probably die before it comes to that."

Cross just looked at him. "This is you trying to cheer me up?"

"This is me telling you how it is. You'll probably survive only a bit longer than the rest of us, if that. But just maybe, you'll go on. And that means you have to go on *now*. No giving up."

"Great speech, coach. How do we do it?"

"You and I have two enemies in common, Cross. The one, I'm going to help you deal with. The other…" Beckett rose and pointed out the window. Cross followed his gesture, and saw a figure standing on a nearby rooftop. A large black man, in a leather jacket and a baseball cap.

"The other," Beckett continued with a smile, "requires a specialist."

"Is that who I think it is?"

"Probably. Tell your people to let him in, and we'll talk."

For the first time in weeks, Jenna Cross smiled.

Lincoln Park Apartments
Chicago, Illinois

The knock on the door was startling, not only because the owner of the apartment was lost in thought, but because he never received visitors. Ever. Warily he rose from the computer desk at which he sat and lifted a heavy Smith & Wesson revolver from a cabinet near the door. A moment's concentration caused his form to blur and fade until he was, for all practical purposes, invisible to mortal (and most immortal) sight. Then and only then did he lean over to glance out the peephole.

For a long moment he simply stared. He hadn't thought to see the person in the hall—at least not in person—for quite some time. Then, coming to a decision, he allowed himself to become visible once more, stuck the gun back on the cabinet, and opened the door.

"Beckett!" he said with a wide grin, stepping aside to allow his friend to enter. "This is quite a surprise. Please come in."

For a moment, however, Beckett did nothing of the sort. Instead, he simply stared. "Well," he said at last, shaking his head in wonderment, "that explains a lot." He finally stepped inside and shut the door behind him. "How are you doing, Okulos?"

"Much better. As you can see, the wounds are all long healed."

Beckett stared his friend in the face. "That's not all that's changed, I see."

He ran a hand over his jaw. "Do you like it?"

Okulos, a Nosferatu formerly as ugly as a nightmare made flesh, now looked almost human. He'd never be handsome—hell, he'd never even reach the heights of "below average"—but his features had realigned themselves, his flesh lost much of its ill hue. In poor lighting or at a quick glance, nobody would think him anything but an unattractive man.

"The withering?" Beckett asked.

Okulos nodded. "I'm one of the—well, lucky ones, you could say. Only a few of my clan have been affected thus. Even fewer were changed as early in the process as I was. I looked like this well before I began to grow weak."

"I see. Lucky." Beckett wandered through the apartment until he stood by the window. He pushed the curtains aside and stared out over the twinkling lights of Chicago.

And there he stood, as though waiting. Finally, just as Okulos opened his mouth to ask, Beckett spoke.

"It was the flare gun that nudged it all into place, Okulos."

Okulos blinked once. "I beg your pardon?"

"The flare gun. You always swore by those. Still had the bandolier when I found you in Kaymakli." Beckett continued to gaze out the window. "Should have used something else when you took down Rayzeel."

"A number of Kindred use flare guns, Beckett."

"Right. But it's rare enough to be memorable, and it was enough to get me thinking. I didn't know 'Samuel,' but he clearly knew me. Knew me well enough to follow me to Vienna. To keep Jenna Cross informed of my progress, to give her the ID number of my plane. To follow me to Iraq. Knew Cesare well enough to fool Theo Bell with an impersonation; Bell didn't know Cesare well, but he's observant by nature. Exactly one person in the world could have done all that, Okulos."

Beckett finally turned. His old friend was gazing at him through half-lidded eyes, standing relatively still in the center of the room.

"Tell me something, Okulos. Why murder Victoria Ash? I've heard that Hardestadt tacked that onto my list of crimes; I'm guessing that was your doing."

"Because she helped you. She pointed you toward the Tremere, and I wasn't going to have her do that again. Plus, she even cared for you somewhere in that black heart of hers."

"And Cross? How did you get Cross on board?"

"Solid tactical advice. I've still got quite a few contacts in the Camarilla echelon, enough to keep her competitive with Hardestadt and his junta. And a little judicious exaggeration of some fears and insecurities."

"To say nothing of a bit of mental tampering."

"That too."

Beckett nodded. "It certainly explains why you could find her when Hardestadt couldn't, doesn't it?" He shook his head, in grudging admiration. "This all can't have been easy, what with the withering. You must have been terrified your mask of Cesare would slip."

"It was worrisome, yes." Okulos still sounded casual, as though they were discussing baseball scores. Beckett realized that he was revealing his secrets so easily because he *wanted* Beckett to understand what he'd done. "But it's amazing what one can do when one has the proper motivation. I only had to hold it long enough to get past that hulking brute."

"And you weren't worried about anyone seeing through your 'Samuel' mask because it wasn't supernatural." Beckett shook his head. "Fake beard?"

"Along with other stage makeup."

"Right. And since you look less monstrous now, a thick beard covered any remaining traces of inhumanity." Beckett's composure broke slightly and he scowled, a low growl forming in his throat. "On the outside, anyway."

Okulos's gaze shifted briefly to the gun on the cabinet. Beckett shook his head again. "Don't even try."

"Why would I? Kill me if you like, Beckett. It won't change anything now. My purpose here was never to kill you, just to ensure that you never found what you were looking for. And now, now it's too late. Chaos moves through Kindred society. One of the great sects has disintegrated, while the other threatens to topple with the slightest nudge. Creatures the likes of which we couldn't even imagine this time last year are among us. There's no way you can find your answers before the end, Beckett, not now that I've forced you to start over from scratch. So kill me, if you will. It just means I die a few months early. I've still won."

The silence in the room grew stiff, almost brittle as the two vampires stared at one another. Clearly, Okulos was waiting for something, for the one specific question he had long looked forward to answering.

Beckett refused to ask it. He didn't have to. He knew why Okulos had done this, should have realized it long before.

In the single night he'd spent in Kaymakli, the wraiths and the images they'd inflicted upon him had infected and warped his dreams like a disease. He'd seen past events through a filter of rage, of hate, of guilt. And in one of those dreams, Okulos's imprisonment was no accident, but the result of a deliberate act of sabotage.

One night. Okulos had been imprisoned in that nightmarish place for years, the constant dreams clashing with his memories until no amount of effort could possibly have separated them. God alone knew what he thought Beckett had done, or why. God alone knew what regrets

Okulos harbored. Perhaps he thought, had he been free, that he might have succeeded where Beckett failed, might have found the answers they'd both sought, might even have found some way to prevent the end before it started. God alone knew how long ago he'd truly gone mad, since the petty and vindictive urges of the Beast had begun to rule even his conscious mind. That he blamed Beckett for his imprisonment, however, was patently obvious.

And what was worse, Beckett had come to a horrifying realization when he'd figured out who Samuel was. In a way, Okulos was right.

No, he hadn't deliberately orchestrated his friend's captivity. But had he *really* done all he could to free him, as he'd sworn he would? For most of the past years, his efforts to free Okulos had occupied only his spare time, only when he had nothing else he was pursuing more actively.

But what had those other pursuits accomplished? Facing Gehenna itself, he was no closer to his answers than he'd ever been, and what little he'd accomplished had happened after Okulos was free. Surely he could have, *should* have, spent more of his time working on the puzzle that was Kaymakli. If he had, if he'd done as he promised rather than wasting his time, could Okulos have walked free earlier? Could he have walked free before the dreams of the dead had driven him mad?

Beckett might not be guilty of the sin for which Okulos had punished him, but his hands were far from clean.

None of which meant, of course, that Beckett would *ever* forgive what Okulos had done since.

"Okulos," Beckett said, "look at me."

"I am. And I like what I see. A broken, defeated—"

"No. *Look.*"

Okulos once had perceptive abilities nearly the equal of Beckett's own. Even now, weakened as he was, he was more than capable of reading auras.

With a vindictive grin, Beckett watched the Nosferatu's expression crumple. "It can't be…" Okulos choked, actually falling back a step.

The aura he saw flickering around Beckett shone with the soft glow of utter calm, utter contentment. Where was the seething anger, the crippling frustration, the deep despondency of failure?

"You showed up too late, Okulos," Beckett told him, each word a blow that seemed to strike Okulos physically in the gut. "You stopped Rayzeel from telling me what I needed to know, but not before she'd mentioned the names of others of her brethren with whom she'd shared her knowledge. It was simple enough to track them down once you disappeared. I knew you wouldn't be watching me any longer."

"No. *No!*"

"Yep. I just wanted to let you know." Beckett brushed past the stammering Nosferatu and opened the door. In the hall, he stopped and looked briefly over his shoulder. "Kill me if you want, Okulos," he said softly. "It doesn't matter. I've won."

The slamming door didn't quite silence Okulos's agonized scream.

Outside the Lincoln Park Apartments
Chicago, Illinois

Kapaneus stood in the parking lot, his face a mask of concentration. Behind him, just far enough back that they could not overhear any hushed conversation, waited Jenna Cross and over a dozen of her closest companions.

Only when Beckett stepped from the darkness before him did the elder allow his concentration to lapse. With a tired expression, he looked up at the newcomer. "Did it work?"

"Seems like. I'm surprised you didn't hear the scream from here."

"I'm glad. Masking one's own aura is a simple enough task. Masking someone else's… I wasn't certain I could maintain it once you left my sight."

"You did just fine, Kapaneus. Okulos actually believes that I'm *not* a hopelessly depressed wreck."

"This is a cruel thing you're doing to him, Beckett. You know that."

"Yup. That's why I'm doing it. The bastard deserves to suffer for a long time for what he did. Unfortunately, we can't let him suffer that long. He might decide to come after me again, once he gets over the shock. And there are a few other folks who have a grudge or two to work out." Beckett turned and waved the others over.

"Apartment 316," he told Cross once the thin-blood drew near. "He's got a revolver near the door, and he's probably got at least one flare gun hidden somewhere in the apartment."

"Don't worry, Beckett. That bastard messed with my mind, sent us after you, and got a number of my friends killed. I *hope* he puts up a fight."

"Are you sure you're up to this, Cross? He's older than any ten of you combined. And we don't know for sure that he hasn't put other safeguards in your head. The fact that you were able to see through his lies is a good sign, but it doesn't prove you're free and clear."

"I wouldn't worry." Jenna Cross grinned nastily and gestured at several of the satchels her friends carried. "I don't plan to get near enough for him to say anything to me. And what we're carrying could take *you* down."

Beckett nodded, and Jenna Cross stepped into the building to have a few final words with "Samuel." Beckett and Kapaneus waited in the parking lot until the shooting stopped—just to be sure—and then disappeared into the night.

The Mission Inn
Riverside, California

Hardestadt never saw it coming.

He was wandering the halls of the Mission Inn, deeply lost in thought, returning to his private rooms after another strategy session with those elders who hadn't yet been slain, disappeared, or fully succumbed to the withering. His list of allies was shrinking at a prodigious rate—which wasn't necessarily a bad thing. He didn't really need them to maintain the assault on the thin-bloods; hell, that was mostly his plan to begin with. And the fewer elders who remained, the less competition he had for the blood of the prisoners, and the easier it would be to reshape the new order fully to his own liking. He wished he knew what had become of Tegyrius, if only out of curiosity, but he didn't especially miss the man.

One moment, Hardestadt was opening the door to his private room, idly contemplating another trip to the nearest incarceration center. The next, pain lanced through his body as several bullets, launched with a hiss from a silenced forty-five, entered his gut.

Mere months ago, Hardestadt could probably have shaken off such an attack. Most Ventrue were blessed with the same resilience and tolerance for injury as the Gangrel, and one as ancient as this could completely ignore what would, even on other Kindred, prove a fatal assault. Now, weakened as he was, the attack hurled him against the wall, the pain wracking him more than enough to keep him from defending himself or even crying out.

His face a mask of fury and agony, Hardestadt looked up. He saw several individuals throughout the room, all armed with firearms and blades both. He focused on the one who stood directly before him, the one who had fired. His eyes widened as he stared up at a dark-skinned face above a heavy leather jacket.

"I didn't expect to see you around here again," Hardestadt offered, his voice steady enough to belie his suffering.

"What can I say?" Bell replied. "I'm unpredictable that way. Jenna Cross says hi, by the way. And bye."

"You think it's that easy, traitor? You know better than anyone, this place is *crawling* with guards. The first sound of combat and they'll be here in seconds."

It took Hardestadt a moment to recognize the deep, rumbling sound coming from his former servant as laughter. "None of the guards on this floor are going to hear anything ever again, Hardestadt. How did you think I even got in here? I know your security better than you do, and I've got this whole team of Cross's people—" and here he gestured at the others around him, "—who were only too happy to back me up on this."

Bell casually stuck the pistol he carried into the waistband of his jeans, and slung his traditional shotgun from over his shoulder.

"Look on the up side, Hardestadt," Bell told him. "Look how successfully the Camarilla took off once your sire was killed."

Your sire? Beckett must have told Bell the truth, the bastard!

"So just imagine," the former archon continued, "how much better it'll be with *you* gone. Hell, I might even be willing to sign back up."

Any response Hardestadt might have made was silenced forever in the deafening blast of a twelve-gauge.

Elsewhere

From Iraq, the great shadow that was Lasombra—in the same way it was Monçada, Leviathan, and every other speck that had fed and shaped the Abyss—flowed outward. It made its way across countries, even across continents, according to no plan or pattern any living mind could recognize. It turned here, drifted there, as though choosing its direction at whim. It vanished for nights at a time, only to reappear thousands of miles and even full oceans away. As news of the strange phenomenon traveled across the globe, panic spread before it like a shockwave. Terror alerts were raised, military and disease-control units scrambled. Before the darkness, people fled. Within the darkness, people prayed, and several of them died.

Where the darkness had passed, the Red Star shone, shone so brightly it was finally visible even to naked, mortal eyes. And in the light of the Red Star, people began to *see*. Their gaze pierced shadows that even sunlight could never penetrate.

In ages past, many had known of the things that shared the night with them, but they had been made to forget. Always, a few had known, but they had been silenced or ignored. In recent years, a few had both seen and been imbued with the ability to fight back, but many of those had gone mad. The few who had not, however, spread the word.

Under the light of the Red Star, and in ever-larger numbers, the living truly saw what had been around them from the very beginning.

Epilogue:
Dawn

There is no salvation in killing,
nor do the Damned ever forget.

—*The Erciyes Fragments,* "Prophecies"

Club ElaZtic
Somewhere in North America

"I'm just not sure what I can do for you, Beckett. You know what things are like right now. I don't keep my head below radar, I'm likely to lose it, you know?"

The two were seated in a booth tucked away in the corner of the club, and Beckett had to lean forward and keep a constant eye on the other vampire's lips to make out his words. The blasting music—a cacophony of electronic noises put together by someone called DJ Anthrax—pumped so loudly the building shook with the bass, and Beckett winced with pain as it assaulted his weakened, but still enhanced, hearing. The dance floor was less crowded than it might once have been, as many people had grown afraid to gather in large groups, but those present thrashed and undulated to the music with an abandon that would have made the maenads proud. Most were drunk or high, and the club's tables were as cluttered with powders and syringes as they were with snacks. Nobody cared. The police had *far* better things to do with their time, if they were doing anything at all.

The room seemed to swim before Beckett's eyes, swaying and swelling in time with the music. He gave himself a mental slap and forced himself to focus. Time enough to collapse later. The scent, the combination of alcohol and coffee and sweat and drug-tainted blood, wasn't helping.

"Look… Richard," Beckett told the leather-clad Kindred before him, barely even able to remember his contact's name, "I'm not asking you to do anything dangerous. I just need to find Archimedes. I know he's here, but the Nosferatu have gone so far underground I don't even know where to look. If you could just introduce me to the prince, I'm sure that he—"

"Forget it. No way."

Beckett's head swam. He gripped the seat beside him, beneath the table where Richard couldn't see, to keep himself steady. "Why not?"

"Come on, man! The only reason I'm not hanging in one of the prince's prisons is because I make myself useful when I can, and stay in the—" Richard stopped long enough to wave off a harried (and stoned) looking waitress who was weaving her way across the dance floor toward them. "—in the shadows when I can't," he concluded a moment later. "Shit, by all rights, I should be reporting that you're in town, Beckett. Vampire your age is a fucking delicacy. But we go back too far for that."

Which meant that Richard would wait until he was out of sight, and *then* report him. Beckett scowled.

"You really think you're likely to wind up on the prince's menu? You're the childe of a primogen, for God's sake."

"Beckett, have you had your eyes *open* while you've been traveling? It's every lick for himself out there, now. The Camarilla's pretty much collapsed completely, and you damn well know it. Ever since Hardestadt's death—say, didn't I hear you had some dealings with him not long before he died?"

Beckett simply waved dismissively.

"Right. Well, you pretty much got your local princes now and nobody standing over them with the whip. Princes do whatever they think they got to do to keep their cities running and their strength up, and ain't anybody saying boo about it. Right now, man, the *last* thing you want to do is attract a prince's notice. And shit, the Nosferatu you're looking for is probably long gone anyway.

"Now I'm getting out of here. For old time's sake, Beckett, I'll give you some advice. Whatever you're looking for, give it up. Get the hell out of Dodge, and stay gone. Not a lot of Kindred your age left anymore, and you don't have a lot of allies. That don't make you a player. That makes you a pizza with extra vitae."

Beckett watched as Richard slid from the booth and made his way toward the door, glancing nervously about him as he went. A moment later another figure stepped from the crowd to sit in Richard's place.

"No luck, I presume," Kapaneus noted.

"None. Again." Beckett slumped and placed his head in his hands, waiting for yet another dizzy spell to pass.

He wondered, idly, how much of the chaos was his fault. Hardestadt hadn't been the Camarilla's only surviving elder, but apparently he'd somehow been a lynchpin all the same. His destruction at the hands of Theo Bell and Cross's thin-bloods had sounded the death knell for the sect. Other elders swiftly disappeared, and while some were no doubt in hiding or in torpor, many more had certainly fallen to younger vampires emboldened by Cross's success. Princes still ruled in the Camarilla's name, but Beckett knew well there was nobody at the rudder.

He'd learned firsthand, in his travels since confronting Okulos, that Sabbat territories were even worse, though not by much. Nothing held the younger vampires of that sect in check anymore, and they didn't even have the memory of the Masquerade to restrain them. Mexico City was a swarm of chaos and violence like nothing seen in the modern world and had been for months. And that violence was spreading. Even the Camarilla territories had gone well beyond "riots and gang warfare." People died by the dozens on a weekly basis in most major cities, as maddened vampires fed indiscriminately or warred with one another. The great shadow swept across the continents, and the official story that it was a rogue biological weapon from the Middle East was just so much chatter. Mortals across the world now locked doors and windows, and bolted crucifixes and other icons to those doors and windows. Groups had taken to patrolling their streets at night, armed to take out an invading army—and not just with guns, but with blades and even wooden stakes. No reputable media had yet used the word "vampire," but the kine had finally awakened to the notion that *something* stalked the night, something that fed on their blood and feared the coming of the dawn. Hell, it was only that the vampiric population was withering and diablerizing itself toward oblivion at breakneck speed that preserved anything even remotely like the Masquerade.

Most of Beckett's contacts were now dead or missing, but what little he still heard told him things had spread beyond the Kindred. He'd heard more stories of wild monsters, haunting, and angelic visitations in the last few months than for the previous decade. Something had stirred the things that even vampires feared—lupines and the like.

And through it all, through the growing chaos and the spreading fire, Beckett had continued his search. The world around him grew terrifying, but he would not yield. He grew weaker now by the night, but he would not yield. He couldn't focus well anymore, couldn't draw upon the strength of his blood. Hell, unless he had Kapaneus or someone to speak to, he found it difficult even to order his thoughts. He couldn't for the unlife of him remember how much time had passed since he'd come so close to his answers with Rayzeel, or even say with any degree of certainty what city he was in. He remembered that he sought a Nosferatu lore-keeper named Archimedes, and that he'd heard Archimedes had come this way, but that was it. And now, now the information was useless; even if the Nosferatu was here, Beckett had no way of finding him.

"I heard something interesting," Kapaneus said, and though his voice was soft Beckett somehow heard him clearly over the pulsing beat. "Apparently the violence in Los Angeles has drastically subsided." He gestured toward a young man at a nearby table, a young man with a radio. "According to the news, the police there have been aided by a large band of civilian volunteers."

"So? The police'll take help from anyone they can

get these—"

"According to the report, the leader of this particular band is a young woman by the name of Jenna Cross."

Beckett raised his head and stared disbelievingly at his companion.

"I suppose it makes some degree of sense," Kapaneus continued thoughtfully. "Anyone with eyes can see that it's only a matter of time before mortals learn of us. Perhaps Cross felt it best to introduce herself first, to make her thin-bloods useful rather than let mortals come to discover them as enemies."

"You think she's told people the truth?"

"I imagine that the police working alongside her and her people must know something is unusual about them. My guess would be that she's revealed herself to certain civil authorities and offered her services.

"It might be the wisest decision she could have made, Beckett," the elder commented as Beckett shook his head. "If any of them survive Gehenna, they will have established allies in the government. They will be able to help control the spread of information about our kind. They may be the best hope for the Kindred."

"There *is* no hope for the Kindred, Kapaneus, and you damn well know it!" Beckett was shouting, suddenly unconcerned with who might hear him; fortunately, the music prevented his voice from carrying. "You know as well as I do that Gehenna is the end. I doubt *any* of us are going to survive it, *certainly* not enough of us to worry about a 'new society.' Cross and the others are kidding themselves."

"And yet you are the one who told her she must strive for this."

"I lied. I needed her cooperation."

Kapaneus shrugged. "A false hope is still better than none."

"No, it's not." Beckett's shoulders slumped. "Look at me, Kapaneus. I've been chasing false hopes for months now, and I'm no closer to my answers than I've ever been. I lost my only chance with Rayzeel, and we both know it. Now… now I'm just marking time until the end."

"And what would you rather be doing, Beckett? Clinging desperately to past glories and fading power, as the princes do? Feeding and killing wantonly, as the neonates do? Fighting to stem the tide of violence alongside the thin-bloods? What would you do, if not seek your answers?"

Beckett's eyes widened, as if he'd been slapped. "I never thought of it that way, I suppose." He sighed once. "You know that I'm not going to find my answers."

"But you'll keep trying."

"But I'll keep trying." Beckett smiled wanly. "For as long as I can stand."

"I will help you, Beckett. I—"

"Caine!"

Kapaneus blinked. "I beg your pardon?"

"Caine must be out there somewhere!" Beckett spoke excitedly. "I never thought about it, because I'm so used to thinking of him as myth! But if Gehenna's truly upon us, and the ancients are really awakening, Caine must be wandering around as well, right? If *anyone* could tell me what I need to know—"

"It would not be he," Kapaneus said softly. "Think, Beckett. Think of all you know of the First Vampire. I would presume that he, of all people, would arguably have the *least* understanding of what it was all for. Remember, according to myth, he never believed he'd done anything wrong."

Beckett seemed to deflate. "You're right, of course." He shook his head. "Besides, it's not like I'd have the slightest clue how to find him." Beckett blinked as his eyes grew unfocused once more. He felt weak, nauseous. The room seemed to spin and twitch with each beat of the speakers.

"I'd bet he could stop all this," he said, more out of a need to keep talking, to keep himself distracted from the pain of the withering, than out of any real desire to converse. "If he wanted to, that is." Beckett chuckled. "What do you suppose he's been up to, all these years?"

"Caine?" Kapaneus' eyes grew distant. "If I had to guess, Beckett… I imagine Caine would long since have grown weary of watching his descendents squabble among one another and torment the kine on whom they fed. I imagine he would long ago have sought out a place of solitude, somewhere he could await the final nights without fear of being disturbed."

Beckett chuckled. "Like you did, you mean." And then, abruptly, the bottom dropped out of Beckett's stomach.

"He might have left the cave occasionally," Kapaneus said, still staring off into space, "sending his spirit out to observe and even occasionally speak to others, to those few with the eyes to see him in that form. But physically, he'd have waited there for centuries. Waited until he was found by someone, someone who offered him one last opportunity to see the world, to see what had become of his descendents before they were no more."

Beckett's eyes bulged, and thought he might pass out. It had to be the withering. He was simply misunderstanding what Kapaneus seemed to be saying. That *had* to be it.

"He would have accompanied this one," Kapaneus said, "allowing him to conduct his own search, interfering only when there was no other option.

"And I think," the elder said, looking directly at Beckett for the first time, "that he might have learned a few things about the nature of the race he had spawned. Things he might otherwise not have known. This younger vampire and his companions might well have taught him, the eldest of us all, something about perseverance and devotion. Something that the eldest, to his shame, had long since forgotten.

"And finally, when they had no more to learn from one another—when the younger vampire had his answers, even if he could not see them—I think then, and only then, would Caine move on."

Beckett stared in complete incomprehension for a long moment, stared at Kapaneus's kindly smile. And then the music went silent, the odor of the club faded, and everything went dark.

A parking lot
Somewhere in North America

He awoke slowly, so slowly, only truly aware of his own consciousness when he realized the light was stinging his eyes even through the lids.

He hadn't really expected to awaken. In a way, he was almost disappointed he had; it would have been so much easier...

He could feel earth beneath him, dry dirt, a bit of dying grass. Shards of broken glass, curved—probably from a bottle of some sort. He smelled garbage, garbage in that putrid, liquid form that only congeals at the base of dumpsters. He smelled urine, vomit, alcohol....

Smoke...

Beckett opened his eyes.

He was, as he suspected, in the lot behind the club, sprawled out at the edge of the property. What he had *not* expected was the fire, burning merrily away beside an old metal drum, that crackled mere feet from his face. Most likely started by some homeless man seeking warmth, something had since knocked it over, covering a portion of the lot in flaming detritus that hadn't yet burned out on its own.

Beckett had already drawn breath to scream, flung his arm up to shield his eyes, before it occurred to him that he really didn't feel the need. Here was this dancing blaze no more than a few feet from where he lay, yet he felt not the slightest hint of panic, not the first trace of the Beast within slamming about in its cage, seeking escape. If anything, the warmth was rather pleasant.

Dusting the soil from his knees—forgetting that his pants were so encrusted with filth already that it couldn't possibly make a difference—Beckett rose to his feet. He was astonished at how easy it was. He'd been so weak, before he finally collapsed inside, hardly able to lift a finger or speak a word. But now he felt strong, stronger than he had in a very long time.

Is *that* why the fire-barrel had been knocked over? Had the Beast broken forth, feeding indiscriminately on the homeless men and women who'd probably been warming themselves around it? It would be so easy in the midst of frenzy to toss a corpse against it or otherwise slam into it without even realizing. Even now, at the end, did he have more deaths on his...?

No. No, that wasn't it. Beckett felt within, delving to the depths of his soul, and found no more trace of an enraged or angry Beast than he had of a frightened one. To say nothing of the fact that the lot was completely empty of corpses or signs of bloodshed.

For just an instant, he thought he recalled a feeling, the impression of someone half leading him, half carrying him out of the club after his collapse. Kapaneus? Yes, it could only have been him. Beckett could still feel the sensation of the other man's arm supporting him; his shoulder, where the elder had laid his hand, still tingled, like a very minor burn.

Beckett felt the world spin around him yet again, but this was emotional, not the affects of the withering. He had thought—hoped—that the realization he had come to in the club was flawed, the ridiculous and laughable result of his weakness and exhaustion. But he knew now, without quite knowing how he knew, that it was not.

No, he had not fed. Kapaneus—Beckett firmly refused to think of the elder by any other name—had granted him the strength he now felt. Just, Beckett suddenly realized, as Kapaneus had protected him from the withering for so long, until even the elder could no longer shield him. It was, in retrospect, the only answer that made sense. Beckett had remained safe from the withering for so long because he had been chosen. He'd just been wrong about *who* had chosen him, and for what.

So why now? Why had the ancient granted him this last bit of strength, steadied him—even if only temporarily—against the worst of the withering?

What was it that Kapaneus still wanted Beckett to do?

Near a city park
Somewhere in North America

He had to figure it out soon. The sun would be up before much longer, and he was sure that, apparent newfound sense of calm aside, he probably still wouldn't react particularly well when it happened.

For hours he had walked aimlessly, his feet choosing the path of their own accord. Though he no longer felt any trace of weakness, his gait was stiff, awkward, like a sleepwalker.

Like the living dead, Beckett thought to himself, and then had to bite his lips until they bled to keep from giggling maniacally.

The club was well behind him now, though had he looked back, he could probably still have seen a thin and greasy plume of smoke from the fire he'd left smoldering in the club's back lot.

Not that he needed to strain to see signs of destruction. The city was lit by more than a handful of conflagrations far larger than the one he'd just left. Sirens wailed ceaselessly in the night, and the people on the street, far less numerous than normal, hurried on their way, their faces twisted in masks of hopelessness and fear.

Beckett didn't know precisely what was happening in the world anymore. He had only half-remembered bits of rumor he'd picked up in his travels. Still, he knew enough. It had finally spilled over onto the kine, and if they didn't yet grasp the enormity of what was to come, it was surely only a matter of time before enough of them figured it out.

And that, Gehenna or no, Antediluvians or no, would be the end.

Beckett shook his head. One way or the other, it was over for the Kindred. They would die in secret, as they had survived these many millennia, or they would die in a paroxysm of humanity's rage and fear, as they had so nearly done before.

Either was fitting, really.

In a way, Beckett found himself envying Lucita. Her death couldn't have been pleasant, but it was swift, over with. And at the end, even if her intentions hadn't been selfless or noble, her sacrifice had meaning. Beckett's death wouldn't even...

He froze on the sidewalk, drawing a mild curse as a rushing pedestrian almost collided with him. His eyes grew wide with shock—and then, almost despite himself, Beckett began to laugh.

It really *was* that simple, wasn't it? Leave it to him, leave it to the Kindred, to complicate matters.

His mind racing—not randomly or desperately now, but toward a very specific destination—Beckett walked once more. He needed to find just the right—

There.

A city park. Not well maintained, but littered with newspaper, magazine pages, used napkins... A single wobbly slide stood above a shallow sandbox, a rusty hand-powered carrousel beside it. Unimpressive, dismal, dirty. But it would do.

Not yet, though. He had to see it, at least the beginnings of it. One last time, he had to see it.

Slowly, stiffly, Beckett turned to face the east.

And now, not walking, not searching, just waiting, he couldn't help but think, his mind finally settling on the conclusions it had been reaching toward for so long.

He had been right—and so terribly wrong. It was

Gehenna; it was the end, yes. He would never again have the opportunity to seek his answers, but that didn't matter anymore. There was *no* hidden meaning behind it, no glorious purpose, no ultimate answer.

And it was his fault.

All his frantic efforts of the past nights, indeed of the long years of his quest, and it was only the words of a mysterious ancient and the final actions of one who had abandoned her humanity, that led to any revelation, any truth of the Kindred purpose. And it was only this:

It didn't matter.

It didn't matter what God had intended when he reached down and smote a farmer who had shed the blood of man. It made no difference what God had intended Caine's offspring to be. An object lesson, a plague on mankind, a catalyst to force the nations of humanity to work together—none of it mattered.

For the Kindred, while cursed, had still enjoyed the greatest of all God's gifts. Free will. The ability to choose, as Lucita did, each his own purpose, his own meaning.

They never had.

Their leaders had squabbled with one another, seeing only what they *wanted*, not what *was*. Their youth had understood only the power they now had, and none of the consequences. Their scholars, including Beckett himself, were the worst of the lot, for they had looked only to the past for answers, never seeking to create their own.

The sky began to lighten in the east, and Beckett—who had, for obvious reasons, not seen a sunrise in hundreds of years—could not tell how much of the dawn's red tint came from the pollutants in the air, and how much from the tears of blood that blurred his vision and ran unchecked down his face. Meaningless, meaningless…

Except for the meaning he could give it *now*, at the end, as Lucita had done.

This was the end of his world—perhaps the end of the world of mortals as well. It was entirely possible, even likely, there would be no tomorrow.

But just maybe there would. Maybe something, some small piece of the world, would survive. Survive, and grow, and begin anew.

And he would be there. By God, he understood now, and he would *make* them see that so long as they looked to the heavens for answers, they could never see the world in front of them. They would get it right at last.

Or not. More likely, these were his last moments, and any other hope was an illusion, a false dream such as the one Jenna Cross chased in LA. But if nothing else, he *knew*. He knew the answer now, even if he could probably never use it.

And Kapaneus had been right after all. A false hope *was* better than none.

Like the joy of a delighted child, Beckett's laughter rang out across the tiny park, echoing off the trees and the rickety slide. For the last time, he felt the power of the blood flow through him as he summoned his strength, felt it pumping as though, for just a moment, his heart beat once more.

As the sun rose on the final night of the Kindred, Beckett called upon the power granted him by an overly proud farmer, sank slowly into the earth, and slept.

About the Author

Ari Marmell has been writing more or less constantly for the past ten years, though he's only been paid for it for the past three. (Whether that makes him determined or simply pigheaded is a matter of perspective.) He is the author of multiple roleplaying game supplements, for both the **World of Darkness** and everyone's favorite fantasy game system. He likes both games very much, and doesn't care that you don't. **Vampire: Gehenna, The Final Night** is his first novel. Ari lives in Austin, Texas, with his wife George, two cats, and seven different neuroses. (If you'd like to adopt one of the neuroses, they're looking for good homes.)

Acknowledgements

What do you say—who do you thank—in your first published novel? If Philippe gave me an entire chapter for it, I'm not sure I could say everything I want to. So, in brief, or as brief as I can, heartfelt thanks: To Ryan, Ron, Gary, both Jasons, Jamie, and Jerel, who gamed with me for many a year and encouraged me to write if that's what I wanted to do. To my mother, Carole, for all the mother-type reasons. To my sister, Naomi, for brutal (and ultimately helpful) honesty. To my wife, George, for patience above and beyond the call. To Philippe Boulle, for encouraging what was good and helping correct what was—well, less good. To Professor Robisson (who will never see this and wouldn't remember me anyway, but I'm doing it because I told him I would), for being honest and for being wrong.

All of these, and many more, mean more to me than I can say. But as this *is* my first published novel, there's one that really needs special attention.

To my father, Howard, who taught me even from childhood that stories come from *somewhere*. That they don't have to end when the credits roll or the cover closes. Without him, and the lessons he taught without (I think) ever realizing he was teaching, God knows *what* I'd be doing right now—but it wouldn't be writing.

Dark Ages

Clan Novel Series

The Call of the Beast

Deep in the wilds of Livonia, the vampire warlord Qarakh has become a power to be reckoned with. But now, the ancient Ventrue Alexander marches toward his lands, with undead knights at his side. This ancient Cainite has crushed many before him. Can Qarakh hope to stand where so many have fallen?

BOOK TEN

GANGREL

BY TIM WAGGONER

ISBN 1-58846-847-X   WW11214

Available in February!

ACT TWO OF THE TIME OF JUDGMENT TRILOGY

THE LAST BATTLE
A novel of the Apocalypse by Bill Bridges

ISBN 1-58846-856-9; WW11911; 352 pages; $7.99

The werewolf Jonas Albrecht and his packmates have felt the approach of their final reckoning more keenly than most. Once an exile from his people, Albrecht has risen to the lofty position of king. But as the prophecies come true and the final call to battle sounds, Albrecht faces the prospect that all he has gained has been for naught. The prophecies are clear: The Last Gaian King will fall to the Wyrm.

Can King Albrecht fight on?

AVAILABLE NOW.

TIME OF JUDGMENT

THE WORLD YOU KNEW IS GONE...
BUT THE DARKNESS REMAINS.

NEW SETTING. NEW SYSTEM.
NEW WORLD OF DARKNESS.

AUGUST 2004

WORLD OF DARKNESS RULEBOOK
VAMPIRE: THE REQUIEM